OXFORD WORLD'S CLASSICS

NORTHANGER ABBEY

JANE AUSTEN was born in 1775 in the village of Steventon, Hampshire, the daughter of an Anglican clergyman. The Austens were cultured but not at all rich, though one of Austen's brothers was adopted by a wealthy relative. Other brothers followed professional careers in the Church, the Navy, and banking. With the exception of two brief periods away at school, Austen and her elder sister Cassandra, her closest friend and confidante, were educated at home. Austen's earliest surviving work, written at Steventon whilst still in her teens, is dedicated to her family and close female friends. Between 1801 and 1809, her least productive period, Austen lived in Bath, where her father died in 1805, and in Southampton. In 1809, she moved with her mother, Cassandra, and their great friend Martha Lloyd to Chawton, Hampshire, her home until her death in Winchester in July 1817. During this time, Austen published four of her major novels: *Sense and Sensibility* (1811), *Pride and Prejudice* (1813), *Mansfield Park* (1814), and *Emma* (1816), visiting London regularly to oversee their publication. *Persuasion* and *Northanger Abbey* were published posthumously in December 1817. *Sanditon*, a new novel, was left unfinished at the time of her death.

THOMAS KEYMER is Chancellor Henry N.R. Jackman University Professor of English at the University of Toronto, where he has also served as Director of Book History & Print Culture and Chair of the Department of English. He was previously Elmore Fellow and Tutor in English at St Anne's College, University of Oxford, where he remains a Supernumerary Fellow. His books include *Jane Austen: Writing, Society, Politics* (2020), *Poetics of the Pillory: English Literature and Seditious Libel 1660–1820* (2019), and, as editor, *The Oxford History of the Novel in English*, vol. i: *Prose Fiction from the Origins of Print to 1750* (2017).

T0284589

OXFORD WORLD'S CLASSICS

*For over 100 years Oxford World's Classics have brought
readers closer to the world's great literature. Now with over 700
titles—from the 4,000-year-old myths of Mesopotamia to the
twentieth century's greatest novels—the series makes available
lesser-known as well as celebrated writing.*

*The pocket-sized hardbacks of the early years contained
introductions by Virginia Woolf, T. S. Eliot, Graham Greene,
and other literary figures which enriched the experience of reading.
Today the series is recognized for its fine scholarship and
reliability in texts that span world literature, drama and poetry,
religion, philosophy, and politics. Each edition includes perceptive
commentary and essential background information to meet the
changing needs of readers.*

OXFORD WORLD'S CLASSICS

JANE AUSTEN

Northanger Abbey

Edited with an Introduction and Notes by
THOMAS KEYMER

OXFORD
UNIVERSITY PRESS

OXFORD
UNIVERSITY PRESS

Great Clarendon Street, Oxford, OX2 6DP,
United Kingdom

Oxford University Press is a department of the University of Oxford.
It furthers the University's objective of excellence in research, scholarship,
and education by publishing worldwide. Oxford is a registered trade mark of
Oxford University Press in the UK and in certain other countries

Editorial material © Thomas Keymer 2024
Chronology © Vivien Jones 2003

Published in the United States of America by Oxford University Press
198 Madison Avenue, New York, NY 10016, United States of America

British Library Cataloguing in Publication Data

Data available

Library of Congress Control Number: 2024930848

ISBN 978-0-19-884106-7

Printed and bound in the UK by
Clays Ltd, Elcograf S.p.A.

MIX
Paper | Supporting
responsible forestry
FSC® C018072

CONTENTS

INTRODUCTION

NORTHANGER ABBEY is a comedy about reading and misreading—reading books, reading the world—and about different kinds of peril, both imagined and real. It is Jane Austen's most self-conscious work in generic terms, grounded in a tradition of metafiction (novels about novels) that looks back two centuries to Cervantes, yet also in the flashiest, most fashionable new writing of Austen's day. It shows her experimenting creatively with form and technique, reworking inherited conventions of authorial commentary and storytelling while developing her signature style of free indirect discourse, where detached narrative comes to bear the impress of a character's voice and perspective. The celebrated fifth chapter of *Northanger Abbey*, in which Austen steps out of her narrative frame to make a bold, eloquent case for the power of novels, is a landmark of literary history, a key moment in the elevation of the genre from dismissive, even hostile, eighteenth-century assumptions on the road to its Victorian prestige.

Yet the achievement of *Northanger Abbey* is more than merely technical, for all the novel's brilliance in formal terms. The absurdities of fashion and conspicuous consumption, with their capacity to corrode social relations, are ever-present motifs in Austen, from the fancily customized toothpick case that obsesses Robert Ferrars in *Sense and Sensibility* to the sumptuous barouche-landau (a high-end convertible carriage) that Mrs Elton purrs about in *Emma*. Yet Austen's satire on voguish ostentation and social competition is nowhere more sustained than in *Northanger Abbey*, set first in shark-infested Bath, the premier health resort and marriage market of the day, and then in a more tranquil, or seemingly tranquil, pocket of rural Gloucestershire that turns out to be contaminated by greed. Austen interlaces her themes of literary fashion and consumer materialism with deftness and verve, and uses both to explore a perennial concern: the navigation by a vulnerable protagonist (Catherine Morland is Austen's youngest primary heroine, not without powers of intuition, but certainly the most naïve) of financial disadvantage, social constraint, and sometimes quite ruthless manipulation. The novel rarely suspends its genial comic tone and mode of teasing indirection, but as the harder edges of Austen's satire came to be appreciated by

post-Victorian readers, *Northanger Abbey* has also been credited with
an underlying seriousness—even a trenchant severity—of purpose.
For the modernist author Rebecca West in her preface to a new edition of 1932, 'the feminism of Jane Austen, to take the expression of
it in *Northanger Abbey*', was marked, conscious, and 'very drastic; it
declares that the position of woman as society dictated it was humili-
ating, dangerous, and founded on lying propositions'.[1]

Composition and Publication

Northanger Abbey is the first of Austen's six full-length novels to have
been accepted for publication, yet also (with *Persuasion*, in a four-
volume set) the last to have been actually published. In criticism, it
tends to be treated as somehow marking the start of Austen's career,
and this habit may derive from *Northanger Abbey*'s affinity with the
madcap parodic skits she wrote in her teens, gleeful spoofs on the
creaking devices and mawkish clichés of circulating-library fiction.[2] As
Freya Johnston points out, studies that line up the major works in
sequence routinely kick off with *Northanger Abbey*, although when
starting work on the book in the 1790s Austen had already drafted two
other novels, and she was still working (or was working again) on it at
a time, almost two decades later, when four of the novels were now in
print. 'We might say of *Northanger Abbey* that it is both an early and
a late work', Johnston suggests.[3] The publishing (or, for what must have
seemed endless years, non-publishing) history is complex, fascinating,
and rich in paradox—'extraordinary', Austen called it herself, biting
her tongue (p. 3)—though also frustratingly indistinct at key points.
This is a history, moreover, that has intriguing consequences for inter-
pretation; more than mere extraneous authorial biography, it connects
intimately, albeit in some ways fortuitously, with the substance of
Northanger Abbey as a book about books (as commodities, as obses-
sions, as snares). In a work satirically concerned with literary fashion,

[1] Jane Austen, *Northanger Abbey*, preface by Rebecca West (London: Jonathan Cape,
1932), p. viii.

[2] Apart from a short specimen, these early manuscripts, 'written . . . for sociable reading and for circulation and performance among family and friends', remained unpublished until the twentieth century (Jane Austen, *Teenage Writings*, ed. Kathryn Sutherland
and Freya Johnston (Oxford: Oxford University Press, 2017), p. xi).

[3] Freya Johnston, *Jane Austen, Early and Late* (Princeton: Princeton University Press,
2021), 92; see also 63.

the marketplace for print, and the unstable reputation of novelists and novels, the publishing history serves to dramatize a key *Northanger Abbey* theme in the dysfunctional real world of authors and booksellers. And although we know little for sure about the exact nature of Austen's last revisions to *Northanger Abbey*, the obstacles she experienced—even the humiliations, the lying propositions—may have sharpened her satire in the version eventually published following her death.

The surviving facts deserve careful attention. According to Austen's sister Cassandra in a memorandum recording composition dates for all six novels, 'North-hanger Abbey was written about the years 98 & 99'.[4] Cassandras are famous for not being believed, but this dating was endorsed by another family insider (' "Northanger Abbey" . . . was certainly first composed in 1798'[5]) and has been broadly accepted by modern scholars. More specifically, Deirdre Le Faye suggests that *Susan* (Austen's original title for *Northanger Abbey*) was composed between August 1798 and late June 1799, with a separate revision stage in winter 1802–3—a stage Le Faye infers from Austen's preliminary statement that 'THIS little work was finished in the year 1803' (p. 3).[6] Publication had to wait, however, until five months after Austen's death, when in December 1817 the London publisher John Murray brought out *Northanger Abbey and Persuasion* in a four-volume edition of 1,750 copies (with 1818 on the title page, as was standard practice for dating end-of-year publications). At a time when circulating libraries and communal reading habits would mean many readers per copy, this was a respectable total, though short of the print runs enjoyed by the 'sister author[s]' (p. 79)—Frances Burney, Maria Edgeworth—with whom Austen aligns herself in *Northanger Abbey*. The novel was not to reach anything like a mass audience until its inclusion in Richard Bentley's affordable, frequently reprinted Standard Novels series (1833), followed by cheap Routledge paperbacks in the 1850s.[7]

[4] *Jane Austen's Fiction Manuscripts*, ed. Kathryn Sutherland (Oxford: Oxford University Press, 2018), v. 297; Sutherland dates Cassandra's memorandum to July–Dec. 1817 and calls it 'the most important source of information for the composition of her sister's novels'.

[5] J. E. Austen-Leigh, *A Memoir of Jane Austen and Other Family Recollections*, ed. Kathryn Sutherland (Oxford: Oxford University Press, 2002), 44.

[6] Deirdre Le Faye, *Jane Austen: A Family Record* (2nd edn, Cambridge: Cambridge University Press, 2004), pp. xxii–xxiv.

[7] William St Clair, *The Reading Nation in the Romantic Period* (Cambridge: Cambridge University Press, 2004), 580. In 1814, Burney's *The Wanderer* and Edgeworth's *Patronage* came out in print runs of 3,000 and 8,000 respectively (St Clair, *Reading Nation*, 584, 597; see also, for Ann Radcliffe, 631).

Assuming Cassandra's memorandum to be correct, *Northanger Abbey* is then the third of Austen's full-length novels to have been drafted, the first two being *Sense and Sensibility* (which began life as *Elinor and Marianne*, probably in 1795) and *Pride and Prejudice* (the original version of which, as *First Impressions*, was completed in 1797, offered to the leading bookseller Thomas Cadell, and rejected sight unseen by return of post: humiliation indeed). *Northanger Abbey* was, however, the first of the novels to be successfully sold to a publisher. This time Austen selected a more realistic target than upscale Cadell: the mid-level London firm of Crosby & Co., whose proprietor, Benjamin Crosby, had published William Godwin's radical novel *Things as They Are; or, The Adventures of Caleb Williams* in 1794, and was now expanding his fiction list to become the fourth most prolific publisher of novels in the 1800–9 decade.[8] The transaction took place sometime in spring 1803 (April seems likely), when Crosby bought Austen's manuscript for £10, possibly via a bookselling associate in Bath, where Austen was now living (she had visited at least twice in the previous decade); her intermediary was a man named William Seymour, attorney to her brother Henry and later reportedly a suitor of Austen herself. This modest sum—£10 would buy you about twenty Crosby novels—was as much as an unconnected first-time author could expect, although it is sometimes noted by comparison that Ann Radcliffe, the star Gothic novelist whose work enthrals Catherine in Bath, was paid £500 for *The Mysteries of Udolpho* (1794) and a record-breaking £800 for *The Italian* (1797). Crosby & Co. published a total of ten new novels in 1803, and between July and September they advertised *Susan* as 'In the Press' in the fashionable *St James's Chronicle* in London and at least seven provincial newspapers, as well as in two of the firm's own books.[9] But *Susan* never appeared.

---

[8] A. A. Mandal, 'Making Austen MAD: Benjamin Crosby and the Non-Publication of *Susan*', *RES* 57/231 (2006), 507–25, at 513.

[9] Mandal transcribes from the *Dorchester & Sherborne Journal* (26 Aug. 1803) an advertisement listing eleven Crosby novels to which is appended 'In the Press—Susan, 2 vols.'. Similar notices were more recently found in the *St James's Chronicle* (23 July), the *Northampton Mercury* (30 July), the *Stamford Mercury* (5 and 19 Aug.), the *Hampshire Chronicle* (8 Aug.), the *Hull Advertiser* (13 Aug.), and the *Derby Mercury* (8 Sept.); for these, and the two advertisements in books, see Margie Burns, *Publishing Northanger Abbey: Jane Austen and the Writing Profession* (Wilmington, DE: Vernon Press, 2021), 4–16, 233–4.

It is sometimes assumed that as a publisher of Gothic fiction himself (his 1803 output included Mary Julia Young's *Moss Cliff Abbey*
and Anne Ker's *The Mysterious Count; or, Montville Castle*), Crosby
was disinclined, on reflection, to proceed further with a send-up of
a genre that was serving him well. But booksellers of the period had
more pressing matters to think about than the curatorial purity of
their lists, and in a profession notorious for high rates of bankruptcy,
few could afford the luxury of overspecializing. With titles such as
Mrs F. C. Patrick's *More Ghosts!* (1798), even William Lane of the
Minerva Press, London's foremost purveyor of Gothic schlock, saw
no contradiction in bringing out spoofs of the genre alongside the real
thing—and in any case the real thing often flirts, on closer inspection,
with the rhetorical overkill of the spoofs. Crosby played the same
game himself with Elisabeth Guénard's *The Three Monks!!!* (1803),
an arch, mildly risqué tale of absent crusaders, randy friars, and bored
ladies who 'were always disposed to receive extremely well, the godly
men who came to *amuse* them'.[10] A more plausible explanation for
Susan's non-appearance is provided by Anthony Mandal, who docu-
ments Crosby's escalating business difficulties in the period following
his purchase of Austen's manuscript, and suggests that these difficulties underlie a sudden drop-off in his production of fiction, with just
two new novels in 1804 (one published late in the year, the other as
part of a consortium). Crosby may have invested £10 in buying
Susan, but that was a small loss to absorb compared with the £100 or
more that he would have had to lay out, at his own risk, to produce the
two-volume novel of an unknown author.[11] And by the time he
returned seriously in 1806 to the fiction market—a world of instant
fashion and urgent sell-by dates—*Susan* was ancient history.

There is no record of Austen's response to the impasse until 1809,
a year often held to mark a revival of her creative energies after the
personal and financial disruptions entailed by her father's death in
1805. But in February that year another two-volume work entitled
Susan: A Novel was published by John Booth, a London bookseller
who also ran a circulating library in the smart West End district of

---

[10] Elizabeth Guénard, trans. H. J. Sarrett, *The Three Monks!!!* (1803), I. 1. (In references to contemporary novels, volume nos. are given in upper-case roman numerals,
chapter nos. in lower-case roman numerals, and page nos. in arabic numerals, with the
different elements separated by spaced points.)

[11] Mandal, 'Making Austen MAD', 518–23.

Portland Place. Austen cannot have mistaken this insipid effort for her own book: as one of Booth's advance notices specifies, the published *Susan* was a fanciful (but of course impeccably moral) romance in which 'the Exclusion of the heroine of this work into a remote isle of Scotland will . . . immediately remind the reader of Elizabeth, the Exile of Siberia, from their unity of interest and elegant simplicity'.[12] She probably saw the novel advertised, however, and may even have seen the text itself—in which case the simplicity would have struck her more than the interest. Perhaps she later saw the *Monthly Review* notice in which Anna Laetitia Barbauld classes *Susan* 'among the blue-winged ephemera' of the year, noting, in nicely judged tones of bored inattention, its dreary plot routines: 'prodigious number of fevers, together with several faintings, two duels, and one or two deaths.'[13] It was in this context that Austen set aside her usual practice of dealing with publishers via male relatives (her father, her brother) and wrote testily to Crosby & Co. under the pseudonym Mrs Ashton Dennis—so enabling the expressive sign-off 'I am Gentlemen &c &c | MAD.—'. In the body of the letter, Austen protests breach of contract ('an early publication was stipulated for at the time of Sale'), offers to send another copy 'supposing the MS by some carelessness to have been lost', and announces herself, in the absence of satisfaction, 'at liberty to secure the publication of my work, by applying elsewhere'. She did not act, however, on a reply in which Crosby's son Richard threatened legal action should she take her retained copy to another publisher, while adding of the copy languishing in his office that 'the MS. Shall be yours for the same as we paid for it'.[14] Still in straitened circumstances, Austen may simply have lacked the ready cash.

It was not until spring 1816 that her brother Henry retrieved the manuscript from Crosby & Co., and at that point Austen composed her 'Advertisement, by the Authoress', with wording that seems to

---

[12] *Bath Chronicle and Weekly Gazette* (12 Jan. 1809); the reference is to Sophie Ristaud Cottin's *Elizabeth; or, The Exiles of Siberia* (1807), a tedious Minerva Press publication translated by Elizabeth Meeke.

[13] *Monthly Review* (July 1809), quoted by Devoney Looser, 'The ABCs of *Northanger Abbey*: Advertisements, Backstories, and Classifications', *Persuasions On-Line*, 40/1 (2019).

[14] *Jane Austen's Letters*, ed. Deirdre Le Faye (4th edn, Oxford: Oxford University Press, 2011), 182 (5 Apr. 1809), 183 (8 Apr. 1809). Further references will be to *Letters*, followed by page no. and date.

envisage immediate publication. At the same time, she made plain her thoughts about Crosby with a flourish of crushing Johnsonese: 'That any bookseller should think it worth while to purchase what he did not think it worth while to publish seems extraordinary' (p. 3). Yet once again the novel failed to appear, and a year later, having completed *Persuasion* and started *Sanditon*, and in failing health, Austen told her niece Fanny Knight that 'Miss Catherine is put upon the Shelve for the present, and I do not know that she will ever come out'.[15] The heroine's new name was no doubt in reaction to the 1809 *Susan*, and Austen was also now using this name as her working title (the still untitled *Persuasion*, she adds, 'is short, about the length of Catherine'). However eloquent the published title *Northanger Abbey* might be, there is no reliable evidence to indicate that Austen devised it herself or planned to use it. It is usually attributed to Henry (in Kathryn Sutherland's words, Austen's 'unofficial literary agent'), who managed her literary reputation after death, notably in an anodyne 'Biographical Notice' prefixed to the posthumous edition.[16]

Terrorist Novel-Writing

In the twentieth-century heyday of formalist criticism, the *Northanger Abbey* title irked readers for whom this was a broken-backed work, a game of two poorly integrated halves (social comedy in the Bath episodes, Gothic parody in the Northanger section) that failed to reach its advertised setting until more than halfway through.[17] It made excellent sense, however, to highlight Austen's inspired name for the Tilney estate, with all its rich implications. In the first place this was (like *Mansfield Park*) a plausible place name, and Cassandra's 'North-hanger' spelling suggests this meaning was uppermost in her own mind. A hanger was a steep-sloped or 'hanging' wood, like Colonel Brandon's idyllic Delaford Hanger in *Sense and Sensibility*, and there was a real-life North Hanger Farm outside Southampton, where Austen lived for a period. When Catherine imagines the abbey

---

[15] *Letters*, 348 (13 Mar. 1817). On creative consequences of the overlap with *Persuasion* and *Sanditon*, see below, pp. xxiii–xxiv.

[16] Kathryn Sutherland, *Jane Austen's Textual Lives: From Aeschylus to Bollywood* (Oxford: Oxford University Press, 2005), 227.

[17] On this once standard objection, see Janine Barchas, *Matters of Fact in Jane Austen: History, Location, and Celebrity* (Baltimore: Johns Hopkins University Press, 2012), 93.

'standing low in a valley, sheltered from the north and east by rising woods of oak' (p. 100), her words suggest a rural idyll, and on arrival the reality appears to match, with 'steep woody hills rising behind . . . beautiful even in the leafless month of March' (p. 127). But the evocation was historical as well as topographical, and here more sinister connotations emerge. For all her professed boredom with history— 'The quarrels of popes and kings . . . in every page' (p. 77)—Catherine knows enough of these quarrels to recognize Northanger as 'a richly-endowed convent at the time of the Reformation . . . fallen into the hands of an ancestor of the Tilneys on its dissolution' (p. 100). '[F]allen into', as though by happy chance—but with all her characteristic lightness of touch, Austen gestures here to the stripped altars and bare ruined choirs of Henrician tyranny, and traces the Tilneys' wealth to a brutal history of coercion and confiscation. A beneficiary of (in Margaret Doody's words) 'the original land grab',[18] General Tilney now seems bent on grabbing Miss Morland; true to the legacy of his forebears, he seeks to enrich his dynasty further via a fat dowry for his son. Until, that is, new information makes him perceive Catherine anew, not as a landed heiress at all, but instead an impecunious parasite or 'hanger-on'—another meaning, current at the time, that lurks within the novel's title.

More pervasively, as Tony Tanner proposed in his classic essay 'Anger in the Abbey', the title suggests the ruling passion of the mercurial General. Or, at least, one of his ruling passions—and 'Northavarice' or 'Northambition' were scarcely options. 'Anger' is the novel's disquieting keyword, with its cognate and synonymous terms: 'his resentful ire'; 'furious in his anger'; 'Enraged with almost every body in the world but himself' (pp. 138, 179). Though distributed between several of Austen's characters (sometimes in negative formulations), the word clusters most emphatically around General Tilney, with decreasing efforts on his side at suppression or concealment. The culmination, near the end of the narrative, is open rage. This is a comedy, Tanner writes, in which patriarchal anger is only tenuously contained by the norms of civility and politeness that we associate with Austen's world: 'There are atrocities and atrocities and they can take on domestic and social forms without thereby ceasing to be atrocities.'[19]

Atrocity was all the rage in literature of the 1790s, from harrowing reports of the revolutionary guillotine in Helen Maria Williams's *Letters from France* (1790–6) to the Gothic craze that surrounded *The Mysteries of Udolpho: A Romance* in 1794 and John Thorpe's favourite, Matthew Lewis's electrifying *The Monk: A Romance* (1796). Some readers even traced a connection, like the 1797 satirist who, styling himself 'a Jacobin Novelist' but deploring 'the tyranny of Robespierre', mused that in the new sensationalist fiction 'we have exactly and faithfully copied the SYSTEM OF TERROR, if not in our streets, and in our fields, at least in our circulating libraries, and in our closets'.[20] Gothic fiction was still being produced at scale when *Northanger Abbey* at last reached print, and in this context the most unmistakable suggestion of the title—amplified in Murray's newspaper ads for *Northanger Abbey, a Romance*, though no such generic marker appeared in the book itself[21]—is that here was yet another imitation of Radcliffe, or, if not, a send-up like Thomas Love Peacock's cerebral satire *Nightmare Abbey* (1818).

Cod-medieval relics and ruins, with their connotations of feudal barbarism and ancient mystery, were essential components of Gothic, and in 1796 the *Critical Review* complained about the formulaic monotony of the genre, though exempting its foremost exponent: 'Since Mrs Radcliffe's justly admired and successful romances, the press has teemed with stories of haunted castles and visionary terrors; the incidents of which are so little diversified, that criticism is at a loss to vary its remarks.'[22] Abbeys were special favourites, with the opportunities they offered for tales of perverted religiosity and inquisitorial torment. Radcliffe-era examples include *The Abbey of St Asaph* (1795), *Roach Abbey* (1796), *The Horrors of Oakendale Abbey* (1797), and *Grasville Abbey* (1798); between 1790 and 1820, at least thirty novels sported eponymous abbeys, alongside *The Haunted Priory*

[19] Tony Tanner, *Jane Austen* (Basingstoke: Macmillan, 1986), 69.

[20] 'Terrorist System of Novel-Writing', *Monthly Magazine* (Aug. 1797), 102–4, at 102.

[21] David Gilson, *A Bibliography of Jane Austen* (new edn, Winchester: St Paul's Bibliographies, 1997), 84.

[22] Angela Wright, *Britain, France and the Gothic, 1764–1820: The Import of Terror* (Cambridge: Cambridge University Press, 2013), quoting the *Critical Review* (Feb. 1796) on *Austenburn Castle*.

(1794), *The Monastery of Gondolfo* (1810), *Convent of Grey Penitents* (1810), and much more.[23] Austen neatly evokes the representational clichés shared by these works to indicate her heroine's fervid anticipation of Northanger. Approaching as dusk falls, Catherine is trained by her reading to be sure of sublime experience: 'every bend in the road was expected with solemn awe to afford a glimpse of its massy walls of grey stone, rising amidst a grove of ancient oaks, with the last beams of the sun playing in beautiful splendour on its high Gothic windows' (p. 114). Her mind's eye reflects blood-curdling shockers like Regina Maria Roche's *The Children of the Abbey* (1796), where the heroine traverses oak woods 'scattered over with relics of druidical antiquity', and then admires from 'the massy door' of the abbey 'the dark and stupendous edifice, whose gloom was now heightened by the shadows of evening, with venerable awe'.[24] Later, Henry Tilney echoes any number of Minerva Press potboilers when teasing Catherine with thoughts of a 'gloomy chamber—too lofty and extensive for you, with only the feeble rays of a single lamp to take in its size—its walls hung with tapestry exhibiting figures as large as life, and the bed, of dark green stuff or purple velvet, presenting even a funereal appearance' (p. 112). His words evoke exactly the predicament of Mary Pilkington's heroine in *Rosina* (1793) on entering 'a large gloomy chamber, hung with old fashioned, but not ill executed tapestry. The curtains of the bed hung in tattered remnants . . . She gazed around her in wild astonishment, until the light burning down into the socket, began to throw its feeble and tremulous gleams on the walls of her dungeon.'[25]

In *Northanger Abbey* as a whole, much of the fun for readers immersed in disposable circulating-library fiction must have arisen from the many further echoes of Gothic tags—'motionless with horror' (p. 121); 'her blood was chilled' (p. 122)—that Austen works into her text. That may be why she worried about her novel's best-before date after years of cultural transition, when 'places, manners, books, and opinions have undergone considerable changes' (p. 3). But in fact Austen's most outrageous Gothic flourishes—'Darkness

[23] See the book listings in Peter Garside, James Raven, and Rainer Schöwerling (eds), *The English Novel, 1770–1829: A Bibliographical Survey*, 2 vols. (Oxford: Oxford University Press, 2000); no doubt further titles like this appeared as magazine serials.
[24] Regina Maria Roche, *The Children of the Abbey* (1796), I. 287, 288.
[25] Mary Pilkington, *Rosina* (1793), IV. 177.

impenetrable and immoveable filled the room' (p. 121)—are timeless enough to sound like *Paradise Lost* and *Frankenstein* all at once. Other passages tweak the routines of the Radcliffe moment in ways that require no exaggeration. Asked by Catherine if Northanger is 'a fine old place, just like what one reads about', Henry replies that they will not need to penetrate 'a hall dimly lighted by the expiring embers of a wood fire' (p. 112); they will not encounter, in other words, the hackneyed thrills and off-the-peg shivers of Richard Warner's *Netley Abbey* (1795), a novel based on a much-visited Cistercian ruin near Southampton that Austen toured herself in 1808. Here the hero, summoned into a gloomy refectory 'by screams of female distress', finds the villainous abbot creepily illuminated, as convention dictated, 'by the expiring embers of a large fire'.[26]

A literature of terror that included in its gory repertoire sensational stories of abduction and imprisonment, spine-tingling supernatural (or apparently supernatural) effects, and a hyperbolic rhetoric of sublime description, the Gothic novel was diversifying rapidly in the 1790s. It had diversified even more by the 1810s, when Walter Scott joked about different possible ways to market his bestselling *Waverley* (1814). He might have evoked the *Udolpho* mode, all lost keys, ruinous precincts and trembling steps, with 'stories of blood and horror . . . heard in the servant's hall'. Alternatively, 'a Romance from the German' would promise 'a profligate abbot, an oppressive duke, a secret and mysterious association of Rosycrucians and illuminati, with all their properties of black cowls, caverns, daggers, electrical machines, trap-doors, and dark-lanterns'.[27] When Catherine first encounters Gothic writing in fashion-obsessed Bath, however, she and her friend Isabella have no time for fine subgeneric distinctions, and they move straight from the black veils and skeletons of Radcliffe's fiction to the 'ten or twelve more of the same kind' noted in Isabella's pocketbook (p. 24). The listed works are 'all horrid', Isabella placidly adds, in a conversation that shifts seamlessly between Gothic novels and coquelicot ribbons, the latest books and the newest fabrics, must-have textiles and texts. It is as though all are

[26] Richard Warner, *Netley Abbey* (1795), I. 145; see Dale Townshend, 'Ruins, Romance and the Rise of Gothic Tourism: The Case of Netley Abbey, 1750–1830', *Journal for Eighteenth-Century Studies*, 37/3 (2014), 377–94.

[27] Walter Scott, *Waverley*, ed. Claire Lamont and Kathryn Sutherland (Oxford: Oxford University Press, 2015), 3–4.

interchangeable consumer trinkets, instances of what Austen calls 'the unmeaning Luxuries of Bath' in her teenage satire 'Love and Freindship'.[28] And while the titles Isabella gives, including *Mysterious Warnings*, *Necromancer of the Black Forest*, and *Horrid Mysteries*, might sound too good to be true, all were real publications of the 1790s, most of them German *Schauerromane* ('shudder-novels') or English imitations from the Minerva Press. Austen knew at least one first hand, having heard her father read aloud from 'the "Midnight Bell", which he has got from the library', during a family trip of 1798. A month later, she was willing enough to be counted with her binge-reading heroine, proclaiming herself and her family (when a local library proprietor disparaged fiction) to be 'great Novel-readers & not ashamed of being so'.[29] Perhaps parody requires not only immersion in the target discourse but also real affection.

Part of the pleasure of Gothic, the emergence of distinct subgenres notwithstanding, was that of eerie repetition, with the iterability of favourite tropes in new but broadly recognizable plot frameworks. The genre overall was characterized by temporally or geographically remote settings—medieval, Renaissance, Mediterranean, Teutonic—in which enlightened modern constraints on plot and action—manners and morals, customs and laws—were conveniently put aside. By locating climactic plot events in the winding labyrinths and gloomy recesses of ancient monasteries or ruined castles, Gothic cultivated an atmosphere laden with enthralling psychosexual connotation. Perhaps Austen plays on this feature with 'the cavity of importance' (p. 120) that Catherine is on the brink of discovering at Northanger, or the 'frightful great rent' (p. 172) in her guardian's lacework at Bath ('It would have been very shocking to have it torn', p. 12); such innuendos recall the notorious 'great slit in my worked muslin gown' that preoccupies Lydia after her elopement with Wickham in *Pride and Prejudice*.[30]

Gothic fiction could also speak, however subliminally, to its political moment, and the 'Jacobin Novelist' cited above was not alone in

---

[28] Austen, *Teenage Writings*, ed. Sutherland and Johnston, 71.

[29] *Letters*, 15 (24 Oct. 1798); 27 (18 Dec. 1798).

[30] Jane Austen, *Pride and Prejudice*, ed. Christina Lupton (Oxford: Oxford University Press, 2019), III. v. 216; on these and other innuendos in *Northanger Abbey*, see Jillian Heydt-Stevenson, *Austen's Unbecoming Conjunctions: Subversive Laughter, Embodied History* (New York: Palgrave Macmillan, 2005), 69–102.

connecting the aesthetic of terror with the most sanguinary phase of the French Revolution, Robespierre's Terror of 1793–4, inaugurated by a widely repeated official declaration 'que la terreur soit à l'ordre du jour'. Another journalist scoffed at novelists for making '*terror* the *order of the day*, by confining the heroes and heroines in old gloomy castles, full of spectres, apparitions, ghosts, and dead men's bones'.[31] But there were more profound ways in which, for the Marquis de Sade in 1799, the imaginative world of Radcliffe and Lewis 'was the necessary offspring of the revolutionary upheaval which affected the whole of Europe'.[32] And if novelistic bloodshed and phantoms somehow registered the public atmosphere of turmoil and shock in which they were born, Gothic settings could also read like so many Bastilles, crumbling embodiments of a doomed *ancien régime*. As William Hazlitt recalled in 1819, it was natural enough 'if amidst the tumult of events crowded into this period, our literature has partaken of the disorder of the time', while more specifically Radcliffe's mouldering castles 'derived part of their interest . . . from the supposed tottering state of all old structures at the time'.[33] With her usual comic brio, Austen makes similar connections when Catherine is thrilled to hear that 'something very shocking indeed, will soon come out of London' (p. 80). She means a new novel, but the mind of her interlocutor Eleanor Tilney, perhaps schooled by her loyalist father in political paranoia, leaps to the horrors of revolutionary violence. When Henry at last clears up the misunderstanding, his words—'the Bank attacked, the Tower threatened, the streets of London flowing with blood' (p. 81)—are reminiscent, in their breathless telegraphese, of an account given by Austen's cousin Eliza de Feuillide of being caught in a London riot of 1792: 'the noise of the populace, the drawn swords & pointed bayonets of the guards, the fragments of brick & mortar thrown on every side, one of which had nearly killed my Coachman,

[31] 'Terrorist Novel Writing', in *The Spirit of the Public Journals for 1797* (1798), 223; for the Paris declaration, see Kenneth R. Johnston, *Unusual Suspects: Pitt's Reign of Alarm and the Lost Generation of the 1790s* (Oxford: Oxford University Press, 2013), pp. xvii, 256.

[32] Marquis de Sade, *The Crimes of Love: Heroic and Tragic Tales, Preceded by An Essay on Novels*, trans. David Howard (Oxford: Oxford University Press, 2005), 13 ('le fruit indispensable des secousses révolutionnaires, dont l'Europe entière se ressentait').

[33] *The Selected Writings of William Hazlitt*, ed. Duncan Wu (London: Pickering & Chatto, 1998), v. 111–12.

the firing at one end of the street.'[34] Revolution in London did not materialize, but the fears were real. Small wonder that Austen's vigilant General, even in his Northanger retirement, pays such close attention to newspapers and pamphlets, 'poring over the affairs of the nation', his eyes 'blinding for the good of others' (p. 134) like some reactionary latter-day Milton.

Throughout this multilayered satire on Gothic, Austen is not playing, of course, on particular novels, but rather on their idiom in general. The exception is the ubiquitous *Udolpho*, a point of reference in both volumes of *Northanger Abbey*, and a work Austen assumes her readers will know, not least for its villain-hero Montoni, a brooding sixteenth-century brigand who starves his wife almost to death in a haunted castle (she is found in a skeletal state and does not survive) and imprisons the orphaned heroine in order to win control of her inheritance via marriage to a sidekick. In the Bath volume, Radcliffe's flamboyant bestseller affords Catherine 'the luxury of a raised, restless, and frightened imagination' (p. 34) when she devours it on Isabella's recommendation; even sophisticated Henry Tilney has read it, with, he jokes, his 'hair standing on end the whole time' (p. 76). More consequentially, *Udolpho* shapes her torrid fantasies about secret murder in the Northanger volume, beguiling her mind from mundane reality to the point of perceiving the General, as the plot nears its climax, as himself a tortured, guilt-stricken villain, discernibly wearing 'the air and attitude of a Montoni' (p. 134).

Traditions and Techniques

Yet for all the prominence of Gothic in general and *Udolpho* in particular, this is far from the full extent of Austen's intertextual repertoire. Long before the circulating libraries of Bath, and while still a mischievous, baseball-playing tomboy, Catherine's mind is shaped by schoolroom staples—the poems of Gray and Pope, the plays of Shakespeare—as mediated by popular anthologies, and also, of course, by novels. In one of *Northanger Abbey*'s many delayed-release ironies, she learns from *Twelfth Night* that a lovelorn woman should

---

[34] To Philadelphia Walter, 7 June 1792, quoted by Deirdre Le Faye, *Jane Austen's 'Outlandish Cousin': The Life and Letters of Eliza de Feuillide* (London: British Library, 2002), 112–13. Eliza's royalist husband was guillotined during the Terror; she later married Austen's brother Henry.

look 'like Patience on a monument | Smiling at Grief'; this tag was frequently quoted in sentimental fiction of the day, and sure enough, we later see Catherine react to a minor setback 'with smiles of most exquisite misery' (pp. 7, 46). Austen sprinkles the opening chapters with jokes about a dizzying range of fictional modes aside from Gothic: foundling novels concerning a dashing 'young man whose origin was unknown' (p. 8); sentimental novels where characters oppress each other 'with sadness, and drown . . . in tears' (p. 9); libertine novels where baronets 'delight in forcing young ladies away to some remote farm-house' (p. 9); epistolary novels where characters exchange 'by every post . . . a detail of every interesting conversation' (p. 9); interpolated tales with gratuitous accounts of 'past adventures and sufferings . . . twenty years before' (p. 20). A wry prediction that Mrs Allen will finally 'reduce poor Catherine to all the desperate wretchedness of which a last volume is capable . . . whether by intercepting her letters, ruining her character, or turning her out of doors' (p. 10) resumes the joke about 'virtue in distress' novels—though again with proleptic irony, since turning out of doors in disgrace is just what lies ahead. Conspicuously, this is the work of an author whose confidence in her entitlement to publish flows from a knowing immersion in all the varieties of modern fiction, and from a sharp sense of the absurdities of each.

It is the work of an author, moreover, whose exclusion from the world of print as she wrote and revised (first hasty Cadell, then inert Crosby) is rhetorically offset by tones of amused condescension, and by flourishes of self-conscious narration that bypass the tired formulas of the day, recalling instead the mid-century sophistication of Henry Fielding. As John Mullan notes, across Austen's corpus as a whole, 'one of the reasons why this novel feels so different . . . is that we are so constantly reminded of the author's presence, arranging and commenting and speaking as herself'.[35] Where elsewhere Austen uses an authorial or quasi-authorial first person very sparingly (and in *Emma* avoids it entirely), *Northanger Abbey* makes at least fourteen first-person interventions in the narrative. Austen plays with witty artificiality on the materiality of her text (the volumes, the pages, the paper), on the interpretative tasks she leaves to readers (their

---

[35] John Mullan, *What Matters in Jane Austen? Twenty Crucial Puzzles Solved* (London: Bloomsbury, 2012), 294.

discernment, their judgement, their sagacity), and on narrative material she finds too cheesy to include, as when, on leaving Bath, 'The embraces, tears, and promises of the parting fair ones may be fancied' (p. 108). When a nobleman appears from nowhere in the final chapter to help wind up the plot, 'the most charming young man in the world is instantly before the imagination of us all'—and since no good novelist neglects the neo-Aristotelian 'rules of composition', Austen will make him the man whose old laundry list Catherine finds earlier in the volume (pp. 181–2).

Gestures like this intensify in the final pages, as Austen contrives the inevitable union of her 'almost pretty' heroine and 'not quite handsome' hero (pp. 6, 14). Most obvious is her parting disavowal—in her inability to decide whether her story will 'recommend parental tyranny, or reward filial disobedience' (p. 182)—of the expected didactic sign-off. All Austen's novels display a degree of amused impatience in their last-chapter sprint to a happy ending—not quite burlesque acceleration, but something approaching it—but *Northanger Abbey* is the wittiest case, mocking bloated courtship novels and their predictable conclusions by directing readers to 'see in the tell-tale compression of the pages before them, that we are all hastening together to perfect felicity' (p. 181). Again the register is unerring, and seasoned novel-readers might have remembered the 'prospects of the most perfect felicity' that open up towards the end of the anonymous *Emilia Belville* (1768), or the happy lovers of Charlotte Smith's *Celestina* (1791), fixed 'in such perfect felicity as is seldom enjoyed'.[36] The odd thing, amidst these wry subversions of convention, is that the first magazine reviewer of *Northanger Abbey and Persuasion* saw no objection to the first novel's satire on parental authority, and instead took aim at the offensive moral of the second, 'which seems to be, that young people should always marry according to their own inclinations and upon their own judgment'.[37]

This emphasis on authorial management and artifice does not mean that *Northanger Abbey* lacks any trace of the free indirect style that Austen perfected in her later work, where detached narrative

---

[36] *The History of Miss Emilia Belville* (1768), II. 214; Charlotte Smith, *Celestina* (1791), IV. 349; see also, for a lumpier anticipation of Austen's joke, Jane West, *A Gossip's Story* (1796), II. 96.

[37] *British Critic* (Mar. 1818), repr. in B. C. Southam (ed.), *Jane Austen: The Critical Heritage*, 2 vols. (London: Routledge & Kegan Paul, 1968–87), i. 93.

shades into conveying—as though infiltrated by, even emanating from—a character's subjective perceptions and idiolect (personal habits of language). However, the effect tends to be felt in snatches and shards, not sustained set pieces, as at several points where what might otherwise be narrative disinformation indicates Catherine's failure to grasp the malignity around her. When the General's children strike her as cowed and reserved, we learn that '*He* could not be accountable for his children's want of spirits' (p. 91)—but of course he could, and he is. When Isabella, though engaged to Catherine's brother, starts leading on swaggering Captain Tilney—'How strange that she should not perceive his admiration!' (p. 104)—not much readerly sagacity is needed to see what Isabella is doing. It has been suggested that passages like this, as technical departures from the dominant mode of *Northanger Abbey*, may indicate late revision as Austen prepared her retrieved manuscript for the press while also completing *Persuasion* and planning *Sanditon*.[38] These works certainly speak to each other in intriguing ways. However fortuitous their eventual pairing as a four-volume set, *Persuasion* seems to mirror or reverse *Northanger Abbey* in key aspects, with its traumatic but finally euphoric return to 'the white glare of Bath' (in this sense the four volumes have a palindromic structure),[39] or the pointed contrast between its benign, upright naval officers (Admiral Croft, Captain Wentworth) and the brutal military men of *Northanger Abbey*. *Persuasion*—a work defined, Deidre Lynch notes, by its sequel-like characteristics, its plot unfolding 'under the shadows cast by a prior story'[40]—also resumes *Northanger Abbey*'s theme of reading and the power of reading to shape the self; even wise, mature Anne Elliot is not immune to Catherine's mistake, and while advising Captain Benwick not to wallow in Romantic verse, she fails to practise what she preaches. In *Sanditon*, Charlotte Heywood is a knowing, vigilant Catherine Morland immune to the snare of novels; *Northanger Abbey*'s attack on reviewers who complain 'of the trash with which the press now groans' (p. 23) finds its evil twin in the flatulent speeches of

[38] See Doody, *Jane Austen's Names*, 251, and, for this argument in detail, Narelle Shaw, 'Free Indirect Speech and Jane Austen's 1816 Revision of Northanger Abbey', *SEL* 30/4 (1990), 591–601.

[39] Jane Austen, *Persuasion*, ed. James Kinsley and Deidre Lynch (Oxford: Oxford University Press, 2008), I. v. 32.

[40] Austen, *Persuasion*, ed. Kinsley and Lynch, p. xviii; see also pp. x–xi.

Sir Edward Denham, who despises 'the mere Trash of the common Circulating Library'.[41] For Kathryn Sutherland, such overlaps are 'the inevitable consequence of a chronology of writing which included alongside new ventures . . . the revision of earlier completed writings, a pattern which leaves us with *Sanditon*, her final work, as the sequel to *Northanger Abbey*, one of her earliest'.[42]

The celebrated defence of fiction may itself be a later addition in whole or part. One of the novels Austen praises as work 'in which the most thorough knowledge of human nature, the happiest delineation of its varieties . . . are conveyed to the world in the best chosen language' (p. 23) had not been published when she drafted *Northanger Abbey*; that was Edgeworth's *Belinda*, a work of 1801. The chapter may also draw on an influential vindication of the genre, Anna Laetitia Barbauld's essay 'On the Origin and Progress of Novel-Writing', first published as the introduction to a multi-volume anthology of 1810, *The British Novelists*; in this context, Sutherland calls Austen's chapter a 'Barbauld-like panegyric to the female novel', while Anne Toner suggests 'the confluence in their thinking and even Austen's direct allusion'.[43] Both authors emphasize a tradition of sophisticated social and moral satire that reaches back through Burney and Edgeworth to mid-century women writers like Charlotte Lennox, whose clever reworking of Cervantes in *The Female Quixote* (1752) Austen read more than once ('I find the work quite equal to what I remembered it', she wrote in 1807).[44] No doubt Lennox's work, in which a protagonist obsessed by voluminous heroic romances (her servant sinks under the weight of them; her suitor dreads having to read them) expects modern life to conform to outlandish chivalric norms, helped inspire *Northanger Abbey*. Even in Austen's opening sentence, on Catherine's unlikely credentials as 'an heroine' (p. 5), a gratuitously fussy indefinite article

[41] Jane Austen, *Sanditon*, ed. Kathryn Sutherland (Oxford: Oxford University Press, 2019), viii. 45.

[42] Sutherland, *Jane Austen's Textual Lives*, 127; on *Sanditon*, see also Deidre Shauna Lynch, *The Economy of Character: Novels, Market Culture, and the Business of Inner Meaning* (Chicago: University of Chicago Press, 1998), 223–7.

[43] Sutherland, *Jane Austen's Textual Lives*, 219; Anne Toner, *Jane Austen's Style: Narrative Economy and the Novel's Growth* (Cambridge: Cambridge University Press, 2020), 59; see also Jocelyn Harris, 'Anna Letitia Barbauld, Jane Austen's Unseen Interlocutor', in William McCarthy and Olivia Murphy (eds), *Anna Letitia Barbauld: New Perspectives* (Lewisburg, PA: Bucknell University Press, 2014), 237–57.

[44] *Letters*, 120 (7 Jan. 1807).

calls to mind Lennox's running (indeed somewhat overplayed) joke about the stereotypes of romance, where 'one never has the Idea of an Heroine older than Eighteen'.[45] That said, Austen seems not to have worried that she was merely recycling, with application to more recent fictional vogues, the basic conceit of Lennox's satire or imitations like Tabitha Gilman Tenney's *Female Quixotism*, an American novel of 1801. When another updating of Lennox, Eaton Stannard Barrett's *The Heroine; or, Adventures of a Fair Romance Reader*, came out in 1813, Austen could enjoy it as 'a delightful burlesque, particularly on the Radcliffe style', without seeming to worry that its appearance might threaten the still unpublished *Northanger Abbey*.[46]

The Spoils of Northanger

That may be because, as well as burlesquing 'the Radcliffe style', Austen had more ambitious uses in mind for Quixotic fiction. Crucial here was the potential of *Don Quixote* itself, the towering prototype of 1605–15, which uses its hero's book-driven madness not only to satirize the romances that detach Quixote from modernity but also, from a romance perspective, to defamiliarize modernity with the aim of seeing it anew. Cervantic satire could cut, in other words, two ways: most obviously on the deranged Quixote and the fanciful reading that obsesses him, but more interestingly on the debased world he rails against. In eighteenth century Britain, this was a potential exploited by the novelist Tobias Smollett, who shared Austen's Tory distaste for commercial mores and Whiggish corruption, and used his novel *Sir Launcelot Greaves* (1760–1) to satirize a range of present-day abuses, from electoral bribery to private madhouses. As the name of Smollett's English Quixote suggests (greaves are a category of medieval armour), Sir Launcelot is mentally locked in a remote chivalric past. But the name also indicates real contemporary evils or ills for which Sir Launcelot grieves.

In what ways might Radcliffe and her imitators open up satirical opportunities of this kind? One might consider the fictional tradition that Austen jokes about when alluding to 'the difficulties and dangers of a six weeks' residence in Bath' (p. 8) and 'our heroine's entrée

[45] Charlotte Lennox, *The Female Quixote*, ed. Margaret Dalziel with an introd. by Margaret Anne Doody (Oxford: Oxford University Press, 2008), III. i. 111.
[46] *Letters*, 267 (2 Mar. 1814).

into life' (p. 10)—a tradition to which Burney contributed in her debut novel *Evelina; or, the History of a Young Lady's Entrance into the World* (1778), but now in need of refreshment. *Evelina* details the codes and conventions stacked against the heroine as she enters society—the rules of the assembly, the protocols of the ballroom—and their exploitation by social or sexual predators. Catherine's Bath experience involves similar patterns of entrapment: forced unwittingly into breaches of propriety that leave her 'restlessly miserable' (p. 65); constrained by conventions in which 'man has the advantage of choice, woman only the power of refusal' (p. 53); compelled by pre-engagement to a suitor she dislikes to deny the suitor she wants to encourage (p. 36). Austen's inspired twist on this tradition is her ongoing hint that Gothic novels—novels of coercion, abduction, and imprisonment—might stand as dramatic metaphors for her social predicament. There is of course a sharp difference of degree between the perils of Udolpho and those of Bath, but it is not an absolute difference of kind, and Austen plays with teasing wit on the parallels. When boorish, manipulative John Thorpe—he of the 'Well hung' carriage (p. 29)—insists on whisking her off in his gig to the tourist destination of Blaise Castle, this is not quite abduction to a Gothic fastness, not only because Thorpe's trophy vehicle fails to make it (he overtasks the horses), but also because Blaise is a folly, a modern fake. Built as a viewpoint and party venue in 1766, it offers not the Gothic experience Catherine craves, all winding vaults and grated doors, but a foretaste of the modern luxury contrived at Northanger: as Humphry Repton, the fashionable landscape designer, said of Blaise, not 'a mouldering castle whose ruined turrets threaten destruction, and revive the horrors of feudal strife; but . . . a mansion of elegance, cheerfulness, and hospitality'.[47] Ironies like this are everywhere, but so is an underlying sense that Catherine, no less than *Udolpho*'s Emily, is an innocent abroad in a predatory world. Even as she reads about the imperilled heroines of Gothic novels, she experiences a modified version of the same thing, constrained by modern civility, but quietly analogous.

It follows that for all the absurdity of taking Gothic fiction literally as a guide to life, the fiction need not be absurd in itself, and when

---

[47] Cynthia Wall, *Grammars of Approach: Landscape, Narrative, and the Linguistic Picturesque* (Chicago: University of Chicago Press, 2019), 54, quoting Humphry Repton, *Red Book for Blaise Castle* (1796), 'The Approach'.

more thoughtfully approached as metaphorical in meaning, may even have a certain explanatory power. For the polite world of a modern spa still has its perils and pains, and through clever deployment of Gothic hyperbole in her opening volume—Catherine suffers 'agony', 'distresses', 'dread', 'misery', 'mortification', 'pangs', 'torment', and more—Austen draws playful analogies between the trials of a Radcliffe heroine and the everyday but no less absorbing tribulations of an ingénue at Bath. Catherine, after all, is manipulated and deceived by Isabella, trapped on one occasion by her brother, and more or less abducted on another; she is constrained, even imprisoned, in a world of regulated proprieties, and exploited by friends who link arms with hers 'though their hearts were at war' (p. 70). Her predicament is not literally that of the novels she reads, yet these novels can still indicate forms of persecution that operate, albeit in new guise, in a world of polite sociability. Eventually, Gothic settings and modern dilemmas coalesce in Catherine's mind, in ways brilliantly evoked as, hurried by Thorpe through the streets of Bath, her thoughts become a swirl of 'broken promises and broken arches, phaetons and false hangings, Tilneys and trap-doors' (p. 60). Gothic is something more interesting here than a frivolous distraction from the real; it offers instead a disquieting new lens on the real.

Tanner was among the first to spell out how the pattern intensifies as Catherine reaches Northanger. Her disappointment with the building starts the process, and in the chapters that follow, Austen's comedy works through studiously bathetic descriptions of mundane actualities—the elegant, light-filled rooms, the consumer durables and modern comforts—that frustrate her novel-fuelled desires. Traces of the medieval remain to be seen, like the pointed arches atop the General's bright replacement windows. But the overall impression is of disappointing rational modernity: swept gravel, regular casements, pretty china; wallpaper and carpets where there should be tapestries and sliding panels. Here Austen deftly exaggerates a familiar eighteenth-century experience. Northanger is not quite the teardown that readers would have known from famous cases like Wanstead Abbey in Essex, rebuilt in Palladian style by a political grandee named Earl Tylney, only for the new building to be demolished after the 1812 marriage of Catherine Tilney-Long, reputedly the wealthiest heiress in England, to a profligate gambler. But less extreme cases came in for criticism with the rise of picturesque aesthetics—a trend, associated

especially with William Gilpin, on which Henry lectures Catherine
on their Beechen Cliff walk. When visiting the former Cistercian
monastery of Forde Abbey in Dorset in the 1790s, Gilpin was dis-
mayed to find the great hall extravagantly retrofitted and the cloister
converted to an orangery: 'Sash windows glare over pointed arches,
and Gothic walls are adorned with Indian paper', he protests, deploring 'the hands of improvement' as agents of depraved taste and
vulgar ostentation.[48] In just this spirit, when Catherine searches for
those traces of past villainy that Gothic buildings should betray—
padlocked crime scenes, cells suited to barbarous proceedings—she
finds only commodious apartments with well-disposed closets.

In some ways, of course, it remains a defensible account of
Northanger Abbey to see it as a straightforward satire on fiction and
delusion à la Lennox: a novel of female education in which a naïve,
novel-obsessed heroine loses her grasp on reality, confuses a modern
gentleman with a Gothic villain, and is instructed out of her errors by
a wise suitor. Part of the cleverness of Austen's second volume lies in
the mixed messages sent out about Northanger's proprietor, but at
one level he seems genial enough, not so much the malign Montoni of
Catherine's imaginings as a harmless Uncle Toby: a retired veteran
whose 'hobby-horse' is growing exotic fruit, and who thoughtfully
procures 'every modern invention to facilitate the labour of the cooks'
(pp. 127, 131). By imagining the General instead in the villainous
Gothic role of uxoricide, Catherine has entertained 'grossly injurious
suspicions' inspired by her reading. But finally her mind is brought
back from 'the alarms of romance' to encounter and recognize, free of
hyperbolic literary distraction, the sober and salutary 'anxieties of
common life' (p. 144). Middle England, Henry instructs her, is not
a Radcliffean realm.

Or is it? On inspection, something looks badly awry on the Tilney
estate. The setting that so alarms Catherine, if not for exactly the
right reason, stands in a long line of grand mansions in eighteenth-
century literature, from Alexander Pope's *Epistle to Burlington* (1731)
to Oliver Goldsmith's *The Deserted Village* (1770), that embody the
depredations of commercial modernity and the hubris of their over-
weening masters. These are places whose owners disavow inherited

---

[48] Doody, *Jane Austen's Names*, 258–9, quoting William Gilpin, *Observations on the
Western Parts of England* (1798); see also, on Catherine Tilney-Long, 85.

responsibilities of communal stewardship, and who fashion their estates instead as self-regarding projections of wealth and power—to the point, in Goldsmith's poem, of appropriating previously common land and deporting the rural poor. A key concept here (as at the real-world Forde Abbey) is that of 'improvement', always a suspect term in Austen, with its connotations of luxurious, self-gratifying ostentation and the displacement of rural tradition by mercantile values. In contrast to Austen milieux where traditional obligations of stewardship still prevail—milieux like Mr Knightley's Donwell, contaminated by 'neither fashion nor extravagance', or Darcy's Pemberton in *Pride and Prejudice*, 'neither gaudy nor uselessly fine'[49]—'improvement' runs riot in morally dubious environments like Lady Cathcrine de Bourgh's Rosings, with its £800 chimneypiece and expensive glazing, or Norland Park, where acquisitive John Dashwood and his appalling wife enclose the village common and fell ancient walnut trees to make way for a voguish new hothouse. Points like this are sometimes thought to indicate a radical strain in Austen's thinking, but as the historian Jeremy Black makes clear, they more plausibly suggest a conservative distaste for the ascendancy of commercial interests and the concomitant erosion of social bonds: 'The reorganization of much of the countryside through enclosure reflected elite power, not least by disrupting traditional rights and expectations. So even more with the demolition of villages to create parkland.'[50]

From this perspective, 'The General's improving hand' (p. 131) at Northanger looks less benign. Too old for a sporty two-seater like John Thorpe, too staid for the newfangled barouche-landau of *Emma*'s leech-like Sucklings, he travels to Northanger in a stately chaise-and-four with all the pomp of 'postilions handsomely liveried' (a pseudo-aristocratic affection) and 'numerous outriders properly mounted' (p. 110). Once there, he alternates between assuring Catherine that he values money only to make others happy—'The brother and sister looked at each other' (p. 148)—while pointing out the 'costly gilding' in a renovated apartment and regretting the antiquity of his breakfast china, 'quite an old set, purchased two years ago'

[49] Jane Austen, *Emma*, ed. John Mullan (Oxford: Oxford University Press, 2022), III. vi. 275; Austen, *Pride and Prejudice*, ed. Lupton, III. i. 182.
[50] Jeremy Black, *England in the Age of Austen* (Bloomington: Indiana University Press, 2021), 57; the classic statement is Alistair M. Duckworth's *The Improvement of the Estate: A Study of Jane Austen's Novels* (Baltimore: Johns Hopkins University Press, 1994).

(pp. 115, 125). Perhaps most telling is his remodelling of the Northanger landscape to project status at the expense of community. Time-honoured practices of rural society give way to assertions of control over nature: 'a village of hot-houses seemed to arise . . . and a whole parish to be at work within the inclosure' (p. 127). Another of the General's humblebrags, this time about tropical fruit—'The pinery had yielded only one hundred in the last year' (p. 127)—aligns him with other domineering landowners in fiction of the day. Perhaps Austen remembered the socially ambitious proprietor of Clarendon Abbey in Mary Robinson's *Angelina* (1796), who boasts of his pineapple crop to Lord Acreland, a visitor whose acres he means to land for his daughter via marriage.[51] And while the hyacinth cultivars also yielded by Northanger's hothouses are not quite the speculative assets of seventeenth-century tulipomania, the implications are still disquieting; Catherine's own treatment, Deidre Lynch observes, is 'linked quite pointedly to the indoor forcing of hyacinths, the consummate example of florists' flowers'.[52] Mere tenants come in for rougher treatment, and in the parish of Woodston (the Tilney living that Henry rather negligently holds), a throwaway comment neatly indicates that improvement here means evicting peasants and demolishing homes. Only when Catherine, invited to 'examine some improvements' at Woodston, admires a picturesque cottage from the window does the General relent from his plan to sanitize the view: 'You like it—you approve it as an object;—it is enough . . . The cottage remains' (p. 154).

It has been suggested, in this novel of marriage markets and transactional courtship, that Austen is quietly playing on famous names, and hinting as the source of the General's designs on Catherine that he confuses her patrons the Allens with heirs of the quarrying magnate Ralph Allen, the wealthiest man in mid-eighteenth-century Bath. When Austen renamed her heroine at revision stage, there may also have been a sly if somewhat incongruous joke about hapless Catherine Tilney-Long. Even the offstage Miss Drummond, the heiress the General courts and marries in his youth (she is worth £20,000, exactly the wealth of the preening Miss Bingleys in *Pride*

[51] Liz Bellamy, *The Language of Fruit: Literature and Horticulture in the Long Eighteenth Century* (Philadelphia: University of Pennsylvania Press, 2019), 157–87.

[52] Deidre Shauna Lynch, ' "Young ladies are delicate plants": Jane Austen and Greenhouse Romanticism', *ELH* 77/3 (2010), 689–729, at 714.

and Prejudice), bears a name that Austen's readers would have associated with money, the Drummonds being a prominent banking dynasty.[53] Matrimony for the General is plainly 'mattermoney' (an eloquent malapropism from another Smollett novel),[54] and the pattern persists to the end of *Northanger Abbey*, with his delight when Eleanor marries a viscount. His avarice and ambition, those quintessentially Machiavellian vices, are beyond question. Yet does that make him, as *Udolpho* leads Catherine to suspect, a criminal Montoni? It is worth dwelling here on Henry's halting denial, which at one level brings Catherine back from romance to reality with a thud, but on inspection offers less clear resolution. The passage is a masterpiece of ironic suggestion, with hints that subtly implicate the General even as Henry defends him:

He loved her, I am persuaded, as well as it was possible for him to—We have not all, you know, the same tenderness of disposition—and I will not pretend to say that while she lived, she might not often have had much to bear, but though his temper injured her, his judgment never did. His value of her was sincere; and, if not permanently, he was truly afflicted by her death. (p. 142)

From the novel's rather obsessive guardian of rigorous usage and transparent language,[55] it is an odd speech, replete with unexpected qualifications and concessions, and with none of Henry's habitual mansplaining confidence. Literally, of course, the General has not locked his wife in a turret or starved her to death. But in spite of himself, Henry's words leave open the possibility of a more mundane, though perhaps little less lethal, version of Montoni's crime on the General's part: imprisoning the former Miss Drummond in a loveless marriage ('We have not all . . . the same tenderness of disposition'), oppressing her everyday life with burdens ('I will not pretend to say that . . . she might not often have had much to bear'), and assailing her with his trademark irrational anger ('his temper injured her'). If not quite killing his long-suffering wife, the General

[53] See Barchas, *Matters of Fact*, 57–92 (Allen), 117–21 (Tilney-Long), 277 n. 34 (Drummond).

[54] Tobias Smollett, *The Expedition of Humphry Clinker*, ed. Lewis M. Knapp and Paul-Gabriel Boucé (Oxford: Oxford University Press, 2009), 352.

[55] On Henry's bossy linguistic prescriptivism, as much the object of Austen's satire as the fashionable jargon he dislikes, see Joe Bray, *The Language of Jane Austen* (Basingstoke: Palgrave Macmillan, 2018), 107–15.

gave her little to live for. And while *Northanger Abbey* is not a Mary Wollstonecraft novel, where transactional marriage leaves a woman 'bastilled . . . for life',[56] it is a work, all the same, in which a widower's 'sincere value' for his late wife is clearly presented as a number—that £20,000 again—much more than a feeling. Happily for the General, the cash the liveried postilions, the costly gilding, the village of hot-houses—has outlasted his grief, even if a second Miss Drummond must now be found for his son.

For Anne Toner, the rhetorical figure of apophasis—where explicit disavowal of a meaning calls attention to its implicit presence—is one of Austen's core techniques: 'a dynamic of denying and disclosing' that galvanized her stylistic thinking and her narrative practice.[57] And so it is, not only with Henry's exquisitely managed speech, but more broadly with Catherine's 'visions of romance' and the sense that 'Charming as were all Mrs. Radcliffe's works . . . it was not in them perhaps that human nature, at least in the midland counties of England, was to be looked for' (pp. 142, 143). Gothic is explicitly dismissed, only to be implicitly validated. For on inspection, little in Henry's speech dispels the intuition of hidden evil that has made Catherine perceive the General through a Gothic lens. Henry goes on to rest his denial on the presence of external constraint in civilized, or more importantly transparent, modern England; 'human nature' has little to do with it. Outrages could not be perpetrated, he says, 'without being known, in a country like this, where social and literary intercourse is on such a footing; where every man is surrounded by a neighbourhood of voluntary spies, and where roads and newspapers lay every thing open' (p. 142). It is an odd place to rest his argument in several ways, not least in wording that recalls the ministerially induced paranoia of the 1790s, when, amidst conspiracy and insurrection alarms, the banning of political associations and the suspension of habeas corpus, 'voluntary spies' were officially recruited to report on suspected incendiaries. In the year of *Northanger Abbey*'s publication, the poet Samuel Taylor Coleridge recalled just such an episode involving himself and Wordsworth, though Wordsworth's

---

[56] Mary Wollstonecraft, *Mary and The Wrongs of Woman*, ed. Gary Kelly (Oxford: Oxford University Press, 2007), 137.

[57] Toner, *Jane Austen's Style*, 83. Toner quotes Nathan Bailey's neat 1721 definition of apophasis as a means 'whereby an Oratour seems to wa[i]ve what he would plainly insinuate' (84).

subversiveness in fact went little further than the radical-chic pose of wearing striped pantaloons.[58]

For all her tears and humiliation, it would seem, Catherine has got something fundamentally right about the structures of power in Northanger, and perhaps—if the General, provincial patriarch and military man, stands in some way for larger authority—beyond it. One might even conclude that it is Radcliffe and her school who have trained Catherine, albeit at first unconsciously, to understand the General more fully than anyone around him, including his son. Her one mistake has been to think of Gothic as literally applicable to a modern world in which there is 'security for the existence even of a wife not beloved, in the laws of the land, and the manners of the age' (pp. 143–4). Conspicuously, Austen leaves her list of securities at that, as though to imply that while laws and manners may have changed, the human capacity for villainy has not, and has merely adjusted its methods to fit the times. Without the rather fragile infrastructure of modern society, with its newspapers, roads, and nosy neighbours, unloved wives might still be done away with, and unsuspecting heiresses fleeced.

In the end, nothing discredits the General more emphatically than his culminating act of malevolence, Catherine's brutal expulsion from Northanger—a clever inversion of Gothic convention (since heroines are normally walled in, not thrown out) that nonetheless reveals an underlying affinity with Radcliffe's villain. Or, as Catherine now sees it, with more than a hint of authorial endorsement, 'in suspecting General Tilney of either murdering or shutting up his wife, she had scarcely sinned against his character, or magnified his cruelty' (p. 179). For Maria Edgeworth, the fellow novelist Austen so admired, this climactic twist of plot was a bridge too far, a violation of plausibility that belonged more to romance than to realist fiction. As she wrote within weeks of the novel's publication, 'the behaviour of the General in Northanger Abbey, packing off the young lady without a servant or the common civilities which any bear of a man, not to say gentleman, would have shown, is quite outrageously out of drawing and out of nature'.[59] But

[58] See Johnston, *Unusual Suspects*, 229–34.

[59] *Maria Edgeworth's Letters from Ireland*, ed. Valerie Pakenham (Dublin: Lilliput Press, 2017), 224 (21 Feb. 1818). Amusingly, Edgeworth calls *Northanger Abbey* 'one of the most stupid, nonsensical fictions I ever read (excepting always the praises of myself & Lady Delacour)'.

that is precisely Austen's point. For all its admirable qualities, verisimilitude of the Edgeworth kind gets us only so far in our knowledge of human nature. We need not only Radcliffe but perhaps even the cheap imitations, 'the trash with which the press now groans', to show us something more.

NOTE ON THE TEXT

FOR the tortuous history of *Northanger Abbey*'s composition and Jane Austen's frustrated efforts to publish it during her lifetime, see the Introduction, pp. viii–xiii. The novel at last appeared in print five months after Austen's death, when in December 1817 the London publisher John Murray brought out *Northanger Abbey and Persuasion* in a four-volume edition of 1,750 copies (with 1818 on the title page, as was standard practice for dating end-of-year publications). Most copies of the first edition were sold within a year, but 282 copies were remaindered in 1821. Beyond a French translation of 1824 and a Philadelphia reprint of 1833 (which, among other changes, removed most of John Thorpe's oaths, tactfully rendered as 'd——' in the original), no further edition appeared until Richard Bentley's inclusion of *Northanger Abbey* in his prominent, affordably priced Standard Novels series of 1833. Like the French and American editions, the Bentley reprint has no textual authority.[1]

The drawn-out history of publication, or for a long time non-publication, implies the existence of at least three manuscripts marking different stages of composition and revision: (1) the original working draft of 1798–9 as remembered by Cassandra Austen; (2) the manuscript sold to Crosby & Co. in 1803 and bought back from them in 1816, presumably a fair copy involving revisions of unknown extent; (3) the retained copy to which Austen refers in her letter to Crosby of 1809, which she may or may not have revised from time to time during the 1803–16 period. The posthumously published edition may have been typeset from the second or third of these manuscripts, apparently with a new layer of revision before Austen put the novel 'upon the Shelve' in March 1817. Or a new fair copy may have been used. None of these manuscripts survives, with the exception of a six-word title-page fragment in Austen's hand ('Susan. | a Novel in Two volumes.'), now in the Morgan Library, New York. In the published text, small smoking guns give evidence of revision post-dating first composition and then the sale to Crosby: praise for Maria

[1] David Gilson, *A Bibliography of Jane Austen* (new edn, Winchester: St Paul's Bibliographies, 1997), 84–6.

Edgeworth's *Belinda*, a novel published in June 1801; more conclusively, a passage reworked from Anna Laetitia Barbauld's edition of *The Correspondence of Samuel Richardson*, which did not appear in print until June 1804, and a reference to Union Passage in Bath, which was not so named until 1807. Datable allusions of this kind are unusual in Austen's writing at the best of times, and these examples of revision or insertion may be the tip of the iceberg. The most obvious and thoroughgoing change is the heroine's renaming from Susan to Catherine, probably in response to publication of another *Susan, A Novel* in 1809, and it has been suggested that the surname Tilney may also be a late introduction.[2] Conjecturally, though quite persuasively, it has been argued that elements of Austen's late style, specifically her use of free indirect discourse to represent characters' speech or thought, are intermittently present throughout the text, with a concentration in the second volume.[3]

In the absence of surviving manuscript witnesses, and in the absence, too, of more than a handful of detectable typographical errors in the posthumous first edition, *Northanger Abbey* presents few complications in textual-editorial terms. The first scholarly treatments were by Katharine Metcalfe in her free-standing Clarendon Press edition of 1923, followed a few months later by Metcalfe's husband R. W. Chapman in vol. v of *The Novels of Jane Austen* (Clarendon Press, 1923; rev. Mary Lascelles, 1965, 1969); both based their text on the first edition and shared the same page settings.[4] The present edition reprints James Kinsley's Oxford English Novels text of 1971, in which Kinsley closely followed Chapman but revised Chapman's textual apparatus and reconsidered his emendations.[5] Substantively, I depart just once from Kinsley's text, restoring 'quizzers' from the first edition in place of the Chapman/Kinsley emendation 'quizzes' (see p. 40 with note). A few minor typographical

[2] Janine Barchas, *Matters of Fact in Jane Austen: History, Location, and Celebrity* (Baltimore: Johns Hopkins University Press, 2012), 116–22.

[3] Narelle Shaw, 'Free Indirect Speech and Jane Austen's 1816 Revision of *Northanger Abbey*', *Studies in English Literature, 1500–1900*, 30/4 (1990), 591–601.

[4] Kathryn Sutherland, *Jane Austen's Textual Lives: From Aeschylus to Bollywood* (Oxford: Oxford University Press, 2005), 43–4; the Metcalfe edition appeared in July, the Chapman edition in Nov.

[5] Jane Austen, *Northanger Abbey and Persuasion*, ed. with introd. by John Davie, textual notes and bibliography by James Kinsley (London: Oxford University Press, 1971); see Kinsley's Note on the Text (xxi) and Textual Notes (471).

errors have been corrected, and some accidentals (specifically variable dash-lengths) have been adjusted to reflect the expressive practice of the first edition more closely than in Kinsley.

One peculiarity of the first edition to modern eyes is the occasional use of quotation marks around passages of indirect or reported speech. Chapman and Kinsley retain these marks except in two cases of incomplete pairs: see pp. 125 and 150, where a quotation closes without first opening. In these two cases, Chapman and Kinsley delete the closing marks; I retain them as indications of indirect discourse, supplying opening partners at lines 3 and 32 respectively. Various positions for these opening partners have been proposed by recent editors; the solutions of Susan J. Wolfson are followed here.[6]

---

[6] For the rationale, see Jane Austen, *Northanger Abbey*, ed. Susan J. Wolfson (Cambridge, MA: Harvard University Press, 2014), 48–9; see also Wolfson's astute discussion of the quizzers/quizzes crux, at 42–3, 49.

SELECT BIBLIOGRAPHY

Editions

Northanger Abbey and Persuasion (London: John Murray, 1818 [published December 1817]).

Northanger Abbey and Persuasion, in *The Novels of Jane Austen*, ed. R. W. Chapman (Oxford: Clarendon Press, 1923; 3rd edn, 1932–4; rev. Mary Lascelles, 1965–6), vol. v.

Northanger Abbey, ed. Barbara M. Benedict and Deirdre Le Faye (Cambridge: Cambridge University Press, 2006).

Textual and Bibliographical Studies

Burns, Margie, 'A Third Publisher's Advertisement for *Susan* Found: Why Didn't Crosby Publish Jane Austen?', *Persuasions*, 39 (2017), 184–202.

Burns, Margie, *Publishing Northanger Abbey: Jane Austen and the Writing Profession* (Wilmington, DE: Vernon Press, 2021).

Gilson, David, *A Bibliography of Jane Austen* (new edn, Winchester: St Paul's Bibliographies, 1997).

Halsey, Katherine, 'Jane Austen', *Oxford Bibliographies Online*, doi: 10.1093/obo/9780199846719-0081 (2012; rev. 2018).

Looser, Devoney, 'The ABCs of *Northanger Abbey*: Advertisements, Backstories, and Classifications', *Persuasions On-Line*, 40/1 (2019).

Mandal, A. A., 'Making Austen MAD: Benjamin Crosby and the Non-Publication of *Susan*', *RES* 57/231 (2006), 507–25.

Shaw, Narelle, 'Free Indirect Speech and Jane Austen's 1816 Revision of *Northanger Abbey*', *SEL* 30/4 (1990), 591–601.

Sutherland, Kathryn, *Jane Austen's Textual Lives: From Aeschylus to Bollywood* (Oxford: Oxford University Press, 2005).

Letters and Biography

Jane Austen's Letters, ed. Deirdre Le Faye (4th edn, Oxford: Oxford University Press, 2011).

Austen-Leigh, J. E., *A Memoir of Jane Austen and Other Family Recollections*, ed. Kathryn Sutherland (Oxford: Oxford University Press, 2002).

Byrne, Paula, *The Real Jane Austen: A Life in Small Things* (London: HarperPress, 2013).

Clery, E. J., *Jane Austen: The Banker's Sister* (London: Biteback Publishing, 2017).

Fergus, Jan, *Jane Austen: A Literary Life* (Basingstoke: Macmillan, 1991).

Honan, Park, *Jane Austen: Her Life* (rev. edn, London: Phoenix Giants, 1997).

Le Faye, Deirdre, *A Chronology of Jane Austen and Her Family, 1600–2000* (rev. edn, Cambridge: Cambridge University Press, 2013).

Le Faye, Deirdre, *Jane Austen: A Family Record* (2nd edn, Cambridge: Cambridge University Press, 2004).

Nokes, David, *Jane Austen: A Life* (London: Fourth Estate, 1997).

Stafford, Fiona, *Jane Austen: A Brief Life* (New Haven: Yale University Press, 2017).

Tomalin, Claire, *Jane Austen: A Life* (London: Viking, 1997).

Historical and Literary Contexts

Allan, David, *A Nation of Readers: The Lending Library in Georgian England* (London: British Library, 2008).

Black, Jeremy, *England in the Age of Jane Austen* (Bloomington: Indiana University Press, 2021).

Bray, Joe, *The Female Reader in the English Novel: From Burney to Austen* (London: Routledge, 2009).

Colley, Linda, *Britons: Forging the Nation, 1707–1837* (New Haven: Yale University Press, 1992).

Copeland, Edward, *Women Writing about Money: Women's Fiction in England, 1790–1820* (Cambridge: Cambridge University Press, 1995).

Downie, J. A. (ed.), *The Oxford Handbook of the Eighteenth-Century Novel* (Oxford: Oxford University Press, 2016).

Garside, Peter, Raven, James, Schöwerling, Rainer, et al., *The English Novel, 1770–1829: A Bibliographical Survey* (Oxford: Oxford University Press, 2000).

Garside, Peter, and O'Brien, Karen (eds), *The Oxford History of the Novel in English*, vol. ii: *English and British Fiction, 1750–1820* (Oxford: Oxford University Press, 2015).

Hilton, Boyd, *A Mad, Bad, and Dangerous People? England 1783–1846* (Oxford: Oxford University Press, 2006).

Looser, Devoney (ed.), *The Cambridge Companion to Women's Writing in the Romantic Period* (Cambridge: Cambridge University Press, 2015).

Lynch, Deidre Shauna, *The Economy of Character: Novels, Market Culture, and the Business of Inner Meaning* (Chicago: University of Chicago Press, 1998).

Pearson, Jacqueline, *Women's Reading in Britain, 1750–1835: A Dangerous Recreation* (Cambridge: Cambridge University Press, 1999).

St Clair, William, *The Reading Nation in the Romantic Period* (Cambridge: Cambridge University Press, 2004).

Vickery, Amanda, *Behind Closed Doors: At Home in Georgian England* (New Haven: Yale University Press, 2010).

Wall, Cynthia, *Grammars of Approach: Landscape, Narrative, and the Linguistic Picturesque* (Chicago: University of Chicago Press, 2019).

Wright, Angela, *Britain, France and the Gothic, 1764–1820: The Import of Terror* (Cambridge: Cambridge University Press, 2013).

Wright, Angela, and Townshend, Dale (eds), *The Cambridge History of the Gothic*, vol. i: *Gothic in the Long Eighteenth Century* (Cambridge: Cambridge University Press, 2020).

Critical Works on Jane Austen

Auerbach, Emily, *Searching for Jane Austen* (Madison: University of Wisconsin Press, 2004).

Barchas, Janine, *Matters of Fact in Jane Austen: History, Location, and Celebrity* (Baltimore: Johns Hopkins University Press, 2012).

Bray, Joe, *The Language of Jane Austen* (Basingstoke: Palgrave Macmillan, 2018).

Butler, Marilyn, *Jane Austen and the War of Ideas* (new edn, Oxford: Clarendon Press, 1987).

Copeland, Edward, and McMaster, Juliet (eds), *The Cambridge Companion to Jane Austen* (Cambridge: Cambridge University Press, 1997; 2nd edn, 2011).

Davidson, Jenny, *Reading Jane Austen* (Cambridge: Cambridge University Press, 2017).

Doody, Margaret, *Jane Austen's Names: Riddles, Persons, Places* (Chicago: University of Chicago Press, 2015).

Duckworth, Alistair M., *The Improvement of the Estate: A Study of Jane Austen's Novels* (rev. edn, Baltimore: Johns Hopkins University Press, 1994).

Dussinger, John, *In the Pride of the Moment: Encounters in Jane Austen's World* (Columbus: Ohio State University Press, 1990).

Emsley, Sarah, *Jane Austen's Philosophy of the Virtues* (Basingstoke: Palgrave Macmillan, 2005).

Gard, Roger, *Jane Austen's Novels: The Art of Clarity* (New Haven: Yale University Press, 1992).

Galperin, William H., *The Historical Austen* (Philadelphia: University of Pennsylvania Press, 2003).

Gilbert, Sandra M., and Gubar, Susan, 'Inside the House of Fiction: Jane Austen's Tenants of Possibility', in Gilbert and Gubar, *The Madwoman in the Attic: The Woman Writer and the Nineteenth-Century Literary Imagination* (2nd edn, New Haven: Yale University Press, 2000), 107–84.

Halsey, Katie, *Jane Austen and Her Readers, 1786–1945* (London: Anthem, 2012).

Harding, D. W., *Regulated Hatred and Other Essays on Jane Austen*, ed. Monica Lawlor (London: Athlone Press, 1998).

Harris, Jocelyn, *Jane Austen's Art of Memory* (Cambridge: Cambridge University Press, 1989).

Heydt-Stevenson, Jillian, *Austen's Unbecoming Conjunctions: Subversive Laughter, Embodied History* (New York: Palgrave Macmillan, 2005).

Hume, Robert D., 'Money in Jane Austen', *RES* 64/264 (2013), 289–310.

Jenkyns, Richard, *A Fine Brush on Ivory: An Appreciation of Jane Austen* (Oxford: Oxford University Press, 2004).

Johnson, Claudia L., *Equivocal Beings: Politics, Gender, and Sentimentality in the 1790s: Wollstonecraft, Radcliffe, Burney, Austen* (Chicago: University of Chicago Press, 1995).

Johnson, Claudia L., *Jane Austen: Women, Politics, and the Novel* (Chicago: University of Chicago Press, 1988).

Johnson, Claudia L., *Jane Austen's Cults and Cultures* (Chicago: University of Chicago Press, 2012).

Johnson, Claudia L., and Tuite, Clara (eds), *A Companion to Jane Austen* (Oxford: Wiley-Blackwell, 2009).

Johnson, Claudia L., and Tuite, Clara, *30 Great Myths about Jane Austen* (Chichester: Wiley-Blackwell, 2020).

Johnston, Freya, *Jane Austen, Early and Late* (Princeton: Princeton University Press, 2021).

Kaplan, Deborah, *Jane Austen among Women* (Baltimore: Johns Hopkins University Press, 1992).

Knox-Shaw, Peter, *Jane Austen and the Enlightenment* (Cambridge: Cambridge University Press, 2004).

Lascelles, Mary, *Jane Austen and Her Art* (Oxford: Oxford University Press, 1939)

Litz, A. Walton, *Jane Austen: A Study of Her Artistic Development* (New York: Oxford University Press, 1965).

Looser, Devoney, *The Making of Jane Austen* (Baltimore: Johns Hopkins University Press, 2017).

Lynch, Deidre Shauna (ed.), *Janeites: Austen's Disciples and Devotees* (Princeton: Princeton University Press, 2000).

Lynch, Deidre Shauna, '"Young ladies are delicate plants": Jane Austen and Greenhouse Romanticism', *ELH* 77/3 (2010), 689–729.

Mandal, Anthony, *Jane Austen and the Popular Novel: The Determined Author* (Basingstoke: Palgrave Macmillan, 2007).

Mazzeno, Laurence W., *Jane Austen: Two Centuries of Criticism* (Rochester, NY: Camden House, 2011).

Miles, Robert, *Jane Austen*, Writers and Their Work (Plymouth: Northcote House, 2003).

Miller, D. A., *Jane Austen, or The Secret of Style* (Princeton: Princeton University Press, 2003).

Moler, Kenneth L., *Jane Austen's Art of Allusion* (Lincoln, NE: University of Nebraska Press, 1968).

Morini, Massimiliano, *Jane Austen's Narrative Techniques: A Stylistic and Pragmatic Analysis* (Farnham: Ashgate, 2009).

Mudrick, Marvin, *Jane Austen: Irony as Defense and Discovery* (Berkeley and Los Angeles: University of California Press, 1952).

Mullan, John, *What Matters in Jane Austen? Twenty Crucial Puzzles Solved* (London: Bloomsbury, 2012).

Murphy, Olivia, *Jane Austen the Reader: The Artist as Critic* (Basingstoke: Palgrave Macmillan, 2013).

Roberts, Warren, *Jane Austen and the French Revolution* (New York: St Martin's Press, 1979).

Sales, Roger, *Jane Austen and Representations of Regency England* (London: Routledge, 1994).

Southam, B. C. (ed.), *Jane Austen: The Critical Heritage*, 2 vols. (London: Routledge & Kegan Paul, 1968–87).

Tandon, Bharat, *Jane Austen and the Morality of Conversation* (London: Anthem, 2003).

Tanner, Tony, *Jane Austen* (Basingstoke: Macmillan, 1986).

Todd, Janet, *The Cambridge Introduction to Jane Austen* (2nd edn, Cambridge: Cambridge University Press, 2015).

Todd, Janet (ed.), *Jane Austen in Context* (Cambridge: Cambridge University Press, 2005).

Toner, Anne, *Jane Austen's Style: Narrative Economy and the Novel's Growth* (Cambridge: Cambridge University Press, 2020).

Tuite, Clara, *Romantic Austen: Sexual Politics and the Literary Canon* (Cambridge: Cambridge University Press, 2002).

Valihora, Karen, *Austen's Oughts: Judgment after Locke and Shaftesbury* (Newark: University of Delaware Press, 2010).

Waldron, Mary, *Jane Austen and the Fiction of Her Time* (Cambridge: Cambridge University Press, 1999).

Wallace, Tara Ghoshal, *Jane Austen and Narrative Authority* (Basingstoke: Macmillan, 1995).

Wilson, Cheryl A., and Frawley, Maria H. (eds), *The Routledge Companion to Jane Austen* (New York: Routledge, 2022).

Wiltshire, John, *The Hidden Jane Austen* (Cambridge: Cambridge University Press, 2014).

Websites

Jane Austen Society of North America: http://jasna.org/
Jane Austen's Fiction Manuscripts Digital Edition: https://janeausten.ac.uk/
Reading with Austen: https://www.readingwithausten.com/

Republic of Pemberley: https://pemberley.com/
What Jane Saw: http://www.whatjanesaw.org/

See also the two journals published by JASNA, *Persuasions* and *Persuasions On-Line* (http://jasna.org/publications/); special issues of both have been devoted to *Northanger Abbey* (*Persuasions*, 32 (2010); *Persuasions On-Line*, 31/1 (Winter 2010)).

Critical Works on Northanger Abbey

Anderson, Walter E., 'From Northanger to Woodston: Catherine's Education to Common Life', *Philological Quarterly*, 63/4 (1984), 493–509.

Barchas, Janine, 'Mapping *Northanger Abbey*: or, Why Austen's Bath of 1803 Resembles Joyce's Dublin of 1904', *RES* 60/245 (2009), 431–59; revised in Barchas, *Matters of Fact in Jane Austen: History, Location, and Celebrity* (Baltimore: Johns Hopkins University Press, 2012), 57–92.

Baudot, Laura, ' "Nothing really in it": Gothic Interiors and the Externals of the Courtship Plot in *Northanger Abbey*', *Eighteenth-Century Fiction*, 24/2 (2011), 325–52.

Benis, Toby R., 'The Neighborhoods of *Northanger Abbey*', *Eighteenth Century*, 56/2 (2015), 179–92.

Bennett, Ashly, 'Shame and Sensibility: Jane Austen's Humiliated Heroines', *Studies in Romanticism*, 54/3 (2015), 377–400.

Massei-Chamayou, Marie-Laure, ' "Oh! Who can ever be tired of Bath?" The Sense of Place in Jane Austen's *Northanger Abbey* and *Persuasion*', in Sophie Chiari and Samuel Delorme (eds), *Spa Culture and Literature in England, 1500–1800* (Cham: Palgrave Macmillan, 2021), 65–85.

Cordón, Joanne, 'Speaking Up for Catherine Morland: Cixous and the Feminist Heroine', *Frontiers*, 32/3 (2011), 41–63.

Erickson, Lee, 'The Economy of Novel Reading: Jane Austen and the Circulating Library', *Studies in English Literature 1500–1900*, 30/4 (1990), 573–90; revised in Erickson, *The Economy of Literary Form: English Literature and the Industrialization of Publishing, 1800–1850* (Baltimore: Johns Hopkins University Press, 1996), 125–41.

Ewers, Chris, '*Northanger Abbey* and Austen's "wandering story" ', in Ewers, *Mobility in the English Novel from Defoe to Austen* (Woodbridge: Boydell & Brewer, 2018), 161–89.

Fergus, Jan, *Jane Austen and the Didactic Novel: Northanger Abbey, Sense and Sensibility, and Pride and Prejudice* (London: Macmillan, 1983).

Heydt-Stevenson, Jillian, '*Northanger Abbey*, *Desmond*, and History', *Wordsworth Circle*, 44/2–3 (2013), 140–8.

Hoeveler, Diane, 'Vindicating *Northanger Abbey*: Mary Wollstonecraft, Jane Austen, and Gothic Feminism', in Devoney Looser (ed.), *Jane Austen and Discourses of Feminism* (New York: St Martin's Press, 1995), 117–35.

Hopkins, Robert, 'General Tilney and Affairs of State: The Political Gothic of *Northanger Abbey*', *Philological Quarterly*, 57 (1978), 213–24.

Jerinic, Maria, 'In Defense of the Gothic: Rereading *Northanger Abbey*', in Devoney Looser (ed.), *Jane Austen and Discourses of Feminism* (New York: St Martin's Press, 1995), 137–49.

Kickel, Katherine, 'General Tilney's Timely Approach to the Improvement of the Estate in Jane Austen's *Northanger Abbey*', *Nineteenth-Century Literature*, 63/2 (2008), 145–69.

Knox-Shaw, Peter, '*Northanger Abbey* and the Liberal Historians', *Essays in Criticism*, 49/4 (1999), 319–43; revised in Knox-Shaw, *Jane Austen and the Enlightenment* (Cambridge: Cambridge University Press, 2004), 108–28.

Kowaleski Wallace, Elizabeth, '"Penance and mortification for ever": Jane Austen and the Ambient Noise of Catholicism', *Tulsa Studies in Women's Literature*, 31/1 (2012), 159–80.

Lansdown, Richard, '"Rare in Burlesque": *Northanger Abbey*', *Philological Quarterly*, 83/1 (2004), 61–81.

Lau, Beth, 'Catherine's Education in Mindreading in *Northanger Abbey*', in Lau (ed.), *Jane Austen and Sciences of the Mind* (Abingdon: Routledge, 2018), 37–57.

Lau, Beth, 'Madeline at *Northanger Abbey*: Keats's Anti-Romances and Gothic Satire', *JEGP* 84/1 (1985), 30–50.

Levine, George, 'Translating the Monstrous: *Northanger Abbey*', *Nineteenth-Century Fiction*, 30 (1975), 335–50; revised in Levine, *The Realistic Imagination: English Fiction from Frankenstein to Lady Chatterley* (Chicago: University of Chicago Press, 1981), 61–80.

Litvak, Joseph, '*Bon Chic, Bon Genre*: Sophistication and History in *Northanger Abbey*', in Litvak, *Strange Gourmets: Sophistication, Theory, and the Novel* (Durham, NC: Duke University Press, 1997), 33–54.

Looser, Devoney, '(Re)Making History and Philosophy: Austen's *Northanger Abbey*', *European Romantic Review*, 4/1 (1993), 34–56; revised in Looser, *British Women Writers and the Writing of History, 1670–1820* (Baltimore: Johns Hopkins University Press, 2000), 178–203.

Loveridge, Mark, '*Northanger Abbey*; or, Nature and Probability', *Nineteenth-Century Literature*, 46/1 (1991), 1–29.

MacMahon, Barbara, 'Metarepresentation and Decoupling in *Northanger Abbey*', *English Studies*, 90/5–6 (2009), 518–44 and 673–94.

Malina, Debra, 'Rereading the Patriarchal Text: *The Female Quixote, Northanger Abbey*, and the Trace of the Absent Mother', *Eighteenth-Century Fiction*, 8/2 (1996), 271–92.

Miall, David. S., 'The Preceptor as Fiend: Radcliffe's Psychology of the Gothic', in Laura Dabundo (ed.), *Jane Austen and Mary Shelley and Their Sisters* (Lanham, MD: University Press of America, 2000), 31–43.

Miller, Christopher R., 'Jane Austen's Aesthetics and Ethics of Surprise', *Narrative*, 13/3 (2005), 238–60; revised in Miller, *Surprise: The Poetics of the Unexpected from Milton to Austen* (Ithaca, NY: Cornell University Press, 2015), 141–70.

Mimma, Shinobu, 'General Tilney and Tyranny: *Northanger Abbey*', *Eighteenth-Century Fiction*, 8/4 (1996), 503–18.

Miskin, Lauren, '"True Indian Muslin" and the Politics of Consumption in Jane Austen's *Northanger Abbey*', *Journal for Early Modern Cultural Studies*, 15 (2015), 5–26.

Molesworth, Jesse, 'Gothic Time, Sacred Time', *Modern Language Quarterly*, 75/1 (2014), 29–55.

Moore, Roger E., 'The Hidden History of *Northanger Abbey*: Jane Austen and the Dissolution of the Monasteries', *Religion & Literature*, 43/1 (2011), 55–80; revised in Moore, *Jane Austen and the Reformation: Remembering the Sacred Landscape* (Abingdon: Routledge, 2016), 79–108.

Morrison, Paul, 'Enclosed in Openness: *Northanger Abbey* and the Domestic Carceral', *Texas Studies in Literature and Language*, 33/1 (1991), 1–23.

Neill, Edward, 'The Secret of *Northanger Abbey*', *Essays in Criticism*, 47/1 (1997), 13–32; revised in Neill, *The Politics of Jane Austen* (Basingstoke: Palgrave Macmillan, 1999), 15–30.

Nelson, James Lindemann, 'How Catherine Does Go On: *Northanger Abbey* and Moral Thought', *Philosophy and Literature*, 34/1 (2010), 188–200.

Ogawa, Kimiyo, '"Roaming Fancy" and Imagination: Gothic Force in Austen's *Northanger Abbey* and Keats's *Isabella*', *SEL* 57 (2016), 23–39.

Paulson, Ronald, 'Gothic Fiction and the French Revolution', *ELH* 48 (1981), 532–54.

Roberts, Bette B., 'The Horrid Novels: *The Mysteries of Udolpho* and *Northanger Abbey*', in Kenneth W. Graham (ed.), *Gothic Fictions: Prohibition/Transgression* (New York: AMS Press, 1989), 89–111.

Robinson, Terry F., '"A mere skeleton of history": Reading Relics in Jane Austen's *Northanger Abbey*', *European Romantic Review*, 17/2 (2006), 215–27.

Southam, B. C. (ed.), *Jane Austen, Northanger Abbey and Persuasion: A Casebook* (London: Macmillan, 1976).

Spongberg, Mary, 'History, Fiction, and Anachronism: *Northanger Abbey*, the Tudor "Past" and the "Gothic" Present', *Textual Practice*, 26/4 (2012), 631–48.

Townshend, Dale, 'Improvement and Repair: Architecture, Romance and the Politics of the Gothic, 1790–1817', *Literature Compass*, 8/10 (2011), 712–38; revised in Townshend, *Gothic Antiquity: History, Romance, and the Architectural Imagination, 1760–1840* (Oxford: Oxford University Press, 2019), 179–220.

Veisz, Elizabeth, 'Writing the Eighteenth-Century Household: Leapor, Austen, and the Old Feudal Spirits', *Tulsa Studies in Women's Literature*, 30/1 (2011), 71–91.

Wallace, Tara Ghoshal, '*Northanger Abbey* and the Limits of Parody', *Studies in the Novel*, 20/3 (1988), 262–73; revised in Wallace, *Jane Austen and Narrative Authority* (Basingstoke: Macmillan, 1995), 17–30.

West, Rebecca, Preface to Jane Austen, *Northanger Abbey* (London: Jonathan Cape, 1932), pp. v–xi.

Williams, Carolyn D., 'General Tilney and the Maidens All Forlorn: Typecasting in *Northanger Abbey*', *Women's Writing*, 5/1 (1998), 41–59.

Wilt, Judith, 'Jane Austen: The Anxieties of Common Life', in Wilt, *Ghosts of the Gothic: Austen, Eliot and Lawrence* (Princeton: Princeton University Press, 1980), 121–72.

Wyett, Jodi L., 'Female Quixotism Refashioned: *Northanger Abbey*, the Engaged Reader, and the Woman Writer', *Eighteenth Century*, 56/2 (2015), 261–76.

Yoon, Sun Lee, 'Austen's Scale-Making', *Studies in Romanticism*, 52/2 (2013), 171–95.

Zlotnick, Susan, 'From Involuntary Object to Voluntary Spy: Female Agency, Novels, and the Marketplace in *Northanger Abbey*', *Studies in the Novel*, 41/3 (2009), 277–92.

Screen Adaptations and Commentaries

Northanger Abbey: writer Maggie Wadley, director Giles Foster; BBC and A&E, 1987.

Northanger Abbey: writer Andrew Davies, director Jon Jones; Granada and WGBH, 2007.

Parrill, Sue, *Jane Austen on Film and Television: A Critical Study of the Adaptations* (Jefferson, NC: McFarland, 2002), 169–88 ('*Northanger Abbey*').

Roberts, Marilyn, 'Adapting Jane Austen's *Northanger Abbey*: Catherine Morland as Gothic Heroine', in Barbara Tepa Lupack (ed.), *Nineteenth-Century Women at the Movies: Adapting Classic Women's Fiction to Film* (Bowling Green, OH: Popular Press, 1999), 129–39.

Stovel, Bruce, '*Northanger Abbey* at the Movies', *Persuasions*, 20 (1998), 236–47.

Further Reading in Oxford World's Classics

Austen, J., *Emma*, ed. John Mullan.
Austen, J., *Lady Susan, The Watsons, and Sanditon: Unfinished Fictions and Other Writings*, ed. Kathryn Sutherland.
Austen, J., *Mansfield Park*, ed. James Kinsley and Jane Stabler.
Austen, J., *Persuasion*, ed. James Kinsley and Deidre Lynch.
Austen, J., *Pride and Prejudice*, ed. Christina Lupton.
Austen, J., *Selected Letters*, ed. Vivien Jones.
Austen, J., *Sense and Sensibility*, ed. John Mullan.
Austen, J., *Teenage Writings*, ed. Kathryn Sutherland and Freya Johnston.
Austen-Leigh, J. E., *A Memoir of Jane Austen and Other Family Recollections*, ed. Kathryn Sutherland.
Burney, F., *Camilla*, ed. Edward A. Bloom and Lillian D. Bloom.
Burney, F., *Cecilia*, ed. Peter Sabor and Margaret Anne Doody.
Burney, F., *Evelina*, ed. Edward A. Bloom and Vivien Jones.
Edgeworth, M., *Belinda*, ed. Linda Bree.
Lennox, C., *The Female Quixote*, ed. Margaret Dalziel and Margaret Anne Doody.
Lewis, M., *The Monk*, ed. Nick Groom.
Radcliffe, A., *The Italian*, ed. Nick Groom.
Radcliffe, A., *The Mysteries of Udolpho*, ed. Bonamy Dobrée and Terry Castle.
Radcliffe, A., *The Romance of the Forest*, ed. Chloe Chard.
Radcliffe, A., *A Sicilian Romance*, ed. Alison Milbank.
Wollstonecraft, M., *Mary and The Wrongs of Woman*, ed. Gary Kelly.
Wollstonecraft, M., *A Vindication of the Rights of Men* and *A Vindication of the Rights of Woman*, ed. Janet Todd.

A CHRONOLOGY OF JANE AUSTEN

Life	*Historical and Cultural Background*
1784 Performance of Sheridan's *The Rivals* at Steventon.	India Act imposes some parliamentary control on East India Company; Prince Regent begins to build Brighton Pavilion; death of Samuel Johnson.
1785 Attends Abbey House School, Reading, with Cassandra.	William Cowper, *The Task*
1786 Brother Francis (1774–1865) enters Royal Naval Academy, Portsmouth; brother Edward on Grand Tour (to 1790); JA and Cassandra leave school for good.	William Gilpin, *Observations, Relative Chiefly to Picturesque Beauty . . . particularly the Mountains, and Lakes of Cumberland, and Westmoreland*
1787 Starts writing stories collected in three notebooks (to 1793); cousin Eliza de Feuillide visits Steventon; performance of Susannah Centlivre's *The Wonder* at Steventon.	American constitution signed.
1788 JA and Cassandra taken on a trip to Kent and London; *The Chances* and *Tom Thumb* performed at Steventon; brother Henry (1771–1850) goes to St John's College, Oxford; brother Francis sails to East Indies on HMS *Perseverance*; cousins Eliza de Feuillide and Philadelphia Walter attend Hastings's trial.	Warren Hastings impeached for corruption in India; George III's first spell of madness.
1789 James and Henry in Oxford produce periodical, *The Loiterer* (to Mar. 1790); JA begins lifelong friendship with Martha Lloyd and sister Mary when their mother rents Deane Parsonage.	Fall of the Bastille marks beginning of French Revolution.
1790 (June) completes 'Love and Friendship'.	Edmund Burke, *Reflections on the Revolution in France*; [Mary Wollstonecraft], *Vindication of the Rights of Men*
1791 Brother Charles enters Royal Naval Academy, Portsmouth; (Nov.) completes 'The History of England'; Edward marries Elizabeth Bridges and they live at Rowling, Kent.	Parliament rejects bill to abolish slave trade. James Boswell, *Life of Johnson*; Ann Radcliffe, *The Romance of the Forest*

Life	*Historical and Cultural Background*
1792 Writes 'Lesley Castle' and 'Evelyn', and begins 'Kitty, or the Bower'; Lloyds leave Deane to make way for James and first wife, Anne Mathew; cousin Jane Cooper marries Capt. Thomas Williams, RN; sister Cassandra engaged to Revd Tom Fowle.	France declared a republic; Warren Hastings acquitted. Mary Wollstonecraft; *Vindication of the Rights of Woman*; Clara Reeve, *Plans of Education*
1793 Birth of eldest nieces, Fanny and Anna, daughters of brothers Edward and James; writes last of entries in the teenage notebooks; brother Henry joins Oxford Militia.	Execution of Louis XVI of France and Marie Antoinette; revolutionary 'Terror' in Paris; Britain declares war on France.
1794 Probably working on *Lady Susan*; cousin Eliza de Feuillide's husband guillotined in Paris.	Suspension of Habeas Corpus; 'Treason Trials' of radicals abandoned by government when juries refuse to convict; failure of harvests keeps food prices high. Uvedale Price, *Essays on the Picturesque*; Ann Radcliffe, *The Mysteries of Udolpho*
1795 Writes 'Elinor and Marianne' (first draft of *Sense and Sensibility*); death of James's wife; JA flirts with Tom Lefroy, as recorded in first surviving letter.	George III's coach stoned; Pitt's 'Two Acts' enforce repression of radical dissent.
1796 Visits Edward at Rowling; (Oct.) begins 'First Impressions'; subscribes to Frances Burney's *Camilla*.	Frances Burney, *Camilla*; Regina Maria Roche, *Children of the Abbey*; Jane West, *A Gossip's Story*
1797 Marriage of James to Mary Lloyd; (Aug.) completes 'First Impressions'; Cassandra's fiancé dies of fever off Santo Domingo; begins revision of 'Elinor and Marianne' into *Sense and Sensibility*; George Austen offers 'First Impressions' to publisher Cadell without success; Catherine Knight gives Edward possession of Godmersham; marriage of Henry and Eliza de Feuillide.	Napoleon becomes commander of French army; failure of French attempt to invade by landing in Wales; mutinies in British Navy, leaders hanged. Ann Radcliffe, *The Italian*

Life	*Historical and Cultural Background*
1798 Starts to write 'Susan' (later *Northanger Abbey*); visits Godmersham; death in driving accident of cousin Lady Williams (Jane Cooper).	Irish Rebellion; defeat of French fleet at Battle of the Nile; French army lands in Ireland; further suspension of Habeas Corpus. Elizabeth Inchbald, *Lovers' Vows*, translation of play by Kotzebue
1799 Visit to Bath; probably finishes 'Susan'; aunt, Mrs Leigh-Perrot, charged with theft and imprisoned in Ilchester Gaol.	Napoleon becomes consul in France. Hannah More, *Strictures on the Modern System of Female Education*; Jane West, *A Tale of the Times*
1800 Stays with Martha Lloyd at Ibthorpe; trial and acquittal of Mrs Leigh-Perrot.	French conquer Italy; British capture Malta; food riots; first iron-frame printing press; copyright law extended to Ireland. Elizabeth Hamilton, *Memoirs of Modern Philosophers*
1801 Austens move to Bath on George Austen's retirement; James and family move into Stevenson Rectory; first of series of holidays in West Country (to 1804), during one of which thought to have had brief romantic involvement with a man who later died; Henry resigns from Oxford Militia and becomes banker and Army agent in London.	Slave rebellion in Santo Domingo led by Toussaint L'Ouverture; Nelson defeats Danes at Battle of Copenhagen; Act of Union joins Britain and Ireland. Maria Edgeworth, *Belinda*
1802 Visits Godmersham; accepts, then the following morning refuses, proposal of marriage from Harris Bigg-Wither; revises 'Susan'.	L'Ouverture's slave rebellion crushed by French; Peace of Amiens with France; founding of William Cobbett's *Political Register*.
1803 With brother Henry's help, 'Susan' sold to publishers Crosby & Co. for £10.	Resumption of war with France.
1804 Starts writing *The Watsons*; (Dec.) death of Anne Lefroy in riding accident.	
1805 (Jan.) death of George Austen; stops work on *The Watsons*.	Battle of Trafalgar. Walter Scott, *The Lay of the Last Minstrel*

Life	*Historical and Cultural Background*
1806 Austens leave Bath; visit relations at Adlestrop and Stoneleigh; Martha Lloyd becomes member of Austen household after death of her mother; brother Francis marries Mary Gibson; JA, Cassandra, and Mrs Austen take lodgings with them in Southampton.	French blockade of continental ports against British shipping; first steam-powered textile mill opens in Manchester. Lady Morgan, *The Wild Irish Girl*
1807 Brother Charles marries Fanny Palmer in Bermuda.	France invades Portugal; slave-trading by British ships outlawed. George Crabbe, *Poems*
1808 JA visits Godmersham; death of Edward's wife Elizabeth after giving birth to eleventh child.	France invades Spain; beginning of Peninsular War. Debrett, *Baronetage* (*Peerage* first published 1802); Hannah More, *Coelebs in Search of a Wife*; Walter Scott, *Marmion*
1809 (Apr.) attempts unsuccessfully to make Crosby publish 'Susan', writing under pseudonym 'Mrs Ashton Dennis' ('MAD.'); visits Godmersham; (July) moves, with Cassandra, Martha, and Mrs Austen, to house owned by Edward at Chawton, Hampshire.	British capture Martinique and Cayenne from France.
1810 Publisher Egerton accepts *Sense and Sensibility*.	British capture Guadeloupe, last French West Indian colony; riots in London in support of parliamentary reform. Walter Scott, *The Lady of the Lake*
1811 (Feb.) begins *Mansfield Park*; stays with Henry and Eliza in London to correct proofs of *Sense and Sensibility*; (Oct.) *Sense and Sensibility*, 'by a Lady', published on commission; revises 'First Impressions' into *Pride and Prejudice*.	Prince of Wales becomes Regent; Luddite antimachine riots in North and Midlands. Mary Brunton, *Self-Control*
1812 Copyright of *Pride and Prejudice* sold to Egerton for £110; Edward's family take name of Knight at death of Catherine Knight.	United States declare war on Britain; French retreat from Moscow; Lord Liverpool becomes Prime Minister after assassination of Spencer Perceval.

Life	*Historical and Cultural Background*
1813 (Jan.) *Pride and Prejudice* published to great acclaim; JA stays in London to nurse Eliza; death of Eliza; in letter, expresses her hatred for Prince Regent; (June) finishes *Mansfield Park*; second editions of *Sense and Sensibility* and *Pride and Prejudice*.	British invasion of France after Wellington's success at Battle of Vittoria. Byron, *The Giaour*, *The Bride of Abydos*; Robert Southey, *Life of Nelson*
1814 (21 Jan.) begins *Emma*; (Mar. and Nov.) visits brother Henry in London, sees Kean play Shylock; (May) Egerton publishes *Mansfield Park* on commission, sold out in six months; death of Fanny Palmer Austen, brother Charles's wife, after childbirth; marriage of niece Anna Austen to Ben Lefroy.	Napoleon defeated and exiled to Elba; George Stevenson builds first steam locomotive; Edmund Kean's first appearance at Drury Lane. Mary Brunton, *Discipline*; Frances Burney, *The Wanderer*; Byron, *The Corsair*; Maria Edgeworth, *Patronage*; Walter Scott, *Waverley*
1815 (29 Mar.) completes *Emma*; (Aug.) begins *Persuasion*; invited to dedicate *Emma* to the Prince Regent; visits Henry in London; (Dec.) *Emma* published by Murray.	Napoleon escapes; finally defeated at Battle of Waterloo and exiled to St Helena; Humphry Davy invents miners' safety lamp.
1816 'Susan' bought back from Crosby and revised as 'Catherine'; failure of Henry's bank; second edition of *Mansfield Park*; (Aug.) JA completes *Persuasion*; health beginning to fail.	Post-war slump inaugurates years of popular agitation for political and social reform.
1817 (Jan.–Mar.) works on *Sanditon*; (Apr.) makes her Will; moves, with Cassandra, to Winchester, to be closer to skilled medical care; (15 July) composes last poem 'When Winchester Races'; (18 July, 4.30 a.m.) dies in Winchester; buried in Winchester Cathedral; (Dec.) publication (dated 1818) of *Northanger Abbey* and *Persuasion*, together with brother Henry's 'Biographical Notice'.	Attacks on Prince Regent at opening of Parliament; death of his only legitimate child, Princess Charlotte.

NORTHANGER ABBEY

ADVERTISEMENT,

BY THE AUTHORESS,

TO

NORTHANGER ABBEY

THIS little work was finished in the year 1803, and intended for immediate publication.* It was disposed of to a bookseller, it was even advertised, and why the business proceeded no farther, the author has never been able to learn. That any bookseller should think it worth while to purchase what he did not think it worth while to publish seems extraordinary. But with this, neither the author nor the public have any other concern than as some observation is necessary upon those parts of the work which thirteen years have made comparatively obsolete. The public are entreated to bear in mind that thirteen years have passed since it was finished, many more since it was begun, and that during that period, places, manners, books, and opinions have undergone considerable changes.

VOLUME I

CHAPTER I

No one who had ever seen Catherine Morland in her infancy, would have supposed her born to be an heroine. Her situation in life, the character of her father and mother, her own person and disposition, were all equally against her. Her father was a clergyman, without being neglected, or poor, and a very respectable man, though his name was Richard*—and he had never been handsome. He had a considerable independence, besides two good livings—and he was not in the least addicted to locking up his daughters.* Her mother was a woman of useful plain sense, with a good temper, and, what is more remarkable, with a good constitution. She had three sons before Catherine was born; and instead of dying in bringing the latter into the world, as any body might expect, she still lived on—lived to have six children more—to see them growing up around her, and to enjoy excellent health herself. A family of ten children will be always called a fine family, where there are heads and arms and legs enough for the number; but the Morlands had little other right to the word, for they were in general very plain, and Catherine, for many years of her life, as plain as any. She had a thin awkward figure, a sallow skin without colour, dark lank hair, and strong features;—so much for her person;—and not less unpropitious for heroism seemed her mind. She was fond of all boys' plays, and greatly preferred cricket not merely to dolls, but to the more heroic enjoyments of infancy, nursing a dormouse, feeding a canary-bird, or watering a rose-bush. Indeed she had no taste for a garden; and if she gathered flowers at all, it was chiefly for the pleasure of mischief—at least so it was conjectured from her always preferring those which she was forbidden to take.—Such were her propensities—her abilities were quite as extraordinary. She never could learn or understand any thing before she was taught; and sometimes not even then, for she was often inattentive, and occasionally stupid. Her mother was three months in teaching her only to repeat the 'Beggar's Petition;'* and after all, her next sister, Sally, could say it better than she did. Not that Catherine was always stupid,—by no means; she learnt the fable of 'The Hare and many Friends,'* as quickly as any girl in England. Her mother wished her to learn music; and Catherine was sure she should like it, for she was very fond of tinkling the keys of the old forlorn spinnet;* so, at eight years old she began. She learnt a year, and could not bear it;—and Mrs. Morland, who did not insist on her daughters being accomplished in spite of incapacity or distaste, allowed her to leave off. The day which dismissed the music-master was one of the happiest of Catherine's life. Her taste for drawing was not superior; though whenever she could obtain the outside of a letter from her mother, or seize upon any other odd piece of paper, she did what she could in that way, by drawing houses and trees, hens and chickens, all very much like one another.—Writing and accounts she was taught by her father; French by her mother: her proficiency in either was not remarkable, and she shirked her lessons in both whenever she could. What a strange, unaccountable character!—for with all these symptoms of profligacy at ten years old, she had neither a bad heart nor a bad temper; was seldom stubborn, scarcely ever quarrelsome, and very kind to the little ones, with few interruptions of tyranny; she was moreover noisy and wild, hated confinement and cleanliness, and loved nothing so well in the world as rolling down the green slope at the back of the house.

Such was Catherine Morland at ten. At fifteen, appearances were mending; she began to curl her hair and long for balls; her complexion improved, her features were softened by plumpness and colour, her eyes gained more animation, and her figure more consequence. Her love of dirt gave way to an inclination for finery, and she grew clean as she grew smart; she had now the pleasure of sometimes hearing her father and mother remark on her personal improvement. 'Catherine grows quite a good-looking girl,—she is almost pretty to day,' were words which caught her ears now and then; and how welcome were the sounds! To look *almost* pretty, is an acquisition of higher delight to a girl who has been looking plain the first fifteen years of her life, than a beauty from her cradle can ever receive.

Mrs. Morland was a very good woman, and wished to see her children every thing they ought to be; but her time was so much occupied in lying-in* and teaching the little ones, that her elder daughters were inevitably left to shift for themselves, and it was not very wonderful that Catherine, who had by nature nothing heroic about her, should prefer cricket, base ball,* riding on horseback, and running about the country at the age of fourteen, to books—or at least books of information—for, provided that nothing like useful knowledge could be gained from them, provided they were all story and no reflection, she had never any objection to books at all. But from fifteen to seventeen she was in training for a heroine; she read all such works as heroines must read to supply their memories with those quotations which are so serviceable and so soothing in the vicissitudes of their eventful lives.

From Pope, she learnt to censure those who

> 'bear about the mockery of woe.'*

From Gray, that

> 'Many a flower is born to blush unseen,
> 'And waste its fragrance on the desert air.'*

From Thompson, that

> ——'It is a delightful task
> 'To teach the young idea how to shoot.'*

And from Shakspeare she gained a great store of information—amongst the rest, that

> ——'Trifles light as air,
> 'Are, to the jealous, confirmation strong,
> 'As proofs of Holy Writ.'

That

> 'The poor beetle, which we tread upon,
> 'In corporal sufferance feels a pang as great
> 'As when a giant dies.'

And that a young woman in love always looks

> ——'like Patience on a monument
> 'Smiling at Grief.'*

So far her improvement was sufficient—and in many other points she came on exceedingly well; for though she could not write sonnets, she brought herself to read them; and though there seemed no chance of her throwing a whole party into raptures by a prelude on the pianoforte, of her own composition, she could listen to other people's performance with very little fatigue. Her greatest deficiency was in the pencil—she had no notion of drawing—not enough even to attempt a sketch of her lover's profile, that she might be detected in the design.* There she fell miserably short of the true heroic height. At present she did not know her own poverty, for she had no lover to pourtray. She had reached the age of seventeen, without having seen one amiable youth who could call forth her sensibility;* without having inspired one real passion, and without having excited even any admiration but what was very moderate and very transient. This was strange indeed! But strange things may be generally accounted for if their cause be fairly searched out. There was not one lord in the neighbourhood; no—not even a baronet. There was not one family among their acquaintance who had reared and supported a boy accidentally found at their door—not one young man whose origin was unknown.* Her father had no ward, and the squire of the parish no children.

But when a young lady is to be a heroine, the perverseness of forty surrounding families cannot prevent her. Something must and will happen to throw a hero in her way.

Mr. Allen, who owned the chief of the property about Fullerton, the village in Wiltshire where the Morlands lived, was ordered to Bath* for the benefit of a gouty constitution;—and his lady, a good-humoured woman, fond of Miss Morland, and probably aware that if adventures will not befal a young lady in her own village, she must seek them abroad, invited her to go with them. Mr. and Mrs. Morland were all compliance, and Catherine all happiness.

CHAPTER II

In addition to what has been already said of Catherine Morland's personal and mental endowments, when about to be launched into all the difficulties and dangers of a six weeks' residence in Bath, it may be stated, for the reader's more certain information, lest the following pages should otherwise fail of giving any idea of what her character is meant to be; that her heart was affectionate, her disposition cheerful and open, without conceit or affectation of any kind—her manners just removed from the awkwardness and shyness of a girl; her person pleasing, and, when in good looks, pretty—and her mind about as ignorant and uninformed as the female mind at seventeen usually is.

When the hour of departure drew near, the maternal anxiety of Mrs. Morland will be naturally supposed to be most severe. A thousand alarming presentiments of evil to her beloved Catherine from this terrific separation must oppress her heart with sadness, and drown her in tears for the last day or two of their being together; and advice of the most important and applicable nature must of course flow from her wise lips in their parting conference in her closet. Cautions against the violence of such noblemen and baronets as delight in forcing young ladies away to some remote farm-house, must, at such a moment, relieve the fulness of her heart. Who would not think so? But Mrs. Morland knew so little of lords and baronets, that she entertained no notion of their general mischievousness, and was wholly unsuspicious of danger to her daughter from their machinations. Her cautions were confined to the following points. 'I beg, Catherine, you will always wrap yourself up very warm about the throat, when you come from the Rooms at night;* and I wish you would try to keep some account of the money you spend;—I will give you this little book on purpose.'

Sally, or rather Sarah, (for what young lady of common gentility will reach the age of sixteen without altering her name as far as she can?) must from situation be at this time the intimate friend and confidante of her sister. It is remarkable, however, that she neither insisted on Catherine's writing by every post, nor exacted her promise of transmitting the character of every new acquaintance, nor a detail of every interesting conversation that Bath might produce.* Every thing indeed relative to this important journey was done, on the part of the Morlands, with a degree of moderation and composure, which seemed rather consistent with the common feelings of common life, than with the refined susceptibilities, the tender emotions which the first separation of a heroine from her family ought always to excite. Her father, instead of giving her an unlimited order on his banker, or even putting an hundred pounds bank-bill into her hands, gave her only ten guineas, and promised her more when she wanted it.

Under these unpromising auspices, the parting took place, and the journey began. It was performed with suitable quietness and uneventful safety. Neither robbers nor tempests befriended them, nor one lucky overturn* to introduce them to the hero. Nothing more alarming occurred than a fear on Mrs. Allen's side, of having once left her clogs behind her at an inn, and that fortunately proved to be groundless.

They arrived at Bath. Catherine was all eager delight;—her eyes were here, there, every where, as they approached its fine and striking environs, and afterwards drove through those streets which conducted them to the hotel. She was come to be happy, and she felt happy already.

They were soon settled in comfortable lodgings in Pulteney-street.*

It is now expedient to give some description of Mrs. Allen, that the reader may be able to judge, in what manner her actions will hereafter tend to promote the general distress of the work, and how she will, probably, contribute to reduce poor Catherine to all the desperate wretchedness of which a last volume is capable—whether by her imprudence, vulgarity, or jealousy—whether by intercepting her letters, ruining her character, or turning her out of doors.

Mrs. Allen was one of that numerous class of females, whose society can raise no other emotion than surprise at there being any men in the world who could like them well enough to marry them. She had neither beauty, genius, accomplishment, nor manner. The air of a gentlewoman, a great deal of quiet, inactive good temper, and a trifling turn of mind, were all that could account for her being the choice of a sensible, intelligent man, like Mr. Allen. In one respect she was admirably fitted to introduce a young lady into public, being as fond of going every where and seeing every thing herself as any young lady could be. Dress was her passion. She had a most harmless delight in being fine; and our heroine's entrée into life* could not take place till after three or four days had been spent in learning what was mostly worn, and her chaperon was provided with a dress of the newest fashion. Catherine too made some purchases herself, and when all these matters were arranged, the important evening came which was to usher her into the Upper Rooms. Her hair was cut and dressed by the best hand, her clothes put on with care, and both Mrs. Allen and her maid declared she looked quite as she should do. With such encouragement, Catherine hoped at least to pass uncensured through the crowd. As for admiration, it was always very welcome when it came, but she did not depend on it.

Mrs. Allen was so long in dressing, that they did not enter the ball-room till late. The season was full,* the room crowded, and the two ladies squeezed in as well as they could. As for Mr. Allen, he repaired directly to the card-room, and left them to enjoy a mob by themselves. With more care for the safety of her new gown than for the comfort of her protegée, Mrs. Allen made her way through the throng of men by the door, as swiftly as the necessary caution would allow; Catherine, however, kept close at her side, and linked her arm too firmly within her friend's to be torn asunder by any common effort of a struggling assembly. But to her utter amazement she found that to proceed along the room was by no means the way to disengage themselves from the crowd; it seemed rather to increase as they went on, whereas she had imagined that when once fairly within the door, they should easily find seats and be able to watch the dances with perfect convenience. But this was far from being the case, and though by unwearied diligence* they gained even the top of the room, their situation was just the same; they saw nothing of the dancers but the high feathers of some of the ladies. Still they moved on—something better was yet in view; and by a continued exertion of strength and ingenuity they found themselves at last in the passage behind the highest bench. Here there was something less of crowd than below; and hence Miss Morland had a comprehensive view of all the company beneath her, and of all the dangers of her late passage through them. It was a splendid sight, and she began, for the first time that evening, to feel herself at a ball; she longed to dance, but she had not an acquaintance in the room. Mrs. Allen did all that she could do in such a case by saying very placidly, every now and then, 'I wish you could dance, my dear,—I wish you could get a partner.' For some time her young friend felt obliged to her for these wishes; but they were repeated so often, and proved so totally ineffectual, that Catherine grew tired at last, and would thank her no more.

They were not long able, however, to enjoy the repose of the eminence they had so laboriously gained.—Every body was shortly in motion for tea, and they must squeeze out like the rest. Catherine began to feel something of disappointment—she was tired of being continually pressed against by people, the generality of whose faces possessed nothing to interest, and with all of whom she was so wholly unacquainted, that she could not relieve the irksomeness of imprisonment by the exchange of a syllable with any of her fellow captives; and when at last arrived in the tea-room, she felt yet more the awkwardness of having no party to join, no acquaintance to claim, no gentleman to assist them.—They saw nothing of Mr. Allen; and after looking about them in vain for a more eligible situation, were obliged to sit down at the end of a table, at which a large party were already placed, without having any thing to do there, or any body to speak to, except each other.

Mrs. Allen congratulated herself, as soon as they were seated, on having preserved her gown from injury. 'It would have been very shocking to have it torn,' said she, 'would not it?—It is such a delicate muslin.—For my part I have not seen any thing I like so well in the whole room, I assure you.'

'How uncomfortable it is,' whispered Catherine, 'not to have a single acquaintance here!'

'Yes, my dear,' replied Mrs. Allen, with perfect serenity, 'it is very uncomfortable indeed.'

'What shall we do?—The gentlemen and ladies at this table look as if they wondered why we came here—we seem forcing ourselves into their party.'

'Aye, so we do.—That is very disagreeable. I wish we had a large acquaintance here.'

'I wish we had *any*;—it would be somebody to go to.'

'Very true, my dear; and if we knew anybody we would join them directly. The Skinners were here last year—I wish they were here now.'

'Had not we better go away as it is?—Here are no tea things for us, you see.'

'No more there are, indeed.—How very provoking! But I think we had better sit still, for one gets so tumbled in such a crowd! How is my head,* my dear?—Somebody gave me a push that has hurt it I am afraid.'

'No, indeed, it looks very nice.—But, dear Mrs. Allen, are you sure there is nobody you know in all this multitude of people? I think you *must* know somebody.'

'I don't upon my word—I wish I did. I wish I had a large acquaintance here with all my heart, and then I should get you a partner.—I should be so glad to have you dance. There goes a strange-looking woman! What an odd gown she has got on!—How old fashioned it is! Look at the back.'

After some time they received an offer of tea from one of their neighbours; it was thankfully accepted, and this introduced a light conversation with the gentleman who offered it, which was the only time that any body spoke to them during the evening, till they were discovered and joined by Mr. Allen when the dance was over.

'Well, Miss Morland,' said he, directly, 'I hope you have had an agreeable ball.'

'Very agreeable indeed,' she replied, vainly endeavouring to hide a great yawn.

'I wish she had been able to dance,' said his wife, 'I wish we could have got a partner for her.—I have been saying how glad I should be if the Skinners were here this winter instead of last; or if the Parrys had come, as they talked of once, she might have danced with George Parry. I am so sorry she has not had a partner!'

'We shall do better another evening I hope,' was Mr. Allen's consolation.

The company began to disperse when the dancing was over— enough to leave space for the remainder to walk about in some comfort; and now was the time for a heroine, who had not yet played a very distinguished part in the events of the evening, to be noticed and admired. Every five minutes, by removing some of the crowd, gave greater openings for her charms. She was now seen by many young men who had not been near her before. Not one, however, started with rapturous wonder on beholding her, no whisper of eager inquiry ran round the room, nor was she once called a divinity by any body.* Yet Catherine was in very good looks, and had the company only seen her three years before, they would *now* have thought her exceedingly handsome.

She *was* looked at however, and with some admiration; for, in her own hearing, two gentlemen pronounced her to be a pretty girl. Such words had their due effect; she immediately thought the evening pleasanter than she had found it before—her humble vanity was contented— she felt more obliged to the two young men for this simple praise than a true quality heroine would have been for fifteen sonnets in celebration of her charms, and went to her chair* in good humour with every body, and perfectly satisfied with her share of public attention.

CHAPTER III

EVERY morning now brought its regular duties;—shops were to be visited; some new part of the town to be looked at; and the Pump-room* to be attended, where they paraded up and down for an hour, looking at every body and speaking to no one. The wish of a numerous acquaintance in Bath was still uppermost with Mrs. Allen, and she repeated it after every fresh proof, which every morning brought, of her knowing nobody at all.

They made their appearance in the Lower Rooms; and here fortune was more favourable to our heroine. The master of the ceremonies* introduced to her a very gentlemanlike young man as a partner;—his name was Tilney.* He seemed to be about four or five and twenty, was rather tall, had a pleasing countenance, a very intelligent and lively eye, and, if not quite handsome, was very near it. His address was good, and Catherine felt herself in high luck. There was little leisure for speaking while they danced; but when they were seated at tea, she found him as agreeable as she had already given him credit for being. He talked with fluency and spirit—and there was an archness and pleasantry in his manner which interested, though it was hardly understood by her. After chatting some time on such matters as naturally arose from the objects around them, he suddenly addressed her with—'I have hitherto been very remiss, madam, in the proper attentions of a partner here; I have not yet asked you how long you have been in Bath; whether you were ever here before; whether you have been at the Upper Rooms, the theatre, and the concert; and how you like the place altogether. I have been very negligent—but are you now at leisure to satisfy me in these particulars? If you are I will begin directly.'

'You need not give yourself that trouble, sir.'

'No trouble I assure you, madam.' Then forming his features into a set smile, and affectedly softening his voice, he added, with a simpering air, 'Have you been long in Bath, madam?'

'About a week, sir,' replied Catherine, trying not to laugh.

'Really!' with affected astonishment.

'Why should you be surprized, sir?'

'Why, indeed!' said he, in his natural tone—'but some emotion must appear to be raised by your reply, and surprize is more easily assumed, and not less reasonable than any other.—Now let us go on. Were you never here before, madam?'

'Never, sir.'

'Indeed! Have you yet honoured the Upper Rooms?'

'Yes, sir, I was there last Monday.'

'Have you been to the theatre?'

'Yes, sir, I was at the play on Tuesday.'

'To the concert?'

'Yes, sir, on Wednesday.'

'And are you altogether pleased with Bath?'

'Yes—I like it very well.'

'Now I must give one smirk, and then we may be rational again.'

Catherine turned away her head, not knowing whether she might venture to laugh.

'I see what you think of me,' said he gravely—'I shall make but a poor figure in your journal to-morrow.'

'My journal!'

'Yes, I know exactly what you will say: Friday, went to the Lower Rooms; wore my sprigged muslin robe* with blue trimmings—plain black shoes—appeared to much advantage; but was strangely harassed by a queer, half-witted man, who would make me dance with him, and distressed me by his nonsense.'

'Indeed I shall say no such thing.'

'Shall I tell you what you ought to say?'

'If you please.'

'I danced with a very agreeable young man, introduced by Mr. King;* had a great deal of conversation with him—seems a most extraordinary genius—hope I may know more of him. *That*, madam, is what I *wish* you to say.'

'But, perhaps, I keep no journal.'

'Perhaps you are not sitting in this room, and I am not sitting by you. These are points in which a doubt is equally possible. Not keep a journal! How are your absent cousins to understand the tenour of your life in Bath without one? How are the civilities and compliments of every day to be related as they ought to be, unless noted down every evening in a journal? How are your various dresses to be remembered, and the particular state of your complexion, and curl of your hair to be described in all their diversities, without having constant recourse to a journal?—My dear madam, I am not so ignorant of young ladies' ways as you wish to believe me; it is this delightful habit of journalizing which largely contributes to form the easy style of writing for which ladies are so generally celebrated. Every body allows that the talent of writing agreeable letters is peculiarly female. Nature may have done something, but I am sure it must be essentially assisted by the practice of keeping a journal.'

'I have sometimes thought,' said Catherine, doubtingly, 'whether ladies do write so much better letters than gentlemen! That is—I should not think the superiority was always on our side.'

'As far as I have had opportunity of judging, it appears to me that the usual style of letter-writing among women is faultless, except in three particulars.'

'And what are they?'

'A general deficiency of subject, a total inattention to stops,* and a very frequent ignorance of grammar.'

'Upon my word! I need not have been afraid of disclaiming the compliment. You do not think too highly of us in that way.'

'I should no more lay it down as a general rule that women write better letters than men, than that they sing better duets, or draw better landscapes. In every power, of which taste is the foundation, excellence is pretty fairly divided between the sexes.'

They were interrupted by Mrs. Allen:—'My dear Catherine,' said she, 'do take this pin out of my sleeve; I am afraid it has torn a hole already; I shall be quite sorry if it has, for this is a favourite gown, though it cost but nine shillings a yard.'

'That is exactly what I should have guessed it, madam,' said Mr. Tilney, looking at the muslin.

'Do you understand muslins, sir?'

'Particularly well; I always buy my own cravats, and am allowed to be an excellent judge; and my sister has often trusted me in the choice of a gown. I bought one for her the other day, and it was pronounced to be a prodigious bargain by every lady who saw it. I gave but five shillings a yard for it, and a true Indian muslin.'

Mrs. Allen was quite struck by his genius. 'Men commonly take so little notice of those things,' said she: 'I can never get Mr. Allen to know one of my gowns from another. You must be a great comfort to your sister, sir.'

'I hope I am, madam.'

'And pray, sir, what do you think of Miss Morland's gown?'

'It is very pretty, madam,' said he, gravely examining it; 'but I do not think it will wash well; I am afraid it will fray.'

'How can you,' said Catherine, laughing, 'be so——' she had almost said, strange.

'I am quite of your opinion, sir,' replied Mrs. Allen: 'and so I told Miss Morland when she bought it.'

'But then you know, madam, muslin always turns to some account or other; Miss Morland will get enough out of it for a handkerchief, or a cap, or a cloak.—Muslin can never be said to be wasted. I have heard my sister say so forty times, when she has been extravagant in buying more than she wanted, or careless in cutting it to pieces.'

'Bath is a charming place, sir; there are so many good shops here.— We are sadly off in the country; not but what we have very good shops in Salisbury, but it is so far to go;—eight miles is a long way; Mr. Allen says it is nine, measured nine; but I am sure it cannot be more than eight; and it is such a fag*—I come back tired to death. Now here one can step out of doors and get a thing in five minutes.'

Mr. Tilney was polite enough to seem interested in what she said; and she kept him on the subject of muslins till the dancing recommenced. Catherine feared, as she listened to their discourse, that he indulged himself a little too much with the foibles of others.—'What are you thinking of so earnestly?' said he, as they walked back to the ball-room;—'not of your partner, I hope, for, by that shake of the head, your meditations are not satisfactory.'

Catherine coloured, and said, 'I was not thinking of any thing.'

'That is artful and deep, to be sure; but I had rather be told at once that you will not tell me.'

'Well then, I will not.'

'Thank you; for now we shall soon be acquainted, as I am authorized to tease you on this subject whenever we meet, and nothing in the world advances intimacy so much.'

They danced again; and, when the assembly closed, parted, on the lady's side at least, with a strong inclination for continuing the acquaintance. Whether she thought of him so much, while she drank her warm wine and water, and prepared herself for bed, as to dream of him when there, cannot be ascertained; but I hope it was no more than in a slight slumber, or a morning doze at most; for if it be true, as a celebrated writer has maintained, that no young lady can be justified in falling in love before the gentleman's love is declared,[1]* it must be very improper that a young lady should dream of a gentleman before the gentleman is first known to have dreamt of her. How proper Mr. Tilney might be as a dreamer or a lover, had not yet perhaps entered Mr. Allen's head, but that he was not objectionable as a common acquaintance for his young charge he was on inquiry satisfied; for he had early in the evening taken pains to know who her partner was, and had been assured of Mr. Tilney's being a clergyman, and of a very respectable family in Gloucestershire.

[1] Vide a letter from Mr. Richardson, No. 97, vol. ii. Rambler.

CHAPTER IV

WITH more than usual eagerness did Catherine hasten to the Pump-room the next day, secure within herself of seeing Mr. Tilney there before the morning were over, and ready to meet him with a smile:—but no smile was demanded—Mr. Tilney did not appear. Every creature in Bath, except himself, was to be seen in the room at different periods of the fashionable hours; crowds of people were every moment passing in and out, up the steps and down; people whom nobody cared about, and nobody wanted to see; and he only was absent. 'What a delightful place Bath is,' said Mrs. Allen, as they sat down near the great clock,* after parading the room till they were tired; 'and how pleasant it would be if we had any acquaintance here.'

This sentiment had been uttered so often in vain, that Mrs. Allen had no particular reason to hope it would be followed with more advantage now; but we are told to 'despair of nothing we would attain,' as 'unwearied diligence our point would gain;'* and the unwearied diligence with which she had every day wished for the same thing was at length to have its just reward, for hardly had she been seated ten minutes before a lady of about her own age, who was sitting by her, and had been looking at her attentively for several minutes, addressed her with great complaisance in these words:—'I think, madam, I cannot be mistaken; it is a long time since I had the pleasure of seeing you, but is not your name Allen?' This question answered, as it readily was, the stranger pronounced her's to be Thorpe; and Mrs. Allen immediately recognized the features of a former school-fellow and intimate, whom she had seen only once since their respective marriages, and that many years ago. Their joy on this meeting was very great, as well it might since they had been contented to know nothing of each other for the last fifteen years. Compliments on good looks now passed; and, after observing how time had slipped away since they were last together, how little they had thought of meeting in Bath, and what a pleasure it was to see an old friend, they proceeded to make inquiries and give intelligence as to their families, sisters, and cousins, talking both together, far more ready to give than to receive information, and each hearing very little of what the other said. Mrs. Thorpe, however, had one great advantage as a talker, over Mrs. Allen, in a family of children; and when she expatiated on the talents of her sons, and the beauty of her daughters,—when she related their different situations and views,—that John was at Oxford, Edward at Merchant-Taylors',* and William at sea,—and all of them more beloved and respected in their different stations than any other three beings ever were, Mrs. Allen had no similar information to give, no similar triumphs to press on the unwilling and unbelieving ear of her friend, and was forced to sit and appear to listen to all these maternal effusions, consoling herself, however, with the discovery, which her keen eye soon made, that the lace on Mrs. Thorpe's pelisse* was not half so handsome as that on her own.

'Here come my dear girls,' cried Mrs. Thorpe, pointing at three smart looking females, who, arm in arm, were then moving towards her. 'My dear Mrs. Allen, I long to introduce them; they will be so delighted to see you: the tallest is Isabella, my eldest; is not she a fine young woman? The others are very much admired too, but I believe Isabella is the handsomest.'

The Miss Thorpes were introduced; and Miss Morland, who had been for a short time forgotten, was introduced likewise. The name seemed to strike them all; and, after speaking to her with great civility, the eldest young lady observed aloud to the rest, 'How excessively like her brother Miss Morland is!'

'The very picture of him indeed!' cried the mother—and 'I should have known her any where for his sister!' was repeated by them all, two or three times over. For a moment Catherine was surprized; but Mrs. Thorpe and her daughters had scarcely begun the history of their acquaintance with Mr. James Morland, before she remembered that her eldest brother had lately formed an intimacy with a young man of his own college, of the name of Thorpe; and that he had spent the last week of the Christmas vacation with his family, near London.

The whole being explained, many obliging things were said by the Miss Thorpes of their wish of being better acquainted with her; of being considered as already friends, through the friendship of their brothers, &c. which Catherine heard with pleasure, and answered with all the pretty expressions she could command; and, as the first proof of amity, she was soon invited to accept an arm of the eldest Miss Thorpe, and take a turn with her about the room. Catherine was delighted with this extension of her Bath acquaintance, and almost forgot Mr. Tilney while she talked to Miss Thorpe. Friendship is certainly the finest balm for the pangs of disappointed love.*

Their conversation turned upon those subjects, of which the free discussion has generally much to do in perfecting a sudden intimacy between two young ladies; such as dress, balls, flirtations, and quizzes.* Miss Thorpe, however, being four years older than Miss Morland, and at least four years better informed, had a very decided advantage in discussing such points; she could compare the balls of Bath with those of Tunbridge;* its fashions with the fashions of London; could rectify the opinions of her new friend in many articles of tasteful attire; could discover a flirtation between any gentleman and lady who only smiled on each other; and point out a quiz through the thickness of a crowd. These powers received due admiration from Catherine, to whom they were entirely new; and the respect which they naturally inspired might have been too great for familiarity, had not the easy gaiety of Miss Thorpe's manners, and her frequent expressions of delight on this acquaintance with her, softened down every feeling of awe, and left nothing but tender affection. Their increasing attachment was not to be satisfied with half a dozen turns in the Pump-room, but required, when they all quitted it together, that Miss Thorpe should accompany Miss Morland to the very door of Mr. Allen's house; and that they should there part with a most affectionate and lengthened shake of hands, after learning, to their mutual relief, that they should see each other across the theatre at night, and say their prayers in the same chapel the next morning. Catherine then ran directly up stairs, and watched Miss Thorpe's progress down the street from the drawing-room window; admired the graceful spirit of her walk, the fashionable air of her figure and dress, and felt grateful, as well she might, for the chance which had procured her such a friend.

Mrs. Thorpe was a widow, and not a very rich one; she was a good-humoured, well-meaning woman, and a very indulgent mother. Her eldest daughter had great personal beauty, and the younger ones, by pretending to be as handsome as their sister, imitating her air, and dressing in the same style, did very well.

This brief account of the family is intended to supersede the necessity of a long and minute detail from Mrs. Thorpe herself, of her past adventures and sufferings, which might otherwise be expected to occupy the three or four following chapters; in which the worthlessness of lords and attornies might be set forth, and conversations, which had passed twenty years before, be minutely repeated.*

CHAPTER V

CATHERINE was not so much engaged at the theatre that evening, in returning the nods and smiles of Miss Thorpe, though they certainly claimed much of her leisure, as to forget to look with an inquiring eye for Mr. Tilney in every box which her eye could reach; but she looked in vain. Mr. Tilney was no fonder of the play than the Pump-room. She hoped to be more fortunate the next day; and when her wishes for fine weather were answered by seeing a beautiful morning, she hardly felt a doubt of it; for a fine Sunday in Bath empties every house of its inhabitants, and all the world appears on such an occasion to walk about and tell their acquaintance what a charming day it is.

As soon as divine service was over, the Thorpes and Allens eagerly joined each other; and after staying long enough in the Pump-room to discover that the crowd was insupportable, and that there was not a genteel face to be seen, which every body discovers every Sunday throughout the season, they hastened away to the Crescent,* to breathe the fresh air of better company. Here Catherine and Isabella, arm in arm, again tasted the sweets of friendship in an unreserved conversation;—they talked much, and with much enjoyment; but again was Catherine disappointed in her hope of re-seeing her partner. He was no where to be met with; every search for him was equally unsuccessful, in morning lounges or evening assemblies; neither at the upper nor lower rooms, at dressed or undressed balls, was he perceivable; nor among the walkers, the horsemen, or the curricle-drivers of the morning. His name was not in the Pump-room book,* and curiosity could do no more. He must be gone from Bath. Yet he had not mentioned that his stay would be so short! This sort of mysteriousness, which is always so becoming in a hero, threw a fresh grace in Catherine's imagination around his person and manners, and increased her anxiety to know more of him. From the Thorpes she could learn nothing, for they had been only two days in Bath before they met with Mrs. Allen. It was a subject, however, in which she often indulged with her fair friend, from whom she received every possible encouragement to continue to think of him; and his impression on her fancy was not suffered therefore to weaken. Isabella was very sure that he must be a charming young man; and was equally sure that he must have been delighted with her dear Catherine, and would therefore shortly return. She liked him the better for being a clergyman, 'for she must confess herself very partial to the profession;' and something like a sigh escaped her as she said it. Perhaps Catherine was wrong in not demanding the cause of that gentle emotion—but she was not experienced enough in the finesse of love, or the duties of friendship, to know when delicate raillery was properly called for, or when a confidence should be forced.

Mrs. Allen was now quite happy—quite satisfied with Bath. She had found some acquaintance, had been so lucky too as to find in them the family of a most worthy old friend; and, as the completion of good fortune, had found these friends by no means so expensively dressed as herself. Her daily expressions were no longer, 'I wish we had some acquaintance in Bath!' They were changed into—'How glad I am we have met with Mrs. Thorpe!'—and she was as eager in promoting the intercourse of the two families, as her young charge and Isabella themselves could be; never satisfied with the day unless she spent the chief of it by the side of Mrs. Thorpe, in what they called conversation, but in which there was scarcely ever any exchange of opinion, and not often any resemblance of subject, for Mrs. Thorpe talked chiefly of her children, and Mrs. Allen of her gowns.

The progress of the friendship between Catherine and Isabella was quick as its beginning had been warm, and they passed so rapidly through every gradation of increasing tenderness, that there was shortly no fresh proof of it to be given to their friends or themselves. They called each other by their Christian name, were always arm in arm when they walked, pinned up each other's train for the dance, and were not to be divided in the set;* and if a rainy morning deprived them of other enjoyments, they were still resolute in meeting in defiance of wet and dirt, and shut themselves up, to read novels together. Yes, novels;—for I will not adopt that ungenerous and impolitic custom so common with novel writers, of degrading by their contemptuous censure the very performances, to the number of which they are themselves adding*—joining with their greatest enemies in bestowing the harshest epithets on such works, and scarcely ever permitting them to be read by their own heroine, who, if she accidentally take up a novel, is sure to turn over its insipid pages with disgust. Alas! if the heroine of one novel be not patronized by the heroine of another, from whom can she expect protection and regard? I cannot approve of it. Let us leave it to the Reviewers to abuse such effusions of fancy at their leisure, and over every new novel to talk in threadbare strains of the trash with which the press now groans.* Let us not desert one another; we are an injured body. Although our productions have afforded more extensive and unaffected pleasure than those of any other literary corporation in the world, no species of composition has been so much decried. From pride, ignorance, or fashion, our foes are almost as many as our readers. And while the abilities of the nine-hundredth abridger of the History of England,* or of the man who collects and publishes in a volume some dozen lines of Milton, Pope, and Prior, with a paper from the Spectator, and a chapter from Sterne,* are eulogized by a thousand pens,—there seems almost a general wish of decrying the capacity and undervaluing the labour of the novelist, and of slighting the performances which have only genius, wit, and taste to recommend them. 'I am no novel reader— I seldom look into novels—Do not imagine that *I* often read novels— It is really very well for a novel.'—Such is the common cant.—'And what are you reading, Miss ——?' 'Oh! it is only a novel!' replies the young lady; while she lays down her book with affected indifference, or momentary shame.—'It is only Cecilia, or Camilla, or Belinda;'* or, in short, only some work in which the greatest powers of the mind are displayed, in which the most thorough knowledge of human nature, the happiest delineation of its varieties, the liveliest effusions of wit and humour are conveyed to the world in the best chosen language. Now, had the same young lady been engaged with a volume of the Spectator, instead of such a work, how proudly would she have produced the book, and told its name; though the chances must be against her being occupied by any part of that voluminous publication, of which either the matter or manner would not disgust a young person of taste: the substance of its papers so often consisting in the statement of improbable circumstances, unnatural characters, and topics of conversation, which no longer concern any one living; and their language, too, frequently so coarse as to give no very favourable idea of the age that could endure it.

CHAPTER VI

THE following conversation, which took place between the two friends in the Pump-room one morning, after an acquaintance of eight or nine days, is given as a specimen of their very warm attachment, and of the delicacy, discretion, originality of thought, and literary taste which marked the reasonableness of that attachment.

They met by appointment; and as Isabella had arrived nearly five minutes before her friend, her first address naturally was—'My dearest creature, what can have made you so late? I have been waiting for you at least this age!'

'Have you, indeed!—I am very sorry for it; but really I thought I was in very good time. It is but just one. I hope you have not been here long?'

'Oh! these ten ages at least. I am sure I have been here this half hour. But now, let us go and sit down at the other end of the room, and enjoy ourselves. I have an hundred things to say to you. In the first place, I was so afraid it would rain this morning, just as I wanted to set off; it looked very showery, and that would have thrown me into agonies! Do you know, I saw the prettiest hat you can imagine, in a shop window in Milsom-street just now—very like yours, only with coquelicot ribbons instead of green;* I quite longed for it. But, my dearest Catherine, what have you been doing with yourself all this morning?—Have you gone on with Udolpho?'

'Yes, I have been reading it ever since I woke; and I am got to the black veil.'*

'Are you, indeed? How delightful! Oh! I would not tell you what is behind the black veil for the world! Are not you wild to know?'

'Oh! yes, quite; what can it be?—But do not tell me—I would not be told upon any account. I know it must be a skeleton, I am sure it is Laurentina's skeleton.* Oh! I am delighted with the book! I should like to spend my whole life in reading it. I assure you, if it had not been to meet you, I would not have come away from it for all the world.'

'Dear creature! how much I am obliged to you; and when you have finished Udolpho, we will read the Italian* together; and I have made out a list of ten or twelve more of the same kind for you.'

'Have you, indeed! How glad I am!—What are they all?'

'I will read you their names directly; here they are, in my pocket-book. Castle of Wolfenbach, Clermont, Mysterious Warnings, Necromancer of the Black Forest, Midnight Bell, Orphan of the Rhine, and Horrid Mysteries.* Those will last us some time.'

'Yes, pretty well; but are they all horrid, are you sure they are all horrid?'

'Yes, quite sure; for a particular friend of mine, a Miss Andrews, a sweet girl, one of the sweetest creatures in the world, has read every one of them. I wish you knew Miss Andrews, you would be delighted with her. She is netting herself the sweetest cloak you can conceive. I think her as beautiful as an angel, and I am so vexed with the men for not admiring her!—I scold them all amazingly about it.'

'Scold them! Do you scold them for not admiring her?'

'Yes, that I do. There is nothing I would not do for those who are really my friends. I have no notion of loving people by halves, it is not my nature. My attachments are always excessively strong. I told Capt. Hunt at one of our assemblies this winter, that if he was to tease me all night, I would not dance with him, unless he would allow Miss Andrews to be as beautiful as an angel. The men think us incapable of real friendship you know, and I am determined to shew them the difference. Now, if I were to hear any body speak slightingly of you, I should fire up in a moment:—but that is not at all likely, for *you* are just the kind of girl to be a great favourite with the men.'

'Oh! dear,' cried Catherine, colouring, 'how can you say so?'

'I know you very well; you have so much animation, which is exactly what Miss Andrews wants, for I must confess there is something amazingly insipid about her. Oh! I must tell you, that just after we parted yesterday, I saw a young man looking at you so earnestly—I am sure he is in love with you.' Catherine coloured, and disclaimed again. Isabella laughed. 'It is very true, upon my honour, but I see how it is; you are indifferent to every body's admiration, except that of one gentleman, who shall be nameless. Nay, I cannot blame you—(speaking more seriously)—your feelings are easily understood. Where the heart is really attached, I know very well how little one can be pleased with the attention of any body else. Every thing is so insipid, so uninteresting, that does not relate to the beloved object! I can perfectly comprehend your feelings.'

'But you should not persuade me that I think so very much about Mr. Tilney, for perhaps I may never see him again.'

'Not see him again! My dearest creature, do not talk of it. I am sure you would be miserable if you thought so.'

'No, indeed, I should not. I do not pretend to say that I was not very much pleased with him; but while I have Udolpho to read, I feel as if nobody could make me miserable. Oh! the dreadful black veil!

My dear Isabella, I am sure there must be Laurentina's skeleton behind it.'

'It is so odd to me, that you should never have read Udolpho before; but I suppose Mrs. Morland objects to novels.'

'No, she does not. She very often reads Sir Charles Grandison* herself; but new books do not fall in our way.'

'Sir Charles Grandison! That is an amazing horrid book, is it not?—I remember Miss Andrews could not get through the first volume.'

'It is not like Udolpho at all; but yet I think it is very entertaining.'

'Do you indeed!—you surprize me; I thought it had not been read-able. But, my dearest Catherine, have you settled what to wear on your head to-night? I am determined at all events to, be dressed exactly like you. The men take notice of *that* sometimes you know.'

'But it does not signify if they do;' said Catherine, very innocently.

'Signify! Oh, heavens! I make it a rule never to mind what they say. They are very often amazingly impertinent if you do not treat them with spirit, and make them keep their distance.'

'Are they?—Well, I never observed *that*. They always behave very well to me.'

'Oh! they give themselves such airs. They are the most conceited creatures in the world, and think themselves of so much importance!— By the bye, though I have thought of it a hundred times, I have always forgot to ask you what is your favourite complexion in a man. Do you like them best dark or fair?'

'I hardly know. I never much thought about it. Something between both, I think. Brown—not fair, and not very dark.'

'Very well, Catherine. That is exactly he. I have not forgot your description of Mr. Tilney;—"a brown skin, with dark eyes, and rather dark hair."—Well, my taste is different. I prefer light eyes, and as to complexion—do you know—I like a sallow better than any other. You must not betray me, if you should ever meet with one of your acquaintance answering that description.'

'Betray you!—What do you mean?'

'Nay, do not distress me. I believe I have said too much. Let us drop the subject.'

Catherine, in some amazement, complied; and after remaining a few moments silent, was on the point of reverting to what inter-ested her at that time rather more than any thing else in the world,

Laurentina's skeleton; when her friend prevented her, by saying,—'For Heaven's sake! let us move away from this end of the room. Do you know, there are two odious young men who have been staring at me this half hour. They really put me quite out of countenance. Let us go and look at the arrivals. They will hardly follow us there.'

Away they walked to the book;* and while Isabella examined the names, it was Catherine's employment to watch the proceedings of these alarming young men.

'They are not coming this way, are they? I hope they are not so impertinent as to follow us. Pray let me know if they are coming. I am determined I will not look up.'

In a few moments Catherine, with unaffected pleasure, assured her that she need not be longer uneasy, as the gentlemen had just left the Pump-room.

'And which way are they gone?' said Isabella, turning hastily round. 'One was a very good-looking young man.'

'They went towards the churchyard.'

'Well, I am amazingly glad I have got rid of them! And now, what say you to going to Edgar's Buildings* with me, and looking at my new hat? You said you should like to see it.'

Catherine readily agreed. 'Only,' she added, 'perhaps we may over-take the two young men.'

'Oh! never mind that. If we make haste, we shall pass by them pres-ently, and I am dying to shew you my hat.'

'But if we only wait a few minutes, there will be no danger of our seeing them at all.'

'I shall not pay them any such compliment, I assure you. I have no notion of treating men with such respect. *That* is the way to spoil them.'

Catherine had nothing to oppose against such reasoning; and therefore, to shew the independence of Miss Thorpe, and her resolution of humbling the sex, they set off immediately as fast as they could walk, in pursuit of the two young men.

CHAPTER VII

HALF a minute conducted them through the Pump-yard to the archway, opposite Union-passage; but here they were stopped. Every body acquainted with Bath may remember the difficulties of crossing Cheap-street* at this point; it is indeed a street of so impertinent a nature, so unfortunately connected with the great London and Oxford roads, and the principal inn of the city, that a day never passes in which parties of ladies, however important their business, whether in quest of pastry, millinery, or even (as in the present case) of young men, are not detained on one side or other by carriages, horsemen, or carts. This evil had been felt and lamented, at least three times a day, by Isabella since her residence in Bath; and she was now fated to feel and lament it once more, for at the very moment of coming opposite to Union-passage, and within view of the two gentlemen who were proceeding through the crowds, and threading the gutters of that interesting alley, they were prevented crossing by the approach of a gig,* driven along on bad pavement by a most knowing-looking coachman with all the vehemence that could most fitly endanger the lives of himself, his companion, and his horse.

'Oh, these odious gigs!' said Isabella, looking up, 'how I detest them.' But this detestation, though so just, was of short duration, for she looked again and exclaimed, 'Delightful! Mr. Morland and my brother!'

'Good heaven! 'tis James!' was uttered at the same moment by Catherine; and, on catching the young men's eyes, the horse was immediately checked with a violence which almost threw him on his haunches, and the servant having now scampered up, the gentlemen jumped out, and the equipage was delivered to his care.

Catherine, by whom this meeting was wholly unexpected, received her brother with the liveliest pleasure; and he, being of a very amiable disposition, and sincerely attached to her, gave every proof on his side of equal satisfaction, which he could have leisure to do, while the bright eyes of Miss Thorpe were incessantly challenging his notice; and to her his devoirs were speedily paid, with a mixture of joy and embarrassment which might have informed Catherine, had she been more expert in the development of other people's feelings, and less simply engrossed by her own, that her brother thought her friend quite as pretty as she could do herself.

John Thorpe, who in the mean time had been giving orders about the horses, soon joined them, and from him she directly received the amends which were her due; for while he slightly and carelessly touched the hand of Isabella, on her he bestowed a whole scrape* and half a short bow. He was a stout young man of middling height, who, with a plain face and ungraceful form, seemed fearful of being too handsome unless he wore the dress of a groom, and too much like a gentleman unless he were easy where he ought to be civil, and impudent where he might be allowed to be easy. He took out his watch: 'How long do you think we have been running it from Tetbury,* Miss Morland?'

'I do not know the distance.' Her brother told her that it was twenty-three miles.

'*Three*-and-twenty!' cried Thorpe; 'five-and-twenty if it is an inch.' Morland remonstrated, pleaded the authority of road-books, inn-keepers, and milestones; but his friend disregarded them all; he had a surer test of distance. 'I know it must be five-and-twenty,' said he, 'by the time we have been doing it. It is now half after one; we drove out of the inn-yard at Tetbury as the town-clock struck eleven; and I defy any man in England to make my horse go less than ten miles an hour in harness; that makes it exactly twenty-five.'

'You have lost an hour,' said Morland; 'it was only ten o'clock when we came from Tetbury.'

'Ten o'clock! it was eleven, upon my soul! I counted every stroke. This brother of yours would persuade me out of my senses, Miss Morland; do but look at my horse; did you ever see an animal so made for speed in your life?' (The servant had just mounted the carriage and was driving off.) 'Such true blood! Three hours and a half indeed coming only three-and-twenty miles! look at that creature, and suppose it possible if you can.'

'He *does* look very hot to be sure.'

'Hot! he had not turned a hair till we came to Walcot Church;* but look at his forehead; look at his loins; only see how he moves; that horse *cannot* go less than ten miles an hour: tie his legs and he will get on. What do you think of my gig, Miss Morland? a neat one, is not it? Well hung; town built; I have not had it a month. It was built for a Christchurch* man, a friend of mine, a very good sort of fellow; he ran it a few weeks, till, I believe, it was convenient to have done with it. I happened just then to be looking out for some light thing of the kind, though I had pretty well determined on a curricle too; but I chanced to meet him on Magdalen Bridge* as he was driving into Oxford, last term: "Ah! Thorpe," said he, "do you happen to want such a little thing as this? it is a capital one of the kind, but I am cursed tired of it." "Oh! d——," said I, "I am your man; what do you ask?" And how much do you think he did, Miss Morland?'

'I am sure I cannot guess at all.'

'Curricle-hung you see; seat, trunk, sword-case, splashing-board, lamps, silver moulding, all you see complete; the iron-work as good as new, or better. He asked fifty guineas; I closed with him directly, threw down the money, and the carriage was mine.'

'And I am sure,' said Catherine, 'I know so little of such things that I cannot judge whether it was cheap or dear.'

'Neither one nor t'other; I might have got it for less I dare say; but I hate haggling, and poor Freeman wanted cash.'

'That was very good-natured of you,' said Catherine, quite pleased.

'Oh! d—— it, when one has the means of doing a kind thing by a friend, I hate to be pitiful.'

An inquiry now took place into the intended movements of the young ladies; and, on finding whither they were going, it was decided that the gentlemen should accompany them to Edgar's Buildings, and pay their respects to Mrs. Thorpe. James and Isabella led the way; and so well satisfied was the latter with her lot, so contentedly was she endeavouring to ensure a pleasant walk to him who brought the double recommendation of being her brother's friend, and her friend's brother, so pure and uncoquettish were her feelings, that, though they overtook and passed the two offending young men in Milsom-street, she was so far from seeking to attract their notice, that she looked back at them only three times.

John Thorpe kept of course with Catherine, and, after a few minutes' silence, renewed the conversation about his gig—'You will find, however, Miss Morland, it would be reckoned a cheap thing by some people, for I might have sold it for ten guineas more the next day; Jackson, of Oriel,* bid me sixty at once; Morland was with me at the time.'

'Yes,' said Morland, who overheard this; 'but you forget that your horse was included.'

'My horse! oh, d—— it! I would not sell my horse for a hundred. Are you fond of an open carriage, Miss Morland?'

'Yes, very; I have hardly ever an opportunity of being in one; but I am particularly fond of it.'

'I am glad of it; I will drive you out in mine every day.'

'Thank you,' said Catherine, in some distress, from a doubt of the propriety of accepting such an offer.

'I will drive you up Lansdown Hill to-morrow.'*

'Thank you; but will not your horse want rest?'

'Rest! he has only come three-and-twenty miles to-day; all nonsense; nothing ruins horses so much as rest; nothing knocks them up so soon. No, no; I shall exercise mine at the average of four hours every day while I am here.'

'Shall you indeed!' said Catherine very seriously, 'that will be forty miles a day.'

'Forty! aye fifty, for what I care. Well, I will drive you up Lansdown to-morrow; mind, I am engaged.'

'How delightful that will be!' cried Isabella, turning round; 'my dearest Catherine, I quite envy you; but I am afraid, brother, you will not have room for a third.'

'A third indeed! no, no; I did not come to Bath to drive my sisters about; that would be a good joke, faith! Morland must take care of you.'

This brought on a dialogue of civilities between the other two; but Catherine heard neither the particulars nor the result. Her companion's discourse now sunk from its hitherto animated pitch, to nothing more than a short decisive sentence of praise or condemnation on the face of every woman they met; and Catherine, after listening and agreeing as long as she could, with all the civility and deference of the youthful female mind, fearful of hazarding an opinion of its own in opposition to that of a self-assured man, especially where the beauty of her own sex is concerned, ventured at length to vary the subject by a question which had been long uppermost in her thoughts; it was, 'Have you ever read Udolpho, Mr. Thorpe?'

'Udolpho! Oh, Lord! not I; I never read novels; I have something else to do.'

Catherine, humbled and ashamed, was going to apologize for her question, but he prevented her by saying, 'Novels are all so full of nonsense and stuff; there has not been a tolerably decent one come out since Tom Jones, except the Monk;* I read that t'other day; but as for all the others, they are the stupidest things in creation.'

'I think you must like Udolpho, if you were to read it; it is so very interesting.'

'Not I, faith! No, if I read any, it shall be Mrs. Radcliff''s; her novels are amusing enough; they are worth reading; some fun and nature in *them*.'

'Udolpho was written by Mrs. Radcliff,' said Catherine, with some hesitation, from the fear of mortifying him.

'No sure; was it? Aye, I remember, so it was; I was thinking of that other stupid book, written by that woman they make such a fuss about, she who married the French emigrant.'*

'I suppose you mean Camilla?'

'Yes, that's the book, such unnatural stuff!—An old man playing at see-saw!* I took up the first volume once, and looked it over, but I soon found it would not do; indeed I guessed what sort of stuff it must be before I saw it: as soon as I heard she had married an emigrant, I was sure I should never be able to get through it.'

'I have never read it.'

'You had no loss I assure you; it is the horridest nonsense you can imagine; there is nothing in the world in it but an old man's playing at see-saw and learning Latin,* upon my soul there is not.'

This critique, the justness of which was unfortunately lost on poor Catherine, brought them to the door of Mrs. Thorpe's lodgings, and the feelings of the discerning and unprejudiced reader of Camilla gave way to the feelings of the dutiful and affectionate son, as they met Mrs. Thorpe, who had descried them from above, in the passage. 'Ah, mother! how do you do?' said he, giving her a hearty shake of the hand: 'where did you get that quiz of a hat, it makes you look like an old witch? Here is Morland and I come to stay a few days with you, so you must look out for a couple of good beds some where near.' And this address seemed to satisfy all the fondest wishes of the mother's heart, for she received him with the most delighted and exulting affection. On his two younger sisters he then bestowed an equal portion of his fraternal tenderness, for he asked each of them how they did, and observed that they both looked very ugly.

These manners did not please Catherine; but he was James's friend and Isabella's brother; and her judgment was further bought off by Isabella's assuring her, when they withdrew to see the new hat, that John thought her the most charming girl in the world, and by John's engaging her before they parted to dance with him that evening. Had she been older or vainer, such attacks might have done little; but, where youth and diffidence are united, it requires uncommon steadiness of reason to resist the attraction of being called the most charming girl in the world, and of being so very early engaged as a partner; and the consequence was, that, when the two Morlands, after sitting an hour with the Thorpes, set off to walk together to Mr. Allen's, and James, as the door was closed on them, said, 'Well, Catherine, how do

you like my friend Thorpe?' instead of answering, as she probably
would have done, had there been no friendship and no flattery in the
case, 'I do not like him at all;' she directly replied, 'I like him very
much; he seems very agreeable.'

'He is as good-natured a fellow as ever lived; a little of a rattle;* but
that will recommend him to your sex I believe: and how do you like
the rest of the family?'

'Very, very much indeed: Isabella particularly.'

'I am very glad to hear you say so; she is just the kind of young
woman I could wish to see you attached to; she has so much good
sense, and is so thoroughly unaffected and amiable; I always wanted
you to know her; and she seems very fond of you. She said the highest
things in your praise that could possibly be; and the praise of such
a girl as Miss Thorpe even you, Catherine,' taking her hand with
affection, 'may be proud of.'

'Indeed I am,' she replied; 'I love her exceedingly, and am delighted
to find that you like her too. You hardly mentioned any thing of her,
when you wrote to me after your visit there.'

'Because I thought I should soon see you myself. I hope you will be
a great deal together while you are in Bath. She is a most amiable girl;
such a superior understanding! How fond all the family are of her;
she is evidently the general favourite; and how much she must be
admired in such a place as this—is not she?'

'Yes, very much indeed, I fancy; Mr. Allen thinks her the prettiest
girl in Bath.'

'I dare say he does; and I do not know any man who is a better judge
of beauty than Mr. Allen. I need not ask you whether you are happy
here, my dear Catherine; with such a companion and friend as Isabella
Thorpe, it would be impossible for you to be otherwise; and the Allens
I am sure are very kind to you?'

'Yes, very kind; I never was so happy before; and now you are come
it will be more delightful than ever; how good it is of you to come so
far on purpose to see *me*.'

James accepted this tribute of gratitude, and qualified his conscience for accepting it too, by saying with perfect sincerity, 'Indeed,
Catherine, I love you dearly.'

Inquiries and communications concerning brothers and sisters,
the situation of some, the growth of the rest, and other family matters, now passed between them, and continued, with only one small

digression on James's part, in praise of Miss Thorpe, till they reached Pulteney-street, where he was welcomed with great kindness by Mr. and Mrs. Allen, invited by the former to dine with them, and summoned by the latter to guess the price and weigh the merits of a new muff and tippet.* A pre-engagement in Edgar's Buildings prevented his accepting the invitation of one friend, and obliged him to hurry away as soon as he had satisfied the demands of the other. The time of the two parties uniting in the Octagon Room* being correctly adjusted, Catherine was then left to the luxury of a raised, restless, and frightened imagination over the pages of Udolpho, lost from all worldly concerns of dressing and dinner, incapable of soothing Mrs. Allen's fears on the delay of an expected dress-maker, and having only one minute in sixty to bestow even on the reflection of her own felicity, in being already engaged for the evening.

CHAPTER VIII

IN spite of Udolpho and the dress-maker, however, the party from Pulteney-street reached the Upper-rooms in very good time. The Thorpes and James Morland were there only two minutes before them; and Isabella having gone through the usual ceremonial of meeting her friend with the most smiling and affectionate haste, of admiring the set of her gown, and envying the curl of her hair, they followed their chaperons, arm in arm, into the ball-room, whispering to each other whenever a thought occurred, and supplying the place of many ideas by a squeeze of the hand or a smile of affection.

The dancing began within a few minutes after they were seated; and James, who had been engaged quite as long as his sister, was very importunate with Isabella to stand up; but John was gone into the card-room to speak to a friend, and nothing, she declared, should induce her to join the set before her dear Catherine could join it too: 'I assure you,' said she, 'I would not stand up without your dear sister for all the world; for if I did we should certainly be separated the whole evening.' Catherine accepted this kindness with gratitude, and they continued as they were for three minutes longer, when Isabella, who had been talking to James on the other side of her, turned again to his sister and whispered, 'My dear creature, I am afraid I must leave you, your brother is so amazingly impatient to begin; I know you will not mind my going away, and I dare say John will be back in a moment, and then you may easily find me out.' Catherine, though a little disappointed, had too much good-nature to make any opposition, and the others rising up, Isabella had only time to press her friend's hand and say, 'Good bye, my dear love,' before they hurried off. The younger Miss Thorpes being also dancing, Catherine was left to the mercy of Mrs. Thorpe and Mrs. Allen, between whom she now remained. She could not help being vexed at the non-appearance of Mr. Thorpe, for she not only longed to be dancing, but was likewise aware that, as the real dignity of her situation could not be known, she was sharing with the scores of other young ladies still sitting down all the discredit of wanting a partner. To be disgraced in the eye of the world, to wear the appearance of infamy while her heart is all purity, her actions all innocence, and the misconduct of another the true source of her debasement, is one of those circumstances which peculiarly belong to the heroine's life, and her fortitude under it what particularly dignifies her character.* Catherine had fortitude too; she suffered, but no murmur passed her lips.

From this state of humiliation, she was roused, at the end of ten minutes, to a pleasanter feeling, by seeing, not Mr. Thorpe, but Mr. Tilney, within three yards of the place where they sat; he seemed to be moving that way, but he did not see her, and therefore the smile and the blush, which his sudden reappearance raised in Catherine, passed away without sullying her heroic importance. He looked as handsome and as lively as ever, and was talking with interest to a fashionable and pleasing-looking young woman, who leant on his arm, and whom Catherine immediately guessed to be his sister; thus unthinkingly throwing away a fair opportunity of considering him lost to her for ever, by being married already. But guided only by what was simple and probable, it had never entered her head that Mr. Tilney could be married; he had not behaved, he had not talked, like the married men to whom she had been used; he had never mentioned a wife, and he had acknowledged a sister. From these circumstances sprang the instant conclusion of his sister's now being by his side; and therefore, instead of turning of a deathlike paleness, and falling in a fit on Mrs. Allen's bosom, Catherine sat erect, in the perfect use of her senses, and with cheeks only a little redder than usual.

Mr. Tilney and his companion, who continued, though slowly, to approach, were immediately preceded by a lady, an acquaintance of

Mrs. Thorpe; and this lady stopping to speak to her, they, as belonging to her, stopped likewise, and Catherine, catching Mr. Tilney's eye, instantly received from him the smiling tribute of recognition. She returned it with pleasure, and then advancing still nearer, he spoke both to her and Mrs. Allen, by whom he was very civilly acknowledged. 'I am very happy to see you again, sir, indeed; I was afraid you had left Bath.' He thanked her for her fears, and said that he had quitted it for a week, on the very morning after his having had the pleasure of seeing her.

'Well, sir, and I dare say you are not sorry to be back again, for it is just the place for young people—and indeed for every body else too. I tell Mr. Allen, when he talks of being sick of it, that I am sure he should not complain, for it is so very agreeable a place, that it is much better to be here than at home at this dull time of year. I tell him he is quite in luck to be sent here for his health.'

'And I hope, madam, that Mr. Allen will be obliged to like the place, from finding it of service to him.'

'Thank you, sir. I have no doubt that he will.—A neighbour of ours, Dr. Skinner, was here for his health last winter, and came away quite stout.'*

'That circumstance must give great encouragement.'

'Yes, sir—and Dr. Skinner and his family were here three months; so I tell Mr. Allen he must not be in a hurry to get away.'

Here they were interrupted by a request from Mrs. Thorpe to Mrs. Allen, that she would move a little to accommodate Mrs. Hughes and Miss Tilney with seats, as they had agreed to join their party. This was accordingly done, Mr. Tilney still continuing standing before them; and after a few minutes consideration, he asked Catherine to dance with him. This compliment, delightful as it was, produced severe mortification to the lady; and in giving her denial, she expressed her sorrow on the occasion so very much as if she really felt it, that had Thorpe, who joined her just afterwards, been half a minute earlier, he might have thought her sufferings rather too acute. The very easy manner in which he then told her that he had kept her waiting, did not by any means reconcile her more to her lot; nor did the particulars which he entered into while they were standing up, of the horses and dogs of the friend whom he had just left, and of a proposed exchange of terriers between them, interest her so much as to prevent her looking very often towards that part of the room where she had left Mr. Tilney. Of her dear Isabella, to whom she particularly longed to point out that gentleman, she could see nothing. They were in different sets. She was separated from all her party, and away from all her acquaintance;—one mortification succeeded another, and from the whole she deduced this useful lesson, that to go previously engaged to a ball, does not necessarily increase either the dignity or enjoyment of a young lady. From such a moralizing strain as this, she was suddenly roused by a touch on the shoulder, and turning round, perceived Mrs. Hughes directly behind her, attended by Miss Tilney and a gentleman. 'I beg your pardon, Miss Morland,' said she, 'for this liberty,—but I cannot any how get to Miss Thorpe, and Mrs. Thorpe said she was sure you would not have the least objection to letting in this young lady by you.' Mrs. Hughes could not have applied to any creature in the room more happy to oblige her than Catherine. The young ladies were introduced to each other, Miss Tilney expressing a proper sense of such goodness, Miss Morland with the real delicacy of a generous mind making light of the obligation; and Mrs. Hughes, satisfied with having so respectably settled her young charge, returned to her party.

Miss Tilney had a good figure, a pretty face, and a very agreeable countenance; and her air, though it had not all the decided pretension, the resolute stilishness of Miss Thorpe's, had more real elegance. Her manners shewed good sense and good breeding; they were neither shy, nor affectedly open; and she seemed capable of being young, attractive, and at a ball, without wanting to fix the attention of every man near her, and without exaggerated feelings of extatic delight or inconceivable vexation on every little trifling occurrence. Catherine, interested at once by her appearance and her relationship to Mr. Tilney, was desirous of being acquainted with her, and readily talked therefore whenever she could think of any thing to say, and had courage and leisure for saying it. But the hindrance thrown in the way of a very speedy intimacy, by the frequent want of one or more of these requisites, prevented their doing more than going through the first rudiments of an acquaintance, by informing themselves how well the other liked Bath, how much she admired its buildings and surrounding country, whether she drew, or played or sang, and whether she was fond of riding on horseback.

The two dances were scarcely concluded before Catherine found her arm gently seized by her faithful Isabella, who in great spirits exclaimed—'At last I have got you. My dearest creature, I have been looking for you this hour. What could induce you to come into this set, when you knew I was in the other? I have been quite wretched without you.'

'My dear Isabella, how was it possible for me to get at you? I could not even see where you were.'

'So I told your brother all the time—but he would not believe me. Do go and see for her, Mr. Morland, said I—but all in vain—he would not stir an inch. Was not it so, Mr. Morland? But you men are all so immoderately lazy! I have been scolding him to such a degree, my dear Catherine, you would be quite amazed.—You know I never stand upon ceremony with such people.'

'Look at that young lady with the white beads round her head,' whispered Catherine, detaching her friend from James—'It is Mr. Tilney's sister.'

'Oh! heavens! You don't say so! Let me look at her this moment. What a delightful girl! I never saw any thing half so beautiful! But where is her all-conquering brother? Is he in the room? Point him out to me this instant, if he is. I die to see him. Mr. Morland, you are not to listen. We are not talking about you.'

'But what is all this whispering about? What is going on?'

'There now, I knew how it would be. You men have such restless curiosity! Talk of the curiosity of women, indeed!*—'tis nothing. But be satisfied, for you are not to know any thing at all of the matter.'

'And is that likely to satisfy me, do you think?'

'Well, I declare I never knew any thing like you. What can it signify to you, what we are talking of? Perhaps we are talking about you, therefore I would advise you not to listen, or you may happen to hear something not very agreeable.'

In this common-place chatter, which lasted some time, the original subject seemed entirely forgotten; and though Catherine was very well pleased to have it dropped for a while, she could not avoid a little suspicion at the total suspension of all Isabella's impatient desire to see Mr. Tilney. When the orchestra struck up a fresh dance, James would have led his fair partner away, but she resisted. 'I tell you, Mr. Morland,' she cried, 'I would not do such a thing for all the world. How can you be so teasing; only conceive, my dear Catherine, what your brother wants me to do. He wants me to dance with him again, though I tell him that it is a most improper thing, and entirely against the rules. It would make us the talk of the place, if we were not to change partners.'

'Upon my honour,' said James, 'in these public assemblies, it is as often done as not.'

'Nonsense, how can you say so? But when you men have a point to carry, you never stick at any thing. My sweet Catherine, do support me, persuade your brother how impossible it is. Tell him, that it would quite shock you to see me do such a thing; now would not it?'

'No, not at all; but if you think it wrong, you had much better change.'

'There,' cried Isabella, 'you hear what your sister says, and yet you will not mind her. Well, remember that it is not my fault, if we set all the old ladies in Bath in a bustle. Come along, my dearest Catherine, for heaven's sake, and stand by me.' And off they went, to regain their former place. John Thorpe, in the meanwhile, had walked away; and Catherine, ever willing to give Mr. Tilney an opportunity of repeating the agreeable request which had already flattered her once, made her way to Mrs. Allen and Mrs. Thorpe as fast as she could, in the hope of finding him still with them—a hope which, when it proved to be fruitless, she felt to have been highly unreasonable. 'Well, my dear,' said Mrs. Thorpe, impatient for praise of her son, 'I hope you have had an agreeable partner.'

'Very agreeable, madam.'

'I am glad of it. John has charming spirits, has not he?'

'Did you meet Mr. Tilney, my dear?' said Mrs. Allen.

'No, where is he?'

'He was with us just now, and said he was so tired of lounging about, that he was resolved to go and dance; so I thought perhaps he would ask you, if he met with you.'

'Where can he be?' said Catherine, looking round; but she had not looked round long before she saw him leading a young lady to the dance.

'Ah! he has got a partner, I wish he had asked *you*,' said Mrs. Allen; and after a short silence, she added, 'he is a very agreeable young man.'

'Indeed he is, Mrs. Allen,' said Mrs. Thorpe, smiling complacently; 'I must say it, though I *am* his mother, that there is not a more agreeable young man in the world.'

This inapplicable answer might have been too much for the comprehension of many; but it did not puzzle Mrs. Allen, for after only

a moment's consideration, she said, in a whisper to Catherine, 'I dare
say she thought I was speaking of her son.'

Catherine was disappointed and vexed. She seemed to have missed
by so little the very object she had had in view; and this persuasion
did not incline her to a very gracious reply, when John Thorpe came
up to her soon afterwards, and said, 'Well, Miss Morland, I suppose
you and I are to stand up and jig it together again.'

'Oh, no; I am much obliged to you, our two dances are over; and,
besides, I am tired, and do not mean to dance any more.'

'Do not you?—then let us walk about and quiz people. Come along
with me, and I will shew you the four greatest quizzers* in the room;
my two younger sisters and their partners. I have been laughing at
them this half hour.'

Again Catherine excused herself; and at last he walked off to quiz
his sisters by himself. The rest of the evening she found very dull;
Mr. Tilney was drawn away from their party at tea, to attend that of
his partner; Miss Tilney, though belonging to it, did not sit near her,
and James and Isabella were so much engaged in conversing together,
that the latter had no leisure to bestow more on her friend than one
smile, one squeeze, and one 'dearest Catherine.'

CHAPTER IX

THE progress of Catherine's unhappiness from the events of the
evening, was as follows. It appeared first in a general dissatisfaction
with every body about her, while she remained in the rooms, which
speedily brought on considerable weariness and a violent desire to go
home. This, on arriving in Pulteney-street, took the direction of
extraordinary hunger, and when that was appeased, changed into an
earnest longing to be in bed; such was the extreme point of her distress; for when there she immediately fell into a sound sleep which
lasted nine hours, and from which she awoke perfectly revived, in
excellent spirits, with fresh hopes and fresh schemes. The first wish
of her heart was to improve her acquaintance with Miss Tilney, and
almost her first resolution, to seek her for that purpose, in the Pump-
room at noon. In the Pump-room, one so newly arrived in Bath must
be met with, and that building she had already found so favourable
for the discovery of female excellence, and the completion of female

intimacy, so admirably adapted for secret discourses and unlimited confidence, that she was most reasonably encouraged to expect another friend from within its walls. Her plan for the morning thus settled, she sat quietly down to her book after breakfast, resolving to remain in the same place and the same employment till the clock struck one; and from habitude very little incommoded by the remarks and ejaculations of Mrs. Allen, whose vacancy of mind and incapacity for thinking were such, that as she never talked a great deal, so she could never be entirely silent; and, therefore, while she sat at her work, if she lost her needle or broke her thread, if she heard a carriage in the street, or saw a speck upon her gown, she must observe it aloud, whether there were any one at leisure to answer her or not. At about half past twelve, a remarkably loud rap drew her in haste to the window, and scarcely had she time to inform Catherine of there being two open carriages at the door, in the first only a servant, her brother driving Miss Thorpe in the second, before John Thorpe came running up stairs, calling out, 'Well, Miss Morland, here I am. Have you been waiting long? We could not come before; the old devil of a coachmaker was such an eternity finding out a thing fit to be got into, and now it is ten thousand to one, but they break down before we are out of the street. How do you do, Mrs. Allen? a famous ball last night, was not it? Come, Miss Morland, be quick, for the others are in a confounded hurry to be off. They want to get their tumble over.'*

'What do you mean?' said Catherine, 'where are you all going to?'

'Going to? why, you have not forgot our engagement! Did not we agree together to take a drive this morning? What a head you have! We are going up Claverton Down.'*

'Something was said about it, I remember,' said Catherine, looking at Mrs. Allen for her opinion; 'but really I did not expect you.'

'Not expect me! that's a good one! And what a dust* you would have made, if I had not come.'

Catherine's silent appeal to her friend, meanwhile, was entirely thrown away, for Mrs. Allen, not being at all in the habit of conveying any expression herself by a look, was not aware of its being ever intended by any body else; and Catherine, whose desire of seeing Miss Tilney again could at that moment bear a short delay in favour of a drive, and who thought there could be no impropriety in her going with Mr. Thorpe, as Isabella was going at the same time with

James, was therefore obliged to speak plainer. 'Well, ma'am, what do you say to it? Can you spare me for an hour or two? shall I go?'

'Do just as you please, my dear,' replied Mrs. Allen, with the most placid indifference. Catherine took the advice, and ran off to get ready. In a very few minutes she re-appeared, having scarcely allowed the two others time enough to get through a few short sentences in her praise, after Thorpe had procured Mrs. Allen's admiration of his gig; and then receiving her friend's parting good wishes, they both hurried down stairs. 'My dearest creature,' cried Isabella, to whom the duty of friendship immediately called her before she could get into the carriage, 'you have been at least three hours getting ready. I was afraid you were ill. What a delightful ball we had last night. I have a thousand things to say to you; but make haste and get in, for I long to be off.'

Catherine followed her orders and turned away, but not too soon to hear her friend exclaim aloud to James, 'What a sweet girl she is! I quite doat on her.'

'You will not be frightened, Miss Morland,' said Thorpe, as he handed her in, 'if my horse should dance about a little at first setting off. He will, most likely, give a plunge or two, and perhaps take the rest for a minute;* but he will soon know his master. He is full of spirits, playful as can be, but there is no vice in him.'

Catherine did not think the portrait a very inviting one, but it was too late to retreat, and she was too young to own herself frightened; so, resigning herself to her fate, and trusting to the animal's boasted knowledge of its owner, she sat peaceably down, and saw Thorpe sit down by her. Every thing being then arranged, the servant who stood at the horse's head was bid in an important voice 'to let him go,' and off they went in the quietest manner imaginable, without a plunge or a caper, or any thing like one. Catherine, delighted at so happy an escape, spoke her pleasure aloud with grateful surprise; and her companion immediately made the matter perfectly simple by assuring her that it was entirely owing to the peculiarly judicious manner in which he had then held the reins, and the singular discernment and dexterity with which he had directed his whip. Catherine, though she could not help wondering that with such perfect command of his horse, he should think it necessary to alarm her with a relation of its tricks, congratulated herself sincerely on being under the care of so excellent a coachman; and perceiving that the animal continued to go on in

the same quiet manner, without shewing the smallest propensity
towards any unpleasant vivacity, and (considering its inevitable pace
was ten miles an hour) by no means alarmingly fast, gave herself up
to all the enjoyment of air and exercise of the most invigorating kind,
in a fine mild day of February, with the consciousness of safety.
A silence of several minutes succeeded their first short dialogue;—it
was broken by Thorpe's saying very abruptly, 'Old Allen is as rich as
a Jew—is not he?'* Catherine did not understand him—and he
repeated his question, adding in explanation, 'Old Allen, the man you
are with.'

'Oh! Mr. Allen, you mean. Yes, I believe, he is very rich.'

'And no children at all?'

'No—not any.'

'A famous thing for his next heirs. He is *your* godfather, is not he?'

'My godfather!—no.'

'But you are always very much with them.'

'Yes, very much.'

'Aye, that is what I meant. He seems a good kind of old fellow
enough, and has lived very well in his time, I dare say; he is not gouty
for nothing. Does he drink his bottle a-day now?'

'His bottle a-day!—no. Why should you think of such a thing? He
is a very temperate man, and you could not fancy him in liquor last
night?'

'Lord help you!—You women are always thinking of men's being
in liquor. Why you do not suppose a man is overset by a bottle? I am
sure of *this*—that if every body was to drink their bottle a-day, there
would not be half the disorders in the world there are now. It would
be a famous good thing for us all.'

'I cannot believe it.'

'Oh! lord, it would be the saving of thousands. There is not the
hundredth part of the wine consumed in this kingdom, that there
ought to be. Our foggy climate wants help.'

'And yet I have heard that there is a great deal of wine drank in
Oxford.'

'Oxford! There is no drinking at Oxford now, I assure you. Nobody
drinks there. You would hardly meet with a man who goes beyond his
four pints at the utmost. Now, for instance, it was reckoned a remarkable thing at the last party in my rooms, that upon an average we
cleared about five pints a head. It was looked upon as something out

of the common way. *Mine* is famous good stuff to be sure. You would not often meet with any thing like it in Oxford—and that may account for it. But this will just give you a notion of the general rate of drinking there.'

'Yes, it does give a notion,' said Catherine, warmly, 'and that is, that you all drink a great deal more wine than I thought you did. However, I am sure James does not drink so much.'

This declaration brought on a loud and overpowering reply, of which no part was very distinct, except the frequent exclamations, amounting almost to oaths, which adorned it, and Catherine was left, when it ended, with rather a strengthened belief of there being a great deal of wine drank in Oxford, and the same happy conviction of her brother's comparative sobriety.

Thorpe's ideas then all reverted to the merits of his own equipage, and she was called on to admire the spirit and freedom with which his horse moved along, and the ease which his paces, as well as the excellence of the springs, gave the motion of the carriage. She followed him in all his admiration as well as she could. To go before, or beyond him was impossible. His knowledge and her ignorance of the subject, his rapidity of expression, and her diffidence of herself put that out of her power; she could strike out nothing new in commendation, but she readily echoed whatever he chose to assert, and it was finally settled between them without any difficulty; that his equipage was altogether the most complete of its kind in England, his carriage the neatest, his horse the best goer, and himself the best coachman.—'You do not really think, Mr. Thorpe,' said Catherine, venturing after some time to consider the matter as entirely decided, and to offer some little variation on the subject, 'that James's gig will break down?'

'Break down! Oh! lord! Did you ever see such a little tittuppy* thing in your life! There is not a sound piece of iron about it. The wheels have been fairly worn out these ten years at least—and as for the body! Upon my soul, you might shake it to pieces yourself with a touch. It is the most devilish little ricketty business I ever beheld!—Thank God! we have got a better. I would not be bound to go two miles in it for fifty thousand pounds.'

'Good heavens!' cried Catherine, quite frightened, 'then pray let us turn back; they will certainly meet with an accident if we go on. Do let us turn back, Mr. Thorpe; stop and speak to my brother, and tell him how very unsafe it is.'

'Unsafe! Oh, lord! what is there in that? they will only get a roll if it does break down; and there is plenty of dirt, it will be excellent falling. Oh, curse it! the carriage is safe enough, if a man knows how to drive it; a thing of that sort in good hands will last above twenty years after it is fairly worn out. Lord bless you! I would undertake for five pounds to drive it to York and back again, without losing a nail.'

Catherine listened with astonishment; she knew not how to reconcile two such very different accounts of the same thing; for she had not been brought up to understand the propensities of a rattle, nor to know to how many idle assertions and impudent falsehoods the excess of vanity will lead. Her own family were plain matter-of-fact people, who seldom aimed at wit of any kind; her father, at the utmost, being contented with a pun, and her mother with a proverb; they were not in the habit therefore of telling lies to increase their importance, or of asserting at one moment what they would contradict the next. She reflected on the affair for some time in much perplexity, and was more than once on the point of requesting from Mr. Thorpe a clearer insight into his real opinion on the subject; but she checked herself, because it appeared to her that he did not excel in giving those clearer insights, in making those things plain which he had before made ambiguous; and, joining to this, the consideration, that he would not really suffer his sister and his friend to be exposed to a danger from which he might easily preserve them, she concluded at last, that he must know the carriage to be in fact perfectly safe, and therefore would alarm herself no longer. By him the whole matter seemed entirely forgotten; and all the rest of his conversation, or rather talk, began and ended with himself and his own concerns. He told her of horses which he had bought for a trifle and sold for incredible sums; of racing matches, in which his judgment had infallibly foretold the winner; of shooting parties, in which he had killed more birds (though without having one good shot) than all his companions together; and described to her some famous day's sport, with the foxhounds, in which his foresight and skill in directing the dogs had repaired the mistakes of the most experienced huntsman, and in which the boldness of his riding, though it had never endangered his own life for a moment, had been constantly leading others into difficulties, which he calmly concluded had broken the necks of many.

Little as Catherine was in the habit of judging for herself, and unfixed as were her general notions of what men ought to be, she could not entirely repress a doubt, while she bore with the effusions of his endless conceit, of his being altogether completely agreeable. It was a bold surmise, for he was Isabella's brother; and she had been assured by James, that his manners would recommend him to all her sex; but in spite of this, the extreme weariness of his company, which crept over her before they had been out an hour, and which continued unceasingly to increase till they stopped in Pulteney-street again, induced her, in some small degree, to resist such high authority, and to distrust his powers of giving universal pleasure.

When they arrived at Mrs. Allen's door, the astonishment of Isabella was hardly to be expressed, on finding that it was too late in the day for them to attend her friend into the house:—'Past three o'clock!' it was inconceivable, incredible, impossible! and she would neither believe her own watch, nor her brother's, nor the servant's; she would believe no assurance of it founded on reason or reality, till Morland produced his watch, and ascertained the fact; to have doubted a moment longer *then*, would have been equally inconceivable, incredible, and impossible; and she could only protest, over and over again, that no two hours and a half had ever gone off so swiftly before, as Catherine was called on to confirm; Catherine could not tell a falsehood even to please Isabella; but the latter was spared the misery of her friend's dissenting voice, by not waiting for her answer. Her own feelings entirely engrossed her; her wretchedness was most acute on finding herself obliged to go directly home.—It was ages since she had had a moment's conversation with her dearest Catherine; and, though she had such thousands of things to say to her, it appeared as if they were never to be together again; so, with smiles of most exquisite misery, and the laughing eye of utter despondency, she bade her friend adieu and went on.

Catherine found Mrs. Allen just returned from all the busy idleness of the morning, and was immediately greeted with, 'Well, my dear, here you are;' a truth which she had no greater inclination than power to dispute; 'and I hope you have had a pleasant airing?'

'Yes, ma'am, I thank you; we could not have had a nicer day.'

'So Mrs. Thorpe said; she was vastly pleased at your all going.'

'You have seen Mrs. Thorpe then?'

'Yes, I went to the Pump-room as soon as you were gone, and there I met her, and we had a great deal of talk together. She says there was hardly any veal to be got at market this morning, it is so uncommonly scarce.'

'Did you see any body else of our acquaintance?'

'Yes; we agreed to take a turn in the Crescent, and there we met Mrs. Hughes, and Mr. and Miss Tilney walking with her.'

'Did you indeed? and did they speak to you?'

'Yes, we walked along the Crescent together for half an hour. They seem very agreeable people. Miss Tilney was in a very pretty spotted muslin, and I fancy, by what I can learn, that she always dresses very handsomely. Mrs. Hughes talked to me a great deal about the family.'

'And what did she tell you of them?'

'Oh! a vast deal indeed; she hardly talked of any thing else.'

'Did she tell you what part of Gloucestershire they come from?'

'Yes, she did; but I cannot recollect now. But they are very good kind of people, and very rich. Mrs. Tilney was a Miss Drummond, and she and Mrs. Hughes were school-fellows; and Miss Drummond had a very large fortune;* and, when she married, her father gave her twenty thousand pounds, and five hundred to buy wedding-clothes. Mrs. Hughes saw all the clothes after they came from the warehouse.'*

'And are Mr. and Mrs. Tilney in Bath?'

'Yes, I fancy they are, but I am not quite certain. Upon recollection, however, I have a notion they are both dead; at least the mother is; yes, I am sure Mrs. Tilney is dead, because Mrs. Hughes told me there was a very beautiful set of pearls that Mr. Drummond gave his daughter on her wedding-day and that Miss Tilney has got now, for they were put by for her when her mother died.'

'And is Mr. Tilney, my partner, the only son?'

'I cannot be quite positive about that, my dear; I have some idea he is; but however, he is a very fine young man Mrs. Hughes says, and likely to do very well.'

Catherine inquired no further; she had heard enough to feel that Mrs. Allen had no real intelligence to give, and that she was most particularly unfortunate herself in having missed such a meeting with both brother and sister. Could she have foreseen such a circumstance, nothing should have persuaded her to go out with the others; and, as it was, she could only lament her ill-luck, and think over what she had lost, till it was clear to her, that the drive had by no means been very pleasant and that John Thorpe himself was quite disagreeable.

CHAPTER X

THE Allens, Thorpes, and Morlands, all met in the evening at the
theatre; and, as Catherine and Isabella sat together, there was then an
opportunity for the latter to utter some few of the many thousand
things which had been collecting within her for communication, in
the immeasurable length of time which had divided them.—'Oh,
heavens! my beloved Catherine, have I got you at last?' was her
address on Catherine's entering the box and sitting by her. 'Now,
Mr. Morland,' for he was close to her on the other side, 'I shall not
speak another word to you all the rest of the evening; so I charge you
not to expect it. My sweetest Catherine, how have you been this long
age? but I need not ask you, for you look delightfully. You really have
done your hair in a more heavenly style than ever: you mischievous
creature, do you want to attract every body? I assure you, my brother
is quite in love with you already; and as for Mr. Tilney—but *that* is
a settled thing—even *your* modesty cannot doubt his attachment
now; his coming back to Bath makes it too plain. Oh! what would not
I give to see him! I really am quite wild with impatience. My mother
says he is the most delightful young man in the world; she saw him
this morning you know: you must introduce him to me. Is he in the
house now?—Look about for heaven's sake! I assure you, I can hardly
exist till I see him.'

'No,' said Catherine, 'he is not here; I cannot see him any where.'

'Oh, horrid! am I never to be acquainted with him? How do you
like my gown? I think it does not look amiss; the sleeves were entirely
my own thought. Do you know I get so immoderately sick of Bath;
your brother and I were agreeing this morning that, though it is vastly
well to be here for a few weeks, we would not live here for millions.
We soon found out that our tastes were exactly alike in preferring the
country to every other place; really, our opinions were so exactly the
same, it was quite ridiculous! There was not a single point in which
we differed; I would not have had you by for the world; you are such
a sly thing, I am sure you would have made some droll remark or
other about it.'

'No, indeed I should not.'

'Oh, yes you would indeed; I know you better than you know yourself. You would have told us that we seemed born for each other, or
some nonsense of that kind, which would have distressed me beyond

conception; my cheeks would have been as red as your roses; I would
not have had you by for the world.'

'Indeed you do me injustice; I would not have made so improper
a remark upon any account; and besides, I am sure it would never
have entered my head.'

Isabella smiled incredulously, and talked the rest of the evening
to James.

Catherine's resolution of endeavouring to meet Miss Tilney again
continued in full force the next morning; and till the usual moment
of going to the Pump-room, she felt some alarm from the dread of
a second prevention. But nothing of that kind occurred, no visitors
appeared to delay them, and they all three set off in good time for the
Pump-room, where the ordinary course of events and conversation
took place; Mr. Allen, after drinking his glass of water, joined some
gentlemen to talk over the politics of the day and compare the
accounts of their newspapers; and the ladies walked about together,
noticing every new face, and almost every new bonnet in the room.
The female part of the Thorpe family, attended by James Morland,
appeared among the crowd in less than a quarter of an hour, and
Catherine immediately took her usual place by the side of her friend.
James, who was now in constant attendance, maintained a similar
position, and separating themselves from the rest of their party, they
walked in that manner for some time, till Catherine began to doubt
the happiness of a situation which confining her entirely to her friend
and brother, gave her very little share in the notice of either. They
were always engaged in some sentimental discussion or lively dispute,
but their sentiment was conveyed in such whispering voices, and their
vivacity attended with so much laughter, that though Catherine's
supporting opinion was not unfrequently called for by one or the
other, she was never able to give any, from not having heard a word
of the subject. At length however she was empowered to disengage
herself from her friend, by the avowed necessity of speaking to
Miss Tilney, whom she most joyfully saw just entering the room
with Mrs. Hughes, and whom she instantly joined, with a firmer
determination to be acquainted, than she might have had courage to
command, had she not been urged by the disappointment of the day
before. Miss Tilney met her with great civility, returned her advances
with equal good will, and they continued talking together as long as
both parties remained in the room; and though in all probability not

an observation was made, nor an expression used by either which had not been made and used some thousands of times before, under that roof, in every Bath season, yet the merit of their being spoken with simplicity and truth, and without personal conceit, might be something uncommon.—

'How well your brother dances!' was an artless exclamation of Catherine's towards the close of their conversation, which at once surprized and amused her companion.

'Henry!' she replied with a smile. 'Yes, he does dance very well.'

'He must have thought it very odd to hear me say I was engaged the other evening, when he saw me sitting down. But I really had been engaged the whole day to Mr. Thorpe.' Miss Tilney could only bow. 'You cannot think,' added Catherine after a moment's silence, 'how surprized I was to see him again. I felt so sure of his being quite gone away.'

'When Henry had the pleasure of seeing you before, he was in Bath but for a couple of days. He came only to engage lodgings for us.'

'*That* never occurred to me; and of course, not seeing him any where, I thought he must be gone. Was not the young lady he danced with on Monday a Miss Smith?'

'Yes, an acquaintance of Mrs. Hughes.'

'I dare say she was very glad to dance. Do you think her pretty?'

'Not very.'

'He never comes to the Pump-room, I suppose?'

'Yes, sometimes; but he has rid out this morning with my father.'

Mrs. Hughes now joined them, and asked Miss Tilney if she was ready to go. 'I hope I shall have the pleasure of seeing you again soon,' said Catherine. 'Shall you be at the cotillion ball* to-morrow?'

'Perhaps we——yes, I think we certainly shall.'

'I am glad of it, for we shall all be there.'—This civility was duly returned; and they parted—on Miss Tilney's side with some knowledge of her new acquaintance's feelings, and on Catherine's, without the smallest consciousness of having explained them.

She went home very happy. The morning had answered all her hopes, and the evening of the following day was now the object of expectation, the future good. What gown and what head-dress she should wear on the occasion became her chief concern. She cannot be justified in it. Dress is at all times a frivolous distinction, and excessive solicitude about it often destroys its own aim. Catherine knew all this very well; her great aunt had read her a lecture on the subject* only the Christmas before; and yet she lay awake ten minutes on Wednesday night debating between her spotted and her tamboured muslin, and nothing but the shortness of the time prevented her buying a new one for the evening. This would have been an error in judgment, great though not uncommon, from which one of the other sex rather than her own, a brother rather than a great aunt might have warned her, for man only can be aware of the insensibility of man towards a new gown. It would be mortifying to the feelings of many ladies, could they be made to understand how little the heart of man is affected by what is costly or new in their attire; how little it is biassed by the texture of their muslin, and how unsusceptible of peculiar tenderness towards the spotted, the sprigged, the mull or the jackonet.* Woman is fine for her own satisfaction alone. No man will admire her the more, no woman will like her the better for it. Neatness and fashion are enough for the former, and a something of shabbiness or impropriety will be most endearing to the latter.—But not one of these grave reflections troubled the tranquillity of Catherine.

She entered the rooms on Thursday evening with feelings very different from what had attended her thither the Monday before. She had then been exulting in her engagement to Thorpe, and was now chiefly anxious to avoid his sight, lest he should engage her again; for though she could not, dared not expect that Mr. Tilney should ask her a third time to dance, her wishes, hopes and plans all centered in nothing less. Every young lady may feel for my heroine in this critical moment, for every young lady has at some time or other known the same agitation. All have been, or at least all have believed themselves to be, in danger from the pursuit of some one whom they wished to avoid; and all have been anxious for the attentions of some one whom they wished to please. As soon as they were joined by the Thorpes, Catherine's agony began; she fidgetted about if John Thorpe came towards her, hid herself as much as possible from his view, and when he spoke to her pretended not to hear him. The cotillions were over, the country-dancing beginning,* and she saw nothing of the Tilneys. 'Do not be frightened, my dear Catherine,' whispered Isabella, 'but I am really going to dance with your brother again. I declare positively it is quite shocking. I tell him he ought to be ashamed of himself, but you and John must keep us in countenance. Make haste, my dear creature, and come to us. John is just walked off, but he will be back in a moment.'

Catherine had neither time nor inclination to answer. The others walked away, John Thorpe was still in view, and she gave herself up for lost. That she might not appear, however, to observe or expect him, she kept her eyes intently fixed on her fan; and a self-condemnation for her folly, in supposing that among such a crowd they should even meet with the Tilneys in any reasonable time, had just passed through her mind, when she suddenly found herself addressed and again solicited to dance, by Mr. Tilney himself. With what sparkling eyes and ready motion she granted his request, and with how pleasing a flutter of heart she went with him to the set, may be easily imagined. To escape, and, as she believed, so narrowly escape John Thorpe, and to be asked, so immediately on his joining her, asked by Mr. Tilney, as if he had sought her on purpose!—it did not appear to her that life could supply any greater felicity.

Scarcely had they worked themselves into the quiet possession of a place, however, when her attention was claimed by John Thorpe, who stood behind her. 'Hey-day; Miss Morland!' said he, 'what is the meaning of this?—I thought you and I were to dance together.'

'I wonder you should think so, for you never asked me.' 'That is a good one, by Jove!—I asked you as soon as I came into the room, and I was just going to ask you again, but when I turned round, you were gone!—this is a cursed shabby trick! I only came for the sake of dancing with *you*, and I firmly believe you were engaged to me ever since Monday. Yes; I remember, I asked you while you were waiting in the lobby for your cloak. And here have I been telling all my acquaintance that I was going to dance with the prettiest girl in the room; and when they see you standing up with somebody else, they will quiz me famously.'

'Oh, no; they will never think of *me*, after such a description as that.'

'By heavens, if they do not, I will kick them out of the room for blockheads. What chap have you there?' Catherine satisfied his curiosity. 'Tilney,' he repeated, 'Hum—I do not know him. A good figure of a man; well put together.—Does he want a horse?—Here is a friend of mine, Sam Fletcher, has got one to sell that would suit any body. A famous clever animal for the road—only forty guineas. I had fifty minds to buy it myself, for it is one of my maxims always to buy

a good horse when I meet with one; but it would not answer my purpose, it would not do for the field. I would give any money for a real
good hunter. I have three now, the best that ever were back'd. I would
not take eight hundred guineas for them. Fletcher and I mean to get
a house in Leicestershire, against the next season.* It is so d——
uncomfortable, living at an inn.'

This was the last sentence by which he could weary Catherine's
attention, for he was just then born off by the resistless pressure of
a long string of passing ladies. Her partner now drew near, and said,
'That gentleman would have put me out of patience, had he staid with
you half a minute longer. He has no business to withdraw the attention of my partner from me. We have entered into a contract of
mutual agreeableness for the space of an evening, and all our agreeableness belongs solely to each other for that time. Nobody can fasten
themselves on the notice of one, without injuring the rights of the
other. I consider a country-dance as an emblem of marriage. Fidelity
and complaisance are the principal duties of both; and those men who
do not chuse to dance or marry themselves, have no business with the
partners or wives of their neighbours.'

'But they are such very different things!—'

'—That you think they cannot be compared together.'

'To be sure not. People that marry can never part, but must go and
keep house together. People that dance, only stand opposite each
other in a long room for half an hour '

'And such is your definition of matrimony and dancing. Taken in
that light certainly, their resemblance is not striking; but I think
I could place them in such a view.—You will allow, that in both, man
has the advantage of choice, woman only the power of refusal;* that in
both, it is an engagement between man and woman, formed for the
advantage of each; and that when once entered into, they belong
exclusively to each other till the moment of its dissolution; that it is
their duty, each to endeavour to give the other no cause for wishing
that he or she had bestowed themselves elsewhere, and their best
interest to keep their own imaginations from wandering towards the
perfections of their neighbours, or fancying that they should have
been better off with any one else. You will allow all this?'

'Yes, to be sure, as you state it, all this sounds very well; but still
they are so very different.—I cannot look upon them at all in the
same light, nor think the same duties belong to them.'

'In one respect, there certainly is a difference. In marriage, the man is supposed to provide for the support of the woman; the woman to make the home agreeable to the man; he is to purvey, and she is to smile. But in dancing, their duties are exactly changed; the agreeableness, the compliance are expected from him, while she furnishes the fan and the lavender water.* *That*, I suppose, was the difference of duties which struck you, as rendering the conditions incapable of comparison.'

'No, indeed, I never thought of that.'

'Then I am quite at a loss. One thing, however, I must observe. This disposition on your side is rather alarming. You totally disallow any similarity in the obligations; and may I not thence infer, that your notions of the duties of the dancing state are not so strict as your partner might wish? Have I not reason to fear, that if the gentleman who spoke to you just now were to return, or if any other gentleman were to address you, there would be nothing to restrain you from conversing with him as long as you chose?'

'Mr. Thorpe is such a very particular friend of my brother's, that if he talks to me, I must talk to him again; but there are hardly three young men in the room besides him, that I have any acquaintance with.'

'And is that to be my only security? alas, alas!'

'Nay, I am sure you cannot have a better; for if I do not know any body, it is impossible for me to talk to them; and, besides, I do not *want* to talk to any body.'

'Now you have given me a security worth having; and I shall proceed with courage. Do you find Bath as agreeable as when I had the honour of making the inquiry before?'

'Yes, quite—more so, indeed.'

'More so!—Take care, or you will forget to be tired of it at the proper time.—You ought to be tired at the end of six weeks.'

'I do not think I should be tired, if I were to stay here six months.'

'Bath, compared with London, has little variety, and so every body finds out every year. "For six weeks, I allow Bath is pleasant enough; but beyond *that*, it is the most tiresome place in the world." You would be told so by people of all descriptions, who come regularly every winter, lengthen their six weeks into ten or twelve, and go away at last because they can afford to stay no longer.'

'Well, other people must judge for themselves, and those who go to London may think nothing of Bath. But I, who live in a small retired village in the country, can never find greater sameness in such a place as this, than in my own home; for here are a variety of amusements, a variety of things to be seen and done all day long, which I can know nothing of there.'

'You are not fond of the country.'

'Yes, I am. I have always lived there, and always been very happy. But certainly there is much more sameness in a country life than in a Bath life. One day in the country is exactly like another.'

'But then you spend your time so much more rationally in the country;'

'Do I?'

'Do you not?'

'I do not believe there is much difference.'

'Here you are in pursuit only of amusement all day long.'

'And so I am at home—only I do not find so much of it. I walk about here, and so I do there;—but here I see a variety of people in every street, and there I can only go and call on Mrs. Allen.'

Mr. Tilney was very much amused. 'Only go and call on Mrs. Allen!' he repeated. 'What a picture of intellectual poverty! However, when you sink into this abyss again, you will have more to say. You will be able to talk of Bath, and of all that you did here.'

'Oh! yes. I shall never be in want of something to talk of again to Mrs. Allen, or any body else. I really believe I shall always be talking of Bath, when I am at home again—I *do* like it so very much. If I could but have papa and mamma, and the rest of them here, I suppose I should be too happy! James's coming (my eldest brother) is quite delightful—and especially as it turns out, that the very family we are just got so intimate with, are his intimate friends already. Oh! who can ever be tired of Bath?'

'Not those who bring such fresh feelings of every sort to it, as you do. But papas and mammas, and brothers and intimate friends are a good deal gone by, to most of the frequenters of Bath—and the honest relish of balls and plays, and every-day sights, is past with them.'

Here their conversation closed; the demands of the dance becoming now too importunate for a divided attention.

Soon after their reaching the bottom of the set, Catherine perceived herself to be earnestly regarded by a gentleman who stood among the lookers-on, immediately behind her partner. He was a very handsome man, of a commanding aspect, past the bloom, but not past the vigour of life; and with his eye still directed towards her, she saw him presently address Mr. Tilney in a familiar whisper. Confused by his notice, and blushing from the fear of its being excited by something wrong in her appearance, she turned away her head. But while she did so, the gentleman retreated, and her partner coming nearer, said, 'I see that you guess what I have just been asked. That gentleman knows your name, and you have a right to know his. It is General Tilney, my father.'

Catherine's answer was only 'Oh!'—but it was an 'Oh!' expressing every thing needful; attention to his words, and perfect reliance on their truth. With real interest and strong admiration did her eye now follow the General, as he moved through the crowd, and 'How handsome a family they are!' was her secret remark.

In chatting with Miss Tilney before the evening concluded, a new source of felicity arose to her. She had never taken a country walk since her arrival in Bath. Miss Tilney, to whom all the commonly-frequented environs were familiar, spoke of them in terms which made her all eagerness to know them too; and on her openly fearing that she might find nobody to go with her, it was proposed by the brother and sister that they should join in a walk, some morning or other. 'I shall like it,' she cried, 'beyond any thing in the world; and do not let us put it off—let us go to-morrow.' This was readily agreed to, with only a proviso of Miss Tilney's, that it did not rain, which Catherine was sure it would not. At twelve o'clock, they were to call for her in Pulteney-street—and 'remember—twelve o'clock,' was her parting speech to her new friend. Of her other, her older, her more established friend, Isabella, of whose fidelity and worth she had enjoyed a fortnight's experience, she scarcely saw any thing during the evening. Yet, though longing to make her acquainted with her happiness, she cheerfully submitted to the wish of Mr. Allen, which took them rather early away, and her spirits danced within her, as she danced in her chair all the way home.

CHAPTER XI

THE morrow brought a very sober looking morning; the sun making only a few efforts to appear; and Catherine augured from it, every thing most favourable to her wishes. A bright morning so early in the

year, she allowed would generally turn to rain, but a cloudy one foretold improvement as the day advanced. She applied to Mr. Allen for
confirmation of her hopes, but Mr. Allen not having his own skies and
barometer about him, declined giving any absolute promise of sunshine. She applied to Mrs. Allen, and Mrs. Allen's opinion was more
positive. 'She had no doubt in the world of its being a very fine day, if
the clouds would only go off, and the sun keep out.'

At about eleven o'clock however, a few specks of small rain upon
the windows caught Catherine's watchful eye, and 'Oh! dear, I do
believe it will be wet,' broke from her in a most desponding tone.

'I thought how it would be,' said Mrs. Allen.

'No walk for me to-day,' sighed Catherine;—'but perhaps it may
come to nothing, or it may hold up before twelve.'

'Perhaps it may, but then, my dear, it will be so dirty.'

'Oh! that will not signify; I never mind dirt.'

'No,' replied her friend very placidly, 'I know you never mind dirt.'

After a short pause, 'It comes on faster and faster!' said Catherine,
as she stood watching at a window.

'So it does indeed. If it keeps raining, the streets will be very wet.'

'There are four umbrellas up already. How I hate the sight of an
umbrella!'

'They are disagreeable things to carry. I would much rather take
a chair at any time.'

'It was such a nice looking morning! I felt so convinced it would be
dry!'

'Any body would have thought so indeed. There will be very few
people in the Pump-room, if it rains all the morning. I hope Mr. Allen
will put on his great coat when he goes, but I dare say he will not, for
he had rather do any thing in the world than walk out in a great coat;
I wonder he should dislike it, it must be so comfortable.'

The rain continued—fast, though not heavy. Catherine went every
five minutes to the clock, threatening on each return that, if it still
kept on raining another five minutes, she would give up the matter as
hopeless. The clock struck twelve, and it still rained.—'You will not
be able to go, my dear.'

'I do not quite despair yet. I shall not give it up till a quarter after
twelve. This is just the time of day for it to clear up, and I do think it
looks a little lighter. There, it is twenty minutes after twelve, and now
I *shall* give it up entirely. Oh! that we had such weather here as they

had at Udolpho, or at least in Tuscany and the South of France!—the night that poor St. Aubin died!—such beautiful weather!'*

At half past twelve, when Catherine's anxious attention to the weather was over, and she could no longer claim any merit from its amendment, the sky began voluntarily to clear. A gleam of sunshine took her quite by surprize; she looked round; the clouds were parting, and she instantly returned to the window to watch over and encourage the happy appearance. Ten minutes more made it certain that a bright afternoon would succeed, and justified the opinion of Mrs. Allen, who had 'always thought it would clear up.' But whether Catherine might still expect her friends, whether there had not been too much rain for Miss Tilney to venture, must yet be a question.

It was too dirty for Mrs. Allen to accompany her husband to the Pump-room; he accordingly set off by himself, and Catherine had barely watched him down the street, when her notice was claimed by the approach of the same two open carriages, containing the same three people that had surprized her so much a few mornings back.

'Isabella, my brother, and Mr. Thorpe, I declare! They are coming for me perhaps—but I shall not go—I cannot go indeed, for you know Miss Tilney may still call.' Mrs. Allen agreed to it. John Thorpe was soon with them, and his voice was with them yet sooner, for on the stairs he was calling out to Miss Morland to be quick. 'Make haste! make haste!' as he threw open the door—'put on your hat this moment—there is no time to be lost—we are going to Bristol.—How d'ye do, Mrs. Allen?'

'To Bristol! Is not that a great way off?*—But, however, I cannot go with you to-day, because I am engaged; I expect some friends every moment.' This was of course vehemently talked down as no reason at all; Mrs. Allen was called on to second him, and the two others walked in, to give their assistance. 'My sweetest Catherine, is not this delightful? We shall have a most heavenly drive. You are to thank your brother and me for the scheme; it darted into our heads at breakfast-time, I verily believe at the same instant; and we should have been off two hours ago if it had not been for this detestable rain. But it does not signify, the nights are moonlight, and we shall do delightfully. Oh! I am in such extasies at the thoughts of a little country air and quiet!—so much better than going to the Lower Rooms. We shall drive directly to Clifton and dine there; and, as soon as dinner is over, if there is time for it, go on to Kingsweston.'*

'I doubt our being able to do so much,' said Morland.

'You croaking fellow!' cried Thorpe, 'we shall be able to do ten times more. Kingsweston! aye, and Blaize Castle too, and any thing else we can hear of; but here is your sister says she will not go.'

'Blaize Castle!' cried Catherine; 'what is that?'*

'The finest place in England—worth going fifty miles at any time to see.'

'What, is it really a castle, an old castle?'

'The oldest in the kingdom.'

'But is it like what one reads of?'

'Exactly—the very same.'

'But now really—are there towers and long galleries?'

'By dozens.'

'Then I should like to see it; but I cannot——I cannot go.'

'Not go!—my beloved creature, what do you mean?'

'I cannot go, because'——(looking down as she spoke, fearful of Isabella's smile) 'I expect Miss Tilney and her brother to call on me to take a country walk. They promised to come at twelve, only it rained; but now, as it is so fine, I dare say they will be here soon.'

'Not they indeed,' cried Thorpe; 'for, as we turned into Broad-street, I saw them—does he not drive a phaeton with bright chesnuts?'*

'I do not know indeed.'

'Yes, I know he does; I saw him. You are talking of the man you danced with last night, are not you?'

'Yes.'

'Well, I saw him at that moment turn up the Lansdown Road,—driving a smart-looking girl.'

'Did you indeed?'

'Did upon my soul; knew him again directly, and he seemed to have got some very pretty cattle* too.'

'It is very odd! but I suppose they thought it would be too dirty for a walk.'

'And well they might, for I never saw so much dirt in my life. Walk! you could no more walk than you could fly! it has not been so dirty the whole winter; it is ancle-deep every where.'

Isabella corroborated it:—'My dearest Catherine, you cannot form an idea of the dirt; come, you must go; you cannot refuse going now.'

'I should like to see the castle; but may we go all over it? may we go up every staircase, and into every suite of rooms?'

'Yes, yes, every hole and corner.'

'But then,—if they should only be gone out for an hour till it is drier, and call by and bye?'

'Make yourself easy, there is no danger of that, for I heard Tilney hallooing to a man who was just passing by on horse-back, that they were going as far as Wick Rocks.'*

'Then I will. Shall I go, Mrs. Allen?'

'Just as you please, my dear.'

'Mrs. Allen, you must persuade her to go,' was the general cry. Mrs. Allen was not inattentive to it:—'Well, my dear,' said she, 'suppose you go.'—And in two minutes they were off.

Catherine's feelings, as she got into the carriage, were in a very unsettled state; divided between regret for the loss of one great pleasure, and the hope of soon enjoying another, almost its equal in degree, however unlike in kind. She could not think the Tilneys had acted quite well by her, in so readily giving up their engagement, without sending her any message of excuse. It was now but an hour later than the time fixed on for the beginning of their walk; and, in spite of what she had heard of the prodigious accumulation of dirt in the course of that hour, she could not from her own observation help thinking, that they might have gone with very little inconvenience. To feel herself slighted by them was very painful. On the other hand, the delight of exploring an edifice like Udolpho, as her fancy represented Blaize Castle to be, was such a counterpoise of good, as might console her for almost any thing.

They passed briskly down Pulteney-street, and through Laura-place, without the exchange of many words. Thorpe talked to his horse, and she meditated, by turns, on broken promises and broken arches, phaetons and false hangings, Tilneys and trap-doors.* As they entered Argyle-buildings,* however, she was roused by this address from her companion, 'Who is that girl who looked at you so hard as she went by?'

'Who?—where?'

'On the right-hand pavement—she must be almost out of sight now.' Catherine looked round and saw Miss Tilney leaning on her brother's arm, walking slowly down the street. She saw them both looking back at her. 'Stop, stop, Mr. Thorpe,' she impatiently cried, 'it is Miss Tilney; it is indeed.—How could you tell me they were gone?—Stop, stop, I will get out this moment and go to them.' But to what purpose did she speak?—Thorpe only lashed his horse into a brisker trot; the Tilneys, who had soon ceased to look after her, were in a moment out of sight round the corner of Laura-place, and in another moment she was herself whisked into the Market-place.* Still, however, and during the length of another street, she intreated him to stop. 'Pray, pray stop, Mr. Thorpe.—I cannot go on.—I will not go on.—I must go back to Miss Tilney.' But Mr. Thorpe only laughed, smacked his whip, encouraged his horse, made odd noises, and drove on; and Catherine, angry and vexed as she was, having no power of getting away, was obliged to give up the point and submit. Her reproaches, however, were not spared. 'How could you deceive me so, Mr. Thorpe?—How could you say, that you saw them driving up the Lansdown-road?—I would not have had it happen so for the world.—They must think it so strange; so rude of me! to go by them, too, without saying a word! You do not know how vexed I am.—I shall have no pleasure at Clifton, nor in any thing else. I had rather, ten thousand times rather get out now, and walk back to them. How could you say, you saw them driving out in a phaeton?' Thorpe defended himself very stoutly, declared he had never seen two men so much alike in his life, and would hardly give up the point of its having been Tilney himself.

Their drive, even when this subject was over, was not likely to be very agreeable. Catherine's complaisance was no longer what it had been in their former airing. She listened reluctantly, and her replies were short. Blaize Castle remained her only comfort; towards *that*, she still looked at intervals with pleasure; though rather than be disappointed of the promised walk, and especially rather than be thought ill of by the Tilneys, she would willingly have given up all the happiness which its walls could supply—the happiness of a progress through a long suite of lofty rooms, exhibiting the remains of magnificent furniture, though now for many years deserted—the happiness of being stopped in their way along narrow, winding vaults, by a low, grated door; or even of having their lamp, their only lamp, extinguished by a sudden gust of wind, and of being left in total darkness.* In the meanwhile, they proceeded on their journey without any mischance; and were within view of the town of Keynsham,* when a halloo from Morland, who was behind them, made his friend pull up, to know what was the matter. The others then came close enough for conversation, and Morland said, 'We had better go back, Thorpe;

it is too late to go on today; your sister thinks so as well as I. We have been exactly an hour coming from Pulteney-street, very little more than seven miles; and, I suppose, we have at least eight more to go. It will never do. We set out a great deal too late. We had much better put it off till another day, and turn round.'

'It is all one to me,' replied Thorpe rather angrily; and instantly turning his horse, they were on their way back to Bath.

'If your brother had not got such a d—— beast to drive,' said he soon afterwards, 'we might have done it very well. My horse would have trotted to Clifton within the hour, if left to himself, and I have almost broke my arm with pulling him in to that cursed broken-winded jade's pace. Morland is a fool for not keeping a horse and gig of his own.'

'No, he is not,' said Catherine warmly, 'for I am sure he could not afford it.'

'And why cannot he afford it?'

'Because he has not money enough.'

'And whose fault is that?'

'Nobody's, that I know of.' Thorpe then said something in the loud, incoherent way to which he had often recourse, about its being a d—— thing to be miserly; and that if people who rolled in money could not afford things, he did not know who could; which Catherine did not even endeavour to understand. Disappointed of what was to have been the consolation for her first disappointment, she was less and less disposed either to be agreeable herself, or to find her companion so; and they returned to Pulteney-street without her speaking twenty words.

As she entered the house, the footman told her, that a gentleman and lady had called and inquired for her a few minutes after her setting off; that, when he told them she was gone out with Mr. Thorpe, the lady had asked whether any message had been left for her; and on his saying no, had felt for a card, but said she had none about her, and went away. Pondering over these heart-rending tidings, Catherine walked slowly up stairs. At the head of them she was met by Mr. Allen, who, on hearing the reason of their speedy return, said, 'I am glad your brother had so much sense; I am glad you are come back. It was a strange, wild scheme.'

They all spent the evening together at Thorpe's. Catherine was disturbed and out of spirits; but Isabella seemed to find a pool of commerce,* in the fate of which she shared, by private partnership with Morland, a very good equivalent for the quiet and country air of an inn at Clifton. Her satisfaction, too, in not being at the Lower Rooms, was spoken more than once. 'How I pity the poor creatures that are going there! How glad I am that I am not amongst them! I wonder whether it will be a full ball or not! They have not begun dancing yet. I would not be there for all the world. It is so delightful to have an evening now and then to oneself. I dare say it will not be a very good ball. I know the Mitchells will not be there. I am sure I pity every body that is. But I dare say, Mr. Morland, you long to be at it, do not you? I am sure you do. Well, pray do not let any body here be a restraint on you. I dare say we could do very well without you; but you men think yourselves of such consequence.'

Catherine could almost have accused Isabella of being wanting in tenderness towards herself and her sorrows; so very little did they appear to dwell on her mind, and so very inadequate was the comfort she offered. 'Do not be so dull, my dearest creature,' she whispered. 'You will quite break my heart. It was amazingly shocking to be sure; but the Tilneys were entirely to blame. Why were not they more punctual? It was dirty, indeed, but what did that signify? I am sure John and I should not have minded it. I never mind going through any thing, where a friend is concerned; that is my disposition, and John is just the same; he has amazing strong feelings. Good heavens! what a delightful hand you have got! Kings, I vow! I never was so happy in my life! I would fifty times rather you should have them than myself.'

And now I may dismiss my heroine to the sleepless couch, which is the true heroine's portion; to a pillow strewed with thorns and wet with tears.* And lucky may she think herself, if she get another good night's rest in the course of the next three months.

CHAPTER XII

'Mrs. Allen,' said Catherine the next morning, 'will there be any harm in my calling on Miss Tilney to-day? I shall not be easy till I have explained every thing.'

'Go by all means, my dear; only put on a white gown; Miss Tilney always wears white.'

Catherine cheerfully complied; and being properly equipped, was more impatient than ever to be at the Pump-room, that she might inform herself of General Tilney's lodgings, for though she believed they were in Milsom-street, she was not certain of the house, and Mrs. Allen's wavering convictions only made it more doubtful. To Milsom-street she was directed; and having made herself perfect in the number, hastened away with eager steps and a beating heart to pay her visit, explain her conduct, and be forgiven; tripping lightly through the church-yard, and resolutely turning away her eyes, that she might not be obliged to see her beloved Isabella and her dear family, who, she had reason to believe, were in a shop hard by. She reached the house without any impediment, looked at the number, knocked at the door, and inquired for Miss Tilney. The man believed Miss Tilney to be at home, but was not quite certain. Would she be pleased to send up her name? She gave her card. In a few minutes the servant returned, and with a look which did not quite confirm his words, said he had been mistaken, for that Miss Tilney was walked out. Catherine, with a blush of mortification, left the house. She felt almost persuaded that Miss Tilney *was* at home, and too much offended to admit her; and as she retired down the street, could not withhold one glance at the drawing-room windows, in expectation of seeing her there, but no one appeared at them. At the bottom of the street, however, she looked back again, and then, not at a window, but issuing from the door, she saw Miss Tilney herself. She was followed by a gentleman, whom Catherine believed to be her father, and they turned up towards Edgar's-buildings. Catherine, in deep mortification, proceeded on her way. She could almost be angry herself at such angry incivility; but she checked the resentful sensation; she remembered her own ignorance. She knew not how such an offence as her's might be classed by the laws of worldly politeness, to what a degree of unforgivingness it might with propriety lead, nor to what rigours of rudeness in return it might justly make her amenable.

Dejected and humbled, she had even some thoughts of not going with the others to the theatre that night; but it must be confessed that they were not of long continuance: for she soon recollected, in the first place, that she was without any excuse for staying at home; and, in the second, that it was a play she wanted very much to see. To the theatre accordingly they all went; no Tilneys appeared to plague or please her; she feared that, amongst the many perfections of the family, a fondness for plays was not to be ranked; but perhaps it was because they were habituated to the finer performances of the London stage, which she knew, on Isabella's authority, rendered every thing else of the kind 'quite horrid.' She was not deceived in her own expectation of pleasure; the comedy so well suspended her care, that no one, observing her during the first four acts, would have supposed she had any wretchedness about her. On the beginning of the fifth, however, the sudden view of Mr. Henry Tilney and his father, joining a party in the opposite box, recalled her to anxiety and distress. The stage could no longer excite genuine merriment—no longer keep her whole attention. Every other look upon an average was directed towards the opposite box; and, for the space of two entire scenes, did she thus watch Henry Tilney, without being once able to catch his eye. No longer could he be suspected of indifference for a play; his notice was never withdrawn from the stage during two whole scenes. At length, however, he did look towards her, and he bowed—but such a bow! no smile, no continued observance attended it; his eyes were immediately returned to their former direction. Catherine was restlessly miserable; she could almost have run round to the box in which he sat, and forced him to hear her explanation. Feelings rather natural than heroic possessed her; instead of considering her own dignity injured by this ready condemnation—instead of proudly resolving, in conscious innocence, to shew her resentment towards him who could harbour a doubt of it, to leave to him all the trouble of seeking an explanation, and to enlighten him on the past only by avoiding his sight, or flirting with somebody else, she took to herself all the shame of misconduct, or at least of its appearance, and was only eager for an opportunity of explaining its cause.

The play concluded—the curtain fell—Henry Tilney was no longer to be seen where he had hitherto sat, but his father remained, and perhaps he might be now coming round to their box. She was right; in a few minutes he appeared, and, making his way through the then thinning rows, spoke with like calm politeness to Mrs. Allen and her friend.—Not with such calmness was he answered by the latter: 'Oh! Mr. Tilney, I have been quite wild to speak to you, and make my apologies. You must have thought me so rude; but indeed it was not my own fault,—was it, Mrs. Allen? Did not they tell me that Mr. Tilney and his sister were gone out in a phaeton together? and then what could I do? But I had ten thousand times rather have been with you; now had not I, Mrs. Allen?'

'My dear, you tumble my gown,' was Mrs. Allen's reply.

Her assurance, however, standing sole as it did, was not thrown away; it brought a more cordial, more natural smile into his countenance, and he replied in a tone which retained only a little affected reserve:—'We were much obliged to you at any rate for wishing us a pleasant walk after our passing you in Argyle-street: you were so kind as to look back on purpose.'

'But indeed I did not wish you a pleasant walk; I never thought of such a thing; but I begged Mr. Thorpe so earnestly to stop; I called out to him as soon as ever I saw you; now, Mrs. Allen, did not——Oh! you were not there; but indeed I did; and, if Mr. Thorpe would only have stopped, I would have jumped out and run after you.'

Is there a Henry in the world who could be insensible to such a declaration? Henry Tilney at least was not. With a yet sweeter smile, he said every thing that need be said of his sister's concern, regret, and dependence on Catherine's honour.—'Oh! do not say Miss Tilney was not angry,' cried Catherine, 'because I know she was; for she would not see me this morning when I called; I saw her walk out of the house the next minute after my leaving it; I was hurt, but I was not affronted. Perhaps you did not know I had been there.'

'I was not within at the time; but I heard of it from Eleanor, and she has been wishing ever since to see you, to explain the reason of such incivility; but perhaps I can do it as well. It was nothing more than that my father——they were just preparing to walk out, and he being hurried for time, and not caring to have it put off, made a point of her being denied. That was all, I do assure you. She was very much vexed, and meant to make her apology as soon as possible.'

Catherine's mind was greatly eased by this information, yet a something of solicitude remained, from which sprang the following question, thoroughly artless in itself, though rather distressing to the gentleman:—'But, Mr. Tilney, why were *you* less generous than your sister? If she felt such confidence in my good intentions, and could suppose it to be only a mistake, why should *you* be so ready to take offence?'

'Me!—I take offence!'

'Nay, I am sure by your look, when you came into the box, you were angry.'

'I angry! I could have no right.'

'Well, nobody would have thought you had no right who saw your face.' He replied by asking her to make room for him, and talking of the play.

He remained with them some time, and was only too agreeable for Catherine to be contented when he went away. Before they parted, however, it was agreed that the projected walk should be taken as soon as possible; and, setting aside the misery of his quitting their box, she was, upon the whole, left one of the happiest creatures in the world.

While talking to each other, she had observed with some surprize, that John Thorpe, who was never in the same part of the house for ten minutes together, was engaged in conversation with General Tilney; and she felt something more than surprize, when she thought she could perceive herself the object of their attention and discourse.* What could they have to say of her? She feared General Tilney did not like her appearance: she found it was implied in his preventing her admittance to his daughter, rather than postpone his own walk a few minutes. 'How came Mr. Thorpe to know your father?' was her anxious inquiry, as she pointed them out to her companion. He knew nothing about it; but his father, like every military man, had a very large acquaintance.

When the entertainment was over, Thorpe came to assist them in getting out. Catherine was the immediate object of his gallantry; and, while they waited in the lobby for a chair, he prevented the inquiry which had travelled from her heart almost to the tip of her tongue, by asking, in a consequential manner, whether she had seen him talking with General Tilney:—'He is a fine old fellow, upon my soul!—stout, active,—looks as young as his son. I have a great regard for him, I assure you: a gentleman-like, good sort of fellow as ever lived.'

'But how came you to know him?'

'Know him!—There are few people much about town that I do not know. I have met him for ever at the Bedford;* and I knew his face again to-day the moment he came into the billiard-room. One of the best players we have, by the bye; and we had a little touch together,* though I was almost afraid of him at first: the odds were five to four against me; and, if I had not made one of the cleanest strokes that perhaps ever was made in this world—I took his ball exactly—but I could not make you understand it without a table;—however I *did* beat him. A very fine fellow; as rich as a Jew. I should like to dine with him; I dare say he gives famous dinners. But what do you think we have been talking of?—You. Yes, by heavens!—and the General thinks you the finest girl in Bath.'

'Oh! nonsense! how can you say so?'

'And what do you think I said?' (lowering his voice) 'Well done, General, said I, I am quite of your mind.'

Here, Catherine, who was much less gratified by his admiration than by General Tilney's, was not sorry to be called away by Mr. Allen. Thorpe, however, would see her to her chair, and, till she entered it, continued the same kind of delicate flattery, in spite of her entreating him to have done.

That General Tilney, instead of disliking, should admire her, was very delightful; and she joyfully thought, that there was not one of the family whom she need now fear to meet.—The evening had done more, much more, for her, than could have been expected.

CHAPTER XIII

MONDAY, Tuesday, Wednesday, Thursday, Friday and Saturday have now passed in review before the reader; the events of each day, its hopes and fears, mortifications and pleasures have been separately stated, and the pangs of Sunday only now remain to be described, and close the week. The Clifton scheme had been deferred, not relinquished, and on the afternoon's Crescent of this day,* it was brought forward again. In a private consultation between Isabella and James, the former of whom had particularly set her heart upon going, and the latter no less anxiously placed his upon pleasing her, it was agreed that, provided the weather were fair, the party should take place on the following morning; and they were to set off very early, in order to be at home in good time. The affair thus determined, and Thorpe's approbation secured, Catherine only remained to be apprized of it. She had left them for a few minutes to speak to Miss Tilney. In that interval the plan was completed, and as soon as she came again, her agreement was demanded; but instead of the gay acquiescence expected by Isabella, Catherine looked grave, was very sorry, but could not go. The engagement which ought to have kept her from joining in the former attempt, would make it impossible for her to accompany them now. She had that moment settled with Miss Tilney to take their promised walk to-morrow; it was quite determined, and she would not, upon any account, retract. But that she *must* and *should* retract, was instantly the eager cry of both the Thorpes; they must go to Clifton to-morrow, they would not go without her, it would be nothing to put off a mere walk for one day longer, and they would not hear of a refusal. Catherine was distressed, but not subdued. 'Do not urge me, Isabella. I am engaged to Miss Tilney. I cannot go.' This availed nothing. The same arguments assailed her again; she must go, she should go, and they would not hear of a refusal. 'It would be so easy to tell Miss Tilney that you had just been reminded of a prior engagement, and must only beg to put off the walk till Tuesday.'

'No, it would not be easy. I could not do it. There has been no prior engagement.' But Isabella became only more and more urgent; calling on her in the most affectionate manner; addressing her by the most endearing names. She was sure her dearest, sweetest Catherine would not seriously refuse such a trifling request to a friend who loved her so dearly. She knew her beloved Catherine to have so feeling a heart, so sweet a temper, to be so easily persuaded by those she loved. But all in vain; Catherine felt herself to be in the right, and though pained by such tender, such flattering supplication, could not allow it to influence her. Isabella then tried another method. She reproached her with having more affection for Miss Tilney, though she had known her so little a while, than for her best and oldest friends; with being grown cold and indifferent, in short, towards herself. 'I cannot help being jealous, Catherine, when I see myself slighted for strangers, I, who love you so excessively! When once my affections are placed, it is not in the power of any thing to change them. But I believe my feelings are stronger than any body's; I am sure they are too strong for my own peace; and to see myself supplanted in your friendship by strangers, does cut me to the quick, I own. These Tilneys seem to swallow up every thing else.'

Catherine thought this reproach equally strange and unkind. Was it the part of a friend thus to expose her feelings to the notice of others? Isabella appeared to her ungenerous and selfish, regardless of every thing but her own gratification. The painful ideas crossed her mind, though she said nothing. Isabella, in the meanwhile, had applied her handkerchief to her eyes; and Morland, miserable at such a sight, could not help saying, 'Nay, Catherine. I think you cannot stand out any longer now. The sacrifice is not much; and to oblige such a friend—I shall think you quite unkind, if you still refuse.'

This was the first time of her brother's openly siding against her, and anxious to avoid his displeasure, she proposed a compromise. If they would only put off their scheme till Tuesday, which they might easily do, as it depended only on themselves, she could go with them, and every body might then be satisfied. But 'No, no, no!' was the immediate answer; 'that could not be, for Thorpe did not know that he might not go to town on Tuesday.' Catherine was sorry, but could do no more; and a short silence ensued, which was broken by Isabella; who in a voice of cold resentment said, 'Very well, then there is an end of the party. If Catherine does not go, I cannot be the only woman. I would not, upon any account in the world, do so improper a thing.'

'Catherine, you must go,' said James.

'But why cannot Mr. Thorpe drive one of his other sisters? I dare say either of them would like to go.'

'Thank ye,' cried Thorpe, 'but I did not come to Bath to drive my sisters about, and look like a fool. No, if you do not go, d—— me if I do. I only go for the sake of driving you.'

'That is a compliment which gives me no pleasure.' But her words were lost on Thorpe, who had turned abruptly away.

The three others still continued together, walking in a most uncomfortable manner to poor Catherine; sometimes not a word was said, sometimes she was again attacked with supplications or reproaches, and her arm was still linked within Isabella's, though their hearts were at war. At one moment she was softened, at another irritated; always distressed, but always steady.

'I did not think you had been so obstinate, Catherine,' said James; 'you were not used to be so hard to persuade; you once were the kindest, best-tempered of my sisters.'

'I hope I am not less so now,' she replied, very feelingly; 'but indeed I cannot go. If I am wrong, I am doing what I believe to be right.'

'I suspect,' said Isabella, in a low voice, 'there is no great struggle.'

Catherine's heart swelled; she drew away her arm, and Isabella made no opposition. Thus passed a long ten minutes, till they were again joined by Thorpe, who coming to them with a gayer look, said, 'Well, I have settled the matter, and now we may all go to-morrow with a safe conscience. I have been to Miss Tilney, and made your excuses.'

'You have not!' cried Catherine.

'I have, upon my soul. Left her this moment. Told her you had sent me to say, that having just recollected a prior engagement of going to Clifton with us to-morrow, you could not have the pleasure of walking with her till Tuesday. She said very well, Tuesday was just as convenient to her; so there is an end of all our difficulties.—A pretty good thought of mine—hey?'

Isabella's countenance was once more all smiles and good-humour, and James too looked happy again.

'A most heavenly thought indeed! Now, my sweet Catherine, all our distresses are over; you are honourably acquitted, and we shall have a most delightful party.'

'This will not do,' said Catherine; 'I cannot submit to this. I must run after Miss Tilney directly and set her right.'

Isabella, however, caught hold of one hand; Thorpe of the other; and remonstrances poured in from all three. Even James was quite angry. When every thing was settled, when Miss Tilney herself said that Tuesday would suit her as well, it was quite ridiculous, quite absurd to make any further objection.

'I do not care. Mr. Thorpe had no business to invent any such message. If I had thought it right to put it off, I could have spoken to Miss Tilney myself. This is only doing it in a ruder way; and how do I know that Mr. Thorpe has——he may be mistaken again perhaps; he led me into one act of rudeness by his mistake on Friday. Let me go, Mr. Thorpe; Isabella, do not hold me.'

Thorpe told her it would be in vain to go after the Tilneys; they were turning the corner into Brock-street, when he had overtaken them, and were at home by this time.*

'Then I will go after them,' said Catherine, 'wherever they are I will go after them. It does not signify talking. If I could not be persuaded into doing what I thought wrong, I never will be tricked into it.' And with these words she broke away and hurried off. Thorpe would have darted after her, but Morland withheld him.

'Let her go, let her go, if she will go.'

'She is as obstinate as——'

Thorpe never finished the simile, for it could hardly have been a proper one.

Away walked Catherine in great agitation, as fast as the crowd would permit her, fearful of being pursued, yet determined to persevere. As she walked, she reflected on what had passed. It was painful to her to disappoint and displease them, particularly to displease her brother; but she could not repent her resistance. Setting her own inclination apart, to have failed a second time in her engagement to Miss Tilney, to have retracted a promise voluntarily made only five minutes before, and on a false pretence too, must have been wrong. She had not been withstanding them on selfish principles alone, she had not consulted merely her own gratification; *that* might have been ensured in some degree by the excursion itself, by seeing Blaize Castle; no, she had attended to what was due to others, and to her own character in their opinion. Her conviction of being right however was not enough to restore her composure, till she had spoken to Miss Tilney she could not be at ease; and quickening her pace when she got clear of the Crescent, she almost ran over the remaining ground till she gained the top of Milsom-street. So rapid had been her movements, that in spite of the Tilneys' advantage in the outset, they were but just turning into their lodgings as she came within view of them; and the servant still remaining at the open door, she used only the ceremony of saying that she must speak with Miss Tilney that moment, and hurrying by him proceeded up stairs. Then, opening the first door before her, which happened to be the right, she immediately found herself in the drawing-room with General Tilney, his son and daughter. Her explanation, defective only in being—from her irritation of nerves and shortness of breath—no explanation at all, was instantly given. 'I am come in a great hurry—It was all a mistake—I never promised to go—I told them from the first I could not go.—I ran away in a great hurry to explain it.—I did not care what you thought of me.—I would not stay for the servant.'

The business however, though not perfectly elucidated by this speech, soon ceased to be a puzzle. Catherine found that John Thorpe *had* given the message; and Miss Tilney had no scruple in owning herself greatly surprized by it. But whether her brother had still exceeded her in resentment, Catherine, though she instinctively addressed herself as much to one as to the other in her vindication, had no means of knowing. Whatever might have been felt before her arrival, her eager declarations immediately made every look and sentence as friendly as she could desire.

The affair thus happily settled, she was introduced by Miss Tilney to her father, and received by him with such ready, such solicitous politeness as recalled Thorpe's information to her mind, and made her think with pleasure that he might be sometimes depended on. To such anxious attention was the general's civility carried, that not aware of her extraordinary swiftness in entering the house, he was quite angry with the servant whose neglect had reduced her to open

the door of the apartment herself. 'What did William mean by it? He
should make a point of inquiring into the matter.' And if Catherine
had not most warmly asserted his innocence, it seemed likely that
William would lose the favour of his master for ever, if not his place,
by her rapidity.

After sitting with them a quarter of an hour,* she rose to take leave,
and was then most agreeably surprized by General Tilney's asking
her if she would do his daughter the honour of dining and spending
the rest of the day with her. Miss Tilney added her own wishes.
Catherine was greatly obliged; but it was quite out of her power.
Mr. and Mrs. Allen would expect her back every moment. The general declared he could say no more; the claims of Mr. and Mrs. Allen
were not to be superseded; but on some other day he trusted, when
longer notice could be given, they would not refuse to spare her to her
friend. 'Oh, no; Catherine was sure they would not have the least
objection, and she should have great pleasure in coming.' The general
attended her himself to the street-door, saying every thing gallant as
they went down stairs, admiring the elasticity of her walk, which cor-
responded exactly with the spirit of her dancing and making her one
of the most graceful bows she had ever beheld, when they parted.

Catherine, delighted by all that had passed, proceeded gaily to
Pulteney-street; walking, as she concluded, with great elasticity,
though she had never thought of it before. She reached home without
seeing any thing more of the offended party, and now that she had
been triumphant throughout, had carried her point and was secure of
her walk, she began (as the flutter of her spirits subsided) to doubt
whether she had been perfectly right. A sacrifice was always noble;
and if she had given way to their entreaties, she should have been
spared the distressing idea of a friend displeased, a brother angry, and
a scheme of great happiness to both destroyed, perhaps through her
means. To ease her mind, and ascertain by the opinion of an unprejudiced person what her own conduct had really been, she took occasion
to mention before Mr. Allen the half-settled scheme of her brother
and the Thorpes for the following day. Mr. Allen caught at it directly.
'Well,' said he, 'and do you think of going too?'

'No; I had just engaged myself to walk with Miss Tilney before they
told me of it; and therefore you know I could not go with them, could I?'

'No certainly not; and I am glad you do not think of it. These
schemes are not at all the thing. Young men and women driving about

the country in open carriages! Now and then it is very well; but going to inns and public places together! It is not right; and I wonder Mrs. Thorpe should allow it. I am glad you do not think of going; I am sure Mrs. Morland would not be pleased. Mrs. Allen, are not you of my way of thinking? Do not you think these kind of projects objectionable?'

'Yes, very much so indeed. Open carriages are nasty things. A clean gown is not five minutes wear in them. You are splashed getting in and getting out; and the wind takes your hair and your bonnet in every direction. I hate an open carriage myself.'

'I know you do; but that is not the question. Do not you think it has an odd appearance, if young ladies are frequently driven about in them by young men, to whom they are not even related?'

'Yes, my dear, a very odd appearance indeed. I cannot bear to see it.'

'Dear madam,' cried Catherine, 'then why did not you tell me so before? I am sure if I had known it to be improper, I would not have gone with Mr. Thorpe at all; but I always hoped you would tell me, if you thought I was doing wrong.'

'And so I should, my dear, you may depend on it; for as I told Mrs. Morland at parting, I would always do the best for you in my power. But one must not be over particular. Young people *will* be young people, as your good mother says herself. You know I wanted you, when we first came, not to buy that sprigged muslin, but you would. Young people do not like to be always thwarted.'

'But this was something of real consequence; and I do not think you would have found me hard to persuade.'

'As far as it has gone hitherto, there is no harm done,' said Mr. Allen; 'and I would only advise you, my dear, not to go out with Mr. Thorpe any more.'

'That is just what I was going to say,' added his wife.

Catherine, relieved for herself, felt uneasy for Isabella; and after a moment's thought, asked Mr. Allen whether it would not be both proper and kind in her to write to Miss Thorpe, and explain the indecorum of which she must be as insensible as herself; for she considered that Isabella might otherwise perhaps be going to Clifton the next day, in spite of what had passed. Mr. Allen however discouraged her from doing any such thing. 'You had better leave her alone, my dear, she is old enough to know what she is about; and if not, has a mother to advise her. Mrs. Thorpe is too indulgent beyond a doubt;

but however you had better not interfere. She and your brother chuse to go, and you will be only getting ill-will.'

Catherine submitted; and though sorry to think that Isabella should be doing wrong, felt greatly relieved by Mr. Allen's approbation of her own conduct, and truly rejoiced to be preserved by his advice from the danger of falling into such an error herself. Her escape from being one of the party to Clifton was now an escape indeed; for what would the Tilneys have thought of her, if she had broken her promise to them in order to do what was wrong in itself? if she had been guilty of one breach of propriety, only to enable her to be guilty of another?

CHAPTER XIV

THE next morning was fair, and Catherine almost expected another attack from the assembled party. With Mr. Allen to support her, she felt no dread of the event: but she would gladly be spared a contest, where victory itself was painful; and was heartily rejoiced therefore at neither seeing nor hearing any thing of them. The Tilneys called for her at the appointed time; and no new difficulty arising, no sudden recollection, no unexpected summons, no impertinent intrusion to disconcert their measures, my heroine was most unnaturally able to fulfil her engagement, though it was made with the hero himself. They determined on walking round Beechen Cliff,* that noble hill, whose beautiful verdure and hanging coppice render it so striking an object from almost every opening in Bath.

'I never look at it,' said Catherine, as they walked along the side of the river, 'without thinking of the south of France.'

'You have been abroad then?' said Henry, a little surprized.

'Oh! no, I only mean what I have read about. It always puts me in mind of the country that Emily and her father travelled through, in the "Mysteries of Udolpho." But you never read novels, I dare say?'

'Why not?'

'Because they are not clever enough for you—gentlemen read better books.'

'The person, be it gentleman or lady, who has not pleasure in a good novel, must be intolerably stupid. I have read all Mrs. Radcliffe's works, and most of them with great pleasure. The Mysteries of

Udolpho, when I had once begun it, I could not lay down again;—I remember finishing it in two days—my hair standing on end the whole time.'

'Yes,' added Miss Tilney, 'and I remember that you undertook to read it aloud to me, and that when I was called away for only five minutes to answer a note, instead of waiting for me, you took the volume into the Hermitage-walk,* and I was obliged to stay till you had finished it.'

'Thank you, Eleanor;—a most honourable testimony. You see, Miss Morland, the injustice of your suspicions. Here was I, in my eagerness to get on, refusing to wait only five minutes for my sister; breaking the promise I had made of reading it aloud, and keeping her in suspense at a most interesting part, by running away with the volume, which, you are to observe, was her own, particularly her own. I am proud when I reflect on it, and I think it must establish me in your good opinion.'

'I am very glad to hear it indeed, and now I shall never be ashamed of liking Udolpho myself. But I really thought before, young men despised novels amazingly.'

'It is *amazingly*; it may well suggest *amazement* if they do—for they read nearly as many as women. I myself have read hundreds and hundreds. Do not imagine that you can cope with me in a knowledge of Julias and Louisas.* If we proceed to particulars, and engage in the never-ceasing inquiry of "Have you read this?" and "Have you read that?" I shall soon leave you as far behind me as—what shall I say?—I want an appropriate simile;—as far as your friend Emily herself left poor Valancourt when she went with her aunt into Italy.* Consider how many years I have had the start of you. I had entered on my studies at Oxford, while you were a good little girl working your sampler at home!'*

'Not very good I am afraid. But now really, do not you think Udolpho the nicest book in the world?'

'The nicest,—by which I suppose you mean the neatest. That must depend upon the binding.'

'Henry,' said Miss Tilney, 'you are very impertinent. Miss Morland, he is treating you exactly as he does his sister. He is for ever finding fault with me, for some incorrectness of language, and now he is taking the same liberty with you. The word "nicest," as you used it, did not suit him; and you had better change it as soon as you can, or

we shall be overpowered with Johnson and Blair* all the rest of
the way.'

'I am sure,' cried Catherine, 'I did not mean to say any thing wrong;
but it *is* a nice book, and why should not I call it so?'

'Very true,' said Henry, 'and this is a very nice day, and we are taking a very nice walk, and you are two very nice young ladies. Oh! it is
a very nice word indeed!—it does for every thing. Originally perhaps
it was applied only to express neatness, propriety, delicacy, or refine-
ment;—people were nice in their dress, in their sentiments, or their
choice. But now every commendation on every subject is comprised
in that one word.'*

'While, in fact,' cried his sister, 'it ought only to be applied to you,
without any commendation at all. You are more nice than wise. Come,
Miss Morland, let us leave him to meditate over our faults in the
utmost propriety of diction, while we praise Udolpho in whatever
terms we like best. It is a most interesting work. You are fond of that
kind of reading?'

'To say the truth, I do not much like any other.'

'Indeed!'

'That is, I can read poetry and plays, and things of that sort, and do
not dislike travels. But history, real solemn history, I cannot be interested in. Can you?'

'Yes, I am fond of history.'

'I wish I were too. I read it a little as a duty, but it tells me nothing
that does not either vex or weary me. The quarrels of popes and kings,
with wars or pestilences, in every page; the men all so good for nothing, and hardly any women at all—it is very tiresome: and yet I often
think it odd that it should be so dull, for a great deal of it must be
invention. The speeches that are put into the heroes' mouths, their
thoughts and designs—the chief of all this must be invention, and
invention is what delights me in other books.'

'Historians, you think,' said Miss Tilney, 'are not happy in their
flights of fancy. They display imagination without raising interest.
I am fond of history—and am very well contented to take the false
with the true. In the principal facts they have sources of intelligence
in former histories and records, which may be as much depended on,
I conclude, as any thing that does not actually pass under one's own
observation; and as for the little embellishments you speak of, they
are embellishments, and I like them as such. If a speech be well drawn

up, I read it with pleasure, by whomsoever it may be made—and probably with much greater, if the production of Mr. Hume or Mr. Robertson, than if the genuine words of Caractacus, Agricola, or Alfred the Great.'*

'You are fond of history!—and so are Mr. Allen and my father; and I have two brothers who do not dislike it. So many instances within my small circle of friends is remarkable! At this rate, I shall not pity the writers of history any longer. If people like to read their books, it is all very well, but to be at so much trouble in filling great volumes, which, as I used to think, nobody would willingly ever look into, to be labouring only for the torment of little boys and girls, always struck me as a hard fate; and though I know it is all very right and necessary, I have often wondered at the person's courage that could sit down on purpose to do it.'

'That little boys and girls should be tormented,' said Henry, 'is what no one at all acquainted with human nature in a civilized state can deny; but in behalf of our most distinguished historians, I must observe, that they might well be offended at being supposed to have no higher aim; and that by their method and style, they are perfectly well qualified to torment readers of the most advanced reason and mature time of life. I use the verb "to torment," as I observed to be your own method, instead of "to instruct," supposing them to be now admitted as synonimous.'

'You think me foolish to call instruction a torment, but if you had been as much used as myself to hear poor little children first learning their letters and then learning to spell, if you had ever seen how stupid they can be for a whole morning together, and how tired my poor mother is at the end of it, as I am in the habit of seeing almost every day of my life at home, you would allow that to *torment* and to *instruct* might sometimes be used as synonimous words.'

'Very probably. But historians are not accountable for the difficulty of learning to read; and even you yourself, who do not altogether seem particularly friendly to very severe, very intense application, may perhaps be brought to acknowledge that it is very well worth while to be tormented for two or three years of one's life, for the sake of being able to read all the rest of it. Consider—if reading had not been taught, Mrs. Radcliffe would have written in vain—or perhaps might not have written at all.'

Catherine assented—and a very warm panegyric from her on that lady's merits, closed the subject.—The Tilneys were soon engaged in another on which she had nothing to say. They were viewing the country with the eyes of persons accustomed to drawing, and decided on its capability of being formed into pictures, with all the eagerness of real taste. Here Catherine was quite lost. She knew nothing of drawing—nothing of taste:—and she listened to them with an attention which brought her little profit, for they talked in phrases which conveyed scarcely any idea to her. The little which she could understand however appeared to contradict the very few notions she had entertained on the matter before. It seemed as if a good view were no longer to be taken from the top of an high hill, and that a clear blue sky was no longer a proof of a fine day. She was heartily ashamed of her ignorance. A misplaced shame. Where people wish to attach, they should always be ignorant. To come with a well-informed mind, is to come with an inability of administering to the vanity of others, which a sensible person would always wish to avoid. A woman especially, if she have the misfortune of knowing any thing, should conceal it as well as she can.*

The advantages of natural folly in a beautiful girl have been already set forth by the capital pen of a sister author,*—and to her treatment of the subject I will only add in justice to men, that though to the larger and more trifling part of the sex, imbecility in females is a great enhancement of their personal charms, there is a portion of them too reasonable and too well informed themselves to desire any thing more in woman than ignorance. But Catherine did not know her own advantages—did not know that a good-looking girl, with an affectionate heart and a very ignorant mind, cannot fail of attracting a clever young man, unless circumstances are particularly untoward. In the present instance, she confessed and lamented her want of knowledge: declared that she would give any thing in the world to be able to draw; and a lecture on the picturesque immediately followed, in which his instructions were so clear that she soon began to see beauty in every thing admired by him, and her attention was so earnest, that he became perfectly satisfied of her having a great deal of natural taste. He talked of fore-grounds, distances, and second distances—side-screens and perspectives—lights and shades;*—and Catherine was so hopeful a scholar, that when they gained the top of Beechen Cliff, she voluntarily rejected the whole city of Bath, as unworthy to make part of a landscape. Delighted with her progress, and fearful of wearying her with too much wisdom at once, Henry suffered the subject to decline, and by an easy transition from a piece of rocky fragment and the withered oak which he had placed near its summit,* to oaks in general, to forests, the inclosure of them, waste lands, crown lands and government, he shortly found himself arrived at politics;* and from politics, it was an easy step to silence. The general pause which succeeded his short disquisition on the state of the nation, was put an end to by Catherine, who, in rather a solemn tone of voice, uttered these words, 'I have heard that something very shocking indeed, will soon come out in London.'

Miss Tilney, to whom this was chiefly addressed, was startled, and hastily replied, 'Indeed!—and of what nature?'

'That I do not know, nor who is the author. I have only heard that it is to be more horrible than any thing we have met with yet.'

'Good heaven!—Where could you hear of such a thing?'

'A particular friend of mine had an account of it in a letter from London yesterday. It is to be uncommonly dreadful. I shall expect murder and every thing of the kind.'

'You speak with astonishing composure! But I hope your friend's accounts have been exaggerated;—and if such a design is known beforehand, proper measures will undoubtedly be taken by government to prevent its coming to effect.'

'Government,' said Henry, endeavouring not to smile, 'neither desires nor dares to interfere in such matters. There must be murder; and government cares not how much.'

The ladies stared. He laughed, and added, 'Come, shall I make you understand each other, or leave you to puzzle out an explanation as you can? No—I will be noble. I will prove myself a man, no less by the generosity of my soul than the clearness of my head. I have no patience with such of my sex as disdain to let themselves sometimes down to the comprehension of yours. Perhaps the abilities of women are neither sound nor acute—neither vigorous nor keen. Perhaps they may want observation, discernment, judgment, fire, genius, and wit.'

'Miss Morland, do not mind what he says;—but have the goodness to satisfy me as to this dreadful riot.'

'Riot!—what riot?'

'My dear Eleanor, the riot is only in your own brain.* The confusion there is scandalous. Miss Morland has been talking of nothing more dreadful than a new publication which is shortly to come out, in three duodecimo volumes, two hundred and seventy-six pages in each, with a frontispiece to the first, of two tombstones and a lantern—do you understand?—And you, Miss Morland—my stupid sister has mistaken all your clearest expressions. You talked of expected horrors in London—and instead of instantly conceiving, as any rational creature would have done, that such words could relate only to a circulating library, she immediately pictured to herself a mob of three thousand men assembling in St. George's Fields; the Bank attacked, the Tower threatened, the streets of London flowing with blood, a detachment of the 12th Light Dragoons, (the hopes of the nation,) called up from Northampton to quell the insurgents, and the gallant Capt. Frederick Tilney, in the moment of charging at the head of his troop, knocked off his horse by a brickbat from an upper window.* Forgive her stupidity. The fears of the sister have added to the weakness of the woman; but she is by no means a simpleton in general.'

Catherine looked grave. 'And now, Henry,' said Miss Tilney, 'that you have made us understand each other, you may as well make Miss Morland understand yourself—unless you mean to have her think you intolerably rude to your sister, and a great brute in your opinion of women in general. Miss Morland is not used to your odd ways.'

'I shall be most happy to make her better acquainted with them.'

'No doubt;—but that is no explanation of the present.'

'What am I to do?'

'You know what you ought to do. Clear your character handsomely before her. Tell her that you think very highly of the understanding of women.'

'Miss Morland, I think very highly of the understanding of all the women in the world—especially of those—whoever they may be—with whom I happen to be in company.'

'That is not enough. Be more serious.'

'Miss Morland, no one can think more highly of the understanding of women than I do. In my opinion, nature has given them so much, that they never find it necessary to use more than half.'

'We shall get nothing more serious from him now, Miss Morland. He is not in a sober mood. But I do assure you that he must be entirely misunderstood, if he can ever appear to say an unjust thing of any woman at all, or an unkind one of me.'

It was no effort to Catherine to believe that Henry Tilney could never be wrong. His manner might sometimes surprise, but his meaning must always be just:—and what she did not understand, she was almost as ready to admire, as what she did. The whole walk was delightful, and though it ended too soon, its conclusion was delightful too;—her friends attended her into the house, and Miss Tilney, before they parted, addressing herself with respectful form, as much to Mrs. Allen as to Catherine, petitioned for the pleasure of her company to dinner on the day after the next. No difficulty was made on Mrs. Allen's side—and the only difficulty on Catherine's was in concealing the excess of her pleasure.

The morning had passed away so charmingly as to banish all her friendship and natural affection; for no thought of Isabella or James had crossed her during their walk. When the Tilneys were gone, she became amiable again, but she was amiable for some time to little effect; Mrs. Allen had no intelligence to give that could relieve her anxiety, she had heard nothing of any of them. Towards the end of the morning however, Catherine having occasion for some indispensable yard of ribbon which must be bought without a moment's delay, walked out into the town, and in Bond-street overtook the second Miss Thorpe, as she was loitering towards Edgar's Buildings between two of the sweetest girls in the world, who had been her dear friends all the morning. From her, she soon learned that the party to Clifton had taken place. 'They set off at eight this morning,' said Miss Anne, 'and I am sure I do not envy them their drive. I think you and I are very well off to be out of the scrape.—It must be the dullest thing in the world, for there is not a soul at Clifton at this time of year.* Belle went with your brother, and John drove Maria.'

Catherine spoke the pleasure she really felt on hearing this part of the arrangement.

'Oh! yes,' rejoined the other, 'Maria is gone. She was quite wild to go. She thought it would be something very fine. I cannot say I admire her taste; and for my part I was determined from the first not to go, if they pressed me ever so much.'

Catherine, a little doubtful of this, could not help answering, 'I wish you could have gone too. It is a pity you could not all go.'

'Thank you; but it is quite a matter of indifference to me. Indeed, I would not have gone on any account. I was saying so to Emily and Sophia when you overtook us.'

Catherine was still unconvinced; but glad that Anne should have the friendship of an Emily and a Sophia to console her, she bade her adieu without much uneasiness, and returned home, pleased that the party had not been prevented by her refusing to join it, and very heartily wishing that it might be too pleasant to allow either James or Isabella to resent her resistance any longer.

CHAPTER XV

EARLY the next day, a note from Isabella, speaking peace and tenderness in every line, and entreating the immediate presence of her friend on a matter of the utmost importance, hastened Catherine, in the happiest state of confidence and curiosity, to Edgar's Buildings.—The two youngest Miss Thorpes were by themselves in the parlour; and, on Anne's quitting it to call her sister, Catherine took the opportunity of asking the other for some particulars of their yesterday's party. Maria desired no greater pleasure than to speak of it; and Catherine immediately learnt that it had been altogether the most delightful scheme in the world; that nobody could imagine how charming it had been, and that it had been more delightful than any body could conceive. Such was the information of the first five minutes; the second unfolded thus much in detail,—that they had driven directly to the York Hotel, ate some soup, and bespoke an early dinner, walked down to the Pump-room, tasted the water, and laid out some shillings in purses and spars;* thence adjourned to eat ice at a pastry-cook's, and hurrying back to the Hotel, swallowed their dinner in haste, to prevent being in the dark; and then had a delightful drive back, only the moon was not up, and it rained a little, and Mr. Morland's horse was so tired he could hardly get it along.

Catherine listened with heartfelt satisfaction. It appeared that Blaize Castle had never been thought of; and, as for all the rest, there was nothing to regret for half an instant.—Maria's intelligence concluded with a tender effusion of pity for her sister Anne, whom she represented as insupportably cross, from being excluded the party.

'She will never forgive me, I am sure; but, you know, how could I help it? John would have me go, for he vowed he would not drive her, because she had such thick ancles. I dare say she will not be in good humour again this month; but I am determined I will not be cross; it is not a little matter that puts me out of temper.'

Isabella now entered the room with so eager a step, and a look of such happy importance, as engaged all her friend's notice. Maria was without ceremony sent away, and Isabella, embracing Catherine, thus began:—'Yes, my dear Catherine, it is so indeed; your penetration has not deceived you.—Oh! that arch eye of yours!—It sees through every thing.'

Catherine replied only by a look of wondering ignorance.

'Nay, my beloved, sweetest friend,' continued the other, 'compose yourself.—I am amazingly agitated, as you perceive. Let us sit down and talk in comfort. Well, and so you guessed it the moment you had my note?—Sly creature!—Oh! my dear Catherine, you alone who know my heart can judge of my present happiness. Your brother is the most charming of men. I only wish I were more worthy of him.—But what will your excellent father and mother say?—Oh! heavens! when I think of them I am so agitated!'

Catherine's understanding began to awake: an idea of the truth suddenly darted into her mind; and, with the natural blush of so new an emotion, she cried out, 'Good heaven!—my dear Isabella, what do you mean? Can you—can you really be in love with James?'

This bold surmise, however, she soon learnt comprehended but half the fact. The anxious affection, which she was accused of having continually watched in Isabella's every look and action, had, in the course of their yesterday's party, received the delightful confession of an equal love. Her heart and faith were alike engaged to James.—Never had Catherine listened to any thing so full of interest, wonder, and joy. Her brother and her friend engaged!—New to such circumstances, the importance of it appeared unspeakably great, and she contemplated it as one of those grand events, of which the ordinary course of life can hardly afford a return. The strength of her feelings she could not express; the nature of them, however, contented her friend. The happiness of having such a sister was their first effusion, and the fair ladies mingled in embraces and tears of joy.

Delighting, however, as Catherine sincerely did in the prospect of the connexion, it must be acknowledged that Isabella far surpassed her in tender anticipations.—'You will be so infinitely dearer to me, my Catherine, than either Anne or Maria: I feel that I shall be so much more attached to my dear Morland's family than to my own.'

This was a pitch of friendship beyond Catherine.

'You are so like your dear brother,' continued Isabella, 'that I quite doated on you the first moment I saw you. But so it always is with me; the first moment settles every thing. The very first day that Morland came to us last Christmas—the very first moment I beheld him—my heart was irrecoverably gone. I remember I wore my yellow gown, with my hair done up in braids; and when I came into the drawing-room, and John introduced him, I thought I never saw anybody so handsome before.'

Here Catherine secretly acknowledged the power of love; for, though exceedingly fond of her brother, and partial to all his endowments, she had never in her life thought him handsome.

'I remember too, Miss Andrews drank tea with us that evening, and wore her puce-coloured sarsenet,* and she looked so heavenly, that I thought your brother must certainly fall in love with her; I could not sleep a wink all night for thinking of it. Oh! Catherine, the many sleepless nights I have had on your brother's account!—I would not have you suffer half what I have done! I am grown wretchedly thin I know; but I will not pain you by describing my anxiety; you have seen enough of it. I feel that I have betrayed myself perpetually;—so unguarded in speaking of my partiality for the church!—But my secret I was always sure would be safe with *you*.'

Catherine felt that nothing could have been safer; but ashamed of an ignorance little expected, she dared no longer contest the point, nor refuse to have been as full of arch penetration and affectionate sympathy as Isabella chose to consider her. Her brother she found was preparing to set off with all speed to Fullerton, to make known his situation and ask consent; and here was a source of some real agitation to the mind of Isabella. Catherine endeavoured to persuade her, as she was herself persuaded, that her father and mother would never oppose their son's wishes.—'It is impossible,' said she, 'for parents to be more kind, or more desirous of their children's happiness; I have no doubt of their consenting immediately.'

'Morland says exactly the same,' replied Isabella; 'and yet I dare not expect it; my fortune will be so small; they never can consent to it. Your brother, who might marry any body!'

Here Catherine again discerned the force of love.

'Indeed, Isabella, you are too humble.—The difference of fortune can be nothing to signify.'

'Oh! my sweet Catherine, in *your* generous heart I know it would signify nothing; but we must not expect such disinterestedness in many. As for myself, I am sure I only wish our situations were reversed. Had I the command of millions, were I mistress of the whole world, your brother would be my only choice.'

This charming sentiment, recommended as much by sense as novelty, gave Catherine a most pleasing remembrance of all the heroines of her acquaintance; and she thought her friend never looked more lovely than in uttering the grand idea.—'I am sure they will consent,' was her frequent declaration; 'I am sure they will be delighted with you.'

'For my own part,' said Isabella, 'my wishes are so moderate, that the smallest income in nature would be enough for me. Where people are really attached, poverty itself is wealth: grandeur I detest: I would not settle in London for the universe. A cottage in some retired village would be extasy. There are some charming little villas about Richmond.'*

'Richmond!' cried Catherine.—'You must settle near Fullerton. You must be near us.'

'I am sure I shall be miserable if we do not. If I can but be near you, I shall be satisfied. But this is idle talking! I will not allow myself to think of such things, till we have your father's answer. Morland says that by sending it to-night to Salisbury, we may have it to-morrow.*— To-morrow?—I know I shall never have courage to open the letter. I know it will be the death of me.'

A reverie succeeded this conviction—and when Isabella spoke again, it was to resolve on the quality of her wedding-gown.

Their conference was put an end to by the anxious young lover himself, who came to breathe his parting sigh before he set off for Wiltshire. Catherine wished to congratulate him, but knew not what to say, and her eloquence was only in her eyes. From them however the eight parts of speech shone out most expressively, and James could combine them with ease. Impatient for the realization of all that he hoped at home, his adieus were not long; and they would have been yet shorter, had he not been frequently detained by the urgent entreaties of his fair one that he would go. Twice was he called almost from the door by her eagerness to have him gone. 'Indeed, Morland, I must drive you away. Consider how far you have to ride. I cannot bear to see you linger so. For Heaven's sake, waste no more time. There, go, go—I insist on it.'

The two friends, with hearts now more united than ever, were inseparable for the day; and in schemes of sisterly happiness the hours flew along. Mrs. Thorpe and her son, who were acquainted with every thing, and who seemed only to want Mr. Morland's consent, to consider Isabella's engagement as the most fortunate circumstance imaginable for their family, were allowed to join their counsels, and add their quota of significant looks and mysterious expressions to fill up the measure of curiosity to be raised in the unprivileged younger sisters. To Catherine's simple feelings, this odd sort of reserve seemed neither kindly meant, nor consistently supported; and its unkindness she would hardly have forborn pointing out, had its inconsistency been less their friend;—but Anne and Maria soon set her heart at ease by the sagacity of their 'I know what;' and the evening was spent in a sort of war of wit, a display of family ingenuity; on one side in the mystery of an affected secret, on the other of undefined discovery, all equally acute.

Catherine was with her friend again the next day, endeavouring to support her spirits, and while away the many tedious hours before the delivery of the letters; a needful exertion, for as the time of reasonable expectation drew near, Isabella became more and more desponding, and before the letter arrived, had worked herself into a state of real distress. But when it did come, where could distress be found? 'I have had no difficulty in gaining the consent of my kind parents, and am promised that every thing in their power shall be done to forward my happiness,' were the first three lines, and in one moment all was joyful security. The brightest glow was instantly spread over Isabella's features, all care and anxiety seemed removed, her spirits became almost too high for controul, and she called herself without scruple the happiest of mortals.

Mrs. Thorpe, with tears of joy, embraced her daughter, her son, her visitor, and could have embraced half the inhabitants of Bath with satisfaction. Her heart was overflowing with tenderness. It was 'dear John,' and 'dear Catherine' at every word;—'dear Anne and dear Maria' must immediately be made sharers in their felicity; and two 'dears' at once before the name of Isabella were not more than that beloved child had now well earned. John himself was no skulker in joy. He not only bestowed on Mr. Morland the high commendation of being one of the finest fellows in the world, but swore off many sentences in his praise.

The letter, whence sprang all this felicity, was short, containing little more than this assurance of success; and every particular was deferred till James could write again. But for particulars Isabella could well afford to wait. The needful was comprised in Mr. Morland's promise; his honour was pledged to make every thing easy; and by what means their income was to be formed, whether landed property were to be resigned, or funded money made over, was a matter in which her disinterested spirit took no concern. She knew enough to feel secure of an honourable and speedy establishment, and her imagination took a rapid flight over its attendant felicities. She saw herself at the end of a few weeks, the gaze and admiration of every new acquaintance at Fullerton, the envy of every valued old friend in Putney, with a carriage at her command, a new name on her tickets, and a brilliant exhibition of hoop rings on her finger.*

When the contents of the letter were ascertained, John Thorpe, who had only waited its arrival to begin his journey to London, prepared to set off. 'Well, Miss Morland,' said he, on finding her alone in the parlour, 'I am come to bid you good bye.' Catherine wished him a good journey. Without appearing to hear her, he walked to the window, fidgetted about, hummed a tune, and seemed wholly self-occupied.

'Shall not you be late at Devizes?'* said Catherine. He made no answer; but after a minute's silence burst out with, 'A famous good thing this marrying scheme, upon my soul! A clever fancy of Morland's and Belle's. What do you think of it, Miss Morland? *I* say it is no bad notion.'

'I am sure I think it a very good one.'

'Do you?—that's honest, by heavens! I am glad you are no enemy to matrimony however. Did you ever hear the old song, "Going to one wedding brings on another?"* I say, you will come to Belle's wedding, I hope.'

'Yes; I have promised your sister to be with her, if possible.'

'And then you know'—twisting himself about and forcing a foolish laugh—'I say, then you know, we may try the truth of this same old song.'

'May we?—but I never sing. Well, I wish you a good journey. I dine with Miss Tilney to-day, and must now be going home.'

'Nay, but there is no such confounded hurry.—Who knows when we may be together again?—Not but that I shall be down again by the end of a fortnight, and a devilish long fortnight it will appear to me.'

'Then why do you stay away so long?' replied Catherine—finding that he waited for an answer.

'That is kind of you, however—kind and good-natured.—I shall not forget it in a hurry.—But you have more good-nature and all that, than any body living I believe. A monstrous deal of good-nature, and it is not only good-nature, but you have so much, so much of every thing; and then you have such—upon my soul I do not know any body like you.'

'Oh! dear, there are a great many people like me, I dare say, only a great deal better. Good morning to you.'

'But I say, Miss Morland, I shall come and pay my respects at Fullerton before it is long, if not disagreeable.'

'Pray do.—My father and mother will be very glad to see you.'

'And I hope—I hope, Miss Morland, *you* will not be sorry to see me.'

'Oh! dear, not at all. There are very few people I am sorry to see. Company is always cheerful.'

'That is just my way of thinking. Give me but a little cheerful company, let me only have the company of the people I love, let me only be where I like and with whom I like, and the devil take the rest, say I.—And I am heartily glad to hear you say the same. But I have a notion, Miss Morland, you and I think pretty much alike upon most matters.'

'Perhaps we may; but it is more than I ever thought of. And as to *most matters*, to say the truth, there are not many that I know my own mind about.'

'By Jove, no more do I. It is not my way to bother my brains with what does not concern me. My notion of things is simple enough. Let me only have the girl I like, say I, with a comfortable house over my head, and what care I for all the rest? Fortune is nothing. I am sure of a good income of my own; and if she had not a penny, why so much the better.'

'Very true. I think like you there. If there is a good fortune on one side, there can be no occasion for any on the other. No matter which has it, so that there is enough. I hate the idea of one great fortune looking out for another.* And to marry for money I think the wickedest thing in existence.—Good day.—We shall be very glad to see you at Fullerton, whenever it is convenient.' And away she went. It was not in the power of all his gallantry to detain her longer. With such news to communicate, and such a visit to prepare for, her departure was not to be delayed by any thing in his nature to urge; and she hurried away, leaving him to the undivided consciousness of his own happy address, and her explicit encouragement.

The agitation which she had herself experienced on first learning her brother's engagement, made her expect to raise no inconsiderable emotion in Mr. and Mrs. Allen, by the communication of the wonderful event. How great was her disappointment! The important affair, which many words of preparation ushered in, had been foreseen by them both ever since her brother's arrival; and all that they felt on the occasion was comprehended in a wish for the young people's happiness, with a remark, on the gentleman's side, in favour of Isabella's beauty, and on the lady's, of her great good luck. It was to Catherine the most surprizing insensibility. The disclosure however of the great secret of James's going to Fullerton the day before, did raise some emotion in Mrs. Allen. She could not listen to that with perfect calmness; but repeatedly regretted the necessity of its concealment, wished she could have known his intention, wished she could have seen him before he went, as she should certainly have troubled him with her best regards to his father and mother, and her kind compliments to all the Skinners.

END OF VOLUME I

VOLUME II

CHAPTER I

CATHERINE'S expectations of pleasure from her visit in Milsom-street were so very high, that disappointment was inevitable; and accordingly, though she was most politely received by General Tilney, and kindly welcomed by his daughter, though Henry was at home, and no one else of the party, she found, on her return, without spending many hours in the examination of her feelings, that she had gone to her appointment preparing for happiness which it had not afforded. Instead of finding herself improved in acquaintance with Miss Tilney, from the intercourse of the day, she seemed hardly so intimate with her as before; instead of seeing Henry Tilney to greater advantage than ever, in the ease of a family party, he had never said so little, nor been so little agreeable; and, in spite of their father's great civilities to her—in spite of his thanks, invitations, and compliments—it had been a release to get away from him. It puzzled her to account for all this. It could not be General Tilney's fault. That he was perfectly agreeable and good-natured, and altogether a very charming man, did not admit of a doubt, for he was tall and handsome, and Henry's father. *He* could not be accountable for his children's want of spirits, or for her want of enjoyment in his company. The former she hoped at last might have been accidental, and the latter she could only attribute to her own stupidity. Isabella, on hearing the particulars of the visit, gave a different explanation: 'It was all pride, pride, insufferable haughtiness and pride! She had long suspected the family to be very high, and this made it certain. Such insolence of behaviour as Miss Tilney's she had never heard of in her life! Not to do the honours of her house with common good-breeding!—To behave to her guest with such superciliousness!—Hardly even to speak to her!'

'But it was not so bad as that, Isabella; there was no superciliousness; she was very civil.'

'Oh! don't defend her! And then the brother, he, who had appeared so attached to you! Good heavens! well, some people's feelings are incomprehensible. And so he hardly looked once at you the whole day?'

'I do not say so: but he did not seem in good spirits.'

'How contemptible! Of all things in the world inconstancy is my aversion. Let me entreat you never to think of him again, my dear Catherine; indeed he is unworthy of you.'

'Unworthy! I do not suppose he ever thinks of me.'

'That is exactly what I say; he never thinks of you.—Such fickleness! Oh! how different to your brother and to mine! I really believe John has the most constant heart.'

'But as for General Tilney, I assure you it would be impossible for any body to behave to me with greater civility and attention; it seemed to be his only care to entertain and make me happy.'

'Oh! I know no harm of him; I do not suspect him of pride. I believe he is a very gentleman-like man. John thinks very well of him, and John's judgment——'

'Well, I shall see how they behave to me this evening; we shall meet them at the rooms.'

'And must I go?'

'Do not you intend it? I thought it was all settled.'

'Nay, since you make such a point of it, I can refuse you nothing. But do not insist upon my being very agreeable, for my heart, you know, will be some forty miles off. And as for dancing, do not mention it I beg; *that* is quite out of the question. Charles Hodges will plague me to death I dare say; but I shall cut him very short. Ten to one but he guesses the reason, and that is exactly what I want to avoid, so I shall insist on his keeping his conjecture to himself.'

Isabella's opinion of the Tilneys did not influence her friend; she was sure there had been no insolence in the manners either of brother or sister; and she did not credit there being any pride in their hearts. The evening rewarded her confidence; she was met by one with the same kindness, and by the other with the same attention as heretofore: Miss Tilney took pains to be near her, and Henry asked her to dance.

Having heard the day before in Milsom-street, that their elder brother, Captain Tilney, was expected almost every hour, she was at no loss for the name of a very fashionable-looking, handsome young man, whom she had never seen before, and who now evidently belonged to their party. She looked at him with great admiration, and even supposed it possible, that some people might think him handsomer than his brother, though, in her eyes, his air was more assuming, and his countenance less prepossessing. His taste and manners were beyond a doubt decidedly inferior; for, within her hearing, he not only protested against every thought of dancing himself, but even laughed openly at Henry for finding it possible. From the latter circumstance it may be presumed, that, whatever might be our heroine's opinion of him, his admiration of her was not of a very dangerous kind; not likely to produce animosities between the brothers, nor persecutions to the lady. *He* cannot be the instigator of the three villains in horsemen's great coats, by whom she will hereafter be forced into a travelling-chaise and four, which will drive off with incredible speed.* Catherine, meanwhile, undisturbed by presentiments of such an evil, or of any evil at all, except that of having but a short set to dance down, enjoyed her usual happiness with Henry Tilney, listening with sparkling eyes to every thing he said; and, in finding him irresistible, becoming so herself.

At the end of the first dance, Captain Tilney came towards them again, and, much to Catherine's dissatisfaction, pulled his brother away. They retired whispering together; and, though her delicate sensibility did not take immediate alarm, and lay it down as fact, that Captain Tilney must have heard some malevolent misrepresentation of her, which he now hastened to communicate to his brother, in the hope of separating them for ever, she could not have her partner conveyed from her sight without very uneasy sensations. Her suspense was of full five minutes' duration; and she was beginning to think it a very long quarter of an hour, when they both returned, and an explanation was given, by Henry's requesting to know, if she thought her friend, Miss Thorpe, would have any objection to dancing, as his brother would be most happy to be introduced to her. Catherine, without hesitation, replied, that she was very sure Miss Thorpe did not mean to dance at all. The cruel reply was passed on to the other, and he immediately walked away.

'Your brother will not mind it I know,' said she, 'because I heard him say before, that he hated dancing; but it was very good-natured in him to think of it. I suppose he saw Isabella sitting down, and fancied she might wish for a partner; but he is quite mistaken, for she would not dance upon any account in the world.'

Henry smiled, and said, 'How very little trouble it can give you to understand the motive of other people's actions.'

'Why?—What do you mean?'

'With you, it is not, How is such a one likely to be influenced? What is the inducement most likely to act upon such a person's feelings, age, situation, and probable habits of life considered?—but, how should *I* be influenced, what would be *my* inducement in acting so and so?'

'I do not understand you.'

'Then we are on very unequal terms, for I understand you perfectly well.'

'Me?—yes; I cannot speak well enough to be unintelligible.'*

'Bravo!—an excellent satire on modern language.'

'But pray tell me what you mean.'

'Shall I indeed?—Do you really desire it?—But you are not aware of the consequences; it will involve you in a very cruel embarrassment, and certainly bring on a disagreement between us.'

'No, no; it shall not do either; I am not afraid.'

'Well then, I only meant that your attributing my brother's wish of dancing with Miss Thorpe to good-nature alone, convinced me of your being superior in good-nature yourself to all the rest of the world.'

Catherine blushed and disclaimed, and the gentleman's predictions were verified. There was a something, however, in his words which repaid her for the pain of confusion; and that something occupied her mind so much, that she drew back for some time, forgetting to speak or to listen, and almost forgetting where she was; till, roused by the voice of Isabella, she looked up and saw her with Captain Tilney preparing to give them hands across.

Isabella shrugged her shoulders and smiled, the only explanation of this extraordinary change which could at that time be given; but as it was not quite enough for Catherine's comprehension, she spoke her astonishment in very plain terms to her partner.

'I cannot think how it could happen! Isabella was so determined not to dance.'

'And did Isabella never change her mind before?'

'Oh! but, because——and your brother!—After what you told him from me, how could he think of going to ask her?'

'I cannot take surprize to myself on that head. You bid me be surprized on your friend's account, and therefore I am; but as for my brother, his conduct in the business, I must own, has been no more than I believed him perfectly equal to. The fairness of your friend was an open attraction; her firmness, you know, could only be understood by yourself.'

'You are laughing; but I assure you, Isabella is very firm in general.'

'It is as much as should be said of any one. To be always firm must be to be often obstinate. When properly to relax is the trial of judgment; and, without reference to my brother, I really think Miss Thorpe has by no means chosen ill in fixing on the present hour.'

The friends were not able to get together for any confidential discourse till all the dancing was over; but then, as they walked about the room arm in arm, Isabella thus explained herself:—'I do not wonder at your surprize; and I am really fatigued to death. He is such a rattle!—Amusing enough, if my mind had been disengaged; but I would have given the world to sit still.'

'Then why did not you?'

'Oh! my dear! it would have looked so particular; and you know how I abhor doing that. I refused him as long as I possibly could, but he would take no denial. You have no idea how he pressed me. I begged him to excuse me, and get some other partner—but no, not he; after aspiring to my hand, there was nobody else in the room he could bear to think of; and it was not that he wanted merely to dance, he wanted to be with *me*. Oh! such nonsense!—I told him he had taken a very unlikely way to prevail upon me; for, of all things in the world, I hated fine speeches and compliments;—and so——and so then I found there would be no peace if I did not stand up. Besides, I thought Mrs. Hughes, who introduced him, might take it ill if I did not: and your dear brother, I am sure he would have been miserable if I had sat down the whole evening. I am so glad it is over! My spirits are quite jaded with listening to his nonsense: and then,—being such a smart young fellow, I saw every eye was upon us.'

'He is very handsome indeed.'

'Handsome!—Yes, I suppose he may. I dare say people would admire him in general; but he is not at all in my style of beauty. I hate a florid complexion and dark eyes in a man. However, he is very well. Amazingly conceited, I am sure. I took him down several times you know in my way.'

When the young ladies next met, they had a far more interesting subject to discuss. James Morland's second letter was then received, and the kind intentions of his father fully explained. A living, of which Mr. Morland was himself patron and incumbent, of about four hundred pounds yearly value, was to be resigned to his son as soon as he should be old enough to take it;* no trifling deduction from the family income, no niggardly assignment to one of ten children. An estate of at least equal value, moreover, was assured as his future inheritance.

James expressed himself on the occasion with becoming gratitude; and the necessity of waiting between two and three years before they could marry, being, however unwelcome, no more than he had expected, was born by him without discontent. Catherine, whose expectations had been as unfixed as her ideas of her father's income, and whose judgment was now entirely led by her brother, felt equally well satisfied, and heartily congratulated Isabella on having every thing so pleasantly settled.

'It is very charming indeed,' said Isabella, with a grave face. 'Mr. Morland has behaved vastly handsome indeed,' said the gentle Mrs. Thorpe, looking anxiously at her daughter. 'I only wish I could do as much. One could not expect more from him you know. If he finds he *can* do more by and bye, I dare say he will, for I am sure he must be an excellent good hearted man. Four hundred is but a small income to begin on indeed,* but your wishes, my dear Isabella, are so moderate, you do not consider how little you ever want, my dear.'

'It is not on my own account I wish for more; but I cannot bear to be the means of injuring my dear Morland, making him sit down upon an income hardly enough to find one in the common necessaries of life. For myself, it is nothing; I never think of myself.'

'I know you never do, my dear; and you will always find your reward in the affection it makes every body feel for you. There never was a young woman so beloved as you are by every body that knows you; and I dare say when Mr. Morland sees you, my dear child—but do not let us distress our dear Catherine by talking of such things. Mr. Morland has behaved so very handsome you know. I always heard he was a most excellent man; and you know, my dear, we are not to suppose but what, if you had had a suitable fortune, he would have come down with something more, for I am sure he must be a most liberal-minded man.'

'Nobody can think better of Mr. Morland than I do, I am sure. But every body has their failing you know, and every body has a right to do what they like with their own money.' Catherine was hurt by these insinuations. 'I am very sure,' said she, 'that my father has promised to do as much as he can afford.'

Isabella recollected herself. 'As to that, my sweet Catherine, there cannot be a doubt, and you know me well enough to be sure that a much smaller income would satisfy me. It is not the want of more money that makes me just at present a little out of spirits; I hate money; and if our union could take place now upon only fifty pounds a year, I should not have a wish unsatisfied.* Ah! my Catherine, you have found me out. There's the sting. The long, long, endless two years and half that are to pass before your brother can hold the living.'

'Yes, yes, my darling Isabella,' said Mrs. Thorpe, 'we perfectly see into your heart. You have no disguise. We perfectly understand the present vexation; and every body must love you the better for such a noble honest affection.'

Catherine's uncomfortable feelings began to lessen. She endeavoured to believe that the delay of the marriage was the only source of Isabella's regret; and when she saw her at their next interview as cheerful and amiable as ever, endeavoured to forget that she had for a minute thought otherwise. James soon followed his letter, and was received with the most gratifying kindness.

CHAPTER II

THE Allens had now entered on the sixth week of their stay in Bath; and whether it should be the last, was for some time a question, to which Catherine listened with a beating heart. To have her acquaintance with the Tilneys end so soon, was an evil which nothing could counterbalance. Her whole happiness seemed at stake, while the affair was in suspense, and every thing secured when it was determined that the lodgings should be taken for another fortnight. What this additional fortnight was to produce to her beyond the pleasure of sometimes seeing Henry Tilney, made but a small part of Catherine's speculation. Once or twice indeed, since James's engagement had taught her what *could* be done, she had got so far as to indulge in a secret 'perhaps,' but in general the felicity of being with him for the present bounded her views: the present was now comprised in another three weeks, and her happiness being certain for that period, the rest of her life was at such a distance as to excite but little interest. In the course of the morning which saw this business arranged, she visited Miss Tilney, and poured forth her joyful feelings. It was doomed to be a day of trial. No sooner had she expressed her delight in Mr. Allen's lengthened stay, than Miss Tilney told her of her father's having just determined upon quitting Bath by the end of another week. Here was a blow! The past suspense of the morning had been ease and quiet to the present disappointment. Catherine's countenance fell, and in a voice of most sincere concern she echoed Miss Tilney's concluding words, 'By the end of another week!'

'Yes, my father can seldom be prevailed on to give the waters what I think a fair trial. He has been disappointed of some friends' arrival whom he expected to meet here, and as he is now pretty well, is in a hurry to get home.'

'I am very sorry for it,' said Catherine dejectedly, 'if I had known this before—'

'Perhaps,' said Miss Tilney in an embarrassed manner, 'you would be so good—it would make me very happy if—'

The entrance of her father put a stop to the civility, which Catherine was beginning to hope might introduce a desire of their corresponding. After addressing her with his usual politeness, he turned to his daughter and said, 'Well, Eleanor, may I congratulate you on being successful in your application to your fair friend?'

'I was just beginning to make the request, sir, as you came in.'

'Well, proceed by all means. I know how much your heart is in it. My daughter, Miss Morland,' he continued, without leaving his daughter time to speak, 'has been forming a very bold wish. We leave Bath, as she has perhaps told you, on Saturday se'nnight. A letter from my steward tells me that my presence is wanted at home; and being disappointed in my hope of seeing the Marquis of Longtown* and General Courteney here, some of my very old friends, there is nothing to detain me longer in Bath. And could we carry our selfish point with you, we should leave it without a single regret. Can you, in short, be prevailed on to quit this scene of public triumph and oblige your friend Eleanor with your company in Gloucestershire? I am almost ashamed to make the request, though its presumption would certainly appear greater to every creature in Bath than yourself. Modesty such as your's—but not for the world would I pain it by open praise. If you can be induced to honour us with a visit, you will make us happy beyond expression. 'Tis true, we can offer you nothing like the gaieties of this lively place; we can tempt you neither by amusement nor splendour, for our mode of living, as you see, is plain and unpretending; yet no endeavours shall be wanting on our side to make Northanger Abbey not wholly disagreeable.'

Northanger Abbey!—These were thrilling words,* and wound up Catherine's feelings to the highest point of extasy. Her grateful and gratified heart could hardly restrain its expressions within the language of tolerable calmness. To receive so flattering an invitation! To have her company so warmly solicited! Every thing honourable and soothing, every present enjoyment, and every future hope was contained in it; and her acceptance, with only the saving clause of papa and mamma's approbation, was eagerly given.—'I will write home directly,' said she, 'and if they do not object, as I dare say they will not'—

General Tilney was not less sanguine, having already waited on her excellent friends in Pulteney-street, and obtained their sanction of his wishes. 'Since they can consent to part with you,' said he, 'we may expect philosophy from all the world.'

Miss Tilney was earnest, though gentle, in her secondary civilities, and the affair became in a few minutes as nearly settled, as this necessary reference to Fullerton would allow.

The circumstances of the morning had led Catherine's feelings through the varieties of suspense, security, and disappointment; but they were now safely lodged in perfect bliss; and with spirits elated to rapture, with Henry at her heart, and Northanger Abbey on her lips, she hurried home to write her letter. Mr. and Mrs. Morland, relying on the discretion of the friends to whom they had already entrusted their daughter, felt no doubt of the propriety of an acquaintance which had been formed under their eye, and sent therefore by return of post their ready consent to her visit in Gloucestershire. This indulgence, though not more than Catherine had hoped for, completed her conviction of being favoured beyond every other human creature, in friends and fortune, circumstance and chance. Every thing seemed to co-operate for her advantage. By the kindness of her first friends the Allens, she had been introduced into scenes, where pleasures of every kind had met her. Her feelings, her preferences had each known the happiness of a return. Wherever she felt attachment, she had been able to create it. The affection of Isabella was to be secured to her in a sister. The Tilneys, they, by whom above all, she desired to be favourably thought of, outstripped even her wishes in the flattering measures by which their intimacy was to be continued. She was to be their chosen visitor, she was to be for weeks under the same roof with the person whose society she mostly prized—and, in addition to all the rest, this roof was to be the roof of an abbey!—Her passion for ancient edifices was next in degree to her passion for Henry Tilney—and castles and abbies made usually the charm of those reveries which his image did not fill. To see and explore either the ramparts and keep of the one, or the cloisters of the other, had been for many weeks a darling wish, though to be more than the visitor of an hour, had seemed too nearly impossible for desire. And yet, this was to happen. With all the chances against her of house, hall, place, park, court, and cottage, Northanger turned up an abbey, and she was to be its inhabitant. Its long, damp passages, its narrow cells and ruined chapel, were to be within her daily reach, and she could not entirely subdue the hope of some traditional legends, some awful memorials of an injured and ill-fated nun.*

It was wonderful that her friends should seem so little elated by the possession of such a home; that the consciousness of it should be so meekly born. The power of early habit only could account for it. A distinction to which they had been born gave no pride. Their superiority of abode was no more to them than their superiority of person.

Many were the inquiries she was eager to make of Miss Tilney; but so active were her thoughts, that when these inquiries were answered, she was hardly more assured than before, of Northanger Abbey having been a richly-endowed convent at the time of the Reformation, of its having fallen into the hands of an ancestor of the Tilneys on its dissolution, of a large portion of the ancient building still making a part of the present dwelling although the rest was decayed, or of its standing low in a valley, sheltered from the north and east by rising woods of oak.*

CHAPTER III

WITH a mind thus full of happiness, Catherine was hardly aware that two or three days had passed away, without her seeing Isabella for more than a few minutes together. She began first to be sensible of this, and to sigh for her conversation, as she walked along the Pump-room one morning, by Mrs. Allen's side, without any thing to say or to hear; and scarcely had she felt a five minutes' longing of friendship, before the object of it appeared, and inviting her to a secret conference, led the way to a seat. 'This is my favourite place,' said she, as they sat down on a bench between the doors, which commanded a tolerable view of every body entering at either, 'it is so out of the way.'

Catherine, observing that Isabella's eyes were continually bent towards one door or the other, as in eager expectation, and remembering how often she had been falsely accused of being arch, thought the present a fine opportunity for being really so; and therefore gaily said, 'Do not be uneasy, Isabella. James will soon be here.'

'Psha! my dear creature,' she replied, 'do not think me such a simpleton as to be always wanting to confine him to my elbow. It would be hideous to be always together; we should be the jest of the place. And so you are going to Northanger!—I am amazingly glad of it. It is one of the finest old places in England, I understand. I shall depend upon a most particular description of it.'

'You shall certainly have the best in my power to give. But who are you looking for? Are your sisters coming?'

'I am not looking for any body. One's eyes must be somewhere, and you know what a foolish trick I have of fixing mine, when my thoughts are an hundred miles off. I am amazingly absent; I believe I am the most absent creature in the world. Tilney says it is always the case with minds of a certain stamp.'

'But I thought, Isabella, you had something in particular to tell me?'

'Oh! yes, and so I have. But here is a proof of what I was saying. My poor head! I had quite forgot it. Well, the thing is this, I have just had a letter from John;—you can guess the contents.'

'No, indeed, I cannot.'

'My sweet love, do not be so abominably affected. What can he write about but yourself? You know he is over head and ears in love with you.'

'With *me*, dear Isabella!'

'Nay, my sweetest Catherine, this is being quite absurd! Modesty, and all that, is very well in its way, but really a little common honesty is sometimes quite as becoming. I have no idea of being so overstrained! It is fishing for compliments. His attentions were such as a child must have noticed. And it was but half an hour before he left Bath, that you gave him the most positive encouragement. He says so in this letter, says that he as good as made you an offer, and that you received his advances in the kindest way; and now he wants me to urge his suit, and say all manner of pretty things to you. So it is in vain to affect ignorance.'

Catherine, with all the earnestness of truth, expressed her astonishment at such a charge, protesting her innocence of every thought of Mr. Thorpe's being in love with her, and the consequent impossibility of her having ever intended to encourage him. 'As to any attentions on his side, I do declare, upon my honour, I never was sensible of them for a moment—except just his asking me to dance the first day of his coming. And as to making me an offer, or any thing like it, there must be some unaccountable mistake. I could not have misunderstood a thing of that kind, you know!—and, as I ever wish to be believed, I solemnly protest that no syllable of such a nature ever passed between us. The last half hour before he went away!—It must be all and completely a mistake—for I did not see him once that whole morning.'

'But *that* you certainly did, for you spent the whole morning in Edgar's Buildings—it was the day your father's consent came—and I am pretty sure that you and John were alone in the parlour, some time before you left the house.'

'Are you?—Well, if you say it, it was so, I dare say—but for the life of me, I cannot recollect it.—I *do* remember now being with you, and seeing him as well as the rest—but that we were ever alone for five minutes—However, it is not worth arguing about, for whatever might pass on his side, you must be convinced, by my having no recollection of it, that I never thought, nor expected, nor wished for any thing of the kind from him. I am excessively concerned that he should have any regard for me—but indeed it has been quite unintentional on my side, I never had the smallest idea of it. Pray undeceive him as soon as you can, and tell him I beg his pardon—that is—I do not know what I ought to say—but make him understand what I mean, in the properest way. I would not speak disrespectfully of a brother of your's, Isabella, I am sure; but you know very well that if I could think of one man more than another—*he* is not the person.' Isabella was silent. 'My dear friend, you must not be angry with me. I cannot suppose your brother cares so very much about me. And, you know, we shall still be sisters.'

'Yes, yes,' (with a blush) 'there are more ways than one of our being sisters.*—But where am I wandering to?—Well, my dear Catherine, the case seems to be, that you are determined against poor John—is not it so?'

'I certainly cannot return his affection, and as certainly never meant to encourage it.'

'Since that is the case, I am sure I shall not tease you any further. John desired me to speak to you on the subject, and therefore I have. But I confess, as soon as I read his letter, I thought it a very foolish, imprudent business, and not likely to promote the good of either; for what were you to live upon, supposing you came together? You have both of you something to be sure, but it is not a trifle that will support a family now-a-days; and after all that romancers may say, there is no doing without money. I only wonder John could think of it; he could not have received my last.'

'You *do* acquit me then of any thing wrong?—You are convinced that I never meant to deceive your brother, never suspected him of liking me till this moment?'

'Oh! as to that,' answered Isabella laughingly, 'I do not pretend to determine what your thoughts and designs in time past may have been. All that is best known to yourself. A little harmless flirtation or so will occur, and one is often drawn on to give more encouragement than one wishes to stand by. But you may be assured that I am the last person in the world to judge you severely. All those things should be allowed for in youth and high spirits. What one means one day, you know, one may not mean the next. Circumstances change, opinions alter.'

'But my opinion of your brother never did alter; it was always the same. You are describing what never happened.'

'My dearest Catherine,' continued the other without at all listening to her, 'I would not for all the world be the means of hurrying you into an engagement before you knew what you were about. I do not think any thing would justify me in wishing you to sacrifice all your happiness merely to oblige my brother, because he is my brother, and who perhaps after all, you know, might be just as happy without you, for people seldom know what they would be at, young men especially, they are so amazingly changeable and inconstant. What I say is, why should a brother's happiness be dearer to me than a friend's? You know I carry my notions of friendship pretty high. But, above all things, my dear Catherine, do not be in a hurry. Take my word for it, that if you are in too great a hurry, you will certainly live to repent it. Tilney says, there is nothing people are so often deceived in, as the state of their own affections, and I believe he is very right. Ah! here he comes; never mind, he will not see us, I am sure.'

Catherine, looking up, perceived Captain Tilney; and Isabella, earnestly fixing her eye on him as she spoke, soon caught his notice. He approached immediately, and took the seat to which her movements invited him. His first address made Catherine start. Though spoken low, she could distinguish, 'What! always to be watched, in person or by proxy!'

'Psha, nonsense!' was Isabella's answer in the same half whisper. 'Why do you put such things into my head? If I could believe it—my spirit, you know, is pretty independent.'

'I wish your heart were independent. That would be enough for me.'

'My heart, indeed! What can you have to do with hearts? You men have none of you any hearts.'

'If we have not hearts, we have eyes; and they give us torment enough.'

'Do they? I am sorry for it; I am sorry they find any thing so disagreeable in me. I will look another way. I hope this pleases you, (turning her back on him,) I hope your eyes are not tormented now.'

'Never more so; for the edge of a blooming cheek is still in view—at once too much and too little.'

Catherine heard all this, and quite out of countenance could listen no longer. Amazed that Isabella could endure it, and jealous for her brother, she rose up, and saying she should join Mrs. Allen, proposed their walking. But for this Isabella shewed no inclination. She was so amazingly tired, and it was so odious to parade about the Pump-room; and if she moved from her seat she should miss her sisters, she was expecting her sisters every moment; so that her dearest Catherine must excuse her, and must sit quietly down again. But Catherine could be stubborn too; and Mrs. Allen just then coming up to propose their returning home, she joined her and walked out of the Pump-room, leaving Isabella still sitting with Captain Tilney. With much uneasiness did she thus leave them. It seemed to her that Captain Tilney was falling in love with Isabella, and Isabella unconsciously encouraging him; unconsciously it must be, for Isabella's attachment to James was as certain and well acknowledged as her engagement. To doubt her truth or good intentions was impossible; and yet, during the whole of their conversation her manner had been odd. She wished Isabella had talked more like her usual self, and not so much about money; and had not looked so well pleased at the sight of Captain Tilney. How strange that she should not perceive his admiration! Catherine longed to give her a hint of it, to put her on her guard, and prevent all the pain which her too lively behaviour might otherwise create both for him and her brother.

The compliment of John Thorpe's affection did not make amends for this thoughtlessness in his sister. She was almost as far from believing as from wishing it to be sincere; for she had not forgotten that he could mistake, and his assertion of the offer and of her encouragement convinced her that his mistakes could sometimes be very egregious. In vanity therefore she gained but little, her chief profit was in wonder. That he should think it worth his while to fancy himself in love with her, was a matter of lively astonishment. Isabella talked of his attentions; *she* had never been sensible of any; but Isabella had said many things which she hoped had been spoken in haste, and would never be said again; and upon this she was glad to rest altogether for present ease and comfort.

CHAPTER IV

A FEW days passed away, and Catherine, though not allowing herself to suspect her friend, could not help watching her closely. The result of her observations was not agreeable. Isabella seemed an altered creature. When she saw her indeed surrounded only by their immediate friends in Edgar's Buildings or Pulteney street, her change of manners was so trifling that, had it gone no farther, it might have passed unnoticed. A something of languid indifference, or of that boasted absence of mind which Catherine had never heard of before, would occasionally come across her; but had nothing worse appeared, *that* might only have spread a new grace and inspired a warmer interest. But when Catherine saw her in public, admitting Captain Tilney's attentions as readily as they were offered, and allowing him almost an equal share with James in her notice and smiles, the alteration became too positive to be past over. What could be meant by such unsteady conduct, what her friend could be at, was beyond her comprehension. Isabella could not be aware of the pain she was inflicting; but it was a degree of wilful thoughtlessness which Catherine could not but resent. James was the sufferer. She saw him grave and uneasy; and however careless of his present comfort the woman might be who had given him her heart, to *her* it was always an object. For poor Captain Tilney too she was greatly concerned. Though his looks did not please her, his name was a passport to her good will, and she thought with sincere compassion of his approaching disappointment; for, in spite of what she had believed herself to overhear in the Pump-room, his behaviour was so incompatible with a knowledge of Isabella's engagement, that she could not, upon reflection, imagine him aware of it. He might be jealous of her brother as a rival, but if more had seemed implied, the fault must have been in her misapprehension. She wished, by a gentle remonstrance, to remind Isabella of her situation, and make her aware of this double unkindness; but for remonstrance, either opportunity or comprehension was always against her. If able to suggest a hint, Isabella could never understand it. In this distress, the intended departure of the Tilney family became her chief consolation; their journey into Gloucestershire was to take place within a few days, and Captain Tilney's removal would at least restore peace to every heart but his own. But Captain Tilney had at present no intention of removing; he was not to be of the party to Northanger, he was to continue at Bath. When Catherine knew this, her resolution was directly made. She spoke to Henry Tilney on the subject, regretting his brother's evident partiality for Miss Thorpe, and entreating him to make known her prior engagement.

'My brother does know it,' was Henry's answer.

'Does he?—then why does he stay here?'

He made no reply, and was beginning to talk of something else; but she eagerly continued, 'Why do not you persuade him to go away? The longer he stays, the worse it will be for him at last. Pray advise him for his own sake, and for every body's sake, to leave Bath directly. Absence will in time make him comfortable again; but he can have no hope here, and it is only staying to be miserable.' Henry smiled and said, 'I am sure my brother would not wish to do that.'

'Then you will persuade him to go away?'

'Persuasion is not at command; but pardon me, if I cannot even endeavour to persuade him. I have myself told him that Miss Thorpe is engaged. He knows what he is about, and must be his own master.'

'No, he does not know what he is about,' cried Catherine; 'he does not know the pain he is giving my brother. Not that James has ever told me so, but I am sure he is very uncomfortable.'

'And are you sure it is my brother's doing?'

'Yes, very sure.'

'Is it my brother's attentions to Miss Thorpe, or Miss Thorpe's admission of them, that gives the pain?'

'Is not it the same thing?'

'I think Mr. Morland would acknowledge a difference. No man is offended by another man's admiration of the woman he loves; it is the woman only who can make it a torment.'

Catherine blushed for her friend, and said, 'Isabella is wrong. But I am sure she cannot mean to torment, for she is very much attached to my brother. She has been in love with him ever since they first met, and while my father's consent was uncertain, she fretted herself almost into a fever. You know she must be attached to him.'

'I understand: she is in love with James, and flirts with Frederick.'

'Oh! no, not flirts. A woman in love with one man cannot flirt with another.'

'It is probable that she will neither love so well, nor flirt so well, as she might do either singly. The gentlemen must each give up a little.'

After a short pause, Catherine resumed with 'Then you do not believe Isabella so very much attached to my brother?'

'I can have no opinion on that subject.'

'But what can your brother mean? If he knows her engagement, what can he mean by his behaviour?'

'You are a very close questioner.'

'Am I?—I only ask what I want to be told.'

'But do you only ask what I can be expected to tell?'

'Yes, I think so; for you must know your brother's heart.'

'My brother's heart, as you term it, on the present occasion, I assure you I can only guess at.'

'Well?'

'Well!—Nay, if it is to be guess-work, let us all guess for ourselves. To be guided by second-hand conjecture is pitiful. The premises are before you. My brother is a lively, and perhaps sometimes a thoughtless young man; he has had about a week's acquaintance with your friend, and he has known her engagement almost as long as he has known her.'

'Well,' said Catherine, after some moments' consideration, '*you* may be able to guess at your brother's intentions from all this; but I am sure I cannot. But is not your father uncomfortable about it?—Does not he want Captain Tilney to go away?—Sure, if your father were to speak to him, he would go.'

'My dear Miss Morland,' said Henry, 'in this amiable solicitude for your brother's comfort, may you not be a little mistaken? Are you not carried a little too far? Would he thank you, either on his own account or Miss Thorpe's, for supposing that her affection, or at least her good-behaviour, is only to be secured by her seeing nothing of Captain Tilney? Is he safe only in solitude?—or, is her heart constant to him only when unsolicited by any one else?—He cannot think this—and you may be sure that he would not have you think it. I will not say, "Do not be uneasy," because I know that you are so, at this moment; but be as little uneasy as you can. You have no doubt of the mutual attachment of your brother and your friend; depend upon it therefore, that real jealousy never can exist between them; depend upon it that no disagreement between them can be of any duration. Their hearts are open to each other, as neither heart can be to you; they know exactly what is required and what can be borne; and you may be certain, that one will never tease the other beyond what is known to be pleasant.'

Perceiving her still to look doubtful and grave, he added, 'Though Frederick does not leave Bath with us, he will probably remain but a very short time, perhaps only a few days behind us. His leave of absence will soon expire, and he must return to his regiment.—And what will then be their acquaintance?—The mess-room will drink Isabella Thorpe for a fortnight, and she will laugh with your brother over poor Tilney's passion for a month.'*

Catherine would contend no longer against comfort. She had resisted its approaches during the whole length of a speech, but it now carried her captive. Henry Tilney must know best. She blamed herself for the extent of her fears, and resolved never to think so seriously on the subject again.

Her resolution was supported by Isabella's behaviour in their parting interview. The Thorpes spent the last evening of Catherine's stay in Pulteney-street, and nothing passed between the lovers to excite her uneasiness, or make her quit them in apprehension. James was in excellent spirits, and Isabella most engagingly placid. Her tenderness for her friend seemed rather the first feeling of her heart; but that at such a moment was allowable; and once she gave her lover a flat contradiction, and once she drew back her hand; but Catherine remembered Henry's instructions, and placed it all to judicious affection. The embraces, tears, and promises of the parting fair ones may be fancied.

CHAPTER V

MR. and Mrs. Allen were sorry to lose their young friend, whose good-humour and cheerfulness had made her a valuable companion, and in the promotion of whose enjoyment their own had been gently increased. Her happiness in going with Miss Tilney, however, prevented their wishing it otherwise; and, as they were to remain only one more week in Bath themselves, her quitting them now would not long be felt. Mr. Allen attended her to Milsom-street, where she was to breakfast, and saw her seated with the kindest welcome among her new friends; but so great was her agitation in finding herself as one of the family, and so fearful was she of not doing exactly what was right, and of not being able to preserve their good opinion, that, in the embarrassment of the first five minutes, she could almost have wished to return with him to Pulteney-street.

Miss Tilney's manners and Henry's smile soon did away some of her unpleasant feelings; but still she was far from being at ease; nor could the incessant attentions of the General himself entirely reassure her. Nay, perverse as it seemed, she doubted whether she might not have felt less, had she been less attended to. His anxiety for her comfort—his continual solicitations that she would eat, and his often-expressed fears of her seeing nothing to her taste—though never in her life before had she beheld half such variety on a breakfast-table—made it impossible for her to forget for a moment that she was a visitor. She felt utterly unworthy of such respect, and knew not how to reply to it. Her tranquillity was not improved by the General's impatience for the appearance of his eldest son, nor by the displeasure he expressed at his laziness when Captain Tilney at last came down. She was quite pained by the severity of his father's reproof, which seemed disproportionate to the offence; and much was her concern increased, when she found herself the principal cause of the lecture; and that his tardiness was chiefly resented from being disrespectful to her. This was placing her in a very uncomfortable situation, and she felt great compassion for Captain Tilney, without being able to hope for his good-will.

He listened to his father in silence, and attempted not any defence, which confirmed her in fearing, that the inquietude of his mind, on Isabella's account, might, by keeping him long sleepless, have been the real cause of his rising late.—It was the first time of her being decidedly in his company, and she had hoped to be now able to form her opinion of him; but she scarcely heard his voice while his father remained in the room; and even afterwards, so much were his spirits affected, she could distinguish nothing but these words, in a whisper to Eleanor, 'How glad I shall be when you are all off.'

The bustle of going was not pleasant.—The clock struck ten while the trunks were carrying down, and the General had fixed to be out of Milsom-street by that hour. His great coat, instead of being brought for him to put on directly, was spread out in the curricle in which he was to accompany his son. The middle seat of the chaise was not drawn out, though there were three people to go in it, and his daughter's maid had so crowded it with parcels, that Miss Morland would not have room to sit; and, so much was he influenced by this apprehension when he handed her in, that she had some difficulty in saving her own new writing-desk from being thrown out into the street.—At last, however, the door was closed upon the three females, and they set off at the sober pace in which the handsome, highly-fed four horses of a gentleman usually perform a journey of thirty miles: such was the distance of Northanger from Bath, to be now divided into two equal stages. Catherine's spirits revived as they drove from the door; for with Miss Tilney she felt no restraint; and, with the interest of a road entirely new to her, of an abbey before, and a curricle behind, she caught the last view of Bath without any regret, and met with every mile-stone before she expected it. The tediousness of a two hours' bait at Petty-France,* in which there was nothing to be done but to eat without being hungry, and loiter about without any thing to see, next followed—and her admiration of the style in which they travelled, of the fashionable chaise-and-four—postilions handsomely liveried,* rising so regularly in their stirrups, and numerous outriders properly mounted, sunk a little under this consequent inconvenience. Had their party been perfectly agreeable, the delay would have been nothing; but General Tilney, though so charming a man, seemed always a check upon his children's spirits, and scarcely any thing was said but by himself; the observation of which, with his discontent at whatever the inn afforded, and his angry impatience at the waiters, made Catherine grow every moment more in awe of him, and appeared to lengthen the two hours into four.—At last, however, the order of release was given; and much was Catherine then surprized by the General's proposal of her taking his place in his son's curricle for the rest of the journey:—'the day was fine, and he was anxious for her seeing as much of the country as possible.'

The remembrance of Mr. Allen's opinion, respecting young men's open carriages, made her blush at the mention of such a plan, and her first thought was to decline it; but her second was of greater deference for General Tilney's judgment; he could not propose any thing improper for her; and, in the course of a few minutes, she found herself with Henry in the curricle, as happy a being as ever existed. A very short trial convinced her that a curricle was the prettiest equipage in the world; the chaise-and-four wheeled off with some grandeur, to be sure, but it was a heavy and troublesome business, and she could not easily forget its having stopped two hours at Petty-France. Half the time would have been enough for the curricle, and so nimbly were the light horses disposed to move, that, had not the General chosen to have his own carriage lead the way, they could have passed it with ease in half a minute. But the merit of the curricle did not all belong to the horses;—Henry drove so well,—so quietly—without making any disturbance, without parading to her, or swearing at them; so different from the only gentleman-coachman whom it was in her power to compare him with!—And then his hat sat so well, and the innumerable capes of his great coat looked so becomingly important!—To be driven by him, next to being dancing with him, was certainly the greatest happiness in the world. In addition to every other delight, she had now that of listening to her own praise; of being thanked at least, on his sister's account, for her kindness in thus becoming her visitor; of hearing it ranked as real friendship, and described as creating real gratitude. His sister, he said, was uncomfortably circumstanced—she had no female companion—and, in the frequent absence of her father, was sometimes without any companion at all.

'But how can that be?' said Catherine, 'are not you with her?'

'Northanger is not more than half my home; I have an establishment at my own house in Woodston, which is nearly twenty miles from my father's, and some of my time is necessarily spent there.'*

'How sorry you must be for that!'

'I am always sorry to leave Eleanor.'

'Yes; but besides your affection for her, you must be so fond of the abbey!—After being used to such a home as the abbey, an ordinary parsonage-house must be very disagreeable.'

He smiled, and said, 'You have formed a very favourable idea of the abbey.'

'To be sure I have. Is not it a fine old place, just like what one reads about?'

'And are you prepared to encounter all the horrors that a building such as "what one reads about" may produce?—Have you a stout heart?—Nerves fit for sliding pannels and tapestry?'*

'Oh! yes—I do not think I should be easily frightened, because there would be so many people in the house—and besides, it has never been uninhabited and left deserted for years, and then the family come back to it unawares, without giving any notice, as generally happens.'

'No, certainly.—We shall not have to explore our way into a hall dimly lighted by the expiring embers of a wood fire*—nor be obliged to spread our beds on the floor of a room without windows, doors, or furniture. But you must be aware that when a young lady is (by whatever means) introduced into a dwelling of this kind, she is always lodged apart from the rest of the family. While they snugly repair to their own end of the house, she is formally conducted by Dorothy the ancient housekeeper up a different staircase, and along many gloomy passages, into an apartment never used since some cousin or kin died in it about twenty years before.* Can you stand such a ceremony as this? Will not your mind misgive you, when you find yourself in this gloomy chamber—too lofty and extensive for you, with only the feeble rays of a single lamp to take in its size—its walls hung with tapestry exhibiting figures as large as life,* and the bed, of dark green stuff or purple velvet, presenting even a funereal appearance. Will not your heart sink within you?'

'Oh! but this will not happen to me, I am sure.'

'How fearfully will you examine the furniture of your apartment!—And what will you discern?—Not tables, toilettes, wardrobes, or drawers, but on one side perhaps the remains of a broken lute, on the other a ponderous chest which no efforts can open, and over the fire-place the portrait of some handsome warrior, whose features will so incomprehensibly strike you, that you will not be able to withdraw your eyes from it. Dorothy meanwhile, no less struck by your appearance, gazes on you in great agitation, and drops a few unintelligible hints. To raise your spirits, moreover, she gives you reason to suppose that the part of the abbey you inhabit is undoubtedly haunted, and informs you

that you will not have a single domestic within call. With this parting
cordial she curtseys off—you listen to the sound of her receding footsteps as long as the last echo can reach you—and when, with fainting
spirits, you attempt to fasten your door, you discover, with increased
alarm, that it has no lock.'

'Oh! Mr. Tilney, how frightful!—This is just like a book!—But it
cannot really happen to me. I am sure your housekeeper is not really
Dorothy.—Well, what then?'

'Nothing further to alarm perhaps may occur the first night. After
surmounting your *unconquerable* horror of the bed, you will retire to
rest, and get a few hour's unquiet slumber.* But on the second, or at
farthest the *third* night after your arrival, you will probably have a violent storm. Peals of thunder so loud as to seem to shake the edifice to
its foundation will roll round the neighbouring mountains—and during the frightful gusts of wind which accompany it, you will probably
think you discern (for your lamp is not extinguished) one part of the
hanging more violently agitated than the rest. Unable of course to
repress your curiosity in so favourable a moment for indulging it, you
will instantly arise, and throwing your dressing-gown around you,
proceed to examine this mystery. After a very short search, you will
discover a division in the tapestry so artfully constructed as to defy
the minutest inspection, and on opening it, a door will immediately
appear—which door being only secured by massy bars and a padlock,
you will, after a few efforts, succeed in opening,—and, with your lamp
in your hand, will pass through it into a small vaulted room.'

'No, indeed; I should be too much frightened to do any such thing.'

'What! not when Dorothy has given you to understand that there is
a secret subterraneous communication between your apartment and
the chapel of St. Anthony,* scarcely two miles off—Could you shrink
from so simple an adventure? No, no, you will proceed into this small
vaulted room, and through this into several others, without perceiving any thing very remarkable in either. In one perhaps there may be
a dagger, in another a few drops of blood, and in a third the remains
of some instrument of torture; but there being nothing in all this out
of the common way, and your lamp being nearly exhausted, you will
return towards your own apartment. In repassing through the small
vaulted room, however, your eyes will be attracted towards a large,
old-fashioned cabinet of ebony and gold, which, though narrowly
examining the furniture before, you had passed unnoticed. Impelled

by an irresistible presentiment, you will eagerly advance to it, unlock its folding doors, and search into every drawer;—but for some time without discovering any thing of importance—perhaps nothing but a considerable hoard of diamonds. At last, however, by touching a secret spring, an inner compartment will open—a roll of paper appears:—you seize it—it contains many sheets of manuscript—you hasten with the precious treasure into your own chamber, but scarcely have you been able to decipher "Oh! thou—whomsoever thou mayst be, into whose hands these memoirs of the wretched Matilda may fall"—when your lamp suddenly expires in the socket, and leaves you in total darkness.'*

'Oh! no, no—do not say so. Well, go on.'

But Henry was too much amused by the interest he had raised, to be able to carry it farther; he could no longer command solemnity either of subject or voice, and was obliged to entreat her to use her own fancy in the perusal of Matilda's woes. Catherine, recollecting herself, grew ashamed of her eagerness, and began earnestly to assure him that her attention had been fixed without the smallest apprehension of really meeting with what he related. 'Miss Tilney, she was sure, would never put her into such a chamber as he had described!—She was not at all afraid.'

As they drew near the end of their journey, her impatience for a sight of the abbey—for some time suspended by his conversation on subjects very different—returned in full force, and every bend in the road was expected with solemn awe to afford a glimpse of its massy walls of grey stone, rising amidst a grove of ancient oaks, with the last beams of the sun playing in beautiful splendour on its high Gothic windows.* But so low did the building stand, that she found herself passing through the great gates of the lodge into the very grounds of Northanger, without having discerned even an antique chimney.

She knew not that she had any right to be surprized, but there was a something in this mode of approach which she certainly had not expected. To pass between lodges of a modern appearance, to find herself with such ease in the very precincts of the abbey, and driven so rapidly along a smooth, level road of fine gravel, without obstacle, alarm or solemnity of any kind, struck her as odd and inconsistent. She was not long at leisure however for such considerations. A sudden scud of rain driving full in her face, made it impossible for her to observe any thing further, and fixed all her thoughts on the welfare of her new straw bonnet:—and she was actually under the Abbey walls, was springing, with Henry's assistance, from the carriage, was beneath the shelter of the old porch, and had even passed on to the hall, where her friend and the General were waiting to welcome her, without feeling one aweful foreboding of future misery to herself, or one moment's suspicion of any past scenes of horror being acted within the solemn edifice. The breeze had not seemed to waft the sighs of the murdered to her; it had wafted nothing worse than a thick mizzling rain; and having given a good shake to her habit, she was ready to be shewn into the common drawing-room, and capable of considering where she was.

An abbey!—yes, it was delightful to be really in an abbey!—but she doubted, as she looked round the room, whether any thing within her observation, would have given her the consciousness. The furniture was in all the profusion and elegance of modern taste. The fireplace, where she had expected the ample width and ponderous carving of former times, was contracted to a Rumford,* with slabs of plain though handsome marble, and ornaments over it of the prettiest English china. The windows, to which she looked with peculiar dependence, from having heard the General talk of his preserving them in their Gothic form with reverential care, were yet less what her fancy had portrayed. To be sure, the pointed arch was preserved—the form of them was Gothic—they might be even casements—but every pane was so large, so clear, so light! To an imagination which had hoped for the smallest divisions, and the heaviest stone-work, for painted glass, dirt and cobwebs, the difference was very distressing.

The General, perceiving how her eye was employed, began to talk of the smallness of the room and simplicity of the furniture, where every thing being for daily use, pretended only to comfort, &c.; flattering himself however that there were some apartments in the Abbey not unworthy her notice—and was proceeding to mention the costly gilding of one in particular, when taking out his watch, he stopped short to pronounce it with surprize within twenty minutes of five! This seemed the word of separation, and Catherine found herself hurried away by Miss Tilney in such a manner as convinced her that the strictest punctuality to the family hours would be expected at Northanger.

Returning through the large and lofty hall, they ascended a broad staircase of shining oak, which, after many flights and many landing-places, brought them upon a long wide gallery. On one side it had a range of doors, and it was lighted on the other by windows which Catherine had only time to discover looked into a quadrangle, before Miss Tilney led the way into a chamber, and scarcely staying to hope she would find it comfortable, left her with an anxious entreaty that she would make as little alteration as possible in her dress.

CHAPTER VI

A MOMENT'S glance was enough to satisfy Catherine that her apartment was very unlike the one which Henry had endeavoured to alarm her by the description of.—It was by no means unreasonably large, and contained neither tapestry nor velvet.—The walls were papered, the floor was carpeted; the windows were neither less perfect, nor more dim than those of the drawing-room below; the furniture, though not of the latest fashion, was handsome and comfortable, and the air of the room altogether far from uncheerful. Her heart instantaneously at ease on this point, she resolved to lose no time in particular examination of any thing, as she greatly dreaded disobliging the General by any delay. Her habit therefore was thrown off with all possible haste, and she was preparing to unpin the linen package, which the chaise-seat had conveyed for her immediate accommodation, when her eye suddenly fell on a large high chest, standing back in a deep recess on one side of the fire-place.* The sight of it made her start; and, forgetting every thing else, she stood gazing on it in motionless wonder, while these thoughts crossed her:—

'This is strange indeed! I did not expect such a sight as this!—An immense heavy chest!—What can it hold?—Why should it be placed here?—Pushed back too, as if meant to be out of sight!—I will look into it—cost me what it may, I will look into it—and directly too—by day-light.—If I stay till evening my candle may go out.' She advanced and examined it closely: it was of cedar, curiously inlaid with some darker wood, and raised, about a foot from the ground, on a carved stand of the same. The lock was silver, though tarnished from age; at each end were the imperfect remains of handles also of silver, broken perhaps prematurely by some strange violence; and, on the centre of the lid, was a mysterious cypher, in the same metal. Catherine bent over it intently, but without being able to distinguish any thing with certainty. She could not, in whatever direction she took it, believe the last letter to be a *T*; and yet that it should be any thing else in that house was a circumstance to raise no common degree of astonishment. If not originally their's, by what strange events could it have fallen into the Tilney family?

Her fearful curiosity was every moment growing greater; and seizing, with trembling hands, the hasp of the lock, she resolved at all hazards to satisfy herself at least as to its contents. With difficulty, for something seemed to resist her efforts, she raised the lid a few inches; but at that moment a sudden knocking at the door of the room made her, starting, quit her hold, and the lid closed with alarming violence. This ill-timed intruder was Miss Tilney's maid, sent by her mistress to be of use to Miss Morland; and though Catherine immediately dismissed her, it recalled her to the sense of what she ought to be doing, and forced her, in spite of her anxious desire to penetrate this mystery, to proceed in her dressing without further delay. Her progress was not quick, for her thoughts and her eyes were still bent on the object so well calculated to interest and alarm; and though she dared not waste a moment upon a second attempt, she could not remain many paces from the chest. At length, however, having slipped one arm into her gown, her toilette seemed so nearly finished, that the impatience of her curiosity might safely be indulged. One moment surely might be spared; and, so desperate should be the exertion of her strength, that, unless secured by supernatural means, the lid in one moment should be thrown back. With this spirit she sprang forward, and her confidence did not deceive her. Her resolute effort threw back the lid, and gave to her astonished eyes the view of a white cotton counterpane, properly folded, reposing at one end of the chest in undisputed possession!

She was gazing on it with the first blush of surprize, when Miss Tilney, anxious for her friend's being ready, entered the room, and to the rising shame of having harboured for some minutes an absurd expectation, was then added the shame of being caught in so idle a search. 'That is a curious old chest, is not it?' said Miss Tilney, as Catherine hastily closed it and turned away to the glass. 'It is impossible to say how many generations it has been here. How it came to be first put in this room I know not, but I have not had it moved, because I thought it might sometimes be of use in holding hats and bonnets. The worst of it is that its weight makes it difficult to open. In that corner, however, it is at least out of the way.'

Catherine had no leisure for speech, being at once blushing, tying her gown, and forming wise resolutions with the most violent dispatch. Miss Tilney gently hinted her fear of being late; and in half a minute they run down stairs together, in an alarm not wholly unfounded, for General Tilney was pacing the drawing-room, his watch in his hand, and having, on the very instant of their entering, pulled the bell with violence, ordered 'Dinner to be on table *directly!*'

Catherine trembled at the emphasis with which he spoke, and sat pale and breathless, in a most humble mood, concerned for his children, and detesting old chests; and the General recovering his politeness as he looked at her, spent the rest of his time in scolding his daughter, for so foolishly hurrying her fair friend, who was absolutely out of breath from haste, when there was not the least occasion for hurry in the world: but Catherine could not at all get over the double distress of having involved her friend in a lecture and been a great simpleton herself, till they were happily seated at the dinner-table, when the General's complacent smiles, and a good appetite of her own, restored her to peace. The dining-parlour was a noble room, suitable in its dimensions to a much larger drawing-room than the one in common use, and fitted up in a style of luxury and expense which was almost lost on the unpractised eye of Catherine, who saw little more than its spaciousness and the number of their attendants. Of the former, she spoke aloud her admiration; and the General, with a very gracious countenance, acknowledged that it was by no means an ill-sized room; and further confessed, that, though as careless on such subjects as most people, he did look upon a tolerably large eating-room as one of the necessaries of life; he supposed, however, 'that she must have been used to much better sized apartments at Mr. Allen's?'

'No, indeed,' was Catherine's honest assurance; 'Mr. Allen's dining-parlour was not more than half as large:' and she had never seen so large a room as this in her life. The General's good-humour increased.—Why, as he *had* such rooms, he thought it would be simple not to make use of them; but, upon his honour, he believed there might be more comfort in rooms of only half their size. Mr. Allen's house, he was sure, must be exactly of the true size for rational happiness.

The evening passed without any further disturbance, and, in the occasional absence of General Tilney, with much positive cheerfulness. It was only in his presence that Catherine felt the smallest fatigue from her journey; and even then, even in moments of languor or restraint, a sense of general happiness preponderated, and she could think of her friends in Bath without one wish of being with them.

The night was stormy; the wind had been rising at intervals the whole afternoon; and by the time the party broke up, it blew and rained violently. Catherine, as she crossed the hall, listened to the tempest with sensations of awe; and, when she heard it rage round a corner of the ancient building and close with sudden fury a distant door, felt for the first time that she was really in an Abbey.—Yes, these were characteristic sounds;—they brought to her recollection a countless variety of dreadful situations and horrid scenes, which such buildings had witnessed, and such storms ushered in; and most heartily did she rejoice in the happier circumstances attending her entrance within walls so solemn!—*She* had nothing to dread from midnight assassins or drunken gallants.* Henry had certainly been only in jest in what he had told her that morning. In a house so furnished, and so guarded, she could have nothing to explore or to suffer; and might go to her bedroom as securely as if it had been her own chamber at Fullerton. Thus wisely fortifying her mind, as she proceeded up stairs, she was enabled, especially on perceiving that Miss Tilney slept only two doors from her, to enter her room with a tolerably stout heart; and her spirits were immediately assisted by the cheerful blaze of a wood fire. 'How much better is this,' said she, as she walked to the fender—'how much better to find a fire ready lit, than to have to wait shivering in the cold till all the family are in bed, as so many poor girls have been obliged to do, and then to have a faithful old servant frightening one by coming in with a faggot! How glad I am that Northanger is what it is! If it had been like some other places, I do not know that, in such a night as this, I could have answered for my courage:—but now, to be sure, there is nothing to alarm one.'

She looked round the room. The window curtains seemed in motion. It could be nothing but the violence of the wind penetrating through the divisions of the shutters; and she stept boldly forward, carelessly humming a tune, to assure herself of its being so, peeped courageously behind each curtain, saw nothing on either low window seat to scare her, and on placing a hand against the shutter, felt the strongest conviction of the wind's force. A glance at the old chest, as she turned away from this examination, was not without its use; she scorned the causeless fears of an idle fancy, and began with a most happy indifference to prepare herself for bed. 'She should take her time; she should not hurry herself; she did not care if she were the last person up in the house. But she would not make up her fire; *that* would seem cowardly, as if she wished for the protection of light after she were in bed.' The fire therefore died away, and Catherine, having spent the best part of an hour in her arrangements, was beginning to think of stepping into bed, when, on giving a parting glance round the room, she was struck by the appearance of a high, old-fashioned black cabinet, which, though in a situation conspicuous enough, had never caught her notice before. Henry's words, his description of the ebony cabinet which was to escape her observation at first, immediately rushed across her; and though there could be nothing really in it, there was something whimsical, it was certainly a very remarkable coincidence! She took her candle and looked closely at the cabinet. It was not absolutely ebony and gold; but it was Japan, black and yellow Japan of the handsomest kind;* and as she held her candle, the yellow had very much the effect of gold. The key was in the door, and she had a strange fancy to look into it; not however with the smallest expectation of finding any thing, but it was so very odd, after what Henry had said. In short, she could not sleep till she had examined it. So, placing the candle with great caution on a chair, she seized the key with a very tremulous hand and tried to turn it; but it resisted her utmost strength. Alarmed, but not discouraged, she tried it another way; a bolt flew, and she believed herself successful; but how strangely mysterious!—the door was still immoveable. She paused a moment in breathless wonder. The wind roared down the chimney, the rain beat in torrents against the windows, and every thing seemed to speak the awfulness of her situation. To retire to bed, however, unsatisfied on such a point, would be vain, since sleep must be impossible with the consciousness of a cabinet so mysteriously closed in her immediate vicinity. Again therefore she applied herself to the key, and after moving it in every possible way for some instants with the determined celerity of hope's last effort, the door suddenly yielded to her hand: her heart leaped with exultation at such a victory, and having thrown open each folding door, the second being secured only by bolts of less wonderful construction than the lock, though in that her eye could not discern any thing unusual, a double range of small drawers appeared in view, with some larger drawers above and below them; and in the centre, a small door, closed also with a lock and key, secured in all probability a cavity of importance.

Catherine's heart beat quick, but her courage did not fail her. With a cheek flushed by hope, and an eye straining with curiosity, her fingers grasped the handle of a drawer and drew it forth. It was entirely empty. With less alarm and greater eagerness she seized a second, a third, a fourth; each was equally empty: Not one was left unsearched, and in not one was any thing found. Well read in the art of concealing a treasure, the possibility of false linings to the drawers did not escape her, and she felt round each with anxious acuteness in vain. The place in the middle alone remained now unexplored; and though she had 'never from the first had the smallest idea of finding any thing in any part of the cabinet, and was not in the least disappointed at her ill success thus far, it would be foolish not to examine it thoroughly while she was about it.' It was some time however before she could unfasten the door, the same difficulty occurring in the management of this inner lock as of the outer; but at length it did open; and not vain, as hitherto, was her search; her quick eyes directly fell on a roll of paper pushed back into the further part of the cavity, apparently for concealment, and her feelings at that moment were indescribable. Her heart fluttered, her knees trembled, and her cheeks grew pale. She seized, with an unsteady hand, the precious manuscript, for half a glance sufficed to ascertain written characters; and while she acknowledged with awful sensations this striking exemplification of what Henry had foretold, resolved instantly to peruse every line before she attempted to rest.'⁕

The dimness of the light her candle emitted made her turn to it with alarm; but there was no danger of its sudden extinction, it had yet some hours to burn; and that she might not have any greater difficulty in distinguishing the writing than what its ancient date might occasion, she hastily snuffed it. Alas! it was snuffed and extinguished in one. A lamp could not have expired with more awful effect. Catherine, for a few moments, was motionless with horror. It was done completely; not a remnant of light in the wick could give hope to the rekindling breath. Darkness impenetrable and immoveable filled the room.⁎ A violent gust of wind, rising with sudden fury, added fresh horror to the moment. Catherine trembled from head to foot. In the pause which succeeded, a sound like receding footsteps and the closing of a distant door struck on her affrighted ear. Human nature could support no more. A cold sweat stood on her forehead, the manuscript fell from her hand, and groping her way to the bed, she jumped hastily in, and sought some suspension of agony by creeping far underneath the clothes. To close her eyes in sleep that night, she felt must be entirely out of the question. With a curiosity so justly awakened, and feelings in every way so agitated, repose must be absolutely impossible. The storm too abroad so dreadful!—She had not been used to feel alarm from wind, but now every blast seemed fraught with awful intelligence. The manuscript so wonderfully found, so wonderfully accomplishing the morning's prediction, how was it to be accounted for?—What could it contain?—to whom could it relate?—by what means could it have been so long concealed?—and how singularly strange that it should fall to her lot to discover it! Till she had made herself mistress of its contents, however, she could have neither repose nor comfort; and with the sun's first rays she was determined to peruse it. But many were the tedious hours which must yet intervene. She shuddered, tossed about in her bed, and envied every quiet sleeper. The storm still raged, and various were the noises, more terrific even than the wind, which struck at intervals on her startled ear. The very curtains of her bed seemed at one moment in motion, and at another the lock of her door was agitated, as if by the attempt of somebody to enter. Hollow murmurs seemed to creep along the gallery, and more than once her blood was chilled by the sound of distant moans. Hour after hour passed away, and the wearied Catherine had heard three proclaimed by all the clocks in the house, before the tempest subsided, or she unknowingly fell fast asleep.

CHAPTER VII

THE housemaid's folding back her window-shutters at eight o'clock the next day, was the sound which first roused Catherine; and she opened her eyes, wondering that they could ever have been closed, on objects of cheerfulness; her fire was already burning, and a bright morning had succeeded the tempest of the night. Instantaneously with the consciousness of existence, returned her recollection of the manuscript; and springing from the bed in the very moment of the maid's going away, she eagerly collected every scattered sheet which had burst from the roll on its falling to the ground, and flew back to enjoy the luxury of their perusal on her pillow. She now plainly saw that she must not expect a manuscript of equal length with the generality of what she had shuddered over in books, for the roll, seeming to consist entirely of small disjointed sheets, was altogether but of trifling size, and much less than she had supposed it to be at first.

Her greedy eye glanced rapidly over a page. She started at its import. Could it be possible, or did not her senses play her false?—An inventory of linen, in coarse and modern characters, seemed all that was before her! If the evidence of sight might be trusted, she held a washing-bill in her hand. She seized another sheet, and saw the same articles with little variation; a third, a fourth, and a fifth presented nothing new. Shirts, stockings, cravats and waistcoats faced her in each. Two others, penned by the same hand, marked an expenditure scarcely more interesting, in letters, hair-powder, shoestring and breeches-ball.* And the larger sheet, which had inclosed the rest, seemed by its first cramp line, 'To poultice chesnut mare,'—a farrier's bill! Such was the collection of papers, (left perhaps, as she could then suppose, by the negligence of a servant in the place whence she had taken them,) which had filled her with expectation and alarm, and robbed her of half her night's rest! She felt humbled to the dust. Could not the adventure of the chest have taught her wisdom? A corner of it catching her eye as she lay, seemed to rise up in judgment against her. Nothing could now be clearer than the absurdity of her recent fancies. To suppose that a manuscript of many generations back could have remained undiscovered in a room such as that, so modern, so habitable!—or that she should be the first to possess the skill of unlocking a cabinet, the key of which was open to all!

How could she have so imposed on herself?—Heaven forbid that Henry Tilney should ever know her folly! And it was in a great measure his own doing, for had not the cabinet appeared so exactly to agree with his description of her adventures, she should never have felt the smallest curiosity about it. This was the only comfort that occurred. Impatient to get rid of those hateful evidences of her folly, those detestable papers then scattered over the bed, she rose directly, and folding them up as nearly as possible in the same shape as before, returned them to the same spot within the cabinet, with a very hearty wish that no untoward accident might ever bring them forward again, to disgrace her even with herself.

Why the locks should have been so difficult to open however, was still something remarkable, for she could now manage them with perfect ease. In this there was surely something mysterious, and she indulged in the flattering suggestion for half a minute, till the possibility of the door's having been at first unlocked, and of being herself its fastener, darted into her head, and cost her another blush.

She got away as soon as she could from a room in which her conduct produced such unpleasant reflections, and found her way with all speed to the breakfast-parlour, as it had been pointed out to her by Miss Tilney the evening before. Henry was alone in it; and his immediate hope of her having been undisturbed by the tempest, with an arch reference to the character of the building they inhabited, was rather distressing. For the world would she not have her weakness suspected; and yet, unequal to an absolute falsehood, was constrained to acknowledge that the wind had kept her awake a little. 'But we have a charming morning after it,' she added, desiring to get rid of the subject; 'and storms and sleeplessness are nothing when they are over. What beautiful hyacinths!—I have just learnt to love a hyacinth.'

'And how might you learn?—By accident or argument?'

'Your sister taught me; I cannot tell how. Mrs. Allen used to take pains, year after year, to make me like them; but I never could, till I saw them the other day in Milsom-street; I am naturally indifferent about flowers.'

'But now you love a hyacinth. So much the better. You have gained a new source of enjoyment, and it is well to have as many holds upon happiness as possible. Besides, a taste for flowers is always desirable in your sex, as a means of getting you out of doors, and tempting you to more frequent exercise than you would otherwise take. And though the love of a hyacinth may be rather domestic, who can tell, the sentiment once raised, but you may in time come to love a rose?'

'But I do not want any such pursuit to get me out of doors. The pleasure of walking and breathing fresh air is enough for me, and in fine weather I am out more than half my time.—Mamma says, I am never within.'

'At any rate, however, I am pleased that you have learnt to love a hyacinth. The mere habit of learning to love is the thing; and a teachableness of disposition in a young lady is a great blessing.—Has my sister a pleasant mode of instruction?'

Catherine was saved the embarrassment of attempting an answer, by the entrance of the General, whose smiling compliments announced a happy state of mind, but whose gentle hint of sympathetic early rising did not advance her composure.

The elegance of the breakfast set forced itself on Catherine's notice when they were seated at table; and, luckily, it had been the General's choice. 'He was enchanted by her approbation of his taste, confessed it to be neat and simple, thought it right to encourage the manufacture of his country; and for his part, to his uncritical palate, the tea was as well flavoured from the clay of Staffordshire, as from that of Dresden or Sève. But this was quite an old set, purchased two years ago. The manufacture was much improved since that time; he had seen some beautiful specimens when last in town, and had he not been perfectly without vanity of that kind, might have been tempted to order a new set. He trusted, however, that an opportunity might ere long occur of selecting one—though not for himself.'* Catherine was probably the only one of the party who did not understand him.

Shortly after breakfast Henry left them for Woodston, where business required and would keep him two or three days. They all attended in the hall to see him mount his horse, and immediately on re-entering the breakfast room, Catherine walked to a window in the hope of catching another glimpse of his figure. 'This is a somewhat heavy call upon your brother's fortitude,' observed the General to Eleanor. 'Woodston will make but a sombre appearance to-day.'

'Is it a pretty place?' asked Catherine.

'What say you, Eleanor?—speak your opinion, for ladies can best tell the taste of ladies in regard to places as well as men. I think it would be acknowledged by the most impartial eye to have many recommendations. The house stands among fine meadows facing the south-east, with an excellent kitchen-garden in the same aspect; the walls surrounding which I built and stocked myself about ten years ago, for the benefit of my son. It is a family living, Miss Morland; and the property in the place being chiefly my own, you may believe I take care that it shall not be a bad one. Did Henry's income depend solely on this living, he would not be ill provided for. Perhaps it may seem odd, that with only two younger children, I should think any profession necessary for him; and certainly there are moments when we could all wish him disengaged from every tie of business. But though I may not exactly make converts of you young ladies, I am sure your father, Miss Morland, would agree with me in thinking it expedient to give every young man some employment. The money is nothing, it is not an object, but employment is the thing. Even Frederick, my eldest son, you see, who will perhaps inherit as considerable a landed property as any private man in the country, has his profession.'

The imposing effect of this last argument was equal to his wishes. The silence of the lady proved it to be unanswerable.

Something had been said the evening before of her being shewn over the house, and he now offered himself as her conductor; and though Catherine had hoped to explore it accompanied only by his daughter, it was a proposal of too much happiness in itself, under any circumstances, not to be gladly accepted; for she had been already eighteen hours in the Abbey, and had seen only a few of its rooms. The netting-box,* just leisurely drawn forth, was closed with joyful haste, and she was ready to attend him in a moment. 'And when they had gone over the house, he promised himself moreover the pleasure of accompanying her into the shrubberies and garden.' She curtsied her acquiescence. 'But perhaps it might be more agreeable to her to make those her first object. The weather was at present favourable, and at this time of year the uncertainty was very great of its continuing so.—Which would she prefer? He was equally at her service.—Which did his daughter think would most accord with her fair friend's wishes?—But he thought he could discern.—Yes, he certainly read in Miss Morland's eyes a judicious desire of making use of the present smiling weather.—But when did she judge amiss?—The Abbey would be always safe and dry.—He yielded implicitly, and would fetch his hat and attend them in a moment.' He left the room, and Catherine, with a disappointed, anxious face, began to speak of her unwillingness that he should be taking them out of doors against his own inclination, under a mistaken idea of pleasing her; but she was stopt by Miss Tilney's saying, with a little confusion, 'I believe it will be wisest to take the morning while it is so fine; and do not be uneasy on my father's account, he always walks out at this time of day.'

Catherine did not exactly know how this was to be understood. Why was Miss Tilney embarrassed? Could there be any unwillingness on the General's side to shew her over the Abbey? The proposal was his own. And was not it odd that he should *always* take his walk so early? Neither her father nor Mr. Allen did so. It was certainly very provoking. She was all impatience to see the house, and had scarcely any curiosity about the grounds. If Henry had been with them indeed!—but now she should not know what was picturesque when she saw it. Such

were her thoughts, but she kept them to herself, and put on her bonnet in patient discontent.

She was struck however, beyond her expectation, by the grandeur
of the Abbey, as she saw it for the first time from the lawn. The whole
building enclosed a large court; and two sides of the quadrangle, rich
in Gothic ornaments, stood forward for admiration. The remainder
was shut off by knolls of old trees, or luxuriant plantations, and the
steep woody hills rising behind to give it shelter, were beautiful even
in the leafless month of March. Catherine had seen nothing to compare with it; and her feelings of delight were so strong, that without
waiting for any better authority, she boldly burst forth in wonder
and praise. The General listened with assenting gratitude; and it
seemed as if his own estimation of Northanger had waited unfixed till
that hour.

The kitchen-garden was to be next admired, and he led the way to
it across a small portion of the park.

The number of acres contained in this garden was such as Catherine
could not listen to without dismay, being more than double the extent
of all Mr. Allen's, as well as her father's, including church-yard and
orchard. The walls seemed countless in number, endless in length;
a village of hot-houses seemed to arise among them, and a whole parish to be at work within the inclosure. The General was flattered by
her looks of surprize, which told him almost as plainly, as he soon
forced her to tell him in words, that she had never seen any gardens at
all equal to them before;—and he then modestly owned that, 'without
any ambition of that sort himself—without any solicitude about
it,—he did believe them to be unrivalled in the kingdom. If he had
a hobby-horse, it was *that*. He loved a garden. Though careless enough
in most matters of eating, he loved good fruit—or if he did not, his
friends and children did. There were great vexations however attending such a garden as his. The utmost care could not always secure the
most valuable fruits. The pinery had yielded only one hundred in the
last year.* Mr. Allen, he supposed, must feel these inconveniences as
well as himself.'

'No, not at all. Mr. Allen did not care about the garden, and never
went into it.'

With a triumphant smile of self-satisfaction, the General wished
he could do the same, for he never entered his, without being vexed in
some way or other, by its falling short of his plan.

'How were Mr. Allen's succession-houses worked?' describing the nature of his own as they entered them.*

'Mr. Allen had only one small hot-house, which Mrs. Allen had the use of for her plants in winter, and there was a fire in it now and then.'

'He is a happy man!' said the General, with a look of very happy contempt.

Having taken her into every division, and led her under every wall, till she was heartily weary of seeing and wondering, he suffered the girls at last to seize the advantage of an outer door, then expressing his wish to examine the effect of some recent alterations about the tea-house, proposed it as no unpleasant extension of their walk, if Miss Morland were not tired. 'But where are you going, Eleanor?— Why do you chuse that cold, damp path to it? Miss Morland will get wet. Our best way is across the park.'

'This is so favourite a walk of mine,' said Miss Tilney, 'that I always think it the best and nearest way. But perhaps it may be damp.'

It was a narrow winding path through a thick grove of old Scotch firs; and Catherine, struck by its gloomy aspect, and eager to enter it, could not, even by the General's disapprobation, be kept from stepping forward. He perceived her inclination, and having again urged the plea of health in vain, was too polite to make further opposition. He excused himself however from attending them:—'The rays of the sun were not too cheerful for him, and he would meet them by another course.' He turned away; and Catherine was shocked to find how much her spirits were relieved by the separation. The shock however being less real than the relief, offered it no injury; and she began to talk with easy gaiety of the delightful melancholy which such a grove inspired.

'I am particularly fond of this spot,' said her companion, with a sigh. 'It was my mother's favourite walk.'

Catherine had never heard Mrs. Tilney mentioned in the family before, and the interest excited by this tender remembrance, shewed itself directly in her altered countenance, and in the attentive pause with which she waited for something more.

'I used to walk here so often with her!' added Eleanor; 'though I never loved it then, as I have loved it since. At that time indeed I used to wonder at her choice. But her memory endears it now.'

'And ought it not,' reflected Catherine, 'to endear it to her husband? Yet the General would not enter it.' Miss Tilney continuing silent, she ventured to say, 'Her death must have been a great affliction!'

'A great and increasing one,' replied the other, in a low voice. 'I was only thirteen when it happened; and though I felt my loss perhaps as strongly as one so young could feel it, I did not, I could not then know what a loss it was.' She stopped for a moment, and then added, with great firmness, 'I have no sister, you know—and though Henry—though my brothers are very affectionate, and Henry is a great deal here, which I am most thankful for, it is impossible for me not to be often solitary.'

'To be sure you must miss him very much.'

'A mother would have been always present. A mother would have been a constant friend; her influence would have been beyond all other.'

'Was she a very charming woman? Was she handsome? Was there any picture of her in the Abbey? And why had she been so partial to that grove? Was it from dejection of spirits?'—were questions now eagerly poured forth;—the first three received a ready affirmative, the two others were passed by; and Catherine's interest in the deceased Mrs. Tilney augmented with every question, whether answered or not. Of her unhappiness in marriage, she felt persuaded. The General certainly had been an unkind husband. He did not love her walk:—could he therefore have loved her? And besides, handsome as he was, there was a something in the turn of his features which spoke his not having behaved well to her.

'Her picture, I suppose,' blushing at the consummate art of her own question, 'hangs in your father's room?'

'No;—it was intended for the drawing-room; but my father was dissatisfied with the painting, and for some time it had no place. Soon after her death I obtained it for my own, and hung it in my bed-chamber—where I shall be happy to shew it you;—it is very like.'—Here was another proof. A portrait—very like—of a departed wife, not valued by the husband!—He must have been dreadfully cruel to her!

Catherine attempted no longer to hide from herself the nature of the feelings which, in spite of all his attentions, he had previously excited; and what had been terror and dislike before, was now absolute aversion. Yes, aversion! His cruelty to such a charming woman made him odious to her. She had often read of such characters; characters, which Mr. Allen had been used to call unnatural and over-drawn; but here was proof positive of the contrary.

She had just settled this point, when the end of the path brought them directly upon the General; and in spite of all her virtuous indignation, she found herself again obliged to walk with him, listen to him, and even to smile when he smiled. Being no longer able however to receive pleasure from the surrounding objects, she soon began to walk with lassitude; the General perceived it, and with a concern for her health, which seemed to reproach her for her opinion of him, was most urgent for returning with his daughter to the house. He would follow them in a quarter of an hour. Again they parted—but Eleanor was called back in half a minute to receive a strict charge against taking her friend round the Abbey till his return. This second instance of his anxiety to delay what she so much wished for, struck Catherine as very remarkable.

CHAPTER VIII

An hour passed away before the General came in, spent, on the part of his young guest, in no very favourable consideration of his character.—'This lengthened absence, these solitary rambles, did not speak a mind at ease, or a conscience void of reproach.'—At length he appeared; and, whatever might have been the gloom of his meditations, he could still smile with *them*. Miss Tilney, understanding in part her friend's curiosity to see the house, soon revived the subject; and her father being, contrary to Catherine's expectations, unprovided with any pretence for further delay, beyond that of stopping five minutes to order refreshments to be in the room by their return, was at last ready to escort them.

They set forward; and, with a grandeur of air, a dignified step, which caught the eye, but could not shake the doubts of the well-read Catherine, he led the way across the hall, through the common drawing-room and one useless anti-chamber,* into a room magnificent both in size and furniture—the real drawing-room, used only with company of consequence.—It was very noble—very grand—very charming!—was all that Catherine had to say, for her indiscriminating eye scarcely discerned the colour of the satin;* and all minuteness of praise, all praise that had much meaning, was supplied by the General: the costliness or elegance of any room's fitting-up could be nothing to her; she cared for no furniture of a more modern date than

the fifteenth century. When the General had satisfied his own curiosity, in a close examination of every well-known ornament, they proceeded into the library, an apartment, in its way, of equal magnificence,
exhibiting a collection of books, on which an humble man might have
looked with pride.—Catherine heard, admired, and wondered with
more genuine feeling than before—gathered all that she could from
this storehouse of knowledge, by running over the titles of half a shelf,
and was ready to proceed. But suites of apartments did not spring up
with her wishes.—Large as was the building, she had already visited
the greatest part; though, on being told that, with the addition of the
kitchen, the six or seven rooms she had now seen surrounded three
sides of the court, she could scarcely believe it, or overcome the suspicion of there being many chambers secreted. It was some relief, however, that they were to return to the rooms in common use, by passing
through a few of less importance, looking into the court, which, with
occasional passages, not wholly unintricate, connected the different
sides;—and she was further soothed in her progress, by being told,
that she was treading what had once been a cloister, having traces of
cells pointed out, and observing several doors, that were neither
opened nor explained to her;—by finding herself successively in
a billiard-room, and in the General's private apartment, without comprehending their connexion, or being able to turn aright when she left
them; and lastly, by passing through a dark little room, owning Henry's
authority, and strewed with his litter of books, guns and great coats.

From the dining-room of which, though already seen, and always
to be seen at five o'clock, the General could not forego the pleasure
of pacing out the length, for the more certain information of
Miss Morland, as to what she neither doubted nor cared for, they
proceeded by quick communication to the kitchen—the ancient
kitchen of the convent, rich in the massy walls and smoke of former
days, and in the stoves and hot closets of the present. The General's
improving hand had not loitered here: every modern invention to
facilitate the labour of the cooks, had been adopted within this, their
spacious theatre; and, when the genius of others had failed, his own
had often produced the perfection wanted. His endowments of this
spot alone might at any time have placed him high among the bene-
factors of the convent.

With the walls of the kitchen ended all the antiquity of the Abbey;
the fourth side of the quadrangle having, on account of its decaying

state, been removed by the General's father, and the present erected
in its place. All that was venerable ceased here. The new building was
not only new, but declared itself to be so; intended only for offices,*
and enclosed behind by stable-yards, no uniformity of architecture
had been thought necessary. Catherine could have raved at the hand
which had swept away what must have been beyond the value of all
the rest, for the purposes of mere domestic economy; and would willingly have been spared the mortification of a walk through scenes so
fallen, had the General allowed it; but if he had a vanity, it was in the
arrangement of his offices; and as he was convinced, that, to a mind
like Miss Morland's, a view of the accommodations and comforts,
by which the labours of her inferiors were softened, must always be
gratifying, he should make no apology for leading her on. They took
a slight survey of all; and Catherine was impressed, beyond her
expectation, by their multiplicity and their convenience. The purposes for which a few shapeless pantries and a comfortless scullery
were deemed sufficient at Fullerton, were here carried on in appropriate divisions, commodious and roomy. The number of servants
continually appearing, did not strike her less than the number of their
offices. Wherever they went, some pattened girl stopped to curtsey, or
some footman in dishabille sneaked off.* Yet this was an Abbey!—How
inexpressibly different in these domestic arrangements from such as
she had read about—from abbeys and castles, in which, though certainly larger than Northanger, all the dirty work of the house was to
be done by two pair of female hands at the utmost. How they could
get through it all, had often amazed Mrs. Allen; and, when Catherine
saw what was necessary here, she began to be amazed herself.

   They returned to the hall, that the chief stair-case might be
ascended, and the beauty of its wood, and ornaments of rich carving
might be pointed out: having gained the top, they turned in an opposite direction from the gallery in which her room lay, and shortly
entered one on the same plan, but superior in length and breadth.
She was here shewn successively into three large bed-chambers, with
their dressing-rooms, most completely and handsomely fitted up;
every thing that money and taste could do, to give comfort and elegance to apartments, had been bestowed on these; and, being furnished within the last five years, they were perfect in all that would be
generally pleasing, and wanting in all that could give pleasure to
Catherine. As they were surveying the last, the General, after slightly

naming a few of the distinguished characters, by whom they had at times been honoured, turned with a smiling countenance to Catherine, and ventured to hope, that henceforward some of their earliest tenants might be 'our friends from Fullerton.' She felt the unexpected compliment, and deeply regretted the impossibility of thinking well of a man so kindly disposed towards herself, and so full of civility to all her family.

The gallery was terminated by folding doors, which Miss Tilney, advancing, had thrown open, and passed through, and seemed on the point of doing the same by the first door to the left, in another long reach of gallery, when the General, coming forwards, called her hastily, and, as Catherine thought, rather angrily back, demanding whither she were going?—And what was there more to be seen?—Had not Miss Morland already seen all that could be worth her notice?—And did she not suppose her friend might be glad of some refreshment after so much exercise? Miss Tilney drew back directly, and the heavy doors were closed upon the mortified Catherine, who, having seen, in a momentary glance beyond them, a narrower passage, more numerous openings, and symptoms of a winding stair-case, believed herself at last within the reach of something worth her notice; and felt, as she unwillingly paced back the gallery, that she would rather be allowed to examine that end of the house, than see all the finery of all the rest.—The General's evident desire of preventing such an examination was an additional stimulant. Something was certainly to be concealed; her fancy, though it had trespassed lately once or twice, could not mislead her here; and what that something was, a short sentence of Miss Tilney's, as they followed the General at some distance down stairs, seemed to point out:—'I was going to take you into what was my mother's room—the room in which she died——' were all her words; but few as they were, they conveyed pages of intelligence to Catherine. It was no wonder that the General should shrink from the sight of such objects as that room must contain; a room in all probability never entered by him since the dreadful scene had passed, which released his suffering wife, and left him to the stings of conscience.

She ventured, when next alone with Eleanor, to express her wish of being permitted to see it, as well as all the rest of that side of the house; and Eleanor promised to attend her there, whenever they should have a convenient hour. Catherine understood her:—the

General must be watched from home, before that room could be entered. 'It remains as it was, I suppose?' said she, in a tone of feeling.

'Yes, entirely.'

'And how long ago may it be that your mother died?'

'She has been dead these nine years.' And nine years, Catherine knew was a trifle of time, compared with what generally elapsed after the death of an injured wife, before her room was put to rights.

'You were with her, I suppose, to the last?'

'No,' said Miss Tilney, sighing; 'I was unfortunately from home.—— Her illness was sudden and short; and, before I arrived it was all over.'

Catherine's blood ran cold with the horrid suggestions which naturally sprang from these words. Could it be possible?—Could Henry's father?——And yet how many were the examples to justify even the blackest suspicions!—And, when she saw him in the evening, while she worked with her friend,* slowly pacing the drawing-room for an hour together in silent thoughtfulness, with downcast eyes and contracted brow, she felt secure from all possibility of wronging him. It was the air and attitude of a Montoni!*—What could more plainly speak the gloomy workings of a mind not wholly dead to every sense of humanity, in its fearful review of past scenes of guilt? Unhappy man!—And the anxiousness of her spirits directed her eyes towards his figure so repeatedly, as to catch Miss Tilney's notice. 'My father,' she whispered, 'often walks about the room in this way; it is nothing unusual.'

'So much the worse!' thought Catherine; such ill-timed exercise was of a piece with the strange unseasonableness of his morning walks, and boded nothing good.

After an evening, the little variety and seeming length of which made her peculiarly sensible of Henry's importance among them, she was heartily glad to be dismissed; though it was a look from the General not designed for her observation which sent his daughter to the bell. When the butler would have lit his master's candle, however, he was forbidden. The latter was not going to retire. 'I have many pamphlets to finish,' said he to Catherine, 'before I can close my eyes; and perhaps may be poring over the affairs of the nation for hours after you are asleep. Can either of us be more meetly employed? *My* eyes will be blinding for the good of others; and *yours* preparing by rest for future mischief.'*

But neither the business alleged, nor the magnificent compliment, could win Catherine from thinking, that some very different object

must occasion so serious a delay of proper repose. To be kept up for
hours, after the family were in bed, by stupid pamphlets, was not very
likely. There must be some deeper cause: something was to be done
which could be done only while the household slept; and the probability that Mrs. Tilney yet lived, shut up for causes unknown, and
receiving from the pitiless hands of her husband a nightly supply of
coarse food, was the conclusion which necessarily followed.* Shocking
as was the idea, it was at least better than a death unfairly hastened, as,
in the natural course of things, she must ere long be released. The
suddenness of her reputed illness; the absence of her daughter, and
probably of her other children, at the time—all favoured the suppos-
ition of her imprisonment.—Its origin—jealousy perhaps, or wanton
cruelty—was yet to be unravelled.

In revolving these matters, while she undressed, it suddenly struck
her as not unlikely, that she might that morning have passed near the
very spot of this unfortunate woman's confinement—might have
been within a few paces of the cell in which she languished out her
days; for what part of the Abbey could be more fitted for the purpose
than that which yet bore the traces of monastic division? In the high-
arched passage, paved with stone, which already she had trodden with
peculiar awe, she well remembered the doors of which the General
had given no account. To what might not those doors lead? In support
of the plausibility of this conjecture, it further occurred to her, that
the forbidden gallery, in which lay the apartments of the unfortunate
Mrs. Tilney, must be, as certainly as her memory could guide her,
exactly over this suspected range of cells, and the stair-case by the
side of those apartments of which she had caught a transient glimpse,
communicating by some secret means with those cells, might well
have favoured the barbarous proceedings of her husband. Down that
stair-case she had perhaps been conveyed in a state of well-prepared
insensibility!

Catherine sometimes started at the boldness of her own surmises,
and sometimes hoped or feared that she had gone too far; but they
were supported by such appearances as made their dismissal
impossible.

The side of the quadrangle, in which she supposed the guilty scene
to be acting, being, according to her belief, just opposite her own, it
struck her that, if judiciously watched, some rays of light from the
General's lamp might glimmer through the lower windows, as he

passed to the prison of his wife; and, twice before she stepped into bed, she stole gently from her room to the corresponding window in the gallery, to see if it appeared; but all abroad was dark, and it must yet be too early. The various ascending noises convinced her that the servants must still be up. Till midnight, she supposed it would be in vain to watch; but then, when the clock had struck twelve, and all was quiet, she would, if not quite appalled by darkness, steal out and look once more. The clock struck twelve—and Catherine had been half an hour asleep.

CHAPTER IX

THE next day afforded no opportunity for the proposed examination of the mysterious apartments. It was Sunday, and the whole time between morning and afternoon service was required by the General in exercise abroad or eating cold meat at home;* and great as was Catherine's curiosity, her courage was not equal to a wish of exploring them after dinner, either by the fading light of the sky between six and seven o'clock, or by the yet more partial though stronger illumination of a treacherous lamp. The day was unmarked therefore by any thing to interest her imagination beyond the sight of a very elegant monument to the memory of Mrs. Tilney, which immediately fronted the family pew. By that her eye was instantly caught and long retained; and the perusal of the highly-strained epitaph, in which every virtue was ascribed to her by the inconsolable husband, who must have been in some way or other her destroyer, affected her even to tears.

That the General, having erected such a monument, should be able to face it, was not perhaps very strange, and yet that he could sit so boldly collected within its view, maintain so elevated an air, look so fearlessly around, nay, that he should even enter the church, seemed wonderful to Catherine. Not however that many instances of beings equally hardened in guilt might not be produced. She could remember dozens who had persevered in every possible vice, going on from crime to crime, murdering whomsoever they chose, without any feeling of humanity or remorse; till a violent death or a religious retirement closed their black career.* The erection of the monument itself could not in the smallest degree affect her doubts of Mrs. Tilney's actual decease. Were she even to descend into the family vault where her ashes were supposed to slumber, were she to behold the coffin in which they were said to be enclosed—what could it avail in such a case? Catherine had read too much not to be perfectly aware of the ease with which a waxen figure might be introduced, and a supposititious funeral carried on.*

The succeeding morning promised something better. The General's early walk, ill-timed as it was in every other view, was favourable here; and when she knew him to be out of the house, she directly proposed to Miss Tilney the accomplishment of her promise. Eleanor was ready to oblige her; and Catherine reminding her as they went of another promise, their first visit in consequence was to the portrait in her bed-chamber. It represented a very lovely woman, with a mild and pensive countenance, justifying, so far, the expectations of its new observer; but they were not in every respect answered, for Catherine had depended upon meeting with features, air, complexion that should be the very counterpart, the very image, if not of Henry's, of Eleanor's;—the only portraits of which she had been in the habit of thinking, bearing always an equal resemblance of mother and child.* A face once taken was taken for generations. But here she was obliged to look and consider and study for a likeness. She contemplated it, however, in spite of this drawback, with much emotion; and, but for a yet stronger interest, would have left it unwillingly.

Her agitation as they entered the great gallery was too much for any endeavour at discourse; she could only look at her companion. Eleanor's countenance was dejected, yet sedate; and its composure spoke her enured to all the gloomy objects to which they were advancing. Again she passed through the folding-doors, again her hand was upon the important lock, and Catherine, hardly able to breathe, was turning to close the former with fearful caution, when the figure, the dreaded figure of the General himself at the further end of the gallery, stood before her! The name of 'Eleanor' at the same moment, in his loudest tone, resounded through the building, giving to his daughter the first intimation of his presence, and to Catherine terror upon terror. An attempt at concealment had been her first instinctive movement on perceiving him, yet she could scarcely hope to have escaped his eye; and when her friend, who with an apologizing look darted hastily by her, had joined and disappeared with him, she ran for safety to her own room, and, locking herself in, believed that she should never have courage to go down again. She remained there at least an hour, in the greatest agitation, deeply commiserating the state of her poor friend, and expecting a summons herself from the angry General to attend him in his own apartment. No summons however arrived; and at last, on seeing a carriage drive up to the Abbey, she was emboldened to descend and meet him under the protection of visitors. The breakfast-room was gay with company; and she was named to them by the General, as the friend of his daughter, in a complimentary style, which so well concealed his resentful ire, as to make her feel secure at least of life for the present. And Eleanor, with a command of countenance which did honour to her concern for his character, taking an early occasion of saying to her, 'My father only wanted me to answer a note,' she began to hope that she had either been unseen by the General, or that from some consideration of policy she should be allowed to suppose herself so. Upon this trust she dared still to remain in his presence, after the company left them, and nothing occurred to disturb it.

In the course of this morning's reflections, she came to a resolution of making her next attempt on the forbidden door alone. It would be much better in every respect that Eleanor should know nothing of the matter. To involve her in the danger of a second detection, to court her into an apartment which must wring her heart, could not be the office of a friend. The General's utmost anger could not be to herself what it might be to a daughter; and, besides, she thought the examination itself would be more satisfactory if made without any companion. It would be impossible to explain to Eleanor the suspicions, from which the other had, in all likelihood, been hitherto happily exempt; nor could she therefore, in *her* presence, search for those proofs of the General's cruelty, which however they might yet have escaped discovery, she felt confident of somewhere drawing forth, in the shape of some fragmented journal, continued to the last gasp. Of the way to the apartment she was now perfectly mistress; and as she wished to get it over before Henry's return, who was expected on the morrow, there was no time to be lost. The day was bright, her courage high; at four o'clock, the sun was now two hours above the horizon, and it would be only her retiring to dress half an hour earlier than usual.

It was done; and Catherine found herself alone in the gallery before the clocks had ceased to strike. It was no time for thought; she hurried on, slipped with the least possible noise through the folding doors,

and without stopping to look or breathe, rushed forward to the one in
question. The lock yielded to her hand, and, luckily, with no sullen
sound that could alarm a human being. On tip-toe she entered; the
room was before her; but it was some minutes before she could
advance another step. She beheld what fixed her to the spot and agitated every feature.—She saw a large, well-proportioned apartment,
an handsome dimity bed, arranged as unoccupied with an housemaid's care, a bright Bath stove,* mahogany wardrobes and neatly-
painted chairs, on which the warm beams of a western sun gaily
poured through two sash windows! Catherine had expected to have
her feelings worked, and worked they were. Astonishment and doubt
first seized them; and a shortly succeeding ray of common sense
added some bitter emotions of shame. She could not be mistaken as
to the room; but how grossly mistaken in every thing else!—in
Miss Tilney's meaning, in her own calculation! This apartment, to which
she had given a date so ancient, a position so awful, proved to be one
end of what the General's father had built. There were two other
doors in the chamber, leading probably into dressing-closets; but she
had no inclination to open either. Would the veil in which Mrs. Tilney
had last walked, or the volume in which she had last read, remain to
tell what nothing else was allowed to whisper? No: whatever might
have been the General's crimes, he had certainly too much wit to let
them sue for detection. She was sick of exploring, and desired but to
be safe in her own room, with her own heart only privy to its folly; and
she was on the point of retreating as softly as she had entered, when
the sound of footsteps, she could hardly tell where, made her pause
and tremble. To be found there, even by a servant, would be unpleasant; but by the General, (and he seemed always at hand when least
wanted,) much worse!—She listened—the sound had ceased; and
resolving not to lose a moment, she passed through and closed the
door. At that instant a door underneath was hastily opened; some one
seemed with swift steps to ascend the stairs, by the head of which she
had yet to pass before she could gain the gallery. She had no power to
move. With a feeling of terror not very definable, she fixed her eyes on
the staircase, and in a few moments it gave Henry to her view.
'Mr. Tilney!' she exclaimed in a voice of more than common astonishment. He looked astonished too. 'Good God!' she continued, not
attending to his address, 'how came you here?—how came you up
that staircase?'

'How came I up that staircase!' he replied, greatly surprised. 'Because it is my nearest way from the stable-yard to my own chamber; and why should I not come up it?'

Catherine recollected herself, blushed deeply, and could say no more. He seemed to be looking in her countenance for that explanation which her lips did not afford. She moved on towards the gallery. 'And may I not, in my turn,' said he, as he pushed back the folding doors, 'ask how *you* came here?—This passage is at least as extraordinary a road from the breakfast-parlour to your apartment, as that staircase can be from the stables to mine.'

'I have been,' said Catherine, looking down, 'to see your mother's room.'

'My mother's room!—Is there any thing extraordinary to be seen there?'

'No, nothing at all.—I thought you did not mean to come back till to-morrow.'

'I did not expect to be able to return sooner, when I went away; but three hours ago I had the pleasure of finding nothing to detain me.—You look pale.—I am afraid I alarmed you by running so fast up those stairs. Perhaps you did not know—you were not aware of their leading from the offices in common use?'

'No, I was not.—You have had a very fine day for your ride.'

'Very;—and does Eleanor leave you to find your way into all the rooms in the house by yourself?'

'Oh! no; she shewed me over the greatest part on Saturday—and we were coming here to these rooms—but only—(dropping her voice)—your father was with us.'

'And that prevented you;' said Henry, earnestly regarding her.—'Have you looked into all the rooms in that passage?'

'No, I only wanted to see——Is not it very late? I must go and dress.'

'It is only a quarter past four, (shewing his watch) and you are not now in Bath. No theatre, no rooms to prepare for. Half an hour at Northanger must be enough.'

She could not contradict it, and therefore suffered herself to be detained, though her dread of further questions made her, for the first time in their acquaintance, wish to leave him. They walked slowly up the gallery. 'Have you had any letter from Bath since I saw you?'

'No, and I am very much surprized. Isabella promised so faithfully to write directly.'

'Promised so faithfully!—A faithful promise!—That puzzles me.— I have heard of a faithful performance. But a faithful promise—the fidelity of promising! It is a power little worth knowing however, since it can deceive and pain you. My mother's room is very commodious, is it not? Large and cheerful-looking, and the dressing closets so well disposed! It always strikes me as the most comfortable apartment in the house, and I rather wonder that Eleanor should not take it for her own. She sent you to look at it, I suppose?'

'No.'

'It has been your own doing entirely?'—Catherine said nothing— After a short silence, during which he had closely observed her, he added, 'As there is nothing in the room in itself to raise curiosity, this must have proceeded from a sentiment of respect for my mother's character, as described by Eleanor, which does honour to her memory. The world, I believe, never saw a better woman. But it is not often that virtue can boast an interest such as this. The domestic, unpretending merits of a person never known, do not often create that kind of fervent, venerating tenderness which would prompt a visit like yours. Eleanor, I suppose, has talked of her a great deal?'

'Yes, a great deal. That is—no, not much, but what she did say, was very interesting. Her dying so suddenly,' (slowly, and with hesitation it was spoken,) 'and you— none of you being at home—and your father, I thought—perhaps had not been very fond of her.'

'And from these circumstances,' he replied, (his quick eye fixed on her's,) 'you infer perhaps the probability of some negligence— some—(involuntarily she shook her head)—or it may be—of something still less pardonable.' She raised her eyes towards him more fully than she had ever done before. 'My mother's illness,' he continued, 'the seizure which ended in her death *was* sudden. The malady itself, one from which she had often suffered, a bilious fever*—its cause therefore constitutional. On the third day, in short as soon as she could be prevailed on, a physician attended her, a very respectable man, and one in whom she had always placed great confidence. Upon his opinion of her danger, two others were called in the next day, and remained in almost constant attendance for four-and-twenty hours. On the fifth day she died. During the progress of her disorder, Frederick and I (*we* were both at home) saw her repeatedly; and from our own observation can bear witness to her having received every possible attention which could spring from the affection of those about her, or which her situation in life could command. Poor Eleanor *was* absent, and at such a distance as to return, only to see her mother in her coffin.'

'But your father,' said Catherine, 'was *he* afflicted?'

'For a time, greatly so. You have erred in supposing him not attached to her. He loved her, I am persuaded, as well as it was possible for him to—We have not all, you know, the same tenderness of disposition—and I will not pretend to say that while she lived, she might not often have had much to bear, but though his temper injured her, his judgment never did. His value of her was sincere; and, if not permanently, he was truly afflicted by her death.'

'I am very glad of it,' said Catherine, 'it would have been very shocking!'——

'If I understand you rightly, you had formed a surmise of such horror as I have hardly words to——Dear Miss Morland, consider the dreadful nature of the suspicions you have entertained. What have you been judging from? Remember the country and the age in which we live. Remember that we are English, that we are Christians. Consult your own understanding, your own sense of the probable, your own observation of what is passing around you—Does our education prepare us for such atrocities? Do our laws connive at them? Could they be perpetrated without being known, in a country like this, where social and literary intercourse is on such a footing; where every man is surrounded by a neighbourhood of voluntary spies, and where roads and newspapers lay every thing open?* Dearest Miss Morland, what ideas have you been admitting?'

They had reached the end of the gallery; and with tears of shame she ran off to her own room.

CHAPTER X

THE visions of romance were over. Catherine was completely awakened. Henry's address, short as it had been, had more thoroughly opened her eyes to the extravagance of her late fancies than all their several disappointments had done. Most grievously was she humbled. Most bitterly did she cry. It was not only with herself that she was sunk—but with Henry. Her folly, which now seemed even criminal, was all exposed to him, and he must despise her for ever. The liberty which her imagination had dared to take with the character of his father, could he ever forgive it? The absurdity of her curiosity and her fears, could they ever be forgotten? She hated herself more than she could express. He had—she thought he had, once or twice before this fatal morning, shewn something like affection for her.—But now—in short, she made herself as miserable as possible for about half an hour, went down when the clock struck five, with a broken heart, and could scarcely give intelligible answer to Eleanor's inquiry, if she was well. The formidable Henry soon followed her into the room, and the only difference in his behaviour to her, was that he paid her rather more attention than usual. Catherine had never wanted comfort more, and he looked as if he was aware of it.

The evening wore away with no abatement of this soothing politeness; and her spirits were gradually raised to a modest tranquillity. She did not learn either to forget or defend the past; but she learned to hope that it would never transpire farther, and that it might not cost her Henry's entire regard. Her thoughts being still chiefly fixed on what she had with such causeless terror felt and done, nothing could shortly be clearer, than that it had been all a voluntary, self-created delusion, each trifling circumstance receiving importance from an imagination resolved on alarm, and every thing forced to bend to one purpose by a mind which, before she entered the Abbey, had been craving to be frightened. She remembered with what feelings she had prepared for a knowledge of Northanger. She saw that the infatuation had been created, the mischief settled long before her quitting Bath, and it seemed as if the whole might be traced to the influence of that sort of reading which she had there indulged.

Charming as were all Mrs. Radcliffe's works, and charming even as were the works of all her imitators, it was not in them perhaps that human nature, at least in the midland counties of England, was to be looked for. Of the Alps and Pyrenees, with their pine forests and their vices, they might give a faithful delineation; and Italy, Switzerland, and the South of France, might be as fruitful in horrors as they were there represented. Catherine dared not doubt beyond her own country, and even of that, if hard pressed, would have yielded the northern and western extremities. But in the central part of England there was surely some security for the existence even of a wife not beloved, in the laws of the land, and the manners of the age. Murder was not tolerated, servants were not slaves, and neither poison nor sleeping potions to be procured, like rhubarb, from every druggist. Among the Alps and Pyrenees, perhaps, there were no mixed characters.* There, such as were not as spotless as an angel, might have the dispositions of a fiend. But in England it was not so; among the English, she believed, in their hearts and habits, there was a general though unequal mixture of good and bad. Upon this conviction, she would not be surprized if even in Henry and Eleanor Tilney, some slight imperfection might hereafter appear; and upon this conviction she need not fear to acknowledge some actual specks in the character of their father, who, though cleared from the grossly injurious suspicions which she must ever blush to have entertained, she did believe, upon serious consideration, to be not perfectly amiable.

Her mind made up on these several points, and her resolution formed, of always judging and acting in future with the greatest good sense, she had nothing to do but to forgive herself and be happier than ever; and the lenient hand of time did much for her by insensible gradations in the course of another day. Henry's astonishing generosity and nobleness of conduct, in never alluding in the slightest way to what had passed, was of the greatest assistance to her; and sooner than she could have supposed it possible in the beginning of her distress, her spirits became absolutely comfortable, and capable, as heretofore, of continual improvement by any thing he said. There were still some subjects indeed, under which she believed they must always tremble;—the mention of a chest or a cabinet, for instance—and she did not love the sight of japan in any shape: but even *she* could allow, that an occasional memento of past folly, however painful, might not be without use.

The anxieties of common life began soon to succeed to the alarms of romance. Her desire of hearing from Isabella grew every day greater. She was quite impatient to know how the Bath world went on, and how the Rooms were attended; and especially was she anxious to be assured of Isabella's having matched some fine netting-cotton, on which she had left her intent; and of her continuing on the best terms with James. Her only dependence for information of any kind was on Isabella. James had protested against writing to her till his return to Oxford; and Mrs. Allen had given her no hopes of a letter till she had got back to Fullerton.—But Isabella had promised and promised

again; and when she promised a thing, she was so scrupulous in per-
forming it! this made it so particularly strange!

For nine successive mornings, Catherine wondered over the repetition
of a disappointment, which each morning became more severe: but, on
the tenth, when she entered the breakfast-room, her first object was a letter, held out by Henry's willing hand. She thanked him as heartily as if he
had written it himself. ''Tis only from James, however,' as she looked at
the direction. She opened it; it was from Oxford; and to this purpose:—

'Dear Catherine,

Though, God knows, with little inclination for writing, I think it
my duty to tell you, that every thing is at an end between Miss Thorpe
and me.—I left her and Bath yesterday, never to see either again.
I shall not enter into particulars, they would only pain you more. You
will soon hear enough from another quarter to know where lies the
blame; and I hope will acquit your brother of every thing but the folly
of too easily thinking his affection returned. Thank God! I am unde-
ceived in time! But it is a heavy blow!—After my father's consent had
been so kindly given—but no more of this. She has made me miserable for ever! Let me soon hear from you, dear Catherine; you are my
only friend; *your* love I do build upon. I wish your visit at Northanger
may be over before Captain Tilney makes his engagement known, or
you will be uncomfortably circumstanced.—Poor Thorpe is in town:
I dread the sight of him; his honest heart would feel so much. I have
written to him and my father. Her duplicity hurts me more than all;
till the very last, if I reasoned with her, she declared herself as much
attached to me as ever, and laughed at my fears. I am ashamed to think
how long I bore with it; but if ever man had reason to believe himself
loved, I was that man. I cannot understand even now what she would
be at, for there could be no need of my being played off to make her
secure of Tilney. We parted at last by mutual consent—happy for me
had we never met! I can never expect to know such another woman!
Dearest Catherine, beware how you give your heart.

Believe me,' &c.

Catherine had not read three lines before her sudden change of
countenance, and short exclamations of sorrowing wonder, declared
her to be receiving unpleasant news; and Henry, earnestly watching
her through the whole letter, saw plainly that it ended no better than

it began. He was prevented, however, from even looking his surprize by his father's entrance. They went to breakfast directly; but Catherine could hardly eat any thing. Tears filled her eyes, and even ran down her cheeks as she sat. The letter was one moment in her hand, then in her lap, and then in her pocket; and she looked as if she knew not what she did. The General, between his cocoa and his newspaper, had luckily no leisure for noticing her; but to the other two her distress was equally visible. As soon as she dared leave the table she hurried away to her own room; but the house-maids were busy in it, and she was obliged to come down again. She turned into the drawing-room for privacy, but Henry and Eleanor had likewise retreated thither, and were at that moment deep in consultation about her. She drew back, trying to beg their pardon, but was, with gentle violence, forced to return; and the others withdrew, after Eleanor had affectionately expressed a wish of being of use or comfort to her.

After half an hour's free indulgence of grief and reflection, Catherine felt equal to encountering her friends; but whether she should make her distress known to them was another consideration. Perhaps, if particularly questioned, she might just give an idea—just distantly hint at it—but not more. To expose a friend, such a friend as Isabella had been to her—and then their own brother so closely concerned in it!—She believed she must wave the subject altogether. Henry and Eleanor were by themselves in the breakfast-room; and each, as she entered it, looked at her anxiously. Catherine took her place at the table, and, after a short silence, Eleanor said, 'No bad news from Fullerton, I hope? Mr. and Mrs. Morland—your brothers and sisters—I hope they are none of them ill?'

'No, I thank you,' (sighing as she spoke,) 'they are all very well. My letter was from my brother at Oxford.'

Nothing further was said for a few minutes; and then speaking through her tears, she added, 'I do not think I shall ever wish for a letter again!'

'I am sorry,' said Henry, closing the book he had just opened; 'if I had suspected the letter of containing any thing unwelcome, I should have given it with very different feelings.'

'It contained something worse than any body could suppose!—Poor James is so unhappy!—You will soon know why.'

'To have so kind-hearted, so affectionate a sister,' replied Henry, warmly, 'must be a comfort to him under any distress.'

'I have one favour to beg,' said Catherine, shortly afterwards, in an agitated manner, 'that, if your brother should be coming here, you will give me notice of it, that I may go away.'

'Our brother!—Frederick!'

'Yes; I am sure I should be very sorry to leave you so soon, but something has happened that would make it very dreadful for me to be in the same house with Captain Tilney.'

Eleanor's work was suspended while she gazed with increasing astonishment; but Henry began to suspect the truth, and something, in which Miss Thorpe's name was included, passed his lips.

'How quick you are!' cried Catherine: 'you have guessed it, I declare!— And yet, when we talked about it in Bath, you little thought of its ending so. Isabella—no wonder *now* I have not heard from her— Isabella has deserted my brother, and is to marry your's! Could you have believed there had been such inconstancy and fickleness, and every thing that is bad in the world?'

'I hope, so far as concerns my brother, you are mis-informed. I hope he has not had any material share in bringing on Mr. Morland's dis- appointment. His marrying Miss Thorpe is not probable. I think you must be deceived so far. I am very sorry for Mr. Morland—sorry that any one you love should be unhappy; but my surprize would be greater at Frederick's marrying her, than at any other part of the story.'

'It is very true, however; you shall read James's letter yourself.— Stay——there is one part——' recollecting with a blush the last line.

'Will you take the trouble of reading to us the passages which con- cern my brother?'

'No, read it yourself,' cried Catherine, whose second thoughts were clearer. 'I do not know what I was thinking of,' (blushing again that she had blushed before,)—'James only means to give me good advice.'

He gladly received the letter; and, having read it through, with close attention, returned it saying, 'Well, if it is to be so, I can only say that I am sorry for it. Frederick will not be the first man who has chosen a wife with less sense than his family expected. I do not envy his situation, either as a lover or a son.'

Miss Tilney, at Catherine's invitation, now read the letter likewise; and, having expressed also her concern and surprize, began to inquire into Miss Thorpe's connexions and fortune.

'Her mother is a very good sort of woman,' was Catherine's answer.

'What was her father?'

'A lawyer, I believe.—They live at Putney.'

'Are they a wealthy family?'

'No, not very. I do not believe Isabella has any fortune at all: but that will not signify in your family —Your father is so very liberal! He told me the other day, that he only valued money as it allowed him to promote the happiness of his children.' The brother and sister looked at each other. 'But,' said Eleanor, after a short pause, 'would it be to promote his happiness, to enable him to marry such a girl?—She must be an unprincipled one, or she could not have used your brother so.—And how strange an infatuation on Frederick's side! A girl who, before his eyes, is violating an engagement voluntarily entered into with another man! Is not it inconceivable, Henry? Frederick too, who always wore his heart so proudly! who found no woman good enough to be loved!'

'That is the most unpromising circumstance, the strongest presumption against him. When I think of his past declarations, I give him up.—Moreover, I have too good an opinion of Miss Thorpe's prudence, to suppose that she would part with one gentleman before the other was secured. It is all over with Frederick indeed! He is a deceased man—defunct in understanding. Prepare for your sister-in-law, Eleanor, and such a sister-in-law as you must delight in!—Open, candid, artless, guileless, with affections strong but simple, forming no pretensions, and knowing no disguise.'

'Such a sister-in-law, Henry, I should delight in,' said Eleanor, with a smile.

'But perhaps,' observed Catherine, 'though she has behaved so ill by our family, she may behave better by your's. Now she has really got the man she likes, she may be constant.'

'Indeed I am afraid she will,' replied Henry; 'I am afraid she will be very constant, unless a baronet should come in her way; that is Frederick's only chance.—I will get the Bath paper, and look over the arrivals.'*

'You think it is all for ambition then?—And, upon my word, there are some things that seem very like it. I cannot forget, that, when she first knew what my father would do for them, she seemed quite disappointed that it was not more. I never was so deceived in any one's character in my life before.'

'Among all the great variety that you have known and studied.'

'My own disappointment and loss in her is very great; but, as for poor James, I suppose he will hardly ever recover it.'

'Your brother is certainly very much to be pitied at present; but we must not, in our concern for his sufferings, undervalue your's. You feel, I suppose, that, in losing Isabella, you lose half yourself: you feel a void in your heart which nothing else can occupy. Society is becoming irksome; and as for the amusements in which you were wont to share at Bath, the very idea of them without her is abhorrent. You would not, for instance, now go to a ball for the world. You feel that you have no longer any friend to whom you can speak with unreserve; on whose regard you can place dependence; or whose counsel, in any difficulty, you could rely on. You feel all this?'

'No,' said Catherine, after a few moments' reflection, 'I do not— ought I? To say the truth, though I am hurt and grieved, that I cannot still love her, that I am never to hear from her, perhaps never to see her again, I do not feel so very, very much afflicted as one would have thought.'

'You feel, as you always do, what is most to the credit of human nature.—Such feelings ought to be investigated, that they may know themselves.'

Catherine, by some chance or other, found her spirits so very much relieved by this conversation, that she could not regret her being led on, though so unaccountably, to mention the circumstance which had produced it.

CHAPTER XI

FROM this time, the subject was frequently canvassed by the three young people; and Catherine found, with some surprize, that her two young friends were perfectly agreed in considering Isabella's want of consequence and fortune as likely to throw great difficulties in the way of her marrying their brother. Their persuasion that the General would, upon this ground alone, independent of the objection that might be raised against her character, oppose the connexion, turned her feelings moreover with some alarm towards herself. She was as insignificant, and perhaps as portionless as Isabella; and if the heir of the Tilney property had not grandeur and wealth enough in himself, at what point of interest were the demands of his younger brother to rest? The very painful reflections to which this thought led, could only be dispersed by a dependence on the effect of that particular partiality, which, as she was given to understand by his words as well as his actions, she had from the first been so fortunate as to excite in the General; and by a recollection of some most generous and disinterested sentiments on the subject of money, which she had more than once heard him utter, and which tempted her to think his disposition in such matters misunderstood by his children.

They were so fully convinced, however, that their brother would not have the courage to apply in person for his father's consent, and so repeatedly assured her that he had never in his life been less likely to come to Northanger than at the present time, that she suffered her mind to be at ease as to the necessity of any sudden removal of her own. But as it was not to be supposed that Captain Tilney, whenever he made his application, would give his father any just idea of Isabella's conduct, it occurred to her as highly expedient that Henry should lay the whole business before him as it really was, enabling the General by that means to form a cool and impartial opinion, and prepare his objections on a fairer ground than inequality of situations. She proposed it to him accordingly; but he did not catch at the measure so eagerly as she had expected. 'No,' said he, 'my father's hands need not be strengthened, and Frederick's confession of folly need not be forestalled. He must tell his own story.'

'But he will tell only half of it.'

'A quarter would be enough.'

A day or two passed away and brought no tidings of Captain Tilney. His brother and sister knew not what to think. Sometimes it appeared to them as if his silence would be the natural result of the suspected engagement, and at others that it was wholly incompatible with it. The General, meanwhile, though offended every morning by Frederick's remissness in writing, was free from any real anxiety about him; and had no more pressing solicitude than that of making Miss Morland's time at Northanger pass pleasantly. He often expressed his uneasiness on this head, 'feared the sameness of every day's society and employments would disgust her with the place, wished the Lady Frasers had been in the country, talked every now and then of having a large party to dinner, and once or twice began even to calculate the number of young dancing people in the neighbourhood. But then it was such a dead time of year, no wild-fowl, no game, and the Lady Frasers were not in the country.' And it all ended, at last, in his telling Henry one morning, that when he next went to

Woodston, they would take him by surprize there some day or other, and eat their mutton with him. Henry was greatly honoured and very happy, and Catherine was quite delighted with the scheme. 'And when do you think, sir, I may look forward to this pleasure?—I must be at Woodston on Monday to attend the parish meeting, and shall probably be obliged to stay two or three days.'

'Well, well, we will take our chance some one of those days. There is no need to fix. You are not to put yourself at all out of your way. Whatever you may happen to have in the house will be enough. I think I can answer for the young ladies making allowance for a bachelor's table. Let me see; Monday will be a busy day with you, we will not come on Monday; and Tuesday will be a busy one with me. I expect my surveyor from Brockham* with his report in the morning; and afterwards I cannot in decency fail attending the club. I really could not face my acquaintance if I staid away now; for, as I am known to be in the country, it would be taken exceedingly amiss; and it is a rule with me, Miss Morland, never to give offence to any of my neighbours, if a small sacrifice of time and attention can prevent it. They are a set of very worthy men. They have half a buck from Northanger twice a year; and I dine with them whenever I can. Tuesday, therefore, we may say is out of the question. But on Wednesday, I think, Henry, you may expect us; and we shall be with you early, that we may have time to look about us. Two hours and three quarters will carry us to Woodston, I suppose; we shall be in the carriage by ten; so, about a quarter before one on Wednesday, you may look for us.'

A ball itself could not have been more welcome to Catherine than this little excursion, so strong was her desire to be acquainted with Woodston; and her heart was still bounding with joy, when Henry, about an hour afterwards, came booted and great coated into the room where she and Eleanor were sitting, and said, 'I am come, young ladies, in a very moralizing strain, to observe that our pleasures in this world are always to be paid for,* and that we often purchase them at a great disadvantage, giving ready-monied actual happiness for a draft on the future, that may not be honoured. Witness myself, at this present hour. Because I am to hope for the satisfaction of seeing you at Woodston on Wednesday, which bad weather, or twenty other causes may prevent, I must go away directly, two days before I intended it.'

'Go away!' said Catherine, with a very long face; 'and why?'

'Why!—How can you ask the question?—Because no time is to be lost in frightening my old housekeeper out of her wits,—because I must go and prepare a dinner for you to be sure.'

'Oh! not seriously!'

'Aye, and sadly too—for I had much rather stay.'

'But how can you think of such a thing, after what the General said? when he so particularly desired you not to give yourself any trouble, because *any thing* would do.'

Henry only smiled. 'I am sure it is quite unnecessary upon your sister's account and mine. You must know it to be so; and the General made such a point of your providing nothing extraordinary:—besides, if he had not said half so much as he did, he has always such an excellent dinner at home, that sitting down to a middling one for one day could not signify.'

'I wish I could reason like you, for his sake and my own. Good bye. As to-morrow is Sunday, Eleanor, I shall not return.'

He went; and, it being at any time a much simpler operation to Catherine to doubt her own judgment than Henry's, she was very soon obliged to give him credit for being right, however disagreeable to her his going. But the inexplicability of the General's conduct dwelt much on her thoughts. That he was very particular in his eating, she had, by her own unassisted observation, already discovered; but why he should say one thing so positively, and mean another all the while, was most unaccountable! How were people, at that rate, to be understood? Who but Henry could have been aware of what his father was at?

From Saturday to Wednesday, however, they were now to be without Henry. This was the sad finale of every reflection:—and Captain Tilney's letter would certainly come in his absence; and Wednesday she was very sure would be wet. The past, present, and future, were all equally in gloom. Her brother so unhappy, and her loss in Isabella so great; and Eleanor's spirits always affected by Henry's absence! What was there to interest or amuse her? She was tired of the woods and the shrubberies—always so smooth and so dry; and the Abbey in itself was no more to her now than any other house. The painful remembrance of the folly it had helped to nourish and perfect, was the only emotion which could spring from a consideration of the building. What a revolution in her ideas! she, who had so longed to be in an abbey! Now, there was nothing so charming to her imagination as the unpretending comfort of a well-connected Parsonage,* something like Fullerton, but better: Fullerton had its faults, but Woodston probably had none.—If Wednesday should ever come!

It did come, and exactly when it might be reasonably looked for. It came—it was fine—and Catherine trod on air. By ten o'clock, the chaise-and-four conveyed the trio* from the Abbey; and, after an agreeable drive of almost twenty miles, they entered Woodston, a large and populous village, in a situation not unpleasant. Catherine was ashamed to say how pretty she thought it, as the General seemed to think an apology necessary for the flatness of the country, and the size of the village; but in her heart she preferred it to any place she had ever been at, and looked with great admiration at every neat house above the rank of a cottage, and at all the little chandler's shops which they passed. At the further end of the village, and tolerably disengaged from the rest of it, stood the Parsonage, a new-built substantial stone house, with its semi-circular sweep and green gates; and, as they drove up to the door, Henry, with the friends of his solitude, a large Newfoundland puppy and two or three terriers, was ready to receive and make much of them.

Catherine's mind was too full, as she entered the house, for her either to observe or to say a great deal; and, till called on by the General for her opinion of it, she had very little idea of the room in which she was sitting. Upon looking round it then, she perceived in a moment that it was the most comfortable room in the world; but she was too guarded to say so, and the coldness of her praise disappointed him.

'We are not calling it a good house,' said he.—'We are not comparing it with Fullerton and Northanger—We are considering it as a mere Parsonage, small and confined, we allow, but decent perhaps, and habitable; and altogether not inferior to the generality;—or, in other words, I believe there are few country parsonages in England half so good. It may admit of improvement, however. Far be it from me to say otherwise; and any thing in reason—a bow thrown out, perhaps—though, between ourselves, if there is one thing more than another my aversion, it is a patched-on bow.'*

Catherine did not hear enough of this speech to understand or be pained by it; and other subjects being studiously brought forward and supported by Henry, at the same time that a tray full of refreshments was introduced by his servant, the General was shortly restored to his complacency, and Catherine to all her usual ease of spirits.

The room in question was of a commodious, well-proportioned size, and handsomely fitted up as a dining parlour; and on their quitting it to walk round the grounds, she was shewn, first into a smaller apartment, belonging peculiarly to the master of the house, and made unusually tidy on the occasion; and afterwards into what was to be the drawing-room, with the appearance of which, though unfurnished, Catherine was delighted enough even to satisfy the General. It was a prettily-shaped room, the windows reaching to the ground, and the view from them pleasant, though only over green meadows; and she expressed her admiration at the moment with all the honest simplicity with which she felt it. 'Oh! why do not you fit up this room, Mr. Tilney? What a pity not to have it fitted up! It is the prettiest room I ever saw;—it is the prettiest room in the world!'

'I trust,' said the General, with a most satisfied smile, 'that it will very speedily be furnished: it waits only for a lady's taste!'

'Well, if it was my house, I should never sit any where else. Oh! what a sweet little cottage there is among the trees—apple trees too! It is the prettiest cottage!'—

'You like it—you approve it as an object;—it is enough. Henry, remember that Robinson is spoken to about it. The cottage remains.'*

Such a compliment recalled all Catherine's consciousness, and silenced her directly; and, though pointedly applied to by the General for her choice of the prevailing colour of the paper and hangings, nothing like an opinion on the subject could be drawn from her. The influence of fresh objects and fresh air, however, was of great use in dissipating these embarrassing associations; and, having reached the ornamental part of the premises, consisting of a walk round two sides of a meadow, on which Henry's genius had begun to act about half a year ago, she was sufficiently recovered to think it prettier than any pleasure-ground she had ever been in before, though there was not a shrub in it higher than the green bench in the corner.

A saunter into other meadows, and through part of the village, with a visit to the stables to examine some improvements, and a charming game of play with a litter of puppies just able to roll about, brought them to four o'clock, when Catherine scarcely thought it could be three. At four they were to dine, and at six to set off on their return. Never had any day passed so quickly!

She could not but observe that the abundance of the dinner did not seem to create the smallest astonishment in the General; nay, that he was even looking at the side-table for cold meat which was not there. His son and daughter's observations were of a different kind. They had seldom seen him eat so heartily at any table but his own; and never before known him so little disconcerted by the melted butter's being oiled.

At six o'clock, the General having taken his coffee, the carriage again received them; and so gratifying had been the tenor of his conduct throughout the whole visit, so well assured was her mind on the subject of his expectations, that, could she have felt equally confident of the wishes of his son, Catherine would have quitted Woodston with little anxiety as to the How or the When she might return to it.

CHAPTER XII

THE next morning brought the following very unexpected letter from Isabella:—

Bath, April—

My dearest Catherine,

I received your two kind letters with the greatest delight, and have a thousand apologies to make for not answering them sooner. I really am quite ashamed of my idleness; but in this horrid place one can find time for nothing. I have had my pen in my hand to begin a letter to you almost every day since you left Bath, but have always been prevented by some silly trifler or other. Pray write to me soon, and direct to my own home. Thank God! we leave this vile place tomorrow. Since you went away, I have had no pleasure in it—the dust is beyond any thing; and everybody one cares for is gone. I believe if I could see you I should not mind the rest, for you are dearer to me than any body can conceive. I am quite uneasy about your dear brother, not having heard from him since he went to Oxford; and am fearful of some misunderstanding. Your kind offices will set all right:—he is the only man I ever did or could love, and I trust you will convince him of it. The spring fashions are partly down; and the hats the most frightful you can imagine. I hope you spend your time pleasantly, but am afraid you never think of me. I will not say all that I could of the family you are with, because I would not be ungenerous, or set you against those you esteem; but it is very difficult to know whom to trust, and young men never know their minds two days together. I rejoice to say, that the young man whom, of all others, I particularly abhor, has left Bath. You will know, from this description, I must mean Captain Tilney, who, as you may remember, was amazingly disposed to follow and tease me, before you went away. Afterwards he got worse, and became quite my shadow. Many girls might have been taken in, for never were such attentions; but I knew the fickle sex too well. He went away to his regiment two days ago, and I trust I shall never be plagued with him again. He is the greatest coxcomb I ever saw, and amazingly disagreeable. The last two days he was always by the side of Charlotte Davis: I pitied his taste, but took no notice of him. The last time we met was in Bath-street, and I turned directly into a shop that he might not speak to me;—I would not even look at him. He went into the Pump-room afterwards; but I would not have followed him for all the world. Such a contrast between him and your brother!—pray send me some news of the latter—I am quite unhappy about him, he seemed so uncomfortable when he went away, with a cold, or something that affected his spirits. I would write to him myself, but have mislaid his direction; and, as I hinted above, am afraid he took something in my conduct amiss. Pray explain every thing to his satisfaction; or, if he still harbours any doubt, a line from himself to me, or a call at Putney when next in town, might set all to rights. I have not been to the Rooms this age, nor to the Play, except going in last night with the Hodges's, for a frolic, at half-price: they teased me into it; and I was determined they should not say I shut myself up because Tilney was gone. We happened to sit by the Mitchells, and they pretended to be quite surprized to see me out. I knew their spite:—at one time they could not be civil to me, but now they are all friendship; but I am not such a fool as to be taken in by them. You know I have a pretty good spirit of my own. Anne Mitchell had tried to put on a turban like mine, as I wore it the week before at the Concert, but made wretched work of it—it happened to become my odd face I believe, at least Tilney told me so at the time, and said every eye was upon me; but he is the last man whose word I would take. I wear nothing but purple now: I know I look hideous in it, but no matter—it is your dear brother's favourite colour. Lose no time, my dearest, sweetest Catherine, in writing to him and to me,

Who ever am, &c.

Such a strain of shallow artifice could not impose even upon Catherine. Its inconsistencies, contradictions, and falsehood, struck her from the very first. She was ashamed of Isabella, and ashamed of having ever loved her. Her professions of attachment were now as disgusting as her excuses were empty, and her demands impudent. 'Write to James on her behalf!—No, James should never hear Isabella's name mentioned by her again.'

On Henry's arrival from Woodston, she made known to him and Eleanor their brother's safety, congratulating them with sincerity on it, and reading aloud the most material passages of her letter with strong indignation. When she had finished it,—'So much for Isabella,' she cried, 'and for all our intimacy! She must think me an idiot, or she could not have written so; but perhaps this has served to make her character better known to me than mine is to her. I see what she has been about. She is a vain coquette, and her tricks have not answered. I do not believe she had ever any regard either for James or for me, and I wish I had never known her.'

'It will soon be as if you never had,' said Henry.

'There is but one thing that I cannot understand. I see that she has had designs on Captain Tilney, which have not succeeded; but I do not understand what Captain Tilney has been about all this time. Why should he pay her such attentions as to make her quarrel with my brother, and then fly off himself?'

'I have very little to say for Frederick's motives, such as I believe them to have been. He has his vanities as well as Miss Thorpe, and the chief difference is, that, having a stronger head, they have not yet injured himself. If the *effect* of his behaviour does not justify him with you, we had better not seek after the cause.'

'Then you do not suppose he ever really cared about her?'

'I am persuaded that he never did.'

'And only made believe to do so for mischief's sake?'

Henry bowed his assent.

'Well, then, I must say that I do not like him at all. Though it has turned out so well for us, I do not like him at all. As it happens, there is no great harm done, because I do not think Isabella has any heart to lose. But, suppose he had made her very much in love with him?'

'But we must first suppose Isabella to have had a heart to lose,— consequently to have been a very different creature; and, in that case, she would have met with very different treatment.'

'It is very right that you should stand by your brother.'

'And if you would stand by *your's*, you would not be much distressed
by the disappointment of Miss Thorpe. But your mind is warped by
an innate principle of general integrity, and therefore not accessible
to the cool reasonings of family partiality, or a desire of revenge.'

Catherine was complimented out of further bitterness. Frederick
could not be unpardonably guilty, while Henry made himself so
agreeable. She resolved on not answering Isabella's letter; and tried to
think no more of it.

CHAPTER XIII

SOON after this, the General found himself obliged to go to London
for a week; and he left Northanger earnestly regretting that any
necessity should rob him even for an hour of Miss Morland's company, and anxiously recommending the study of her comfort and
amusement to his children as their chief object in his absence. His
departure gave Catherine the first experimental conviction that a loss
may be sometimes a gain. The happiness with which their time now
passed, every employment voluntary, every laugh indulged, every
meal a scene of ease and good-humour, walking where they liked and
when they liked, their hours, pleasures and fatigues at their own command, made her thoroughly sensible of the restraint which the
General's presence had imposed, and most thankfully feel their present release from it. Such ease and such delights made her love the
place and the people more and more every day; and had it not been
for a dread of its soon becoming expedient to leave the one, and an
apprehension of not being equally beloved by the other, she would at
each moment of each day have been perfectly happy; but she was now
in the fourth week of her visit; before the General came home, the
fourth week would be turned, and perhaps it might seem an intrusion
if she staid much longer. This was a painful consideration whenever
it occurred; and eager to get rid of such a weight on her mind, she
very soon resolved to speak to Eleanor about it at once, propose going
away, and be guided in her conduct by the manner in which her proposal might be taken.

Aware that if she gave herself much time, she might feel it difficult
to bring forward so unpleasant a subject, she took the first opportunity of being suddenly alone with Eleanor, and of Eleanor's being in

the middle of a speech about something very different, to start forth her obligation of going away very soon. Eleanor looked and declared herself much concerned. She had 'hoped for the pleasure of her company for a much longer time—had been misled (perhaps by her wishes) to suppose that a much longer visit had been promised—and could not but think that if Mr. and Mrs. Morland were aware of the pleasure it was to her to have her there, they would be too generous to hasten her return.'—Catherine explained.—'Oh! as to *that*, papa and mamma were in no hurry at all. As long as she was happy, they would always be satisfied.'

'Then why, might she ask, in such a hurry herself to leave them?'

'Oh! because she had been there so long.'

'Nay, if you can use such a word, I can urge you no farther. If you think it long—'

'Oh! no, I do not indeed. For my own pleasure, I could stay with you as long again.'—And it was directly settled that, till she had, her leaving them was not even to be thought of. In having this cause of uneasiness so pleasantly removed, the force of the other was likewise weakened. The kindness, the earnestness of Eleanor's manner in pressing her to stay, and Henry's gratified look on being told that her stay was determined, were such sweet proofs of her importance with them, as left her only just so much solicitude as the human mind can never do comfortably without. She did—almost always—believe that Henry loved her, and quite always that his father and sister loved and even wished her to belong to them; and believing so far, her doubts and anxieties were merely sportive irritations.

Henry was not able to obey his father's injunction of remaining wholly at Northanger in attendance on the ladies, during his absence in London; the engagements of his curate at Woodston obliging him to leave them on Saturday for a couple of nights. His loss was not now what it had been while the General was at home; it lessened their gaiety, but did not ruin their comfort; and the two girls agreeing in occupation, and improving in intimacy, found themselves so well-sufficient for the time to themselves, that it was eleven o'clock, rather a late hour at the Abbey, before they quitted the supper-room on the day of Henry's departure. They had just reached the head of the stairs, when it seemed, as far as the thickness of the walls would allow them to judge, that a carriage was driving up to the door, and the next moment confirmed the idea by the loud noise of the house-bell. After the first perturbation of surprize had passed away, in a 'Good Heaven! what can be the matter?' it was quickly decided by Eleanor to be her eldest brother, whose arrival was often as sudden, if not quite so unseasonable, and accordingly she hurried down to welcome him

Catherine walked on to her chamber, making up her mind as well as she could, to a further acquaintance with Captain Tilney, and comforting herself under the unpleasant impression his conduct had given her, and the persuasion of his being by far too fine a gentleman to approve of her, that at least they should not meet under such circumstances as would make their meeting materially painful. She trusted he would never speak of Miss Thorpe; and indeed, as he must by this time be ashamed of the part he had acted, there could be no danger of it; and as long as all mention of Bath scenes were avoided, she thought she could behave to him very civilly. In such considerations time passed away, and it was certainly in his favour that Eleanor should be so glad to see him, and have so much to say, for half an hour was almost gone since his arrival, and Eleanor did not come up.

At that moment Catherine thought she heard her step in the gallery, and listened for its continuance; but all was silent. Scarcely, however, had she convicted her fancy of error, when the noise of something moving close to her door made her start; it seemed as if some one was touching the very doorway—and in another moment a slight motion of the lock proved that some hand must be on it. She trembled a little at the idea of any one's approaching so cautiously; but resolving not to be again overcome by trivial appearances of alarm, or misled by a raised imagination, she stepped quietly forward, and opened the door. Eleanor, and only Eleanor, stood there. Catherine's spirits however were tranquillized but for an instant, for Eleanor's cheeks were pale, and her manner greatly agitated. Though evidently intending to come in, it seemed an effort to enter the room, and a still greater to speak when there. Catherine, supposing some uneasiness on Captain Tilney's account, could only express her concern by silent attention; obliged her to be seated, rubbed her temples with lavender-water, and hung over her with affectionate solicitude. 'My dear Catherine, you must not—you must not indeed—' were Eleanor's first connected words. 'I am quite well. This kindness distracts me— I cannot bear it—I come to you on such an errand!'

'Errand!—to me!'

'How shall I tell you!—Oh! how shall I tell you!'

A new idea now darted into Catherine's mind, and turning as pale as her friend, she exclaimed, ''Tis a messenger from Woodston!'

'You are mistaken, indeed,' returned Eleanor, looking at her most compassionately—'it is no one from Woodston. It is my father himself.' Her voice faltered, and her eyes were turned to the ground as she mentioned his name. His unlooked for return was enough in itself to make Catherine's heart sink, and for a few moments she hardly supposed there were any thing worse to be told. She said nothing; and Eleanor endeavouring to collect herself and speak with firmness, but with eyes still cast down, soon went on. 'You are too good, I am sure, to think the worse of me for the part I am obliged to perform. I am indeed a most unwilling messenger. After what has so lately passed, so lately been settled between us—how joyfully, how thankfully on my side!—as to your continuing here as I hoped for many, many weeks longer, how can I tell you that your kindness is not to be accepted—and that the happiness your company has hitherto given us is to be repaid by——but I must not trust myself with words. My dear Catherine, we are to part. My father has recollected an engagement that takes our whole family away on Monday. We are going to Lord Longtown's, near Hereford, for a fortnight. Explanation and apology are equally impossible. I cannot attempt either.'

'My dear Eleanor,' cried Catherine, suppressing her feelings as well as she could, 'do not be so distressed. A second engagement must give way to a first. I am very, very sorry we are to part—so soon, and so suddenly too; but I am not offended, indeed I am not. I can finish my visit here you know at any time; or I hope you will come to me. Can you, when you return from this lord's, come to Fullerton?'

'It will not be in my power, Catherine.'

'Come when you can, then.'—

Eleanor made no answer; and Catherine's thoughts recurring to something more directly interesting, she added, thinking aloud, 'Monday—so soon as Monday;—and you *all* go. Well, I am certain of——I shall be able to take leave however. I need not go till just before you do, you know. Do not be distressed, Eleanor, I can go on Monday very well. My father and mother's having no notice of it is of very little consequence. The General will send a servant with me, I dare say, half the way—and then I shall soon be at Salisbury, and then I am only nine miles from home.'

'Ah, Catherine! were it settled so, it would be somewhat less intolerable, though in such common attentions you would have received but half what you ought. But—how can I tell you?—Tomorrow morning is fixed for your leaving us, and not even the hour is left to your choice; the very carriage is ordered, and will be here at seven o'clock, and no servant will be offered you.'*

Catherine sat down, breathless and speechless. 'I could hardly believe my senses, when I heard it;—and no displeasure, no resentment that you can feel at this moment, however justly great, can be more than I myself——but I must not talk of what I felt. Oh! that I could suggest any thing in extenuation! Good God! what will your father and mother say! After courting you from the protection of real friends to this—almost double distance from your home, to have you driven out of the house, without the considerations even of decent civility! Dear, dear Catherine, in being the bearer of such a message, I seem guilty myself of all its insult; yet, I trust you will acquit me, for you must have been long enough in this house to see that I am but a nominal mistress of it, that my real power is nothing.'

'Have I offended the General?' said Catherine in a faltering voice.

'Alas! for my feelings as a daughter, all that I know, all that I answer for is, that you can have given him no just cause of offence. He certainly is greatly, very greatly discomposed; I have seldom seen him more so. His temper is not happy, and something has now occurred to ruffle it in an uncommon degree; some disappointment, some vexation, which just at this moment seems important; but which I can hardly suppose you to have any concern in, for how is it possible?'

It was with pain that Catherine could speak at all; and it was only for Eleanor's sake that she attempted it. 'I am sure,' said she, 'I am very sorry if I have offended him. It was the last thing I would willingly have done. But do not be unhappy, Eleanor. An engagement you know must be kept. I am only sorry it was not recollected sooner, that I might have written home. But it is of very little consequence.'

'I hope, I earnestly hope that to your real safety it will be of none; but to every thing else it is of the greatest consequence; to comfort, appearance, propriety, to your family, to the world. Were your friends, the Allens, still in Bath, you might go to them with comparative ease; a few hours would take you there; but a journey of seventy miles, to be taken post by you, at your age, alone, unattended!'

'Oh, the journey is nothing. Do not think about that. And if we are to part, a few hours sooner or later, you know, makes no difference. I can be ready by seven. Let me be called in time.' Eleanor saw that she wished to be alone; and believing it better for each that they should avoid any further conversation, now left her with 'I shall see you in the morning.'

Catherine's swelling heart needed relief. In Eleanor's presence friendship and pride had equally restrained her tears, but no sooner was she gone than they burst forth in torrents. Turned from the house, and in such a way!—Without any reason that could justify, any apology that could atone for the abruptness, the rudeness, nay, the insolence of it. Henry at a distance—not able even to bid him farewell. Every hope, every expectation from him suspended, at least, and who could say how long?—Who could say when they might meet again?—And all this by such a man as General Tilney, so polite, so well-bred, and heretofore so particularly fond of her! It was as incomprehensible as it was mortifying and grievous. From what it could arise, and where it would end, were considerations of equal perplexity and alarm. The manner in which it was done so grossly uncivil; hurrying her away without any reference to her own convenience, or allowing her even the appearance of choice as to the time or mode of her travelling; of two days, the earliest fixed on, and of that almost the earliest hour, as if resolved to have her gone before he was stirring in the morning, that he might not be obliged even to see her. What could all this mean but an intentional affront? By some means or other she must have had the misfortune to offend him. Eleanor had wished to spare her from so painful a notion, but Catherine could not believe it possible that any injury or any misfortune could provoke such ill-will against a person not connected, or, at least, not supposed to be connected with it.

Heavily past the night. Sleep, or repose that deserved the name of sleep, was out of the question. That room, in which her disturbed imagination had tormented her on her first arrival, was again the scene of agitated spirits and unquiet slumbers. Yet how different now the source of her inquietude from what it had been then—how mournfully superior in reality and substance! Her anxiety had foundation in fact, her fears in probability; and with a mind so occupied in the contemplation of actual and natural evil, the solitude of her situation, the darkness of her chamber, the antiquity of the building were

felt and considered without the smallest emotion; and though the
wind was high, and often produced strange and sudden noises
throughout the house, she heard it all as she lay awake, hour after
hour, without curiosity or terror.

Soon after six Eleanor entered her room, eager to show attention or
give assistance where it was possible; but very little remained to be
done. Catherine had not loitered; she was almost dressed, and her
packing almost finished. The possibility of some conciliatory message
from the General occurred to her as his daughter appeared. What so
natural, as that anger should pass away and repentance succeed it?
and she only wanted to know how far, after what had passed, an apology might properly be received by her. But the knowledge would have
been useless here, it was not called for; neither clemency nor dignity
was put to the trial—Eleanor brought no message. Very little passed
between them on meeting; each found her greatest safety in silence,
and few and trivial were the sentences exchanged while they remained
up stairs, Catherine in busy agitation completing her dress, and
Eleanor with more good-will than experience intent upon filling the
trunk. When every thing was done they left the room, Catherine
lingering only half a minute behind her friend to throw a parting
glance on every well-known cherished object, and went down to the
breakfast-parlour, where breakfast was prepared. She tried to eat, as
well to save herself from the pain of being urged, as to make her friend
comfortable; but she had no appetite, and could not swallow many
mouthfuls. The contrasts between this and her last breakfast in that
room, gave her fresh misery, and strengthened her distaste for every
thing before her. It was not four-and-twenty hours ago since they had
met there to the same repast, but in circumstances how different! With
what cheerful ease, what happy, though false security, had she then
looked around her, enjoying every thing present, and fearing little in
future, beyond Henry's going to Woodston for a day! Happy, happy
breakfast! for Henry had been there, Henry had sat by her and helped
her. These reflections were long indulged undisturbed by any address
from her companion, who sat as deep in thought as herself; and the
appearance of the carriage was the first thing to startle and recall them
to the present moment. Catherine's colour rose at the sight of it; and
the indignity with which she was treated striking at that instant on her
mind with peculiar force, made her for a short time sensible only of
resentment. Eleanor seemed now impelled into resolution and speech.

'You *must* write to me, Catherine,' she cried, 'you *must* let me hear from you as soon as possible. Till I know you to be safe at home, I shall not have an hour's comfort. For *one* letter, at all risks, all hazards, I must entreat. Let me have the satisfaction of knowing that you are safe at Fullerton, and have found your family well, and then, till I can ask for your correspondence as I ought to do, I will not expect more. Direct to me at Lord Longtown's, and, I must ask it, under cover to Alice.'

'No, Eleanor, if you are not allowed to receive a letter from me, I am sure I had better not write. There can be no doubt of my getting home safe.'

Eleanor only replied, 'I cannot wonder at your feelings. I will not importune you. I will trust to your own kindness of heart when I am at a distance from you.' But this, with the look of sorrow accompanying it, was enough to melt Catherine's pride in a moment, and she instantly said, 'Oh, Eleanor, I *will* write to you indeed.'

There was yet another point which Miss Tilney was anxious to settle, though somewhat embarrassed in speaking of. It had occurred to her, that after so long an absence from home, Catherine might not be provided with money enough for the expenses of her journey, and, upon suggesting it to her with most affectionate offers of accommodation, it proved to be exactly the case. Catherine had never thought on the subject till that moment; but, upon examining her purse, was convinced that but for this kindness of her friend, she might have been turned from the house without even the means of getting home; and the distress in which she must have been thereby involved filling the minds of both, scarcely another word was said by either during the time of their remaining together. Short, however, was that time. The carriage was soon announced to be ready; and Catherine, instantly rising, a long and affectionate embrace supplied the place of language in bidding each other adieu; and, as they entered the hall, unable to leave the house without some mention of one whose name had not yet been spoken by either, she paused a moment, and with quivering lips just made it intelligible that she left 'her kind remembrance for her absent friend.' But with this approach to his name ended all possibility of restraining her feelings; and, hiding her face as well as she could with her handkerchief, she darted across the hall, jumped into the chaise, and in a moment was driven from the door.

CHAPTER XIV

CATHERINE was too wretched to be fearful. The journey in itself had
no terrors for her; and she began it without either dreading its length,
or feeling its solitariness. Leaning back in one corner of the carriage,
in a violent burst of tears, she was conveyed some miles beyond the
walls of the Abbey before she raised her head; and the highest point
of ground within the park was almost closed from her view before she
was capable of turning her eyes towards it. Unfortunately, the road
she now travelled was the same which only ten days ago she had so
happily passed along in going to and from Woodston; and, for
fourteen miles, every bitter feeling was rendered more severe by the
review of objects on which she had first looked under impressions so
different. Every mile, as it brought her nearer Woodston, added to
her sufferings, and when within the distance of five, she passed the
turning which led to it, and thought of Henry, so near, yet so unconscious, her grief and agitation were excessive.

The day which she had spent at that place had been one of the
happiest of her life. It was there, it was on that day that the General
had made use of such expressions with regard to Henry and herself,
had so spoken and so looked as to give her the most positive conviction of his actually wishing their marriage. Yes, only ten days ago had
he elated her by his pointed regard—had he even confused her by his
too significant reference! And now—what had she done, or what had
she omitted to do, to merit such a change?

The only offence against him of which she could accuse herself,
had been such as was scarcely possible to reach his knowledge. Henry
and her own heart only were privy to the shocking suspicions which
she had so idly entertained; and equally safe did she believe her secret
with each. Designedly, at least, Henry could not have betrayed her. If,
indeed, by any strange mischance his father should have gained intelligence of what she had dared to think and look for, of her causeless
fancies and injurious examinations, she could not wonder at any
degree of his indignation. If aware of her having viewed him as
a murderer, she could not wonder at his even turning her from his
house. But a justification so full of torture to herself, she trusted
would not be in his power.

Anxious as were all her conjectures on this point, it was not, however, the one on which she dwelt most. There was a thought yet nearer,

a more prevailing, more impetuous concern. How Henry would think, and feel, and look, when he returned on the morrow to Northanger and heard of her being gone, was a question of force and interest to rise over every other, to be never ceasing, alternately irritating and soothing; it sometimes suggested the dread of his calm acquiescence, and at others was answered by the sweetest confidence in his regret and resentment. To the General, of course, he would not dare to speak; but to Eleanor—what might he not say to Eleanor about her?

In this unceasing recurrence of doubts and inquiries, on any one article of which her mind was incapable of more than momentary repose, the hours passed away, and her journey advanced much faster than she looked for. The pressing anxieties of thought, which prevented her from noticing any thing before her, when once beyond the neighbourhood of Woodston, saved her at the same time from watching her progress; and though no object on the road could engage a moment's attention, she found no stage of it tedious. From this, she was preserved too by another cause, by feeling no eagerness for her journey's conclusion; for to return in such a manner to Fullerton was almost to destroy the pleasure of a meeting with those she loved best, even after an absence such as her's—an eleven weeks absence. What had she to say that would not humble herself and pain her family; that would not increase her own grief by the confession of it, extend an useless resentment, and perhaps involve the innocent with the guilty in undistinguishing ill-will? She could never do justice to Henry and Eleanor's merit; she felt it too strongly for expression; and should a dislike be taken against them, should they be thought of unfavourably, on their father's account, it would cut her to the heart.

With these feelings, she rather dreaded than sought for the first view of that well-known spire which would announce her within twenty miles of home.* Salisbury she had known to be her point on leaving Northanger; but after the first stage she had been indebted to the post-masters for the names of the places which were then to conduct her to it; so great had been her ignorance of her route. She met with nothing, however, to distress or frighten her. Her youth, civil manners and liberal pay, procured her all the attention that a traveller like herself could require; and stopping only to change horses, she travelled on for about eleven hours without accident or alarm, and between six and seven o'clock in the evening found herself entering Fullerton.

A heroine returning, at the close of her career, to her native village, in all the triumph of recovered reputation, and all the dignity of a countess, with a long train of noble relations in their several phaetons, and three waiting-maids in a travelling chaise-and-four, behind her, is an event on which the pen of the contriver may well delight to dwell; it gives credit to every conclusion, and the author must share in the glory she so liberally bestows.—But my affair is widely different; I bring back my heroine to her home in solitude and disgrace; and no sweet elation of spirits can lead me into minuteness. A heroine in a hack post-chaise, is such a blow upon sentiment, as no attempt at grandeur or pathos can withstand. Swiftly therefore shall her postboy drive through the village, amid the gaze of Sunday groups, and speedy shall be her descent from it.

But, whatever might be the distress of Catherine's mind, as she thus advanced towards the Parsonage, and whatever the humiliation of her biographer in relating it, she was preparing enjoyment of no every-day nature for those to whom she went; first, in the appearance of her carriage—and secondly, in herself. The chaise of a traveller being a rare sight in Fullerton, the whole family were immediately at the window; and to have it stop at the sweep-gate was a pleasure to brighten every eye and occupy every fancy—a pleasure quite unlooked for by all but the two youngest children, a boy and girl of six and four years old, who expected a brother or sister in every carriage. Happy the glance that first distinguished Catherine!—Happy the voice that proclaimed the discovery!—But whether such happiness were the lawful property of George or Harriet could never be exactly understood.

Her father, mother, Sarah, George, and Harriet, all assembled at the door, to welcome her with affectionate eagerness, was a sight to awaken the best feelings of Catherine's heart; and in the embrace of each, as she stepped from the carriage, she found herself soothed beyond any thing that she had believed possible. So surrounded, so caressed, she was even happy! In the joyfulness of family love every thing for a short time was subdued, and the pleasure of seeing her, leaving them at first little leisure for calm curiosity, they were all seated round the tea-table, which Mrs. Morland had hurried for the comfort of the poor traveller, whose pale and jaded looks soon caught her notice, before any inquiry so direct as to demand a positive answer was addressed to her.

Reluctantly, and with much hesitation, did she then begin what might perhaps, at the end of half an hour, be termed by the courtesy of her hearers, an explanation; but scarcely, within that time, could they at all discover the cause, or collect the particulars of her sudden return. They were far from being an irritable race;* far from any quickness in catching, or bitterness in resenting affronts:—but here, when the whole was unfolded, was an insult not to be overlooked, nor, for the first half hour, to be easily pardoned. Without suffering any romantic alarm, in the consideration of their daughter's long and lonely journey, Mr. and Mrs. Morland could not but feel that it might have been productive of much unpleasantness to her; that it was what they could never have voluntarily suffered; and that, in forcing her on such a measure, General Tilney had acted neither honourably nor feelingly—neither as a gentleman nor as a parent. Why he had done it, what could have provoked him to such a breach of hospitality, and so suddenly turned all his partial regard for their daughter into actual ill-will, was a matter which they were at least as far from divining as Catherine herself; but it did not oppress them by any means so long; and, after a due course of useless conjecture, that, 'it was a strange business, and that he must be a very strange man,' grew enough for all their indignation and wonder; though Sarah indeed still indulged in the sweets of incomprehensibility, exclaiming and conjecturing with youthful ardour. 'My dear, you give yourself a great deal of needless trouble,' said her mother at last; 'depend upon it, it is something not at all worth understanding.'

'I can allow for his wishing Catherine away, when he recollected this engagement,' said Sarah, 'but why not do it civilly?'

'I am sorry for the young people,' returned Mrs. Morland; 'they must have a sad time of it; but as for any thing else, it is no matter now; Catherine is safe at home, and our comfort does not depend upon General Tilney.' Catherine sighed. 'Well,' continued her philosophic mother, 'I am glad I did not know of your journey at the time; but now it is all over perhaps there is no great harm done. It is always good for young people to be put upon exerting themselves; and you know, my dear Catherine, you always were a sad little shatter-brained creature; but now you must have been forced to have your wits about you, with so much changing of chaises and so forth; and I hope it will appear that you have not left any thing behind you in any of the pockets.'

Catherine hoped so too, and tried to feel an interest in her own amendment, but her spirits were quite worn down; and, to be silent and alone becoming soon her only wish, she readily agreed to her mother's next counsel of going early to bed. Her parents seeing nothing in her ill-looks and agitation but the natural consequence of mortified feelings, and of the unusual exertion and fatigue of such a journey, parted from her without any doubt of their being soon slept away; and though, when they all met the next morning, her recovery was not equal to their hopes, they were still perfectly unsuspicious of there being any deeper evil. They never once thought of her heart, which, for the parents of a young lady of seventeen, just returned from her first excursion from home, was odd enough!

As soon as breakfast was over, she sat down to fulfil her promise to Miss Tilney, whose trust in the effect of time and distance on her friend's disposition was already justified, for already did Catherine reproach herself with having parted from Eleanor coldly; with having never enough valued her merits or kindness; and never enough commiserated her for what she had been yesterday left to endure. The strength of these feelings, however, was far from assisting her pen; and never had it been harder for her to write than in addressing Eleanor Tilney. To compose a letter which might at once do justice to her sentiments and her situation, convey gratitude without servile regret, be guarded without coldness, and honest without resentment—a letter which Eleanor might not be pained by the perusal of—and, above all, which she might not blush herself, if Henry should chance to see, was an undertaking to frighten away all her powers of performance; and, after long thought and much perplexity, to be very brief was all that she could determine on with any confidence of safety. The money therefore which Eleanor had advanced was inclosed with little more than grateful thanks, and the thousand good wishes of a most affectionate heart.

'This has been a strange acquaintance,' observed Mrs. Morland, as the letter was finished; 'soon made and soon ended.—I am sorry it happens so, for Mrs. Allen thought them very pretty kind of young people; and you were sadly out of luck too in your Isabella. Ah! poor James! Well, we must live and learn; and the next new friends you make I hope will be better worth keeping.'

Catherine coloured as she warmly answered, 'No friend can be better worth keeping than Eleanor.'

'If so, my dear, I dare say you will meet again some time or other; do not be uneasy. It is ten to one but you are thrown together again in the course of a few years; and then what a pleasure it will be!'

Mrs. Morland was not happy in her attempt at consolation. The hope of meeting again in the course of a few years could only put into Catherine's head what might happen within that time to make a meeting dreadful to her. She could never forget Henry Tilney, or think of him with less tenderness than she did at that moment; but he might forget her; and in that case to meet!——Her eyes filled with tears as she pictured her acquaintance so renewed; and her mother, perceiving her comfortable suggestions to have had no good effect, proposed, as another expedient for restoring her spirits, that they should call on Mrs. Allen.

The two houses were only a quarter of a mile apart; and, as they walked, Mrs. Morland quickly dispatched all that she felt on the score of James's disappointment. 'We are sorry for him,' said she; 'but otherwise there is no harm done in the match going off; for it could not be a desirable thing to have him engaged to a girl whom we had not the smallest acquaintance with, and who was so entirely without fortune; and now, after such behaviour, we cannot think at all well of her. Just at present it comes hard to poor James; but that will not last for ever; and I dare say he will be a discreeter man all his life, for the foolishness of his first choice.'

This was just such a summary view of the affair as Catherine could listen to; another sentence might have endangered her complaisance, and made her reply less rational; for soon were all her thinking powers swallowed up in the reflection of her own change of feelings and spirits since last she had trodden that well-known road. It was not three months ago since, wild with joyful expectation, she had there run backwards and forwards some ten times a-day, with an heart light, gay, and independent; looking forward to pleasures untasted and unalloyed, and free from the apprehension of evil as from the knowledge of it. Three months ago had seen her all this; and now, how altered a being did she return!

She was received by the Allens with all the kindness which her unlooked-for appearance, acting on a steady affection, would naturally call forth; and great was their surprize, and warm their displeasure, on hearing how she had been treated,—though Mrs. Morland's account of it was no inflated representation, no studied appeal to their passions. 'Catherine took us quite by surprize yesterday evening,' said she. 'She travelled all the way post by herself, and knew nothing of coming till Saturday night; for General Tilney, from some odd fancy or other, all of a sudden grew tired of having her there, and almost turned her out of the house. Very unfriendly, certainly; and he must be a very odd man;—but we are so glad to have her amongst us again! And it is a great comfort to find that she is not a poor helpless creature, but can shift very well for herself.'

Mr. Allen expressed himself on the occasion with the reasonable resentment of a sensible friend; and Mrs. Allen thought his expressions quite good enough to be immediately made use of again by herself. His wonder, his conjectures, and his explanations, became in succession her's, with the addition of this single remark—'I really have not patience with the General'—to fill up every accidental pause. And, 'I really have not patience with the General,' was uttered twice after Mr. Allen left the room, without any relaxation of anger, or any material digression of thought. A more considerable degree of wandering attended the third repetition; and, after completing the fourth, she immediately added, 'Only think, my dear, of my having got that frightful great rent in my best Mechlin* so charmingly mended, before I left Bath, that one can hardly see where it was. I must shew it you some day or other. Bath is a nice place, Catherine, after all. I assure you I did not above half like coming away. Mrs. Thorpe's being there was such a comfort to us, was not it? You know you and I were quite forlorn at first.'

'Yes, but *that* did not last long,' said Catherine, her eyes brightening at the recollection of what had first given spirit to her existence there.

'Very true: we soon met with Mrs. Thorpe, and then we wanted for nothing. My dear, do not you think these silk gloves wear very well? I put them on new the first time of our going to the Lower Rooms, you know, and I have worn them a great deal since. Do you remember that evening?'

'Do I! Oh! perfectly.'

'It was very agreeable, was not it? Mr. Tilney drank tea with us, and I always thought him a great addition, he is so very agreeable. I have a notion you danced with him, but am not quite sure. I remember I had my favourite gown on.'

Catherine could not answer; and, after a short trial of other subjects, Mrs. Allen again returned to—'I really have not patience with the General! Such an agreeable, worthy man as he seemed to be! I do not suppose, Mrs. Morland, you ever saw a better-bred man in your life. His lodgings were taken the very day after he left them, Catherine. But no wonder; Milsom-street you know.'—

As they walked home again, Mrs. Morland endeavoured to impress on her daughter's mind the happiness of having such steady well-wishers as Mr. and Mrs. Allen, and the very little consideration which the neglect or unkindness of slight acquaintance like the Tilneys ought to have with her, while she could preserve the good opinion and affection of her earliest friends. There was a great deal of good sense in all this; but there are some situations of the human mind in which good sense has very little power; and Catherine's feelings contradicted almost every position her mother advanced. It was upon the behaviour of these very slight acquaintance that all her present happiness depended; and while Mrs. Morland was successfully confirming her own opinions by the justness of her own representations, Catherine was silently reflecting that *now* Henry must have arrived at Northanger; *now* he must have heard of her departure; and *now*, perhaps, they were all setting off for Hereford.

CHAPTER XV

CATHERINE'S disposition was not naturally sedentary, nor had her habits been ever very industrious; but whatever might hitherto have been her defects of that sort, her mother could not but perceive them now to be greatly increased. She could neither sit still, nor employ herself for ten minutes together, walking round the garden and orchard again and again, as if nothing but motion was voluntary; and it seemed as if she could even walk about the house rather than remain fixed for any time in the parlour. Her loss of spirits was a yet greater alteration. In her rambling and her idleness she might only be a caricature of herself; but in her silence and sadness she was the very reverse of all that she had been before.

For two days Mrs. Morland allowed it to pass even without a hint; but when a third night's rest had neither restored her cheerfulness, improved her in useful activity, nor given her a greater inclination for needle-work, she could no longer refrain from the gentle reproof of, 'My dear Catherine, I am afraid you are growing quite a fine lady. I do not know when poor Richard's cravats would be done, if he had no friend but you. Your head runs too much upon Bath; but there is a time for every thing—a time for balls and plays, and a time for work.* You have had a long run of amusement, and now you must try to be useful.'

Catherine took up her work directly, saying, in a dejected voice, that 'her head did not run upon Bath——much.'

'Then you are fretting about General Tilney, and that is very simple of you: for ten to one whether you ever see him again. You should never fret about trifles.' After a short silence—'I hope, my Catherine, you are not getting out of humour with home because it is not so grand as Northanger. That would be turning your visit into an evil indeed. Wherever you are you should always be contented, but especially at home, because there you must spend the most of your time. I did not quite like, at breakfast, to hear you talk so much about the French-bread at Northanger.'

'I am sure I do not care about the bread. It is all the same to me what I eat.'

'There is a very clever Essay in one of the books up stairs upon much such a subject, about young girls that have been spoilt for home by great acquaintance—"The Mirror," I think.* I will look it out for you some day or other, because I am sure it will do you good.'

Catherine said no more, and, with an endeavour to do right, applied to her work; but, after a few minutes, sunk again, without knowing it herself, into languor and listlessness, moving herself in her chair, from the irritation of weariness, much oftener than she moved her needle.—Mrs. Morland watched the progress of this relapse; and seeing, in her daughter's absent and dissatisfied look, the full proof of that repining spirit to which she had now begun to attribute her want of cheerfulness, hastily left the room to fetch the book in question, anxious to lose no time in attacking so dreadful a malady. It was some time before she could find what she looked for; and other family matters occurring to detain her, a quarter of an hour had elapsed ere she returned down stairs with the volume from which so much was hoped. Her avocations above having shut out all noise but what she created herself, she knew not that a visitor had arrived within the last few minutes, till, on entering the room, the first object she beheld was a young man whom she had never seen before. With a look of much respect, he immediately rose, and being introduced to her by her

conscious daughter as 'Mr. Henry Tilney,' with the embarrassment
of real sensibility began to apologise for his appearance there, acknow-
ledging that after what had passed he had little right to expect a welcome at Fullerton, and stating his impatience to be assured of
Miss Morland's having reached her home in safety, as the cause of
his intrusion. He did not address himself to an uncandid judge or
a resentful heart. Far from comprehending him or his sister in their
father's misconduct, Mrs. Morland had been always kindly disposed
towards each, and instantly, pleased by his appearance, received him
with the simple professions of unaffected benevolence; thanking him
for such an attention to her daughter, assuring him that the friends of
her children were always welcome there, and intreating him to say not
another word of the past.

He was not ill inclined to obey this request, for, though his heart
was greatly relieved by such unlooked-for mildness, it was not just at
that moment in his power to say any thing to the purpose. Returning
in silence to his seat, therefore, he remained for some minutes most
civilly answering all Mrs. Morland's common remarks about the
weather and roads. Catherine meanwhile,—the anxious, agitated,
happy, feverish Catherine,—said not a word; but her glowing cheek
and brightened eye made her mother trust that this good-natured
visit would at least set her heart at ease for a time, and gladly therefore
did she lay aside the first volume of the Mirror for a future hour.

Desirous of Mr. Morland's assistance, as well in giving encouragement, as in finding conversation for her guest, whose embarrassment
on his father's account she earnestly pitied, Mrs. Morland had very
early dispatched one of the children to summon him; but Mr. Morland
was from home—and being thus without any support, at the end of
a quarter of an hour she had nothing to say. After a couple of minutes
unbroken silence, Henry, turning to Catherine for the first time since
her mother's entrance, asked her, with sudden alacrity, if Mr. and
Mrs. Allen were now at Fullerton? and on developing, from amidst all
her perplexity of words in reply, the meaning, which one short syllable
would have given, immediately expressed his intention of paying his
respects to them, and, with a rising colour, asked her if she would
have the goodness to shew him the way. 'You may see the house from
this window, sir,' was information on Sarah's side, which produced
only a bow of acknowledgment from the gentleman, and a silencing
nod from her mother; for Mrs. Morland, thinking it probable, as

a secondary consideration in his wish of waiting on their worthy neighbours, that he might have some explanation to give of his father's behaviour, which it must be more pleasant for him to communicate only to Catherine, would not on any account prevent her accompanying him. They began their walk, and Mrs. Morland was not entirely mistaken in his object in wishing it. Some explanation on his father's account he had to give; but his first purpose was to explain himself, and before they reached Mr. Allen's grounds he had done it so well, that Catherine did not think it could ever be repeated too often. She was assured of his affection; and that heart in return was solicited, which, perhaps, they pretty equally knew was already entirely his own; for, though Henry was now sincerely attached to her, though he felt and delighted in all the excellencies of her character and truly loved her society, I must confess that his affection originated in nothing better than gratitude, or, in other words, that a persuasion of her partiality for him had been the only cause of giving her a serious thought. It is a new circumstance in romance, I acknowledge, and dreadfully derogatory of an heroine's dignity; but if it be as new in common life, the credit of a wild imagination will at least be all my own.

A very short visit to Mrs. Allen, in which Henry talked at random, without sense or connection, and Catherine, wrapt in the contemplation of her own unutterable happiness, scarcely opened her lips, dismissed them to the extasies of another tête-à-tête; and before it was suffered to close, she was enabled to judge how far he was sanctioned by parental authority in his present application. On his return from Woodston, two days before, he had been met near the Abbey by his impatient father, hastily informed in angry terms of Miss Morland's departure, and ordered to think of her no more.

Such was the permission upon which he had now offered her his hand. The affrighted Catherine, amidst all the terrors of expectation, as she listened to this account, could not but rejoice in the kind caution with which Henry had saved her from the necessity of a conscientious rejection, by engaging her faith before he mentioned the subject; and as he proceeded to give the particulars, and explain the motives of his father's conduct, her feelings soon hardened into even a triumphant delight. The General had had nothing to accuse her of, nothing to lay to her charge, but her being the involuntary, unconscious object of a deception which his pride could not pardon, and which a better pride would have been ashamed to own. She was guilty only of being less rich than he had supposed her to be. Under a mistaken persuasion of her possessions and claims, he had courted her acquaintance in Bath, solicited her company at Northanger, and designed her for his daughter in law. On discovering his error, to turn her from the house seemed the best, though to his feelings an inadequate proof of his resentment towards herself, and his contempt of her family.

John Thorpe had first misled him. The General, perceiving his son one night at the theatre to be paying considerable attention to Miss Morland, had accidentally inquired of Thorpe, if he knew more of her than her name. Thorpe, most happy to be on speaking terms with a man of General Tilney's importance, had been joyfully and proudly communicative;—and being at that time not only in daily expectation of Morland's engaging Isabella, but likewise pretty well resolved upon marrying Catherine himself, his vanity induced him to represent the family as yet more wealthy than his vanity and avarice had made him believe them. With whomsoever he was, or was likely to be connected, his own consequence always required that theirs should be great, and as his intimacy with any acquaintance grew, so regularly grew their fortune. The expectations of his friend Morland, therefore, from the first over-rated, had ever since his introduction to Isabella, been gradually increasing, and by merely adding twice as much for the grandeur of the moment, by doubling what he chose to think the amount of Mr. Morland's preferment, trebling his private fortune, bestowing a rich aunt, and sinking half the children, he was able to represent the whole family to the General in a most respectable light. For Catherine, however, the peculiar object of the General's curiosity, and his own speculations, he had yet something more in reserve, and the ten or fifteen thousand pounds which her father could give her, would be a pretty addition to Mr. Allen's estate. Her intimacy there had made him seriously determine on her being handsomely legacied hereafter; and to speak of her therefore as the almost acknowledged future heiress of Fullerton naturally followed. Upon such intelligence the General had proceeded; for never had it occurred to him to doubt its authority. Thorpe's interest in the family, by his sister's approaching connection with one of its members, and his own views on another, (circumstances of which he boasted with almost equal openness,) seemed sufficient vouchers for his truth; and to these were added the absolute facts of the Allens being wealthy and childless, of Miss Morland's being under their care, and—as soon as his acquaintance allowed him to judge—of their treating her with parental kindness. His resolution was soon formed. Already had he discerned a liking towards Miss Morland in the countenance of his son; and thankful for Mr. Thorpe's communication, he almost instantly determined to spare no pains in weakening his boasted interest and ruining his dearest hopes. Catherine herself could not be more ignorant at the time of all this, than his own children. Henry and Eleanor, perceiving nothing in her situation likely to engage their father's particular respect, had seen with astonishment the suddenness, continuance and extent of his attention; and though latterly, from some hints which had accompanied an almost positive command to his son of doing every thing in his power to attach her, Henry was convinced of his father's believing it to be an advantageous connection, it was not till the late explanation at Northanger that they had the smallest idea of the false calculations which had hurried him on. That they were false, the General had learnt from the very person who had suggested them, from Thorpe himself, whom he had chanced to meet again in town, and who, under the influence of exactly opposite feelings, irritated by Catherine's refusal, and yet more by the failure of a very recent endeavour to accomplish a reconciliation between Morland and Isabella, convinced that they were separated for ever, and spurning a friendship which could be no longer serviceable, hastened to contradict all that he had said before to the advantage of the Morlands;—confessed himself to have been totally mistaken in his opinion of their circumstances and character, misled by the rhodomontade* of his friend to believe his father a man of substance and credit, whereas the transactions of the two or three last weeks proved him to be neither; for after coming eagerly forward on the first overture of a marriage between the families, with the most liberal proposals, he had, on being brought to the point by the shrewdness of the relator, been constrained to acknowledge himself incapable of giving the young people even a decent support. They were, in fact, a necessitous family; numerous too almost beyond example; by no means respected in their own neighbourhood, as he had lately had particular opportunities of discovering; aiming at a style of life which their fortune could not warrant; seeking to better themselves by wealthy connexions; a forward, bragging, scheming race.

The terrified General pronounced the name of Allen with an inquiring look; and here too Thorpe had learnt his error. The Allens, he believed, had lived near them too long, and he knew the young man on whom the Fullerton estate must devolve. The General needed no more. Enraged with almost every body in the world but himself, he set out the next day for the Abbey, where his performances have been seen.

I leave it to my reader's sagacity to determine how much of all this it was possible for Henry to communicate at this time to Catherine, how much of it he could have learnt from his father, in what points his own conjectures might assist him, and what portion must yet remain to be told in a letter from James. I have united for their ease what they must divide for mine.* Catherine, at any rate, heard enough to feel, that in suspecting General Tilney of either murdering or shutting up his wife, she had scarcely sinned against his character, or magnified his cruelty.

Henry, in having such things to relate of his father, was almost as pitiable as in their first avowal to himself. He blushed for the narrow-minded counsel which he was obliged to expose. The conversation between them at Northanger had been of the most unfriendly kind. Henry's indignation on hearing how Catherine had been treated, on comprehending his father's views, and being ordered to acquiesce in them, had been open and bold. The General, accustomed on every ordinary occasion to give the law in his family, prepared for no reluctance but of feeling, no opposing desire that should dare to clothe itself in words, could ill brook the opposition of his son, steady as the sanction of reason and the dictate of conscience could make it. But, in such a cause, his anger, though it must shock, could not intimidate Henry, who was sustained in his purpose by a conviction of its justice. He felt himself bound as much in honour as in affection to Miss Morland, and believing that heart to be his own which he had been directed to gain, no unworthy retraction of a tacit consent, no reversing decree of unjustifiable anger, could shake his fidelity, or influence the resolutions it prompted.

He steadily refused to accompany his father into Herefordshire, an engagement formed almost at the moment, to promote the dismissal of Catherine, and as steadily declared his intention of offering her his hand. The General was furious in his anger, and they parted in dreadful disagreement. Henry, in an agitation of mind which many solitary hours were required to compose, had returned almost instantly to Woodston; and, on the afternoon of the following day, had begun his journey to Fullerton.

CHAPTER XVI

MR. and Mrs. Morland's surprize on being applied to by Mr. Tilney, for their consent to his marrying their daughter, was, for a few minutes, considerable; it having never entered their heads to suspect an attachment on either side; but as nothing, after all, could be more natural than Catherine's being beloved, they soon learnt to consider it with only the happy agitation of gratified pride, and, as far as they alone were concerned, had not a single objection to start. His pleasing manners and good sense were self-evident recommendations; and having never heard evil of him, it was not their way to suppose any evil could be told. Good-will supplying the place of experience, his character needed no attestation. 'Catherine would make a sad heedless young housekeeper to be sure,' was her mother's foreboding remark; but quick was the consolation of there being nothing like practice.

There was but one obstacle, in short, to be mentioned; but till that one was removed, it must be impossible for them to sanction the engagement. Their tempers were mild, but their principles were steady, and while his parent so expressly forbad the connexion, they could not allow themselves to encourage it. That the General should come forward to solicit the alliance, or that he should even very heartily approve it, they were not refined enough to make any parading stipulation; but the decent appearance of consent must be yielded, and that once obtained—and their own hearts made them trust that it could not be very long denied—their willing approbation was instantly to follow. His *consent* was all that they wished for. They were no more inclined than entitled to demand his *money*. Of a very considerable fortune, his son was, by marriage settlements, eventually secure; his present income was an income of independence and comfort, and under every pecuniary view, it was a match beyond the claims of their daughter.

The young people could not be surprized at a decision like this. They felt and they deplored—but they could not resent it; and they parted, endeavouring to hope that such a change in the General, as each believed almost impossible, might speedily take place, to unite them again in the fullness of privileged affection. Henry returned to what was now his only home, to watch over his young plantations, and extend his improvements for her sake, to whose share in them he looked anxiously forward; and Catherine remained at Fullerton to cry. Whether the torments of absence were softened by a clandestine correspondence, let us not inquire. Mr. and Mrs. Morland never did—they had been too kind to exact any promise; and whenever Catherine received a letter, as, at that time, happened pretty often, they always looked another way.

The anxiety, which in this state of their attachment must be the portion of Henry and Catherine, and of all who loved either, as to its final event, can hardly extend, I fear, to the bosom of my readers, who will see in the tell-tale compression of the pages before them, that we are all hastening together to perfect felicity.* The means by which their early marriage was effected can be the only doubt; what probable circumstance could work upon a temper like the General's? The circumstance which chiefly availed, was the marriage of his daughter with a man of fortune and consequence, which took place in the course of the summer—an accession of dignity that threw him into a fit of good-humour, from which he did not recover till after Eleanor had obtained his forgiveness of Henry, and his permission for him 'to be a fool if he liked it!'

The marriage of Eleanor Tilney, her removal from all the evils of such a home as Northanger had been made by Henry's banishment, to the home of her choice and the man of her choice, is an event which I expect to give general satisfaction among all her acquaintance. My own joy on the occasion is very sincere. I know no one more entitled, by unpretending merit, or better prepared by habitual suffering, to receive and enjoy felicity. Her partiality for this gentleman was not of recent origin; and he had been long withheld only by inferiority of situation from addressing her. His unexpected accession to title and fortune had removed all his difficulties; and never had the General loved his daughter so well in all her hours of companionship, utility, and patient endurance, as when he first hailed her, 'Your Ladyship!' Her husband was really deserving of her; independent of his peerage, his wealth, and his attachment, being to a precision the most charming young man in the world. Any further definition of his merits must be unnecessary; the most charming young man in the world is instantly before the imagination of us all. Concerning the one in question therefore I have only to add—(aware that the rules of composition forbid the introduction of a character not connected with my fable)*—that this was the very gentleman whose negligent servant left behind him that collection of washing-bills, resulting from a long visit at Northanger, by which my heroine was involved in one of her most alarming adventures.

The influence of the Viscount and Viscountess in their brother's behalf was assisted by that right understanding of Mr. Morland's circumstances which, as soon as the General would allow himself to be informed, they were qualified to give. It taught him that he had been scarcely more misled by Thorpe's first boast of the family wealth, than by his subsequent malicious overthrow of it; that in no sense of the word were they necessitous or poor, and that Catherine would have three thousand pounds. This was so material an amendment of his late expectations, that it greatly contributed to smooth the descent of his pride; and by no means without its effect was the private intelligence, which he was at some pains to procure, that the Fullerton estate, being entirely at the disposal of its present proprietor, was consequently open to every greedy speculation.

On the strength of this, the General, soon after Eleanor's marriage, permitted his son to return to Northanger, and thence made him the bearer of his consent, very courteously worded in a page full of empty professions to Mr. Morland. The event which it authorized soon followed: Henry and Catherine were married, the bells rang and every body smiled; and, as this took place within a twelvemonth from the first day of their meeting, it will not appear, after all the dreadful delays occasioned by the General's cruelty, that they were essentially hurt by it. To begin perfect happiness at the respective ages of twenty-six and eighteen, is to do pretty well; and professing myself moreover convinced, that the General's unjust interference, so far from being really injurious to their felicity, was perhaps rather conducive to it, by improving their knowledge of each other, and adding strength to their attachment, I leave it to be settled by whomsoever it may concern, whether the tendency of this work be altogether to recommend parental tyranny, or reward filial disobedience.*

FINIS

EXPLANATORY NOTES

THE tradition of annotation and commentary established by R. W. Chapman's edition of *Northanger Abbey* (in *The Novels of Jane Austen*, Clarendon Press, 1923) has been expanded and enriched in this century by Claire Grogan (Broadview Literary Texts, 2002), Claudia L. Johnson (Oxford World's Classics, 2003), Marilyn Gaull (Longman Cultural Editions, 2005), Barbara M. Benedict and Deirdre Le Faye (Cambridge University Press, 2006), David M. Shapard (Anchor Books, 2013), and Susan J. Wolfson (Belknap Press, 2014). I gratefully acknowledge their work and that of earlier editors on whom they drew; I also thank the able research assistants (Dana Lew, Kevin Liu, Austin Long, Ryan Park, Philip Trotter, Rachael Tu) who contributed to the notes that follow. With prose of such teasing delicacy and comic finesse, explanatory annotation is an exercise in tact; failures are all my own. *Northanger Abbey* is cited by page number from this edition; Austen's other novels are cited by volume, chapter, and page numbers from current editions in the Oxford World's Classics series; correspondence is cited by page and date from *Jane Austen's Letters*, ed. Deirdre Le Faye (4th edn, Oxford University Press, 2011). Unless otherwise indicated, further primary sources are cited from first editions (volume nos. are given in upper-case roman numerals, chapter nos. in lower-case roman numerals, and page nos. in arabic numerals, separated by spaced points, e.g. II. ix. 62).

3 *THIS little work . . . immediate publication*: for the tangled history of composition and publication, see the Introduction, pp. viii–xiii. In spring 1803, Austen sold *Northanger Abbey* (as 'Susan', from a manuscript drafted *c*.1798–9) to the publisher Benjamin Crosby, who advertised the novel as in the press but failed to proceed further. She later protested to Crosby & Co. that 'an early publication was stipulated for at the time of Sale' (*Letters*, 182: 5 Apr. 1809), but was unable to buy back the copyright until early 1816. Austen then hoped to publish very soon, or so (in specifying a thirteen-year lag) the present Advertisement suggests. However, a year later, having renamed the novel's heroine, she told her niece Fanny Knight that 'Miss Catherine is put upon the Shelve for the present, and I do not know that she will ever come out' (*Letters*, 348: 13 Mar. 1817). *Northanger Abbey* appeared posthumously in December 1817.

5 *very respectable man, though his name was Richard*: the name is thought to have been a family in-joke. 'Mʳ Richard Harvey's match is put off, till he has got a Better Christian name', Austen tells her sister Cassandra (*Letters*, 10: 15 Sept. 1796); see also her teenage 'History of England' (composed 1791), which ironically calls Richard III, supposed murderer of his nephews and wife, 'a very respectable Man' (*Teenage Writings*, p. 124). There is possibly a private dig at Richard Crosby, boorish son of the non-publisher of 'Susan',

who threatened Austen with legal action should she bring her novel out else-where without compensating Crosby & Co. (*Letters*, 183: 8 Apr. 1809).

5 *independence . . . livings . . . locking up his daughters*: independent income from land or investments; church benefices (usually as parson of a parish) conferring property or income. Here, and throughout the chapter, Austen plays on familiar plot routines from eighteenth-century fiction; Samuel Richardson's *Clarissa* (1747–8) and Ann Radcliffe's *The Mysteries of Udolpho* (1794) are only the most distinguished of many novels featuring a father or other patriarchal figure who imprisons the heroine.

Beggar's Petition: a didactic poem by the Revd Thomas Moss, urging sym-pathy and charity for the poor. First published in Moss's *Poems upon Several Occasions* (1769), it was widely anthologized and used as a school-room recitation exercise.

6 *The Hare and many Friends*: a satirical poem, from John Gay's *Fables* (1727), about fair-weather friends who find reasons not to help a hunted hare. In *Emma*, dim-witted Mrs Elton quotes the bull's excuse ('For when a lady's in the case, | You know all other things give place', III. xvi. 349), apparently not realizing that the bull means he has to go and pleasure his favourite cow.

spinnet: a domestic keyboard instrument, resembling a harpsichord, but smaller, cheaper, and somewhat passé. The instrument of choice was now the more modern and versatile pianoforte, as when, in *Emma*, Jane Fairfax (who previously has 'not even the pitifullest old spinnet . . . to amuse herself with') mysteriously receives a high-end piano from London (II. viii. 165).

lying-in: confinement before and after childbirth.

7 *cricket, base ball*: cricket, already a widespread and popular sport, was now approaching its modern form, with flighted bowling and straight bats replacing trundled deliveries and curved sticks. 'Base-Ball, (an infant Game)', as John Kidgell calls it in his 1755 novel *The Card* (I. ii. 9), was a simple precursor of modern rounders and baseball.

bear about the mockery of woe: Alexander Pope, 'Elegy to the Memory of an Unfortunate Lady' (1717), line 57 (*bear* meaning *carry*).

Many a flower . . . desert air: slightly misquoting Thomas Gray's already canonical *Elegy Written in a Country Churchyard* (1751), lines 55–6 ('Full many a flow'r is born to blush unseen, | And waste its sweetness on the desert air'). Pretentious Mrs Elton quotes the same lines in *Emma* (II. xv. 216), again with 'fragrance' for 'sweetness'; this misquotation may have spread from William Hayley's *Life and Posthumous Writings of William Cowper* (1803), vol. i, 39.

It is a delightful task . . . to shoot: adapting a much-anthologized passage about rural home-schooling from James Thomson's *The Seasons* (1730): 'Delightful Task! to rear the tender Thought, | To teach the young Idea how to shoot' (*Spring* (first published 1728), lines 1152–3, *shoot* meaning *sprout*).

Trifles light as air . . . Smiling at Grief: see *Othello*, III. iii. 316–18; *Measure for Measure*, III. i. 76–8; *Twelfth Night*, II. iv. 111–12. All three passages were staples of popular anthologies such as *The Poetical Preceptor* (1777), *Elegant Extracts* (1783), and other compilations of the kind Austen dispar- ages below (see p. 23 with note). The same Shakespeare tags were also routinely quoted or adapted in sentimental, Gothic, and other subgenres of fiction between 1760 and 1800, at least fifty times in the case of 'smiling at grief' (an act Catherine goes on to perform in a later chapter: see p. 46).

8 *her lover's profile . . . detected in the design*: a familiar occurrence in Gothic novels such as Charlotte Smith's *Emmeline, The Orphan of the Castle* (1788), I. xvi, and Regina Maria Roche's *Clermont, A Tale* (1798), I. iii.

one amiable youth . . . call forth her sensibility: Austen channels the hack- neyed diction of circulating-library novels, as in her parodic teenage writ- ings; see, for example, 'Love and Freindship', where the heroine's 'natural Sensibility' is aroused by 'the most beauteous and amiable Youth, I had ever beheld' (letter v).

boy accidentally found . . . whose origin was unknown: the enabling premise of Henry Fielding's *The History of Tom Jones, A Foundling* (1749) was widely imitated in later novels. 'Henry & Eliza', in which Sir George and Lady Harcourt rear a baby they find concealed in a haystack, is one of several teenage skits in which Austen sends up this plot device; years later, Lady Harcourt suddenly remembers leaving the baby there herself.

Fullerton . . . Wiltshire . . . Bath: Fullerton, Wiltshire, is a fictional location in southern England (8 or 9 miles from Salisbury, we learn below, p. 17), though there was a real Fullerton in neighbouring Hampshire. Bath, just west of the Wiltshire–Somerset boundary and about 100 miles from London, was England's most fashionable spa resort, famed since Roman times for its medicinal springs. Austen stayed in Bath at least twice in the 1790s, resided there between 1801 and 1805, and describes the city with specificity in the chapters that follow. Bath is also a key setting in *Persuasion*, composition of which overlapped with Austen's retrieval and final revision of *Northanger Abbey*; the novels were then published together as a four-volume set.

9 *Rooms at night*: Bath's two sets of Assembly Rooms (the Lower Rooms, built in 1709, and the palatial Upper Rooms of 1771) were the principal social hubs of the resort, where balls, concerts, and other (often very crowded) evening entertainments took place.

writing by every post . . . Bath might produce: Austen plays on the enabling convention of epistolary fiction, the now somewhat stale narrative form in which more than 40 per cent of novels published in Britain between 1770 and 1790 were cast. 'She made me promise to send her a letter every post', writes the heroine of Frances Burney's *Evelina* (1778) in one of many such instances (II. ix. 62).

overturn: carriage accident. Austen was not above using this plot device herself; see the opening chapter of her unfinished *Sanditon* (1817).

10 *Pulteney-street*: opened in 1789, Great Pulteney Street was part of an ambitious speculative development extending Bath eastwards across the

river to Bathwick. 'On the farther side of the Avon is a new creation of architectural beauties, which may vie with any thing in the world', gushed a prominent guidebook (John Feltham, *A Guide to All the Watering and Sea Bathing Places, For 1813* (1813), 59). In practice, the new neighbourhood struggled to compete with established central locations, and the Allens would have found it an affordable choice.

10 *entrée into life*: recalling the subtitle of *Evelina; or, A Young Lady's Entrance into the World* (1778) by Frances Burney, whose later novels *Cecilia* and *Camilla* Austen praises below (see p. 23 with note).

season was full: Catherine visits Bath in February, midway through a social season that ran from September to May, with a lull in the hot summer months (when fashionable visitors preferred Clifton and Bristol Hotwells: see p. 82 with note).

11 *unwearied diligence*: for this phrase, see p. 18 with note.

12 *my head*: like the high-feathered ladies mentioned earlier in this chapter, Mrs Allen presumably sports an elaborate coiffure or headdress.

13 *called a divinity by any body*: a routine hyperbole in sentimental novels. See, for example, Jane Purbeck's *Honoria Sommerville* (1789), in which one character 'has worn her hair in ringlets without powder, ever since my brother told her she looked like a divinity' (I. xi. 206); also the anonymous *Adeline; or, The Orphan* (1790): 'What a divinity! exclaimed the Marquis (with the air of a man who thought himself charming) when he was introduced to Adeline' (III. xlviii. 58).

her chair: a sedan chair on poles, carried by two porters; Bath's often steep gradients posed problems for horse-drawn carriages.

Pump-room: built in the Corinthian style between 1789 and 1799, the Grand Pump Room replaced a more modest original building of 1704–6. It was Bath's main daytime social hub, where visitors could see and be seen while drinking the waters, listening to music, conversing, and promenading.

14 *master of the ceremonies*: an elective office made famous by Richard 'Beau' Nash (1674–1761), who facilitated social interaction and oversaw the protocols of decorum at public assemblies. When Catherine and the Allens visit, the Master of Ceremonies in the Lower Rooms would have been the Irishman James King, who presided there from 1785 before moving to the Upper Rooms in 1805.

his name was Tilney: for some readers, this surname may have evoked the famously wealthy Tylney family of Draycot, Wiltshire. One of its members, Catherine Tilney-Long (1789–1825), was said to be the richest heiress in England at the time of her marriage to William Pole-Wellesley, a spendthrift nephew of the Duke of Wellington, in 1812.

15 *sprigged muslin robe*: lightweight cotton gown embroidered (or by this time often printed) with sprays or sprigs of leaves or flowers.

Mr. King: see note to p. 14.

16 *stops*: punctuation marks; cf. Charlotte Brontë's *Jane Eyre* (1847), in which Jane's doomed schoolfriend Helen 'had been at the top of the class, but for some error of pronunciation or some inattention to stops, she was suddenly sent to the very bottom' (I. vi. 92).

17 *fag*: fatigue (a relatively new slang term; the earliest occurrence recorded in the *OED* is from Frances Burney's journal for Apr. 1780).

celebrated writer . . . love is declared: 'That a young lady should be in love, and the love of the young gentleman undeclared, is an heterodoxy which prudence, and even policy, must not allow' (*Rambler*, no. 97, 19 Feb. 1751). This starchy letter was contributed to Samuel Johnson's periodical *The Rambler* by the novelist Samuel Richardson, whose heroines in *Pamela* (1740), *Clarissa* (1747–8), and *Sir Charles Grandison* (1753–4) all break his rule one way or another. Austen had already drafted *Northanger Abbey* when this letter was first attributed to Richardson in a printed source (Alexander Chalmers's multi-volume anthology of 1802–3, *The British Essayists*), but Johnson's original headnote drops a heavy hint, and Richardson's authorship was widely assumed.

18 *great clock*: a 10-foot-tall longcase clock by the master craftsman Thomas Tompion (1639–1713), presented by Tompion to the city in 1709 and still in situ in the Grand Pump Room.

despair of nothing . . . unwearied diligence . . . point would gain: this well-known distich comes from Thomas Dyche's much-reprinted schoolbook of 1707, *A Guide to the English Tongue* ('Alphabet 2, Of Two-line Pieces', 126 in Dyche's 2nd edn of 1710). Deirdre Le Faye suggests that Austen may have stitched the same words into a surviving embroidered sampler dated 1794 ('*Northanger Abbey* and Mrs Allen's Maxims', *Notes and Queries*, 46/4 (1999), 449–50). However, the sampler in question has the signature 'Ann Gross Agd 7' (Bristol Museum and Art Gallery, Object No. T95).

19 *Merchant-Taylors'*: a London grammar school, founded by cloth merchants in 1561, whose mainly middling-sort (non-elite) pupils would often go on to St John's College, Oxford.

pelisse: a long cloak for women, often made of luxurious fabric and trimmed with lace or fur, with details evoking the style of military uniform.

Friendship . . . the finest balm for the pangs of disappointed love: mimicking the formulaic diction of sentimental novels such as *Ianthé* (1798) by Emily Clark ('her sympathetic feelings soothed the pangs of disappointed love', I. 198) and *The Letters of Maria*, a 1790 imitation of Sterne by Miss Street, where even 'the sweet balm of consolation' offered by Yorick cannot 'heal the pangs of disappointed love' (letter xxvi, p. 68). See also Austen's parodic teenage writings such as 'Love and Freindship' ('the endearing Intercourse of Freindship', 'the pleasing Pangs of Love') and 'Evelyn' ('the friendly balm of comfort').

20 *quizzes*: people (or sometimes things) of eccentric or risible appearance. See note to p. 40.

20 *Tunbridge*: Tunbridge Wells, Kent, was a rival spa town in south-east
England, closer to London and promoted by Beau Nash, but never eclips-
ing Bath as a fashionable destination.

past adventures and sufferings . . . minutely repeated: novels of the period
were often padded with interpolated memoirs by minor characters, a feature Austen targets in her early parody 'Jack & Alice'. Grasping attorneys
and the lords they act for are especially prominent in novels by Charlotte
Smith such as *Marchmont* (1796), which features an attorney named
Vampyre.

21 *Crescent*: the Royal Crescent, designed and built by John Wood the
Younger in 1767–75, was 'a majestic assemblage of buildings of an ellip-
tical form, with a single order of Ionic pillars . . . It consists of thirty elegant houses, with a fine lawn in front, declining towards the [River] Avon,
and commands very extensive prospects over the city and the opposite
hills' (Feltham, *Guide*, 58). The grand architecture and elevated situation
of the Crescent made it one of Bath's most prestigious addresses and
a favourite spot for taking the air.

Pump-room book: the registration ledger in the Pump Room, signed by
visitors to assist the Master of Ceremonies in making introductions, also
served informally as a social noticeboard and finding aid (the use to which
Catherine puts it again on pp. 27 and 64).

22 *the set*: A number of pairs lined up in rows to perform a dance. The number could vary; Catherine later fears 'having but a short set to dance down'
(p. 93).

degrading . . . performances, to . . . which they are themselves adding: at a time
when the novel genre had not yet attained its Victorian prestige, even the
authors Austen praises in this chapter would sometimes disparage their
fellow novelists. See Burney's defensive Preface to *Evelina*, or the
Advertisement in which Maria Edgeworth defines *Belinda* (1801) as 'a
Moral Tale—the author not wishing to acknowledge a Novel'.

23 *Reviewers . . . trash with which the press now groans*: Austen precisely catches
the haughty style of book reviewers; see, for example, the entry on Mary
Robinson's *Angelina* (1796) in the *Monthly Review* (Mar. 1796), 350: 'Of
the host of novels, with which the press groans, the generality are of so
very inferior a nature as hardly to deserve notice.' *Northanger Abbey* failed
to kill off this cliché, and in July 1820 the *Monthly Review* was still deploring imitations of Sir Walter Scott 'with which the press actually labours
and groans' (327). See also Sir Edward Denham's disdain, in *Sanditon*, for
'the mere Trash of the common Circulating Library' (viii. 136).

nine-hundredth abridger of the History of England: there were numerous
cheap abridgements on the market, including Oliver Goldsmith's *An
Abridgment of the History of England* (1774), based on his own four-volume
The History of England (1771). A copy of the full version survives in the
Austen family with extensive marginalia in her hand; these annotations
inform her earlier mockery of the genre and its shortcomings in her

manuscript skit of 1791, 'The History of England . . . By a partial, prejudiced, & ignorant Historian'.

man who collects . . . chapter from Sterne: the collapse of perpetual copyright in 1774 opened the floodgates to opportunistic compilations of passages from canonical verse (John Milton, 1608–74; Alexander Pope, 1688–1744; Matthew Prior, 1664–1721), essay periodicals (*The Spectator* (1711–12, 1714) by Joseph Addison, Richard Steele, and others), and similar sources. The novelist Laurence Sterne (1713–68) was often included for his sentimental vignettes, but not for his satire or bawdry. The best-known anthologies were by Vicesimus Knox (1752–1821), whose *Elegant Extracts; or, Useful and Entertaining Passages in Prose* (1784) and *Elegant Extracts . . . in Poetry* (1789) reached respectively their 10th and 8th London editions in 1816. Austen was not entirely hostile; she gave *Elegant Extracts* to a niece in 1801, and she makes it a favourite with *Emma*'s worthy yeoman farmer Robert Martin, who by day reads 'the Agricultural Reports' and by night 'the Elegant Extracts' (I. iv. 23).

Cecilia, or Camilla, or Belinda: Frances Burney, *Cecilia; or, Memoirs of an Heiress* (1782); Burney, *Camilla; or, A Picture of Youth* (1796); Maria Edgeworth, *Belinda* (1801). *Camilla* was published by subscription and includes 'Miss J. Austen, Steventon' in its list of advance purchasers. The date of *Belinda* means that Austen added this reference, and perhaps other parts of the chapter, some time after first drafting the novel in *c*.1798–9.

24 *Milsom-street . . . coquelicot ribbons instead of green*: Milsom Street, built in 1762–8, was an upscale address in Bath, known for its fashionable shops and circulating libraries; coquelicot (from the French) was the orange-tinged red hue of a wild poppy. The *OED*'s earliest illustration dates from 1795; the next is from a letter to Cassandra in which Austen plans to replace the black military feather in her cap with 'the Coquelicot one, as being smarter;—& besides Coquelicot is to be all the fashion this winter' *(Letters*, 26–7: 18 Dec. 1798).

Udolpho . . . the black veil: Isabella has started the second volume of Ann Radcliffe's four-volume *The Mysteries of Udolpho* (1794), the most celebrated Gothic novel of the era and a key intertext for *Northanger Abbey*. Exploring remote chambers in the Castle of Udolpho, the heroine Emily faints on lifting a black silk veil, without Radcliffe disclosing what she sees (II. vi). It may be the remains of Signora Laurentini, whose ghost is believed to haunt the castle, but it later turns out to be a waxwork corpse, sculpted as a penitential memento mori.

Laurentina's skeleton: not Laurentina but Laurentini, and the skeleton Catherine anticipates will be a mere waxwork (see note above).

the Italian: *The Italian; or, The Confessional of the Black Penitents* (1797) was Ann Radcliffe's follow-up to *The Mysteries of Udolpho*, and the last of her novels to be published within Austen's (and Radcliffe's own) lifetime.

Castle of Wolfenbach . . . Horrid Mysteries: these are genuine titles from the Gothic craze of the 1790s, all but one of them issued by William Lane's Minerva Press, a prolific publisher of sensationalist fiction. There is a German cast to the examples Austen chooses: Eliza Parsons, *Castle of Wolfenbach, A German Story* (1793); Regina Maria Roche, *Clermont, A Tale* (1798); Eliza Parsons, *The Mysterious Warning, A German Tale* (1796); Karl Friedrich Kahlert, *The Necromancer; or, The Tale of the Black Forest* (1794); Eleanor Sleath, *The Orphan of the Rhine, A Romance* (1798), Peter Will (trans.), *Horrid Mysteries, A Story, from the German of the Marquis of Grosse* (1796). The odd book out is Francis Lathom's *The Midnight Bell, A German Story* (1798), published by Henry Delahoy Symonds, a radical bookseller who had recently spent years in prison for seditious libel. Writing to Cassandra, Austen describes her father reading *The Midnight Bell* from a library copy; he would probably have done so aloud (*Letters*, 15: 14 Oct. 1798).

26 *Sir Charles Grandison*: Austen jokes here about Richardson's seven-volume work of 1753–4, with its prolix circumstantial realism and glacial narrative pace. Even so, this was reportedly among her favourite novels: 'Every circumstance narrated in Sir Charles Grandison, all that was ever said or done in the cedar parlour, was familiar to her; and the wedding days of Lady L. and Lady G. were as well remembered as if they had been living friends' (J. E. Austen-Leigh et al., *A Memoir of Jane Austen and Other Family Recollections*, ed. Kathryn Sutherland (Oxford: Oxford University Press, 2002), 71).

27 *walked to the book*: the registration ledger; see note to p. 21.

   Edgar's Buildings: a terrace of large town houses across the top of Milsom Street—a desirable address, somewhat better than the Allens' in Great Pulteney Street, but not as good as that of the Tilneys, who turn out to be staying in prime Milsom Street (p. 64).

28 *Union-passage . . . Cheap-street*: Cheap Street was a major thoroughfare between the Pump Room and Union Passage (or Cock Lane, as the passage was known until 1807: one of several details indicating later revision by Austen).

   gig: a sporty two-seater with two wheels, drawn by a single horse (though John Thorpe attends to 'the horses' a few paragraphs below).

   scrape: 'An awkward bow or salutation in which the foot is drawn backwards on the ground' (*OED*).

29 *Tetbury*: a small town on the road between Bath and Oxford—which is where Thorpe and James Morland should really be. It is February, we learn below (p. 43), midway through Oxford's Hilary Term.

   not turned a hair . . . Walcot Church: St Swithin's church, Walcot, was on the northern side of Bath; Austen's parents married there in 1764, and her father was buried in the crypt in 1805. The *OED* gives this passage as its earliest instance of 'not to turn a hair: *literal* of a horse, not to show sweat by the roughening of his hair'; *forehand* is 'that part of a horse which is before the rider'.

   Christchurch: Christ Church was one of the grandest and wealthiest Oxford colleges, founded in 1546 by Henry VIII.

curricle . . . on Magdalen Bridge: Magdalen Bridge, strengthened and rebuilt in the 1780s, was the gateway into Oxford from the London road; a curricle was a speedy two-horse carriage, more fashionable and costly than the second-hand (but still expensive) gig Thorpe buys from his indebted friend.

30 *Oriel*: another Oxford college, socially less prestigious than Christ Church, but with a higher academic reputation.

31 *doubt of the propriety . . . Lansdown Hill to-morrow*: extending north-west from Bath in the direction of Bristol, Lansdown Hill was soon to be the site of Lansdown (or Beckford's) Tower, an extravagant folly built in the 1820s for William Beckford, the wealthy author of *Vathek* (1786). With no room in the gig for a chaperone, Catherine's doubt about propriety is well founded.

Tom Jones . . . the Monk: Henry Fielding's urbane, risqué *Tom Jones* (1749) and Matthew Lewis's supercharged Gothic novel *The Monk* (1796) are stereotypically masculine picks, both thought scandalous in their day.

32 *she who married the French emigrant*: in 1793 Frances Burney married General Alexandre-Jean-Baptiste Piochard, comte d'Arblay, a liberal constitutionalist who had fled revolutionary France the previous year. For *Camilla*, see note to p. 23.

old man playing at see-saw: see note below.

playing at see-saw and learning Latin: Thorpe has indeed not got far through Burney's five-volume novel; Sir Hugh Tyrold plays with his nieces and nephew in the second chapter and starts learning Latin in the fifth.

33 *rattle*: 'A person who talks incessantly in a lively or inane manner' (*OED*); often used with a connotation of bluster or bragging (as below, p. 45). In *Pride and Prejudice*, it is among Mr Darcy's virtues that 'he does not rattle away like other young men' (III. i. 184).

34 *muff and tippet*: a hand-warmer and scarf-like shawl or cape, typically fur or fur-lined, like the 'Ermine Tippet' worn by Austen in the London snow in 1814 (*Letters*, 271: 7 Mar.).

Octagon Room: the Great Octagon in Bath's Upper Assembly Rooms was a spectacular gathering place originally used for card games; Anne Elliot and Captain Wentworth have a pivotal encounter here in *Persuasion* (II. viii).

35 *To be disgraced . . . dignifies her character*: as Austen's wording suggests, calumny and unearned disgrace are occupational hazards for the protagonists of sentimental novels. See, for example, Mary Pilkington's *Rosina* (1793), in which the heroine's slanderer 'either willingly devoted the innocent object of his aversion to actual infamy . . . or vilely sought to degrade the purity of her character with a fictitious stigma' (I. xxvi. 202).

36 *stout*: not portly but robust and vigorous, like the 'stout girl of all works' recommended by Mrs Jennings in *Sense and Sensibility* as a way to cut costs on domestic servants (III. ii. 202).

38 *curiosity of women, indeed*: the conversation is about mere inquisitiveness, but Isabella's words allude to criticisms of intellectual women. On this satirical trope, see L. Cottegnies, S. Parageau, and J. J. Thompson (eds), *Women and Curiosity in Early Modern England and France* (Leiden: Brill, 2016).

40 *four greatest quizzers*: in modern editions, the original 1817 reading ('quizzers') is usually emended to read 'quizzes'. But the first edition has relatively few misprints and may be correct here. Perhaps Thorpe simply identifies his sisters and their partners as 'quizzes' (ludicrous people, fit for mockery). He may be attempting a paradox, however: that by setting up as 'quizzers' (i.e. by ridiculing others, a sense illustrated in *OED* by examples from 1797 and 1798) they invite mockery themselves.

41 *get their tumble over*: their jolting carriage ride, but Thorpe also slips in a sexual hint (*tumble* being a euphemism for sex, as in Henry Fielding's innuendo-laden farce of 1736, *Tumble-down Dick*).

our engagement . . . Claverton Down: Claverton Down was a picturesque spot to the south-east of Bath; the proposed engagement (to which Catherine has not in fact agreed) was for Lansdown Hill in the opposite direction.

dust: more of Thorpe's sophomoric slang, meaning disturbance, uproar, or fuss.

42 *take the rest for a minute*: stubbornly refuse to go forward.

43 *Old Allen is as rich as a Jew—is not he?*: Thorpe's loutish question may betray a confusion of identities between the Fullerton Allens and the heirs of Ralph Allen of Bath (1693–1764), a wealthy entrepreneur and philanthropist who made his fortune by reforming the postal system and quarrying stone. On the death in 1796 of Allen's niece and principal heir, much speculation surrounded the inheritance, which had passed to obscure collateral descendants bearing the Allen name (see Janine Barchas, *Matters of Fact in Jane Austen: History, Location, and Celebrity* (Baltimore: Johns Hopkins University Press, 2012), ch. 2). Thorpe later shares his assumptions with General Tilney (p. 67; see also p. 177).

44 *tittuppy*: perhaps Thorpe's coinage or an otherwise unrecorded piece of undergraduate slang. The *OED* gives this passage as its earliest illustration, with 'characterized by bouncing movement; unsteady, shaky, rickety' as the definition.

47 *Miss Drummond . . . large fortune*: perhaps evoking the wealthy banking dynasty founded in 1717 by Andrew Drummond, a London-based goldsmith who cannily avoided the political entanglements of his brother William, Viscount Strathallan, a Jacobite rebel killed at the Battle of Culloden in 1746. By 1795 the annual profits of Messrs Drummond were £30,000; a later partner in the bank, Andrew Berkeley Drummond, was Privy Purse to George III between 1812 and 1818.

warehouse: a somewhat pretentious synonym for shop, used in *Pride and Prejudice* by pushy Mrs Bennet, who has to tell unworldly Lydia 'which are the best warehouses' (III. v. 213).

50 *cotillion ball*: cotillion balls, featuring a French style of choreographed dance for four pairs, became popular in the 1770s and were held weekly in Bath's Upper Rooms. Their appeal began to wane in the 1790s, and by the time *Northanger Abbey* appeared in 1817, cotillions had been largely superseded by quadrilles.

51 *Dress is at all times a frivolous distinction . . . lecture on the subject*: Austen may be alluding to a particular didactic source (as is clear in a comparable passage below: see p. 174 with note), or she may be mimicking the sententious style of conduct literature in general. For all its irony, this whole paragraph has intriguing similarities with the chapter 'Of Vanity' in Germaine de Staël's *A Treatise on the Influence of the Passions, upon the Happiness of Individuals and of Nations* (1798); Staël discusses female fashion as a futile form of self-torment, especially at assemblies and 'in the ball room, where the most frivolous claims to distinction display the effects of vanity in their warmest colours' (118).

tamboured muslin . . . the jackonet: sprigs and spots were decorations hand-stitched (tamboured) or printed on light muslin shirts (mulls) and heavier cotton outer garments (Jackonets), both made from imported Indian fabrics.

country-dancing beginning: in the later part of the Bath evening, cotillions would give way to country dancing, which was more informal but not necessarily rustic; the term was often conflated with 'the *French contre-danse*, where a number of persons placing themselves *opposite* one to another begin a figure' (*Gentleman's Magazine* (Apr. 1758), 174).

53 *Leicestershire . . . season*: a Midlands county known for fox-hunting; the season ran from mid-autumn to early spring.

advantage of choice . . . power of refusal: Henry pinpoints a dilemma lengthily explored in Richardson's *Sir Charles Grandison* and central to the tragedy of *Clarissa*, in which the heroine insists on 'the liberty of *refusal*, which belongs to my Sex'; according to her coercive brother, 'the liberty of *refusing* . . . is denied you, because we are all sensible, that the liberty of *chusing*, to every one's dislike, must follow' (3rd edn (1751), I. xliii. 307; II. vii. 35).

54 *fan and the lavender water*: used to cool or calm overheated dancers; cf. *Sense and Sensibility*, in which Elinor screens distraught Marianne 'from the observation of others, while reviving her with lavender water' (II. vi. 132).

58 *night that poor St. Aubin died!—such beautiful weather!*: Catherine blurs the details of Radcliffe's deathbed scene in *The Mysteries of Udolpho*, in which St Aubert (not St Aubin) 'lingered till about three o'clock in the afternoon' (I. vii. 218). St Aubins feature in other novels of the period including Agnes Musgrave's *Cicely; or, The Rose of Raby*, a Minerva Press publication of 1795.

Bristol . . . a great way off: it was 12 or 13 miles' distance from Bath to Bristol, a port city central to the slave trade until slaving voyages were outlawed in 1807.

58 *Clifton . . . Kingsweston*: Clifton was a grand hilltop suburb to the west of
Bristol, above Bristol's own spa (the Hot-wells); Kingsweston, more than
3 miles further north-west, was known for its sweeping views across the
Avon estuary and into Wales. With his claim to drive at 10 miles per hour
or more (p. 29), Thorpe is being ambitious.

59 *Blaize Castle! . . . what is that?*: Blaise Castle, a popular destination 4 miles
north of Bristol, was not the real thing (as Thorpe believes or affects to
believe) but a modern folly. It had distinct slave-trade associations. Built
in 1766 by Thomas Farr, a Bristol merchant whose wealth derived from
sugar plantations and enslaved labour, it was acquired in 1789 by John
Scandrett Harford, a Quaker banker and leading Bristol abolitionist,
whose son of the same name, a close ally of William Wilberforce, went on
to make the Blaise estate a hub of the abolitionist campaign.

phaeton with bright chesnuts: a fashionable four-wheeled open carriage,
built for speed, and drawn in this case by two chestnut horses.

cattle: 'In the language of the stable, applied to horses' (*OED*).

60 *Wick Rocks*: another celebrated beauty spot, between Bath and Bristol,
known for its limestone crags.

broken promises . . . trap-doors: Catherine's mind alternates between her
own difficulties in modern Bath (broken promises, phaetons, Tilneys) and
the trials of a heroine in Gothic settings (broken arches, false hangings,
trapdoors).

Laura-place . . . Argyle-buildings: parts of the new Bathwick development,
completed in 1794 (Laura Place) and 1789 (Argyle Buildings, now Argyle
Street). Catherine's party is still to the east of Pulteney Bridge and Bath
proper, whereas Thorpe claims to have seen the Tilneys heading north out
of the city via Lansdown Road.

61 *Market-place*: Catherine has now crossed the Avon into the main part of
Bath.

narrow, winding vaults . . . total darkness: Catherine imagines herself
as a Gothic protagonist, though a less prudent one than the hero of
Mrs Martin's *Reginald; or, The House of Mirandola* (1799), who, exploring
the narrow passages, spiral staircases, and subterranean dungeons of an
ancient castle, 'now placed his lamp out of the reach of the sudden gust of
wind that might rush forth on opening the door' (II. i. 47).

town of Keynsham: about 7 miles west of Bath in the Bristol direction.

63 *pool of commerce*: a fashionable card game resembling poker. Austen was
wary when playing this game herself on a visit to Bath, and wrote to
Cassandra that she declined to enter a second pool, 'for the Stake was three
shillings, & I cannot afford to lose that, twice in an even^g' (*Letters*, 149:
7 Oct. 1808).

pillow strewed with thorns and wet with tears: proverbial, and frequently
used in Gothic and sentimental fiction; see, for example, Mary Robinson,
Vancenza (1792), I. vi. 75 ('found her pillow covered with thorns');

Charlotte Smith, *Marchmont* (1796), IV. x. 300 ('strewed his pillow with thorns').

67 *object of their attention and discourse*: see note to p. 43.

Bedford: a celebrated coffee house in Covent Garden, London.

billiard-room . . . little touch together: billiards was becoming a fashionable game (as in *Sense and Sensibility*, I. xx) and was often played for high stakes. To *touch* is to strike the ball lightly or gently, as in *The Sylph* (1779), a novel sometimes attributed to Georgiana Cavendish, Duchess of Devonshire, but probably by Sophia Briscoe: 'let us have a little touch at billiards . . . I'll bet you five hundred, Biddulph, that I pocket your ball in five minutes' (II. xxxix. 96–7).

68 *the afternoon's Crescent of this day*: the characters now promenade on the Royal Crescent, as was a fashionable Sunday activity (see note to p. 21).

71 *Brock-street . . . home by this time*: Brock Street leads from the Crescent towards the Circus and, below it, the centre of Bath; the Tilneys are heading home to Milsom Street.

73 *quarter of an hour*: the conventionally approved span of time. Violations of the norm are a running joke in *Emma*, from the breezy discourtesy of Frank Churchill ('Ten minutes would have been all that was necessary', II. vi. 152) to the perils of stopping by with Miss Bates ('Mrs. Cole had just been there, just called in for ten minutes, and had been so good as to sit an hour with them', II. i. 119).

75 *Beechen Cliff*: to the south of Bath, a steep wooded hill (sometimes known as a hanging wood or hanger) offering celebrated views across the city.

76 *Hermitage-walk*: an artificial hermit's retreat, often constructed as a ruin, was a fashionable elements of picturesque landscape design; in *Pride and Prejudice* (III. iv), Mrs Bennet hopes to impress Lady Catherine de Bourgh with hers. Eleanor probably means the gloomy 'path through a thick grove of old Scotch firs' that inspires Catherine with 'delightful melancholy' when she tours Northanger (p. 128).

Julias and Louisas: standard names for sentimental heroines in novels such as (within just a few seasons) Elizabeth Helme's *Louisa; or, The Cottage on the Moor* (1787), Cassandra Hawkes's *Julia de Gramont* (1788), the anonymous *Louisa Forrester* (1789), the anonymous *Seymour Castle; or, The History of Julia and Cecilia* (1789), Helen Maria Williams's *Julia, A Novel* (1790), Elizabeth Hervey's *Louisa, A Novel* (1790), and the anonymous *Louisa; or, The Reward of an Affectionate Daughter* (1790). Austen works several Julias and Louisas into her teenage parodies, including the idealized Julia of 'The Female Philosopher' ('with a Countenance in which Modesty, Sense & Dignity are happily blended') and the false Louisa of 'Lesley Castle' ('Never was there a sweeter face, a finer form, or a less amiable Heart than Louisa owned!').

Emily . . . Valancourt . . . her aunt into Italy: referring to Radcliffe's *The Mysteries of Udolpho*, in which, packed off to Venice to detach her from her suitor Valancourt, Emily laments 'the distance that would separate them—the Alps, those tremendous barriers! would rise, and whole countries extend between the regions where each must exist!' (I. xiv. 403).

76 *your sampler at home*: 'A beginner's exercise in embroidery; a piece of canvas embroidered by a girl or woman as a specimen of skill, usually containing the alphabet and some mottos worked in ornamental characters' (*OED*).

77 *Johnson and Blair*: Samuel Johnson's *A Dictionary of the English Language* (1755) and Hugh Blair's *Lectures on Rhetoric and Belles Lettres* (1784) were seen as authoritative guides to usage and style, though neither work was simply prescriptive.

every commendation . . . in that one word: with its satire on vacuous, voguish cant, this passage seems to echo a whimsical letter of *c*.November 1749 in which the novelist Samuel Richardson is asked by his correspondent Lady Bradshaigh 'what, in your opinion, is the meaning of the word *sentimental*, so much in vogue amongst the polite, both in town and country? . . . Every thing clever and agreeable is comprehended in that word . . . I am frequently astonished to hear such a one is a *sentimental* man; we were a *sentimental* party; I have been taking a *sentimental* walk.' This letter was first printed in 1804 (*The Correspondence of Samuel Richardson*, ed. Anna Laetitia Barbauld, vol. iv, 282–3), which again suggests later revision on Austen's part.

78 *If a speech be well drawn up . . . Alfred the Great*: David Hume's *The History of England* (1754–61) and William Robertson's *The History of Scotland* (1759) were among the major achievements of Scottish Enlightenment historiography. Historians since antiquity had been inventing or embellishing battlefield orations; the classic instance, from the *Agricola* of Tacitus, is the rousing speech of Calgacus at Mons Graupius.

79 *well-informed mind . . . conceal it as well as she can*: Austen's sarcasm may be aimed at John Gregory's much-reprinted conduct manual *A Father's Legacy to His Daughters* (1774), which advises marriageable young women to be 'even cautious in displaying your good sense . . . But if you happen to have any learning, keep it a profound secret, especially from the men, who generally look with a jealous and malignant eye on a woman of great parts, and a cultivated understanding' (31–2). Even in the case of enlightened men, it is unwise 'to shew the full extent of your knowledge' because 'the great art of pleasing in conversation consists in making the company pleased with themselves. You will more readily hear than talk yourselves into their good graces' (32–3).

sister author: probably Frances Burney, whose *Camilla* (see note to p. 23) features a shallow but captivating beauty named Indiana Lynmere.

lecture on the picturesque . . . lights and shades: Austen pokes fun here at picturesque taste, though her brother reports that she was personally 'enamoured of Gilpin on the Picturesque' (Austen-Leigh et al., *Memoir*, 140–1), meaning the aesthetic theories of William Gilpin in, most influentially, *Three Essays: On Picturesque Beauty, on Picturesque Travel, and on Sketching Landscape* (1792). In this work, Gilpin instructs the painter 'in massing, and graduating both his lights, and shades' (vol. i, 20), and analyses the three parts of landscape composition: 'the foreground—the second ground—and the distance' (vol. ii, 27). Perhaps Henry has also been reading Gilpin's *Observations on the River Wye* (1782), in which the banks of the Wye form *'two side-screens . . . and mark the perspective'* (8).

80 *withered oak . . . near its summit*: another cliché of picturesque aesthetics, also singled out in *Sense and Sensibility*, where Edward Ferrars likes 'a fine prospect, but not on picturesque principles', and dislikes 'crooked, twisted, blasted trees' (I. xviii. 72). Gilpin's advice to artists is in fact quite even-handed: 'If a withered stump suit the form of his landscape better than the spreading oak, which he finds in nature, he may make the exchange—or he may make it, if he wish for a spreading oak, where he finds a withered trunk' (*Observations, Relative Chiefly to Picturesque Beauty, Made in the Year 1772* (1786), vol. i, p. xxviii).

inclosure . . . politics: the rural landscape was transformed between 1750 and 1850 by more than 4,000 Enclosure Acts, roughly half of them passed during the Revolutionary and Napoleonic Wars. The beneficiaries were large landowners, whereas labourers lost customary rights to graze livestock, hunt game, and gather firewood on previously common land. In this context, expanses of picturesque landscape could bespeak dispossession. As Mary Wollstonecraft asked, 'Why are huge forests still allowed to stretch out with idle pomp and all the indolence of Eastern grandeur? Why does the brown waste meet the traveller's view, when men want work?' (*A Vindication of the Rights of Men* (2nd edn, 1790), 148). For the labouring-class poet John Clare in the years following Austen's death, 'Inclosure came and trampled on the grave | Of labour's rights and left the poor a slave' ('The Mores', lines 19–20); in another poem, 'Inclosure like a Buonaparte let not a thing remain | It levelled every bush and tree and levelled every hill | And hung the moles for traitors' ('Remembrances', lines 67–9).

riot is only in your own brain: perhaps another memory of Johnson's *Rambler* essays, in which uncontrolled imagination (or strictly speaking 'fancy' or 'dream') is called 'this invisible riot of the mind' (no. 89, 22 Jan. 1751).

81 *mob of three thousand men . . . brickbat from an upper window*: St George's Fields in Southwark, south of the Thames, had been the launchpad for large-scale political riots in 1768, when soldiers fired on up to 15,000 Wilkesite protesters, and 1780 (the Gordon Riots), when anti-Catholic mobs attacked Parliament, the Bank of England, and other targets. The Gordon Riots involved perhaps 60,000 and lasted several days; order was only restored on the deployment of regular soldiers, who killed at least 285 protesters. Smaller riots occurred in the wake of the French Revolution, including the 1792 Mount Street Riot, which caught up Austen's cousin Eliza de Feuillide; she describes 'the noise of the populace, the drawn

swords & pointed bayonets of the guards, the fragments of brick & mortar thrown on every side, one of which had nearly killed my Coachman, the firing at one end of the street' (letter to Philadelphia Walter, 7 June 1792; see above, Introduction). St George's Fields continued to be used for mass meetings in this decade; a minor but widely reported riot was put down by the military there in 1795. Closer to time to the publication of *Northanger Abbey*, the Spa Fields Riots of 1816 involved a plan by revolutionary Spenceans to seize control of the Bank of England and the Tower of London as respectively the financial and military centres of state power. The 12th Light Dragoons, a celebrated regiment, were stationed at Nottingham (not Northampton) during the winter of 1795–6; they were in Portugal by the time Austen drafted the novel in *c*.1798–9 and in Ireland when she sold it to Crosby & Co. in 1803.

82 *Clifton at this time of year*: unlike Bath, Clifton and nearby Bristol Hotwells were quiet in winter but favoured in summer for 'the concomitant advantages of air and exercise, which may be enjoyed more compleatly in this season' (William Saunders, *A Treatise on the Chemical History and Medical Powers of . . . Mineral Waters* (1800), 126).

83 *York Hotel . . . spars*: an upscale new hotel (opened 1790) in Gloucester Place, Clifton. Spars were crystalline fragments mined in the nearby Avon Gorge and sold as souvenirs.

85 *sarsenet*: a dress made of fine, soft silk, in this case brownish-purple (puce); Austen owned a 'lilac sarsenet . . . a very useful gown, happy to go anywhere' (*Letters*, 269: 6 Mar. 1814).

86 *charming little villas about Richmond*: Richmond upon Thames, about 9 miles west of London, was a fashionable resort for aristocrats, gentry, and wealthy professionals and tradesmen, known for its grandiose riverside mansions.

Salisbury . . . to-morrow: the cathedral city of Salisbury in south-east Wiltshire formed a node in the post-road network. The crossroad from Salisbury to Bath extended for 38 miles; Royal Mail coaches could average 7 to 8 miles per hour.

88 *Putney . . . name on her tickets . . . hoop rings on her finger*: on the south bank of the Thames between Richmond and London, Putney was still a village at this time, fashionable and desirable, but without Richmond's special cachet; nearby Putney Heath was notorious for highwaymen and duelling Londoners. Isabella imagines the married name on her visiting cards; hoop rings were simple gold bands or solitaire rings, worn stacked on the finger for effect.

Devizes: a Wiltshire market town that served as a staging post between London and Bath (18 miles further west).

Going to one wedding brings on another: this dictum was already familiar by the time of John Gay's 1713 comedy *The Wife of Bath* ('One Wedding, the Proverb says, begets another', I. i); it recurs in several late eighteenth-century novels including Eliza Parsons's *Women as They Are*, a Minerva

Press publication of 1796: 'for the old song says, "Going to one wedding begetteth another"' (II. viii. 67).

89 *one great fortune looking out for another*: the consolidation of wealth via transactional marriage, sometimes with tragic consequences, had been a standard theme of novels since Richardson's *Clarissa*. Catherine's wording also recalls William Congreve's comedy *Love for Love* (1695): 'great Fortunes either expect another great Fortune, or a Fool' (I. viii).

93 *villains in horsemen's great coats . . . incredible speed*: abduction by coach is an occupational hazard for heroines of sentimental fiction; see, for example, E. O'Connor, *Emily Benson* (Dublin, 1791), in which 'two men, whose faces were disguised, forced me into a carriage . . . the carriage drove with incredible speed all night, and the succeeding day, at the close of which they stopped; but where, alas! I know not!' (letter xviii, p. 43).

94 *cannot speak well enough to be unintelligible*: cf. Henry Mackenzie's periodical *The Mirror*, in which 'Ignoramus' (a reader struggling with Mackenzie's Latin tags) prompts a wry observation that 'many great personages contrive to be unintelligible in order to be respected' (no. 9, 23 Feb. 1779). Mrs Morland cites *The Mirror* in a later chapter (see p. 174 with note).

95 *old enough to take it*: there was a minimum age of 24 for ordination into the Anglican priesthood.

96 *Four hundred . . . small income to begin on indeed*: not really. One historian estimates the 'Nominal Annual Earnings' of clergymen in 1797 to have been £238; another gives £150 as a 'reasonable' clerical income in 1810. Austen's clergyman father brought in about £600 per annum in his best years, but this came from two parishes and also included income from investments and tutoring (Robert D. Hume, 'Money in Jane Austen', *RES* 64/264 (2013), 289–310, at 290).

97 *fifty pounds . . . not have a wish unsatisfied*: more nonsense from Isabella; £50 per annum was at best an artisan's income.

98 *Marquis of Longtown*: a marquis or marquess was a high-ranking nobleman, second only to a duke in precedence. The General later specifies Longtown in Herefordshire (p. 161), a remote village on the border with Wales, where in reality the main local (but absentee) landowner was Henry Nevill, Earl of Abergavenny.

99 *Northanger Abbey! . . . thrilling words*: abbeys were favourite settings for Gothic fiction, and between Richard Warner's *Netley Abbey* (1795) and Sarah Wilkinson's *The Spectre of Lanmere Abbey* (1820) this 'thrilling' word featured in the title of at least thirty new novels (alongside assorted priories, monasteries, and convents). Northanger is a fictional location about 30 miles north of Bath in Gloucestershire, though there was a real-life North Hanger Farm near Southampton, Hampshire, where Austen lived between 1806 and 1809. A hanger is a steep-sided wood, like picturesque Delaford Hanger in *Sense and Sensibility*. *Anger* (the alarmingly recurrent mood of the abbey's owner) and *hanger-on* (his later view of the heroine as a parasite) are also suggested, perhaps with a glance at *danger*.

100 *ill-fated nun*: another cliché of Gothic fiction, as in Catharine Selden's *The English Nun*, a Minerva Press novel of 1797, which lingers in lachrymose style on 'the misery of the destiny that awaited her' (51) or again 'my unhappy fate' (127) The ill-fated nun in Radcliffe's *The Mysteries of Udolpho* is Sister Agnes, a tragic recluse who, on her death in the novel's final volume, is revealed to be the heiress Signora Laurentini di Udolpho (see note to p. 24).

Reformation . . . dissolution . . . rising woods of oak: during the English Reformation of the sixteenth century, the dissolution of monasteries, beginning under Henry VIII in 1536, involved large-scale expropriation of monastic buildings; many later became private houses, like Northanger or *Emma*'s Donwell Abbey, or picturesque ruins, like the Tintern Abbey of William Wordsworth's 1798 poem. In her teenage 'History of England', Austen wryly notes of Henry VIII 'that his abolishing Religious Houses & leaving them to the ruinous depredations of time has been of infinite use to the landscape of England' (*Teenage Writings*, p. 126). Here Catherine imagines Northanger through the lens of Gothic novels such as the anonymous *Waldeck Abbey* (1795), which places the forbidding Waldeck 'on the declivity of a hill . . . sheltered on the back by towering woods and groves' (I. iii. 49).

102 *more ways than one of our being sisters*: i.e. sisters-in-law, as they would become if Catherine were to marry John Thorpe, or if Isabella were to marry James Morland, or (as Isabella seems now to be thinking) if she and Catherine were each to marry a Tilney brother.

108 *mess-room will drink Isabella . . . for a month*: the officers' mess will toast Isabella; she and James will laugh for a month about Frederick Tilney's passion, or (Henry's ambiguous wording suggests) his passion will last just a month.

110 *bait at Petty-France*: fodder for the horses at Petty France, a minor staging post 14 miles north of Bath, roughly halfway to the fictional Northanger. There was something to see at Petty France after 1812, when Lord Liverpool, the new prime minister, built a manor house there as his country seat.

chaise-and-four—postilions handsomely liveried: a closed travelling carriage with four horses, driven by mounted postilions rather than a coachman seated on the carriage itself. Liveried servants, with embroidered uniforms derived from heraldic arms, were associated with noble families; they are an affectation for Sir Walter Elliot, a mere baronet (*Persuasion*, I. iii), and even more so for General Tilney, a commoner.

111 *Woodston . . . time is necessarily spent there*: not the real Woodston in Huntingdonshire, but a fictional location within three hours' drive, somewhere to the south of Northanger (pp. 151, 166). Henry does not share Sir Thomas Bertram's view, in *Mansfield Park* (II. vii. 194), that 'a parish has wants and claims which can be known only by a clergyman constantly resident, and which no proxy can be capable of satisfying to the same extent'; we later learn that Henry relies on a resident curate (p. 159).

112 *stout heart . . . sliding pannels and tapestry*: see, for example, Catherine Selden's *The Count de Santerre* (1797), in which the protagonists enter a tapestry-lined chamber 'and raising the hangings, discovered a sliding pannel' leading to a hidden chamber (I. xix. 271). 'Stout' hearts are essential survival equipment in Gothic environments, as in Radcliffe's *The Mysteries of Udolpho* (III. vi. 189) and Roche's *Clermont* (II. vii. 124). Here and for the next few paragraphs, Henry gleefully mimics the standard tropes and diction of 1790s Gothic, with a few glances at Radcliffe specifically, but evoking the genre and its signature effects more broadly.

expiring embers of a wood fire: see, for example, Richard Warner's *Netley Abbey* (1795), in which the hero, summoned by 'screams of female distress' into a gloomy refectory, finds the villainous abbot creepily illuminated 'by the expiring embers of a large fire' (I. viii. 145).

Dorothy . . . twenty years before: Dorothée is the ancient, superstitious housekeeper who, in *The Mysteries of Udolpho*, conducts Emily to a disused chamber containing 'the bed on which the Marchioness was said to have died'; there Emily shudders on perceiving by lamplight 'the high canopied tester of dark green damask, with the curtains . . . half drawn, and remaining apparently as they had been left twenty years before; and over the whole bedding was thrown a counterpane, or pall, of black velvet, that hung down to the floor' (IV. iv. 57). *Udolpho* is the obvious prototype for Henry's pastiche, but he might equally have been reading Roche's *Clermont*, which finds Madeline 'in a gloomy chamber, remote from every inhabited one, and assailed by noises from the long unoccupied apartment of a murdered relative' (III. vi. 245). Or compare George Moore's *Grasville Abbey* (1797), in which Matilda and Alfred 'crossed several apartments, till they came to the passage . . . which led to the gloomy chamber that, it was supposed, had formerly contained a corpse lying in state' (II. xxxii. 216).

gloomy chamber . . . figures as large as life: or perhaps Henry remembers Mary Pilkington's *Rosina* (1793), which finds the heroine in 'a large gloomy chamber, hung with old fashioned, but not ill executed tapestry. The curtains of the bed hung in tattered remnants . . . She gazed around her in wild astonishment, until the light burning down into the socket, began to throw its feeble and tremulous gleams on the walls of her dungeon. A group of figures in the tapestry caught her attention, and the dying flame just then aspiring with a sudden glow, revealed it plainly to her view' (IV. xxi. 177). The next few paragraphs are a similar mash-up of Gothic clichés, just about every phrase of which might be found in Radcliffe or her imitators.

113 *unquiet slumber*: amidst the pervasive mock-Gothic diction of this chapter, Austen also slips in an echo of Shakespeare's *Richard III* ('unquiet slumbers', III. ii. 24)—though this phrase also recurs in Gothic novels such as Charlotte Smith's *Montalbert* (1795; II. xvii. 95), Catharine Selden's *The Count de Santerre* (1797; II. xxxv. 213), and Mary Pilkington's *The Subterranean Cavern* (1798; IV. xxi. 225).

113 *subterraneous communication . . . chapel of St. Anthony*: as an early satirist of
Gothic clichés noted, 'the principal incidents must be carried on in *subterraneous* passages' ('On the Terrorist System of Novel-Writing', *Monthly
Magazine* (Aug. 1797), 104). Secret tunnels are a standard feature of
novels such as Radcliffe's *The Castles of Athlin and Dunbayne* (1789),
A Sicilian Romance (1790), and *The Italian* (1797); sometimes they lead to
mysterious sanctuaries, as in Joseph Fox's *Tancred* (1791), where 'the
ancient builder of Rothsay-Castle . . . had contrived a subterraneous passage which led from the Castle to the Chapel of St. Mary' (II. 3).

114 *the wretched Matilda . . . total darkness*: suffering Matildas feature promin-
ently in two major precursors of 1790s Gothic, Horace Walpole's *The
Castle of Otranto* (1764) and Sophia Lee's *The Recess* (1783–5), as well as
in Radcliffe's debut novel, *The Castles of Athlin and Dunbayne*. Among
other beleaguered namesakes, see 'the wretched Matilda' of Isabella
Kelly's *The Ruins of Avondale Priory* (1796), III. xi. 177, or again 'wretched
Matilda' in Matthew Lewis's *The Monk* (1796), II. vi. 180.

solemn awe . . . high Gothic windows: compare, for example, Regina Maria
Roche's *The Children of the Abbey* (1796), where the heroine traverses oak
woods 'scattered over with relics of druidical antiquity', and then views
from 'the massy door' of the abbey 'the dark and stupendous edifice,
whose gloom was now heightened by the shadows of evening, with venerable awe' (I. xv. 287–8).

115 *Rumford*: one of General Tilney's state-of-the-art appliances, invented by
Sir Benjamin Thompson, an American-born inventor who was ennobled
by the Elector of Bavaria as Count Rumford. Rumford fireplaces had
a narrow throat designed to expel smoke efficiently while concentrating
heat inside the room.

116 *large high chest . . . in a deep recess on one side of the fire-place*: as in, for
example, Radcliffe's *The Romance of the Forest* (1791), in which La Motte
'looked into the recess. Upon the ground within it, stood a large chest,
which he went forward to examine, and, lifting the lid, he saw the remains
of a human skeleton. Horror struck upon his heart, and he involuntarily
stepped back' (I. iv. 137).

119 *midnight assassins or drunken gallants*: perhaps alluding to an episode in *The
Mysteries of Udolpho*, in which Verezzi and Bertolini, two dissolute favourites of the villain Montoni, terrify the heroine by roaming drunkenly
through the castle in search of her bedchamber (II. vi). Montoni's most
alarming friend is 'Orsino, the assassin' (IV. iii. 30), a Venetian cavalier
who is on the run after having an enemy 'way-laid and poniarded by hired
assassins' (II. iv. 146).

120 *black and yellow Japan of the handsomest kind*: hard, glossy lacquerwork,
typically black with gilt detail, Japanese in origin but by this time produced in quantity by English manufacturers in the West Midlands.

121 *roll of paper . . . attempted to rest*: playing again on novels such as *The
Romance of the Forest*, in which, roaming a desolate abbey on a stormy

night, Radcliffe's heroine Adeline finds 'a small roll of paper, tied with a string, and covered with dust' (II. viii. 14); her attempts to decipher the manuscript, and the 'curiosity and terror' it inspires in her (II. viii. 15), are dwelt on at length.

121 *Darkness impenetrable and immoveable filled the room*: a Gothic cliché popularized by Radcliffe in *The Mysteries of Udolpho* ('Impenetrable darkness again involved the scene', III. xi. 394), targeted by William Beckford in his 1798 parody *Azemia* (II. ix. 174; II. x. 195), and resumed by Mary Shelley in *Frankenstein* (1818), I. vii. 148 ('the scene was enveloped in an impenetrable darkness'). The melodramatic inversion ('darkness impenetrable') also suggests *Paradise Lost*, i. 63 ('No light, but rather darkness visible').

123 *breeches-ball*: an alkaline composition 'for cleaning Leather Breeches, which by dry rubbing them takes out all grease and spots, gives them a most beautiful colour, and is a great preserver of the leather' (*Morning Chronicle*, 5 Sept. 1783).

125 *clay of Staffordshire . . . Dresden or Sêve . . . not for himself*: Dresden and Sèvres, leading Continental centres for the production of fine porcelain, were now rivalled for quality and prestige by the Staffordshire manufactures of Josiah Wedgwood (1730–95), Josiah Spode (1733–97), and others. The Wedgwood and Spode companies innovated tirelessly, traded on their elite international clientele, and maintained fashionable London showrooms: just the place, the General hints, to order a wedding gift.

126 *netting-box*: needlework case.

127 *pinery . . . only one hundred in the last year*: hothouse for growing pineapples (pines), an exotic luxury. Pineapples were notoriously difficult to grow in English latitudes; with his yield of 'only one hundred', the General performs a humblebrag.

128 *succession-houses . . . entered them*: here General Tilney resembles Sir Robert Stamford, an exploitative, self-aggrandizing landowner in Charlotte Smith's *Desmond* (1792), who clears ancient woods to make way for 'an immense range of forcing and succession houses, where not only pines are produced, but where different buildings, and different degrees of heat, are adapted to the ripening cherries in March, and peaches in April' (II. ix. 93). See also the arriviste proprietor of Clarendon Abbey in Mary Robinson's *Angelina* (1796), who boasts to Lord Acreland (with whose family he seeks a marriage alliance) 'that my pinery is one of the first in the kingdom . . . it has cost me a world of money' (I. xiii. 147).

130 *anti-chamber*: antechamber. This widespread though etymologically false spelling also appears in *Pride and Prejudice*, where Lady Catherine de Bourgh holds court behind a similarly intimidating but otherwise useless room (II. vi. 122).

satin: silk fabric suggesting luxury and expense. After touring Blenheim, Chatsworth, and other great houses in *Pride and Prejudice*, Elizabeth Bennet 'really had no pleasure in fine carpets or satin curtains' (II. xix. 179).

132 *offices*: rooms devoted to household service and storage (laundry, pantry, scullery, etc.).

pattened girl . . . footman in dishabille sneaked off: the deferential maidservant wears wooden overshoes; the evasive footman does not wear his liveried uniform.

134 *worked with her friend*: i.e. at sewing or embroidery.

air and attitude of a Montoni: Montoni is the haughty, brooding villain of *The Mysteries of Udolpho*, conspicuous for 'the severity of his temper and the gloominess of his pride' (I. xiv. 382). In one phase of Radcliffe's novel, 'Montoni was often more thoughtful than usual; sometimes the deep workings of his mind entirely abstracted him from surrounding objects, and threw a gloom over his visage that rendered it terrible; at others, his eyes seemed almost to flash fire, and all the energies of his soul appeared to be roused for some great enterprise' (II. iii. 78). Catherine may be recalling a later scene in which 'he paced the room with thoughtful steps' while Emily, the heroine, views 'by the glimmer of the single lamp, placed near a large Venetian mirror, that duskily reflected the scene . . . the tall figure of Montoni passing slowly along, his arms folded, and his countenance shaded' (II. v. 176).

meetly employed . . . future mischief: meetly (fittingly, suitably) was rarely used after 1700 except as a deliberate archaism. The General's antiquated diction suggests some play on a prior source, but there is no obvious precursor in the Bible or Milton (in whose *Paradise Lost*, however, the poet loses his sight for the good of the nation, while Eve works mischief with her eyes).

135 *probability that Mrs. Tilney yet lived . . . necessarily followed*: in *The Mysteries of Udolpho*, Montoni, in order to force his wife to sign over property to him, confines her under guard in a turret 'and, without pity or remorse, had suffered her to lie, forlorn and neglected, under a raging fever'; Emily searches the castle and finds her alive, but with 'a pale and emaciated face' and 'skeleton hand' (III. iii. 67, 65), and she succumbs soon afterwards. Catherine may also remember Radcliffe's *A Sicilian Romance*, which opens with uncertainty about the fate of Louisa Bernini, first wife of the villainous Marquis of Mazzini, of whom 'it was by many persons believed, that his unkindness and neglect put a period to her life' (I. i. 5). Eventually, the marchioness is discovered half starved in a castle dungeon: 'The door opened, and [Julia, the heroine] beheld in a small room, which received its feeble light from a window above, the pale and emaciated figure of a woman, seated, with half closed eyes' (II. xiv. 158).

136 *cold meat at home*: on Sundays, kitchen staff might have time off for worship or rest.

violent death or a religious retirement . . . black career: violent death or religious retirement (to a monastery or similar) is the stereotypical fate of a Gothic villain; some of the most hardened—witness Matthew Lewis's Ambrosio in *The Monk*—take both routes.

137 *waxen figure . . . supposititious funeral carried on*: for the waxwork corpse in Radcliffe's *The Mysteries of Udolpho*, see note to p. 24. Towards the end of *A Sicilian Romance*, the marchioness learns 'that in obedience to the marquis's order . . . I had been buried in effigy at a neighbouring church, with all the pomp of funeral honour due to my rank' (II. xiv. 166).

equal resemblance of mother and child: once again, Catherine's expectations are formed by Gothic novels, in which ancestral portraits disclosing kinship relations are a recurrent motif. The device is central to the denouement of *The Mysteries of Udolpho*, which turns on comparisons between portraits, miniatures, and living faces; 'you surely are her daughter: such striking resemblance is never found but among near relations' (IV. xvi. 354).

139 *dimity . . . Bath stove*: functional cotton cloth, often used for bed upholstery. Bath stoves, less modern and fuel-efficient than the new Rumfords (see note to p. 115), were fitted above the grate with an iron plate in which a small aperture drew smoke into the chimney.

141 *bilious fever*: a somewhat catch-all humoral term, still applied in Austen's day to any febrile condition accompanied by bilious vomiting or diarrhoea; modern diagnoses for 'bilious fever' symptoms would include cholera, hepatitis, malaria, sepsis, typhoid fever, and typhus.

142 *voluntary spies . . . every thing open*: alongside expanding infrastructure (the transport network, the periodical press), Henry's wording evokes the counter-revolutionary paranoia of the 1790s, and in particular the operation of a surveillance network including volunteer informers as well as government agents. The public were encouraged by a royal proclamation of 21 May 1792 (reinforced by later legislation) to report 'seditious' or 'tumultuous' activities, and zealous loyalists were still doing so as Austen drafted *Northanger Abbey*. In a well-known anecdote from Samuel Taylor Coleridge's *Biographia Literaria* (1817), he and Wordsworth, when staying on the Somerset coast in 1797, were suspected by locals of being French agents scouting for an invasion site; a Home Office spy was sent to monitor their activities, eventually concluding that this was 'no French Affair but a mischievuous gang of disaffected Englishmen' (Nicholas Roe, *Wordsworth and Coleridge: The Radical Years* (2nd edn, Oxford: Oxford University Press, 2018), 245–59).

144 *Alps and Pyrenees . . . mixed characters*: in the neoclassical aesthetics of Johnson, Blair, and others, 'mixed characters' had their prototypes in Homeric figures such as Helen, 'that mixed female character, which we partly condemn, and partly pity' (Blair, *Lectures on Rhetoric and Belles Lettres*, lecture xliii). In novels, mixed character was associated especially with the moral and psychological complexities of Richardson's fiction, and above all with the figure of Lovelace, the charismatic villain-hero of *Clarissa*. Reviewers of the 1790s often deplored, by contrast, the black-and-white construction of Gothic novels, with their exaggerated characters and sublime settings (Alps, Pyrenees).

148 *Bath paper . . . the arrivals*: prominent new visitors were listed in the *Bath Chronicle*, which Austen consulted herself when in Bath in 1799, writing to Cassandra that 'There was a very long list of Arrivals here, in the Newspaper yesterday, so that we need not immediately dread absolute Solitude' (*Letters*, 42: 17 May).

151 *Brockham*: probably, like Woodston, a fictional location. However, there was a real Brockhampton in Herefordshire, 45 miles or so north of the fictional Northanger—a long way, though for Mr Darcy in *Pride and Prejudice*, 50 miles is on good roads 'Little more than half a day's journey . . . a *very* easy distance' (II. ix. 134).

     pleasures . . . paid for: Henry plays on the standard rhetoric of sermons and conduct books; see, for example, George Fothergill's warning that 'pleasures must be dearly paid for, either in bitter repentance and remorse here, or in something far more dreadful hereafter' (Vicesimus Knox (ed.), *Family Lectures; or, Domestic Divinity* (1791), II. vii. 517).

153 *well-connected Parsonage*: probably meaning a parsonage with a convenient floor-plan—a clergyman's dwelling with good flow. However, Austen sometime uses *well connected* in the newer and now dominant social sense, as when the heroine of *Emma* forms schemes for the advancement of Harriet Smith: 'I want to see you permanently well connected' (I. iv. 25).

     the trio: editors sometimes retain the first-edition reading ('the two'), but a misprint seems likely at this point. Eleanor as well as Catherine is expected to join the General on the trip ('the young ladies', p. 151), and she is there at the end of the chapter (p. 155). For Austen's comparable use of 'trio' elsewhere, see *Mansfield Park*, II. xi. 224 ('They were now a miserable trio').

     bow thrown out . . . patched-on bow: a bow window added to the existing design.

154 *cottage remains*: the General has presumably been planning to improve the view by evicting some peasants; fashionable designers would often recommend 'taking down a few miserable cottages', as Humphry Repton put it in 1794 (*Sketches and Hints on Landscape Gardening*, 53).

162 *carriage is ordered . . . no servant will be offered you*: a blatant discourtesy, and perhaps an imperilling one, since Catherine will have to change post-chaises alone at unknown inns on a journey lasting eleven hours. Austen's fellow novelist Maria Edgeworth was shocked by this passage: 'The behaviour of the General in *Northanger Abbey*, packing off the young lady without a servant or the common civilities which any bear of a man, not to say gentleman, would have shown, is quite outrageously out of drawing and out of nature' (letter to Margaret Ruxton, 21 Feb. 1818; see above, Introduction). Cf. *Pride and Prejudice*, where for Lady Catherine 'the idea of two young women travelling post by themselves' is a breach of safety as well as propriety since 'young women should always be properly guarded and attended'; Elizabeth reassures her that 'my uncle is to send a servant for us' (II. xiv. 158). Austen reluctantly accepted such constraints herself:

'*I* want to go in a Stage Coach, but Frank will not let me' (*Letters*, 11: 16
Sept. 1796); 'I want to go with him . . . but the unpleasantness of returning
by myself deters me' (*Letters*, 38: 21 Jan. 1799).

167 *well-known spire . . . twenty miles of home*: Salisbury Cathedral, frequently
painted by John Constable in the years after Austen's death, was best
known for its 400-foot spire, visible at distance across flat meadows.

169 *irritable race*: playing on a much-quoted tag from the Roman satirist
Horace, *genus irritabile vatum*, or in Christopher Smart's translation of
1767, 'the irritable race of poets' (*Epistles*, II. ii. 102).

172 *frightful great rent in my best Mechlin*: a delicate Flemish lace from the city
of Mechlin, often used to edge gowns and other garments; cf., in *Pride and
Prejudice*, Lydia's much-analysed 'great slit in my worked muslin gown'
(III. v. 216).

174 *time for balls and plays . . . time for work*: dancing and needlework (as above,
note to p. 134). Mrs Morland plays on a famous sequence of verses in
Ecclesiastes 3:1–8 ('To every thing there is a season . . . a time of war, and
a time of peace'), with perhaps a faint echo of John 9:4 ('I must work the
works of him that sent me, while it is day: the night cometh, when no man
can work').

"The Mirror," I think: the obvious candidate from this periodical is no. 12
(6 Mar. 1779), which warns of the 'Consequence to little folks of intimacy
with great ones, in a letter from John Homespun'. *The Mirror* was edited
and mainly written by Henry Mackenzie, best known as author of the
influential sentimental novel *The Man of Feeling* (1771).

178 *rhodomontade*: variant spelling of *rodomontade*, extravagant boasting, from
the figure of Rodomonte, a swaggering braggart in Renaissance epic.

179 *my reader's sagacity . . . united for their ease what they must divide for mine*:
formulations associated especially with Fielding's playful narrator in *Tom
Jones*, who declares that by leaving narrative gaps 'we do not only consult
our own Dignity and Ease; but the Good and Advantage of the Reader:
For . . . we give him at all such Seasons an Opportunity of employing that
wonderful Sagacity, of which he is Master, by filling up these vacant
Spaces of Time with his own Conjectures' (III. i. 152).

181 *tell-tale compression . . . perfect felicity*: reworking a hackneyed last-chapter
phrase from novels of the period such as Charlotte Smith's *Celestina*
(1791), which leaves its protagonists 'in such perfect felicity as is seldom
enjoyed' (IV. xiii. 349). Austen may be recalling Jane West's novel
A Gossip's Story (1796), which scoffs at 'the perfect excellence and perfect
felicity which exists in the land of Hymen; as described in the Utopian
geography of many modern novelists' (II. xxviii. 96), but she punctures
the cliché more deftly.

182 *rules of composition . . . connected with my fable*: mimicking the efforts of late
eighteenth-century critics to apply neoclassical principles to the novel
genre. See, for example, Henry James Pye's defence, in *A Commentary*

Illustrating the Poetic of Aristotle, by Examples Taken Chiefly from the Modern Poets (1792), of apparently extraneous characters and events in Cervantes and Fielding: 'The story of "Cardenio and Lucinda" in Don Quixote, and still more "Nightingale and Mrs. Miller's Daughter" in Tom Jones, are episodes connected with the fable' (447).

182 *parental tyranny . . . filial disobedience*: a central topic of debate in novels since Richardson's *Clarissa*, still conspicuous in 1790s titles such as *The Penitent Father; or, Injured Innocence Triumphant over Parental Tyranny* (anonymous, 1793) and Frances Jacson's *Disobedience: A Novel* (a Minerva Press publication of 1797).

American Literature

British and Irish Literature

Children's Literature

Classics and Ancient Literature

Colonial Literature

Eastern Literature

European Literature

Gothic Literature

History

Medieval Literature

Oxford English Drama

Philosophy

Poetry

Politics

Religion

The Oxford Shakespeare

A complete list of Oxford World's Classics, including Authors in Context, Oxford English Drama, and the Oxford Shakespeare, is available in the UK from the Marketing Services Department, Oxford University Press, Great Clarendon Street, Oxford OX2 6DP, or visit the website at www.oup.com/uk/worldsclassics.

In the USA, visit www.oup.com/us/owc for a complete title list.

Oxford World's Classics are available from all good bookshops.

TROLLOPE IN   **OXFORD WORLD'S CLASSICS**

Anthony Trollope   **The American Senator**
An Autobiography
Barchester Towers
Can You Forgive Her?
Cousin Henry
Doctor Thorne
The Duke's Children
The Eustace Diamonds
Framley Parsonage
He Knew He Was Right
Lady Anna
The Last Chronicle of Barset
Orley Farm
Phineas Finn
Phineas Redux
The Prime Minister
Rachel Ray
The Small House at Allington
The Warden
The Way We Live Now

A SELECTION OF **OXFORD WORLD'S CLASSICS**

ANTON CHEKHOV	**About Love and Other Stories**
	Early Stories
	Five Plays
	The Princess and Other Stories
	The Russian Master and Other Stories
	The Steppe and Other Stories
	Twelve Plays
	Ward Number Six and Other Stories
FYODOR DOSTOEVSKY	**Crime and Punishment**
	Devils
	A Gentle Creature and Other Stories
	The Idiot
	The Karamazov Brothers
	Memoirs from the House of the Dead
	Notes from the Underground and The Gambler
NIKOLAI GOGOL	**Dead Souls**
	Plays and Petersburg Tales
MIKHAIL LERMONTOV	**A Hero of Our Time**
ALEXANDER PUSHKIN	**Boris Godunov**
	Eugene Onegin
	The Queen of Spades and Other Stories
LEO TOLSTOY	**Anna Karenina**
	The Kreutzer Sonata and Other Stories
	The Raid and Other Stories
	Resurrection
	War and Peace
IVAN TURGENEV	**Fathers and Sons**
	First Love and Other Stories
	A Month in the Country